PRAISE FOR THE NOVELS OF RUTH GLICK
(WRITING AS REBECCA YORK)

"A compulsive read."   —*Publishers Weekly*

"York has penned a convincing and sensual paranormal romance, and readers who fell in love with the characters in her last book, *Killing Moon*, will be glad to meet them again."   —*Booklist*

"Mesmerizing action and passions that leap from the pages with the power of a wolf's coiled spring."   —*Bookpage*

"*Killing Moon* is a delightful supernatural private investigator romance starring two charming lead characters."
                                              —*Midwest Book Review*

"Rebecca York delivers page-turning suspense."
                                              —Nora Roberts

"Glick's prose is smooth, literate, and fast-moving; her love scenes are tender yet erotic; and there's always a happy ending."   —*The Washington Post Book World*

continued . . .

"A true master of intrigue." —*Rave Reviews*

"No one sends more chills down your spine than the very creative and imaginative Ms. York!" —*Romantic Times*

"She writes a fast-paced, satisfying thriller." —*UPI*

"*Edge of the Moon* is clever and a great read. I can't wait to read the final book in this wonderful series."
—*Paranormal Romance Reviews*

Don't miss these other werewolf romantic suspense novels from Rebecca York

KILLING MOON
A P.I. with a preternatural talent for tracking
finds his prey: a beautiful genetic researcher
who may be his only hope for a future . . .

EDGE OF THE MOON
A police detective and a woman who files a missing
persons report become the pawns of an unholy
serial killer in a game of deadly attraction . . .

WITCHING MOON
A werewolf and a sexy biologist investigate a swamp
steeped in superstition, legend, and death . . .

CRIMSON MOON

REBECCA YORK

BERKLEY SENSATION, NEW YORK

THE BERKLEY PUBLISHING GROUP
Published by the Penguin Group
Penguin Group (USA) Inc.
375 Hudson Street, New York, New York 10014, USA
Penguin Group (Canada), 10 Alcorn Avenue, Toronto, Ontario M4V 3B2, Canada
(a division of Pearson Penguin Canada Inc.)
Penguin Books Ltd., 80 Strand, London WC2R 0RL, England
Penguin Group Ireland, 25 St. Stephen's Green, Dublin 2, Ireland (a division of Penguin Books Ltd.)
Penguin Group (Australia), 250 Camberwell Road, Camberwell, Victoria 3124, Australia
(a division of Pearson Australia Group Pty. Ltd.)
Penguin Books India Pvt. Ltd., 11 Community Centre, Panchsheel Park, New Delhi—110 017, India
Penguin Group (NZ), Cnr. Airborne and Rosedale Roads, Albany, Auckland 1310, New Zealand
(a division of Pearson New Zealand Ltd.)
Penguin Books (South Africa) (Pty.) Ltd., 24 Sturdee Avenue, Rosebank, Johannesburg 2196,
South Africa

Penguin Books Ltd., Registered Offices: 80 Strand, London WC2R 0RL, England

This is a work of fiction. Names, characters, places, and incidents either are the product of the author's imagination or are used fictitiously, and any resemblance to actual persons, living or dead, business establishments, events, or locales is entirely coincidental.

CRIMSON MOON

A Berkley Sensation Book / published by arrangement with the author

PRINTING HISTORY
Berkley Sensation edition / January 2005

Copyright © 2005 by Ruth Glick.
Excerpt from *Depth Perception* copyright © 2005 by Linda Castillo.
Cover design by Brad Springer.

ISBN: 0-425-19995-9

BERKLEY® SENSATION
Berkley Sensation Books are published by The Berkley Publishing Group,
a division of Penguin Group (USA) Inc.,
375 Hudson Street, New York, New York 10014.
BERKLEY SENSATION and the "B" design
are trademarks belonging to Penguin Group (USA) Inc.

PRINTED IN THE UNITED STATES OF AMERICA

10 9 8 7 6 5 4 3 2 1

PROLOGUE

IF I'M DEAD, why does it hurt so much?

The question echoed in his mind as he lay on the hard slab. His eyes blinked open, or as open as the swelling would allow. A field of white covered his face. Clouds? A sheet?

Every square inch of his body throbbed from punches and kicks. He shifted slightly, testing. Ribs and kidneys screamed in agony.

That wasn't the worst. Memories flitted in and out of his brain. The beer. The knockdown, drag-out fight. He'd tried to match the bikers drink for drink. That had been a bad mistake. Not his first.

A loudspeaker crackled to life. An urgent voice assaulted his ears.

"Dr. Pearson to ER. Stat. Dr. Pearson to ER. Stat."

He was in a hospital. But why was his face covered? Why was the bed so hard and the air so cold?

Out in the hall, running feet. Voices. He caught snatches of conversation.

". . . three-car pileup."

"We've got all those busted-up bikers, too."

"Triage."

He tried to hang on to consciousness. It slipped away.

Sometime later, he woke again. This time he remembered the babble of excited voices he'd heard as he lay bleeding on the barroom floor.

"Jesus! Roy's dead."

"What happened?"

"Looks like he hit his head on a table when he went down."

More voices, punctuated by loud exclamations of dismay.

"What the hell are we gonna do?"

"Shit, I don't know!"

"Tell the cops the Marshall kid did it. Serves him right for bringing his sorry ass in here."

"Yeah." A boot kicked at his ribs, but he couldn't muster the effort to groan in pain. "He can't say otherwise."

"You think he's dead?"

"What does it matter? We all give the cops the same story, he's dogmeat."

Satisfied laughter.

And now the hard table.

Inching a hand upward, he pulled the sheet off his face. He was lying in a dark room.

In the distance, an ambulance siren wailed.

Had he heard that before? He didn't know. His brain was too bruised.

Cautiously he tried to sit up and gasped as agony caught him in an iron grip. But he was tough. Too tough, maybe. He'd dedicated the first twenty-two years of his life to screwing himself up.

Somewhere in the recesses of his addled brain, through the fogging pain, he saw an opportunity to escape—for good.

Teeth gritted, he managed to lower himself to the cold tile floor and passed out.

Later, his eyes snapped open again. It was still dark. The hospital loudspeaker crackled again.

The staff was busy.

Could he stand the pain of transformation? He must.

He had lost one shoe. It took centuries to work the other one off, then struggle out of jeans and T-shirt caked with dried blood. Centuries to crawl naked to the door, then raise his arm high enough to turn the knob and push the door open a crack. The effort sapped most of his strength, and he sat with his head thrown back against the wall and cold air rasping in and out of his lungs.

But he couldn't stay here long. Eyes closed, he gathered his inner resources, calling on rituals passed from father to son back to the time before written records.

He had learned the words on his sixteenth birthday—the way his brothers had before him. Only two of them were still alive. The ones who were tough enough to survive.

"Taranis, Epona, Cerridwen," he whispered through split, swollen lips, then repeated the same phrase and went on to another.

"Ga. Feart. Cleas. Duais. Aithriocht. Go gcumhdai is dtreorai na deithe thu."

Pain flashed like lightning in his brain. As bad as the first time. No—worse, because his body was too battered to abide the change. He forced himself to endure the agony because he must.

As they had throughout his adult life, the ancient words helped him through the torture of transformation, opened his mind, freed him from the bonds of his human shape.

His brother, Ross, had told him the words were Gaelic. An appeal to Druid deities for powers no man should possess. He didn't care what they were—so long as they helped center his being.

The human part of his mind screamed in protest when he felt his jaw elongate, his teeth sharpen, his body jerk as limbs and muscles transformed into a different shape that, still, was as familiar to him as his human form. Gray hair formed along his flanks, covering his body in a thick, silver-tipped pelt. The color and structure of his eyes changed. And when he forced himself to stand, he was on all fours.

He had been a man. Now he was an animal.

A wolf.

If anybody saw him, maybe they'd think he was a big dog. Or maybe they'd be too busy to notice him. If he was lucky.

The pain was almost too much to bear, but he forced himself to hang onto consciousness. Forced himself to poke his head out the door and reconnoiter in the hallway. He could see an open doorway, where the ambulances unloaded the injured and the dying.

Mustering every ounce of resolve he possessed, he staggered toward the exit.

Someone behind him shouted. "What the hell?"

He kept going, into the night. Into the woods.

HE holed up in an old shed until he was strong enough to hunt. With deer meat in his belly and only a vague plan in mind, he transformed back to his human persona. He stole a car and drove west, changing his name, courtesy of a convenient gravestone in a cemetery in Canton, Ohio. He vowed to stay out of trouble from now on.

Thirty miles west of Denver, he detoured onto a narrow

mountain road, drawn by the majestic scenery, so different from the rolling countryside around Baltimore. At the edge of a pine forest, he stopped to stretch his legs. Or perhaps, fate had tapped him on the shoulder.

As he stood in the sun-dappled forest, he realized something was badly wrong. No birds chirped in the trees. The small animals he expected to hear in the underbrush were strangely quiet. Even the insects seemed to have abandoned the area. The only sound was that of water gurgling over rocks.

A hundred yards from the road, goose bumps rose on his arms when he found a she-wolf and her pups, sheltered by a small cave of rock—all dead. The pups nestled against their mother's belly fur as she lay on her side, her eyes closed. The little family looked as if they were sleeping. Still, he knew the smell of death, knew they would never get up and run free, breathing in the scent of pine and earth and game.

His vision blurred as a profound sense of loss washed over him. Was it for the lifeless wolves—or for himself?

As he dragged in a draft of the forest air, he knew the wolf and her pups were not the only dead creatures here. There were others—too many to count.

Some disaster had befallen the land, as if an evil magician had put the forest under a spell.

Which, he reminded himself, was none of his business, even if it were true. He looked back toward the old Chevy he had liberated from Jack's back lot of half-dead wrecks. He had left his own problems behind. He didn't need anyone else's. Still, something compelled him to walk farther into the shade of the tall pines, feeling their needles crunch under his feet. Sheltered by the forest, he probed for danger, but he knew he was alone. And he knew he wasn't going to leave until he found out what had happened.

Swiftly, he removed all of his clothing. Then, in the light shifting through the tree branches, he ran his hand down his ribs. His body was healing. He could see taut skin and firm muscles, although various parts of his anatomy were still marred by yellow bruises. He'd stopped peeing blood, though. The cut on his forehead, covered by a lock of dark hair, was healing, as was his split upper lip. He was damned lucky he hadn't lost any teeth.

For the first time since leaving Baltimore, he uttered the words that brought the change upon him. Unlike the last time when he'd barely been able to speak, his voice was strong and sure as he rode above the pain.

Transformed, he stood and sniffed the air. Usually in the woods, he felt a raw, primal joy at his change from man to wolf. Today that pleasure was tainted by the air around him. Something raw and ugly wafted from the surface of the water where it splashed over the rocks.

Poison, his sharp sense of smell told him. His human intellect wondered why the she-wolf had drunk the water. Maybe the smell had changed gradually, so she hadn't known what was happening. Maybe a sudden discharge of chemicals had taken her by surprise. Or perhaps she simply hadn't recognized the danger.

The animal in him wanted to flee from the evil that hung like tainted fog over the landscape. The man he was overrode that instinct and forced the wolf to stay, forced him to follow the creek upstream.

He was hardly aware of time and distance passing as he traveled through a nightmare landscape. Everywhere he looked, he saw evidence of man's obscenity, illuminated by the rays of the setting sun. Death and destruction followed the creek.

A doe tried to run from him and floundered on legs that wouldn't hold her weight. A raccoon stared with glazed eyes. He found fish floating in the water and a family of dead foxes. As he picked his way along the riverbank, heading upstream, the water changed. It had been clear, but it began to have a brown tinge. Farther on, scum clung to the rocks, and farther still, the smell of poison began to clog his nostrils.

Then, in the distance, he saw a scar on the face of the land. Smoke belched from a tall chimney, where a mining or logging operation defiled the land.

A sign warned: PRIVATE PROPERTY, KEEP OUT.

He ignored the admonition, but he never got close enough to discover what man-made nightmare was changing the pristine forest into a charnel house.

He sniffed the scent of a man on the wind at the same instant a sound like a firecracker split the air, and something plowed into the trunk of a nearby tree. A bullet.

The wolf was no fool. He turned and ran for his life. But he knew he would come back. If not in person, then in spirit.

CHAPTER
ONE

A UNIFORMED RENT-A-COP directed Sam Morgan to a grassy parking spot beside the curving driveway. He pulled his sleek Jaguar next to a boxy Volvo, then got out and clicked the remote control lock. It was precaution he always took, although he was probably the only thief attending the Wilson Woodlock party.

He'd garnered an invitation to the Montecito, California, mansion through one of the tony organizations he belonged to for the purpose of mingling with the well-to-do, especially the ones who raped the earth for their own gain. The ones who killed animals and savaged forests. The ones who poisoned water and air and earth. Liberating some of their ill-gotten wealth was his chosen profession, as well as one of his chief pleasures.

His next target was Wilson Woodlock, whose company was currently denuding a stand of timber in Washington

State with the enthusiasm of a termite nest on steroids. Woodlock. It should be Woodkiller.

"Enjoy your evening, sir," the rent-a-cop said as Sam strolled up the driveway.

"I certainly will," he answered, with the right touch of enthusiasm.

A middle-aged couple in evening dress joined him on the curved drive, and the perfume wafting off the woman almost knocked him to the blacktop. Holding his breath, he dropped several paces behind them, pretending to admire the scenery.

The house sat in the middle of a walled park big enough to swallow a good-sized townhouse development. Instead of cookie-cutter dwellings for the masses, wide lawns with artfully naturalized plantings stretched into the darkness.

A blaze of lights and the buzz of conversation at the end of the driveway announced the mansion. The structure was typical of the upscale southern California neighborhood— Spanish grandee, with wrought iron balustrades and a red tile roof.

As Sam stepped into the entrance hall, a waiter immediately approached with graceful flutes on a silver tray.

"Champagne."

"No, thanks," he answered politely. He hadn't touched a drop of alcohol since the long-ago disaster in the Baltimore bikers' bar. Back then he'd been rough and tumble Johnny Marshall wearing a black T-shirt and an attitude. Now he was Sam Morgan who felt as much at home in a tuxedo as he did in his wolf's skin.

From saloon to salon in eight years. It was amazing how easily he'd taken on the veneer of civilization—once he'd put his mind to it.

Johnny would have been intimidated by the size of the house and covered his discomfort with a derisive sneer. But

Sam fit easily into the posh surroundings. He didn't have to prove anything—to himself or anyone else.

And he silently complimented his host on the small engraved sign at the front of the hallway: THANK YOU FOR NOT SMOKING. At least Woodlock shared one of his values. Like alcohol, cigarettes were on his Don't-even-think-about-it list. Smoke made him sick, even secondhand.

At the bar in the conservatory, he requested his usual: "Soda water with lime." Then, drink in hand, he wove his way through the partygoers. He recognized many of the faces—some from *Newsweek* or the California papers. Others were from households he'd robbed. But why not? A man with Woodlock's environmental record would have friends of the same persuasion.

He greeted a few acquaintances but kept moving. When he felt the hair on the back of his neck prickle, he went still. Casually he stopped to look at a Picasso print hanging over a Bombay chest. Then, just as casually, he turned. When he saw no one staring at him, he continued on his way.

He encountered his host in the dining room. The lumber baron, a balding sixty-five-year-old man with a shallow chest and stooped shoulders, was propped against a sideboard, talking to several cronies. He seemed almost inert, except for his eyes, which were bright. Too bright. It looked like the guy had fortified himself with something potent in order to withstand his own party.

When Woodlock looked in his direction, Sam pasted a smile on his face and came forward. "I'm pleased to have this chance to meet you," he said, holding out his hand. "I'm Sam Morgan."

"Oh, yes. From the Glendora Fund list. So glad you could come."

The other man's palm was damp and pudgy against his, and Sam had to work to keep a look of disgust off his face.

They chatted for a few minutes; then Sam said he'd like to see his host's famous pre-Columbian art collection, the one that had been written up recently in *Smithsonian Magazine.*

The man flushed with pride and directed him toward the back of the house, leaving him to find his own way while he kept up his host's duties.

Sam easily found the small gallery. It was full of glass display cases that held a wealth of miniature carved and sculpted figures, produced by skilled artisans before the arrival of Columbus in the New World. He bent to look at a woman with large breasts and exaggerated sex organs, then studied the alarm system on the case. When he'd seen what he needed to see, he moved on to other figures—a man riding a llama and a mountain cat, ready to spring. Sixteen little gems were exquisitely rendered. And all were too distinctive to sell on the open market. But he wasn't interested in their cash value. Simply depriving Woodlock of his fabulously expensive tchotchkes would be enough of a reward.

He switched his attention from the art objects to the room itself, looking for a control panel for the alarm system. Although he saw nothing, he'd studied the house plans and had made an educated guess. As he'd hoped, the keypad was in a closet that backed up to the gallery. Once inside, he turned on the small flashlight he'd brought. Taking a piece of special paper from a case in his pocket, he carefully laid it over the keys, then replaced it and slipped the case into his pocket again.

His task completed, he strode to the buffet table and enjoyed a slice of rare roast beef on a cocktail bun. But the crush of people was starting to oppress him. There were too many bodies. Too much heat and noise. Too many smells. If somebody on the other side of the room farted, he knew it.

When he found a closed door, he opened it and stepped into the family room, where he could be alone for a few minutes of decompression.

The shelves behind the boxy chenille sofa were filled with an interesting assortment of books and knickknacks. Mentally he noted a couple of figurines he was pretty sure were Limoges. Nice, but probably not worth his time and trouble.

French doors at the side of the room led to a terrace. He thought he might step outside and give the back of the house a quick inspection. Before he could open the door, however, the swish of a silk skirt stopped him.

"So what do you think of Romberg's chances in the primary?" a woman asked.

He was about to say that he thought the man would be the Republican candidate for governor, but the words froze in his throat as he turned to gaze into the most extraordinary pair of green eyes he had ever seen. Automatically his mind catalogued other details. She was about five foot six, slender, with delicate features and long golden brown hair swept back from her face and held by antique platinum clips studded with tiny diamonds. A matching pendant hung from a slender chain around her throat, dipping toward the cleavage just visible at the top of the softly draped bodice of her ice-blue cocktail dress.

"Very nice," he murmured.

When she gave him a quizzical look, he realized his response hadn't exactly meshed with her question.

He cleared his throat and tried not to sound like a tongue-tied teenager. "Romberg is going to get the votes of people who are worried about raising taxes."

She played with a strand of her hair. "He can't run on one issue."

Sam wanted to say something intelligent. But the

woman's enticing scent wafted toward him—not perfume but her own delicious essence, wrapping him in a seductive embrace. He felt her green eyes stripping away his carefully cultivated veneer, and he couldn't help wondering if she saw all the way down to the wolf lurking deep inside.

Impossible. Nobody could detect the wolf—unless he wanted them to.

He knew who she was. He'd been intrigued enough to dig up every scrap of information on her that he could find.

Some people photographed well. She was just the opposite. As they stood face-to-face, he saw that all the cameras pointed her way had failed her utterly. None had managed to capture her subtle beauty.

Before he could speak, she filled the silence. "I don't think we've met. I'm Olivia Woodlock."

"Sam Morgan," he answered, then heard himself asking, "Were you following me around?"

Did a little flash of guilt cross her features? Before he could analyze her expression, she dipped her head and looked up at him through a screen of lashes.

Her voice turned flirtatious. "You caught my attention."

"I try to blend into the woodwork," he answered.

"You couldn't."

Her tone sent a little jolt along his nerve endings, which he tried to ignore. Starting anything with Woodlock's daughter would be insane. His best option was to put some distance between them, but she took a step closer, moving so that she was facing him.

"I'm glad you stopped by," she murmured.

"Why?"

"I get tired of the same old faces, the same conversations. Do you live nearby?"

"I drove down for the evening," he answered easily.

"From where?"

He almost told her where he lived before quashing the impulse. "North," he said, and left it at that.

It was difficult to keep his focus on her face. He wanted to look at the place where that diamond pendant decorated her cleavage.

He should excuse himself and blend back in to the crowd. He and Olivia Woodlock were standing too close, getting too involved. He didn't want to be attracted to Wilson Woodlock's daughter. And he didn't want her to remember him later.

Too late for that. They were reacting on too basic a level—a very sexual level.

Below the surface of the conversation, he was feeling his own guilt, since his purpose in her home wasn't exactly honorable. Then he reminded himself sternly that she had been brought up in solitary splendor in a house that hundreds of people would be happy to share. Her bedroom alone could probably house three families.

Her bedroom. If he asked her to go up there with him, would she accept the invitation?

The outrageous thought shocked him. Since the bad old days in Baltimore, he'd learned caution. He'd learned to focus on what was important at each moment of his existence. Olivia Woodlock was muddying his brain, tempting him to break the ironclad rules he'd made for himself. He knew by the tension crackling between them that he wasn't the only one sexually interested.

"Do you often play with fire?" he asked, hearing the thickness in his own voice.

"Never."

"Then what are we doing now?"

She licked her lips, and his gaze followed the movement of her tongue.

"We're getting to know each other."

"And then what?"

He waited for a snappy rejoinder. Before she had a chance to continue the conversation, a loud thumping noise and a shout from somewhere outside the room made her eyes go wide.

The blood drained from her face. Pushing past him, she rushed out the door.

CHAPTER
TWO

OLIVIA BOLTED FROM the room, her pulse pounding in her throat, her high heels clicking on the Mexican tiles as she rushed down the hall.

She sensed Sam Morgan behind her but didn't spare him a glance. Several partygoers turned in astonishment, and she rudely shouldered past, tossing out a perfunctory "sorry" as she made for the front hall. When she saw a crowd of people facing the bottom of the steps, her heart stopped, then started again in double time.

"Let it be a waiter who spilled a tray of hors d'oeuvres," she whispered, without much hope.

As she reached the front of the crowd, she caught a glimpse of dress shoes and black trouser legs halfway down the stairs.

"Oh, Colin," she breathed.

Her brother didn't have the brains God had given a hamster—at least when it came to common sense, she amended quickly. He was brilliant with computers; the guest list for the party would have been somewhat different if it hadn't been for his research. But he'd gotten sick and had to go to bed. Still, she'd been afraid he'd try to come down, anyway.

Following the pants legs upward, she saw he had lost his footing somewhere between the landing and the middle of the flight. His partner, Brice, was bending over him, looking as worried as she felt.

Scrambling up the steps, she dropped to her knees beside her brother. "Are you all right?" she asked urgently.

Colin's eyes went from Brice to her. "I'm fine." With his jaw clenched, he pushed himself up, then flushed as he glanced at the onlookers.

She cupped her hand over his shoulder. "You're hurting."

"Not much. Just my ankle." He dragged in a breath, then grabbed the banister and tried to stand. But his leg crumpled beneath him, and he sat down heavily again. From the corner of her eye, she saw her father hugging the wall, probably too embarrassed to step out of the crowd. For him, appearance was everything. The sight of his son sprawled on the stairs did not make a pretty picture. Particularly with Colin's male lover leaning over him like an anxious wife.

Inclining her head toward the onlookers, she raised her voice. "My brother is fine. He has a touch of the flu, and he got dizzy on the stairs." As she spoke, she was thinking how good she'd become at telling lies. Smiling, she added, "I'll be with you shortly."

"Yes, yes. Nothing to get excited about," her father finally chimed in as he ushered some of his guests back toward the bar. "Just an unfortunate mishap. Come, have a drink."

To her relief, the gawkers began to clear the hall—all but one. Sam Morgan, of all people, came up the stairs toward them. As he climbed, he stopped and picked up Colin's glasses, which she hadn't noticed and might well have trampled.

"Let me help you," he said, handing the glasses to Colin, who put them back on to stare at the newcomer.

She watched recognition dawn in his eyes. He hid it quickly, clearing his throat and asking, "Do I know you?"

"Sam Morgan."

Olivia tried to interrupt. "We can manage."

But Morgan was already pushing up Colin's pants leg to look at his ankle. "It's swollen. Either it's sprained or broken," he said.

"Sprained," Colin answered instantly.

"You should have it X-rayed," Morgan said.

"I think ice will take care of it," her brother answered as he turned to Brice. "Could you get me some in a plastic bag?"

"Of course." Brice scurried off, probably glad to be useful.

She wanted to tell Morgan to join the other guests. He was too aggressive, too distracting. She couldn't prevent her response to him, even when her full attention should be on Colin. She was aware of Morgan's every movement and his indisputable masculinity. Aware of the clean, woodsy scent of his body, his strength, his assessing dark gaze, the nearly black hair that needed a trim . . . the mouth that hinted of carnal knowledge.

She blinked, chagrined that her mind was wandering down such paths at a time like this.

Morgan helped her brother stand, then steadied him when he wavered. Colin hobbled slowly up the steps, leaning heavily on the other man.

"Which way?" Morgan asked.

Colin hesitated for a split second. "Right."

The computer room. The last place she'd have taken him.

She bit back a protest, as she followed them down the hall and into the room, her gaze darting immediately to the piles of printouts. Some of them might be papers Sam Morgan shouldn't see.

Colin sighed in relief as he dropped onto the leather couch. Brice arrived with the ice pack in time to help him get settled, with his leg propped on the glass and brass coffee table, a pillow beneath it and the ice pack placed carefully over it.

While Brice was fussing over her brother, Olivia scanned the papers on the desk and decided they were safe.

Then, turning, she crossed to the sofa and inspected her brother's outstretched leg, making a critical assessment of his condition, thinking how much their roles had changed. After their mother had left, he'd been the one who'd cleaned her scraped knees and administered first aid for bee stings. Now she was tending to him. He looked shaken, and perspiration filmed his forehead. She wanted to shout at him that he should be taking better care of himself. But she wasn't going to do it in front of Morgan.

Colin and Brice exchanged a very private glance.

The warmth in that look sent a stab of envy through Olivia. Not that she begrudged her brother the comfort of the relationship. It was just that no one had ever looked at her like that. Maybe no one ever would. If her father had his way, she was doomed to a loveless marriage.

Well, she and Colin were going to do something about Dad's cowardly plans. Of course, she could get herself killed in the process. But she'd decided that would be better than ending up as the wife of a man who wanted only to wield his power over her.

Her brother interrupted her dark thoughts, and she realized he was speaking to Morgan.

"Thank you for your help." He laughed. "Although I would have picked a less dramatic way to meet."

"Glad I was here," Morgan replied.

"I should introduce you to my very good friend, Brice Brayman."

"Nice to meet you."

Olivia watched them shake, aware that they were assessing each other. Undoubtedly, Morgan had picked up on Colin and Brice's relationship, but he wasn't going to pass judgment, at least not overtly. Brice joined his partner on the couch, reaching for his hand and knitting their fingers together. "Morgan's right. Maybe you should get that X-rayed," he murmured.

"If the swelling doesn't go down," Colin answered grudgingly.

Maybe Morgan was embarrassed to be intruding on the family scene, because he turned away and stared at the long desk, taking in the computer, the various peripherals and the custom-sized screen that helped compensate for Colin's reduced vision.

"Quite a setup you have."

Colin grinned. "It keeps me in touch with the world."

"Yeah." To Olivia's relief, Morgan added, "I should be going."

"You don't need to rush off," Colin countered, and she wanted to take him by the shoulders and shake some sense into him.

But Morgan was already heading toward the door. When Olivia started after him, he shook his head. "I can find my own way out."

His broad back disappeared down the hall.

Olivia waited several beats before asking, "I don't suppose you pulled that falling down the steps act on purpose?"

"Oh, come on. I twisted my ankle *on purpose*?"

"Maybe that part was an accident."

"You think I'd risk having Dad furious at me? You know damn well he's going to come charging up here later and chew the hell out of me."

"Yes," she answered, quietly. She didn't envy Colin. Years ago he would have gotten lashed with a riding crop. Now it would simply be a tongue lashing.

Surprising herself with her calm voice, she gave Brice instructions for the cold pack. "You're supposed to alternate twenty minutes on and twenty minutes off with the ice."

"I will."

She wanted to stay and make sure Colin was all right. He was getting sicker more quickly than any of them had expected.

He caught the look in her eye and probably knew what she was thinking. He said only, "I'll be fine."

"I hope so," she answered with sincerity.

He gave her a mischievous look. "You go on down and act like nothing happened. You're good at that."

She wanted to protest that she hated playacting. Instead she left the room.

In the hallway, she started for the steps, then stopped short when she felt a sudden wave of dizziness. Clenching her teeth, she braced her hand against the wall to steady herself and stood with the world swaying around her.

"No. Stop it this minute!" she ordered herself.

Standing in the hall, she waited until she was feeling almost normal. The dizzy episode lasted only a moment, but it was an excellent reminder of why she'd persuaded Colin to help her embark on the biggest lie of her life. Still, it felt as if she and her brother had set a doomsday machine streaking down a mountainside. All they could do was make the best of the ride and hope they didn't crash-land at the bottom.

Once she'd rejoined the guests, she wove her way among them, her progress slowed by frequent questions about her brother. She gave them all the flu story again, but her eyes scanned the crowd, searching for the man she had encountered in the family room.

He wasn't there, nor did she find him anywhere else. She fought a mixture of relief and disappointment. It seemed he had left, and she couldn't shake the disturbing feeling that he had taken some part of her with him.

CHAPTER
THREE

FIGHTING THE RESTLESS rush of blood through her veins, Olivia stood in the dining room, watching people from the catering company help Irene and Jefferies clean up after the party.

Her gaze wandered to a Marc Chagall lithograph in the small gallery collection over the buffet. It showed an exuberant man flying through the air toward his beloved, his neck at an odd angle and a bouquet of flowers in his hand. In an art history class she'd taken at the University of California at Santa Barbara, the professor had explained that Chagall was depicting his wildly ebullient feelings for the woman he would marry, that he often painted a fantasy representation of life. Years ago, her father had liked that quality in the artist. Probably he walked past the picture now without seeing it. For her, the unbridled joy of the man in the painting was a reminder that the Woodlock family no longer possessed the joie de vivre it once had.

"Is there anything I can do for you, Miss Olivia?" Jefferies asked. He was lean and gray-haired now. And his features had aged over the years. But his face was still the one she pictured when she needed warmth and comfort.

She quickly rearranged her own features. "Oh, no. Thank you." Olivia still felt uncomfortable being called "Miss" by a man who had been her substitute parent when she was a child, but she knew she would only embarrass him by trying to put the two of them on a more familiar basis.

"We have some of that raspberry chocolate mousse cake left. It's one of Mr. Colin's favorites," he said.

"Yes. Thanks. I'll take him a piece."

She followed Jefferies into the kitchen, where he put a generous slice of cake onto a dessert plate. She knew he was as upset about her brother as she was.

When their parents had been out of town or out for the evening, Jefferies was the man who had played Monopoly and Clue with them and taken them to riding and tennis lessons. It was he who had bought her sanitary pads and told her what she would need them for. They'd both been embarrassed, but he'd done it because he knew nobody else would.

She touched his arm. "Thank you."

"I'm glad there's some left."

The exchange was warm but brief. She didn't want to linger because he needed to finish up, so he could get some sleep. And she could see Irene, the maid, waiting to ask him a question.

Plate in hand, Olivia headed upstairs. In the upper hall, she could see a flickering light from what had once been a bedroom—until Brice had taken it over.

Drawn to the doorway, she looked at the fat candles set in holders on three carved chests that had been in the attic for years. A golden Buddhist altar stood between the heavily curtained windows. On it, several sticks of incense burned in shallow dishes. An antique rug that had probably adorned a desert nomad's tent covered the floor.

Colin sprawled against several of the pillows, his ice-draped ankle resting on a bolster.

"How do you feel?" she asked.

"Fine."

She wanted to say, "Sure," but she kept the sarcastic comment to herself. Brice, still wearing his tuxedo minus the tie, reclined against another bunch of the rich pillows. Between the men, a square Hermés scarf with a pattern in mauve, gold, and red drew attention to a selection of small objects arranged on top of it.

She knew Brice was propitiating the gods. Or calling on the realm of magic. Or perhaps both.

"Is it okay for Colin to eat a piece of cake in here?" she asked.

Brice looked torn. Probably, eating didn't fit in with his idea of the room's ceremonial purpose. On the other hand, he wanted his partner to get some nourishment. After several seconds hesitation, he nodded his acquiescence.

She handed Colin the plate, collected her own mound of pillows, and took a seat between the two men, her knees tucked up to accommodate the skirt of the cocktail dress.

Brice had set out a strange collection of objects on the scarf. One was a lifelike rendition of a human eye in white and blue glass—an amulet to ward off evil. She knew he'd bought it in Los Angeles, from a shop in the community of Middle Eastern immigrants.

Next to it was a sixteenth-century ornamental brass padlock from China. Brice had told her it was meant to be hung from a child's neck to lock up the youngster's soul and protect it from harm.

He had borrowed a small Aztec statuette from the museum downstairs—a figure of Tlazolteotl, goddess of sexual pleasure, giving birth to the maize god. She sat next to a carved Indonesian male figure with a huge penis and testicles. An ivory Buddha from Burma faced them. And there was something she hadn't seen before—a paperback novel called *Guards! Guards!* by Terry Pratchett.

"What's this doing here?" she asked.

"It's for inspiration," Brice explained.

"Like how?" Olivia asked, aware that he appreciated the interest in his projects.

"It starts with a group of ordinary men who come together to create magic," Brice said. "They each bring objects that might have a little bit of power. And the aggregate adds up to more than the sum of its parts."

"What did they do?"

"Summoned a fire-breathing dragon."

Colin chewed and swallowed a forkful of cake. "I read the book. Unfortunately, the guys couldn't control the dragon. It flew around the city incinerating citizens."

Brice shot him an annoyed look.

"What does it matter?" she couldn't stop herself from saying. "It's just a story, isn't it?"

"Sometimes fiction can be an entrée into all-embracing truth," Brice told her, his voice low and serious.

She didn't argue. She knew how much he wanted it to be true. He thought that divine intervention might be the way to save Colin. But being Brice, he hadn't simply gone to a Christian church and prayed to the Holy Trinity or, maybe, asked the Blessed Virgin to intercede with Jesus for Colin's sake. He'd come up with his own method of asking for supernatural assistance.

She picked up the lock and turned it in her hand before

returning it to the altar. Brice immediately moved the talisman back into the position he'd decided was important.

"So you think you can work magic with these objects?" she inquired.

"Well, I asked the gods to bring you into our circle. And you came. Three is a magic number, you know."

She restrained herself from saying the flickering candles had drawn her to the room. Nor did she point out how bizarre it seemed for the three of them, all dressed to the nines, to be lounging on the floor in front of a makeshift altar full of a bunch of spiritual and secular objects—all laid out on a Hermés scarf.

Colin set aside the half-finished cake, so they could join hands. When Brice nodded his approval, she gave him a small smile. He was so serious. So beyond her experience. And he was totally devoted to Colin.

He was going to be devastated when Colin died.

She cancelled that thought. Colin was going to make it. He had to. And if this magic ceremony could help, she was willing to give it a try.

Brice began to speak in a low, steady voice. "On this winter night, we ask the guidance of the gods who watch over the universe. We ask for protection. And we ask for special favors for a man who has done no wrong, yet terrible tortures have fallen on his shoulders."

Olivia closed her eyes, trying to convince herself that they could make something real happen.

"As the candles flicker, his life flickers. As the world turns, his fate hangs in the balance. But the gods or the fates have the power to set him on a new course. Do not deny him the chance. Let your love and mercy shine down on him all the days of his long life."

As Brice continued to speak, she tried to coax a kind of

hopeful anticipation into her being. Magic was real. If you could just find the key to using it.

Please, she silently begged. *Please let it happen.*

As Brice's prayer wafted over her, she glanced at him, then at Colin, from under lowered lashes. Involuntarily, her hand tightened on her brother's.

They'd both been raised to fulfill certain roles in life. She'd balked at the restrictions. She'd been intimidated by the obligations. Then she'd been angry that the responsibilities weren't going to fall equally on her brother's shoulders.

But her anger had been nothing compared to the wrath of Big Daddy Woodlock when his only son had picked the family's Thanksgiving dinner to announce that he was gay.

Then and there, her father had called his only son every insulting name he could dredge up—from fag to nancy boy to queer. Later, he'd threatened to disinherit him. And Colin had coolly told him that he could make a very good living as a stock market analyst.

Olivia wondered if Colin secretly wished he were the son their father wanted. She knew she wished he hadn't focused on her as the only hope of carrying on the Woodlock line.

Brice stopped talking, and the room was suddenly silent. "I can tell that neither one of you is taking this seriously," he complained.

"I'm trying," Olivia murmured.

"Maybe if you tried harder, it would work."

"We all know what would work," she shot back. When she realized they were still holding hands, she detached herself from the two men.

Colin shifted against the pillows, making himself more comfortable. Silence filled the room. She was wondering what to say, when her brother asked, "So what did you think of Sam Morgan?"

Olivia felt a dart of warmth spear through her. She wasn't

going to tell Colin that Morgan turned her on. Instead she allowed, "He's too sure of himself."

"He's been very successful at his chosen profession. It's made him very rich."

Brice picked up the evil eye and turned it around in his hand. "He exudes sexuality."

"You would notice that," Colin muttered.

"You didn't?"

"Yeah, but I also noticed he's as straight as a knight's lance."

"A nice phallic image."

Olivia listened to the two men banter. Once she had resented Brice. Now she accepted him as one of the family—and trusted him implicitly.

"We can control him," Colin said with the confidence that sometimes drove her crazy.

"With magic?" she asked, then gave a shaky laugh.

"I think you've got a better way to control Sam Morgan."

She blanched. "What do you expect me to do?"

"As much as you want. By all accounts, he's very good in bed."

"Colin!"

"I saw the sparks leaping back and forth between you two," her brother murmured.

She sighed. "You don't miss much. Even when you're in pain."

"I know you pretty well. I like seeing you come alive."

"You won't like trying to work with Morgan. He does what he wants, when he wants, and for his own reasons," Olivia answered, rubbing her hands on the suddenly prickly flesh of her bare arms. In one of their late-night strategy sessions, she had come up with the idea of getting help to steal back their family heritage from Luther Ethridge, the man who had snatched it from them.

Colin had eagerly begun looking for the right candidate. Sam Morgan stood head and shoulders above the others he'd found.

Had sexual attraction swayed her judgment? She'd been obsessing over Sam Morgan since she'd first read Colin's biography of the man and looked at his photograph. Really, she should have stayed away from him tonight, but she hadn't been able to resist following him into the family room.

Realizing the two men were looking at her, she deliberately lowered her hands. Colin thought they'd hit the jackpot with Sam Morgan, but she wasn't so sure it was going to work out the way anybody expected.

She was savvy enough to recognize that Morgan had stirred something hot and sensual inside her. Too bad she couldn't whip up a witch's spell that would keep him under control.

A sudden noise made her head jerk toward the door. An instant later, her dad came blasting through it. He'd taken another hit of coke, or whatever he was using now, and his eyes were manic.

UNCONTROLLABLE anger surged through Wilson as he charged into the room. They were in there again. Doing one of their fake magic ceremonies. And the thought of Woodlocks sinking so low made his blood froth.

He was the head of this family. And they were defying him. A few years ago nobody would have dared. But now they had no shame.

"What the hell is going on?" he demanded, because he wanted to hear their half-baked answer.

Colin blanched, but he kept his voice even. "An after-party conversation."

"Fuck this! Stop this crap. Stop it, do you hear!"

With some part of his mind, he watched himself. And there was still enough rationality left in him to be appalled at his own behavior.

But once the anger took him, it was in control. Striding across the room, he grabbed Brice by the arm and yanked him to his feet. "Get out. Go on, git. I want to talk to my son without his fag lover and chief wizard hovering around."

Anger gathered on Brice's face. But a warning look from Colin had him stalking out of the room like the good little lapdog that he was.

With the fag lover gone, Wilson focused on Olivia. "I expected better of you."

"Sorry," she whispered.

"Sorry isn't good enough." To keep from striking her, he paced to the window, then whirled and faced Colin again, almost knocking over one of the candles.

Olivia reached to steady it, as Wilson let loose with a torrent of words. "If you'd married Demeter Ethridge, the family wouldn't be in this mess," he shouted at his son.

"Demeter Ethridge has the IQ of a stalagmite," Colin shot back.

"You didn't have to discuss quantum physics with her. You just had to fuck her," he shouted.

"I didn't want to fuck her, as you so delicately put it."

The boy's insolence only fired his rage. "Didn't *want* to? Or *couldn't* get it up for a woman? Couldn't you just pretend she was a boy, and that you were fucking her in the ass?"

"Are we going through all this again?" Colin asked in a weary voice.

"Don't smart-mouth me, sonny. You may beat me out on an IQ test, but I was still in charge of this family, the last time I looked." Unable to stop himself, he charged across the room, this time scattering the magic objects spread on the scarf.

He felt Olivia grab his arm and try to yank him away.

He could hear her voice buzzing in his ears, "Get off! Get off him!" she shouted, pounding on his shoulders with her fists. Though he paid no attention to her, the exertion was too much for him. Unable to support his own weight, he sank down heavily in a nest of pillows, panting, watching Colin fall back against the wall.

Olivia's first words were for Colin.

"Are you all right?" she asked urgently.

"Yes," he answered, reaching to shove his glasses back into place.

Only then did she turn to her father—the man who should have been her first concern. "Dad, you need to rest."

He felt tears stinging the backs of his eyes, and he fought to keep his children from seeing them. Somewhere deep inside himself, he hated his behavior, hated his weakness, hated the way he'd lost control of himself and his family.

He'd been holding everything together. Doing his best for himself and for his children. Suddenly, it was all slipping away.

And he was too tired to do anything about it. When Olivia took his arm, he let her help him up. Trying not to lean on her too heavily, he allowed his daughter to help him toward the door.

Still, he needed to make something clear. "I need one of you to do your duty," he growled. "If not Colin, then you."

"My marrying Luther Ethridge won't accomplish what you think it will."

"He'll give us what we need."

She sighed. "He'll enslave me and kill you and Colin and Uncle Darwin."

"No," he said. He'd thought of that. He'd thought of a

way to keep it from happening. But now he couldn't remember what it was.

"Come on. Let's get you to bed," she said.

LUTHER Ethridge was sweating. But it was a good sweat.
He'd spent a half hour on the stair climber and was two
minutes away from finishing his hour on the weight ma-
chines that occupied the spacious gym on the lower level of
his home.

The house—well, no, it was a castle, really, with a front
designed to resemble a medieval fortress and stone walls reinforced against earthquakes—was built into a mountain
overlooking La Jolla. Long ago, he'd bought himself the
home and almost everything else that he deserved. All
through his childhood, he'd been held by his parents to standards set by the Woodlocks, and he'd always rated second
best. Well, he wasn't second best to anyone now. The Woodlocks' fate was in his hands, and he planned to keep it that
way. Through the floor-to-ceiling, bulletproof windows of
the gym, he looked out at the lights of the city and the black
vista beyond, which would metamorphose into an expanse
of the Pacific Ocean as the sun rose. He was waiting for his
contact at the Woodlock house to call. He knew it might be
hours before his spy could slip away, but that knowledge
didn't curb his impatience. This was a big night for Wilson.
The old man had scheduled a formal party, and Luther was
eager to know how it had gone.

After wiping his face on a butter-yellow towel, he
snatched the portable phone from the chrome-and-steel
credenza and strode into the dressing room. With efficient
movements, he pulled off his damp shorts and shirt and
carefully stowed them in the wicker hamper. Naked, he
stood in front of the mirror, inspecting his body. At forty,

he was in excellent shape and worked with single-minded intensity to keep it that way.

For just a moment, another image flickered in his mind: the scrawny kid who had been the butt of practical jokes at the exclusive Dickensen Preparatory School for Boys.

"Go away," he muttered, angry that the persona he'd obliterated long ago still had the power to leap into his mind when he least expected it.

Once again he was a ten-year-old kid, his heart pounding as he walked into the hushed entrance foyer of the school where the Woodlock boys had gone for generations. He'd thought Dickensen Prep would change his life.

He laughed, an angry, grating sound. It had done that, all right.

He'd been weedy and awkward then—the last guy picked for any team. The kid nobody wanted for a roommate. The butt of countless jokes and insults. His first six years at Dickensen had been a living hell. But over the summer before his junior year, when his body had metamorphosed from boy to man, he'd seen an opportunity to change his life. He'd vowed to turn himself into a guy nobody would dare mess with, and he'd started working out in the gym, determined to return to school in the fall with new muscles and a new attitude. He'd accomplished those goals. And he'd been working his ass off ever since—in the gym and in every other venue where he could excel. He was strong and competent, in control. A millionaire many times over. He was proud of what he'd accomplished in life all by himself. He'd learned the value of hard work. The value of instilling fear. The value of focusing on a goal and doing whatever it took to get what he wanted.

He made a small face as he patted his abdomen. No matter how many hours he spent in the gym, he couldn't rid himself of the little paunch below his waist. But he could fix that easily. Time for a trip to Dr. Tomaso in Tijuana. The town had a bad reputation as a tourist trap, but he wasn't going there for painted pottery or jai alai. The city across the border from San Diego was also the perfect location for the luxury clinic that his favorite plastic surgeon ran. Dr. Tomaso was a very talented man. Luther had been there half a dozen times for minor procedures. Like the chin implant and liposuction that had given his face a more masculine profile. And the neat little operation that had lowered the interior shaft of his penis so that two more inches hung down. The kids at school had teased him about his small dick. Well, the hell with them. He looked fine now. Potent. Masculine. Although, another two inches would be even better. Too bad those pills and patches he kept seeing ads for on the Internet were dangerous.

Tomorrow he'd get his secretary to schedule a quick session to take care of his midsection. He'd be in and out of the clinic in twenty-four hours, tops.

Reaching into the large shower stall, he turned on the water and adjusted the temperature, then stepped in, enjoying the feel of the six sprays hitting his body. Afterward, he toweled dry and turned to the closet where he selected Yves Saint Laurent jeans, a soft baby blue knit silk pullover by Armani, and a pair of alligator loafers he had had made at a small factory in Genoa.

The phone rang as he was fixing a health drink.

"Yes?"

"I can't talk long."

"Understood."

"The party was a success. Except for the unfortunate incident where Colin fell down the steps."

"Did he?" Luther chuckled. "The poor boy. What about the others?"

"Wilson is maintaining himself on stimulants."

"And Uncle Darwin?"

"He's showing definite signs of mental instability."

"Good."

"After the party, Wilson gave Colin hell for not agreeing to marry your sister."

"Leave her out of this!"

"Yes, sir."

"And get me the guest list. I mean those who actually attended."

"Yes, sir."

He rang off, thinking that his plan was going very well. Soon he'd have the Woodlocks exactly where he wanted them. Especially Olivia. He wanted her in bed—under him, on her back, on her stomach, any and all ways he could think of.

But meanwhile, it was time to go have some fun with the special visitor in his tower room.

CHAPTER
FOUR

THE DRESS REHEARSALS were over. If he was going to change his mind, now was the time.

In wolf form, Sam approached the Woodlock estate from the mountains above the property, wending his way easily down the steep slope that would be difficult for a man to navigate. In the shadow of a small grove of trees, he sniffed the chilly night air, searching for anything that might threaten him in the immediate environment. Many animals had been here—raccoons, magpies, sparrows, deer—but no other human had visited this patch of ground in the past few weeks.

A car passed on a nearby road, its headlights cutting through the early morning darkness. The gray wolf waited until he was alone in the blackness again. Then, in the shadows under the trees, he silently said the ancient chant that would change him from wolf to man.

With the transformation complete, the wind sent a

shiver over his bare skin. Quickly he scooped up the layer of pine needles covering a newly dug hole in the ground, then brought out a large plastic trash bag with his clothing and equipment.

Minutes later, dressed in black sweats, he slung a knapsack over his shoulder and crossed the hundred yards to the back wall of the estate. There, he threw a grappling hook attached to a rope to the top of the wall and climbed over.

On the other side, he lowered himself to the ground and cautiously approached the mansion, skirting the pavilion that housed the swimming pool. From under the branches of an oak tree, he studied the house as he had on so many nights. At two in the morning, it was dark and still. But that didn't guarantee all of the occupants were tucked in their beds. Colin had trouble sleeping. So did Wilson. Other people lived here, too: Wilson's brother and three servants. A big crowd for a house that Sam planned to rob.

His eyes darted to Olivia's window. Sometimes she stood in the darkness, looking out, as though searching for something. He wanted to believe she was looking for him. She wasn't visible in her window, but the thought that he might see her if he waited long enough made him suddenly breathless. Was it she, not the little figurines in the art gallery, who drew him back here night after night?

He tried in vain to stomp out the question and the even more useless train of thought. He was here to rob the place, dammit.

Yet Olivia continued to invade his mind. Vivid pictures danced in his head: the two of them, naked and aroused. It was easy to conjure the scene he had dreamed so many times since the party, where he'd first laid eyes on her. In his fantasy, he leaned back against a solid stone wall and splayed his legs, equalizing their heights as he gathered her in, so that there was no space between his body and hers.

Yet she inched closer, pressing her breasts tightly against his chest and her belly against his groin, his erection nestled in the cleft at the top of her legs. In his imagination, he swayed her body in his arms, cupped her bottom so he could rub her sex against his aching cock, at the same time he angled his head to feast from her mouth.

Five tortured minutes later, he was hot and hard and cursing himself for a fool. He dragged in air and let it out in a rush. When he was sure his attention was focused where it belonged, he looked at the mansion again. On some deep, instinctive level, he sensed that bailing out of the Woodlock job would be a good idea. But somewhere along the line, it had become more personal than any other heist he'd undertaken, and not only because of Olivia. The further he'd dug into Wilson Woodlock's business dealings, the more he despised the man. He'd traveled north and seen the Woodlock logging business for himself. It was destroying a habitat where thousands of animals lived, and nobody was doing anything to stop it—especially not the government.

Of course, robbing the man's estate wouldn't stop the destruction. Maybe Greenpeace or the Sierra Club could get the EPA to act against Woodlock Industries. He'd given both of them large sums of money—and he would give them more—designating the contributions to fight the wholesale leasing of public lands to logging operations. He hoped the money, combined with the organizations' political clout, would be enough to take care of Woodlock.

Meanwhile, Sam wanted the lumber baron to feel a sense of violation akin to his violation of the land. And ravaging his priceless collection of pre-Columbian artifacts would certainly do the trick.

Sam strained his eyes and ears toward the house. As far as he could tell, no one was on the first floor. "Let's roll," he muttered under his breath, then slipped through the shrubbery at the edge of the wide lawn, heading for the patio.

He was operating by the book he'd written. First, he checked to make sure that the motion detectors were off. Then, he stood for a long time, listening for sounds of movement. Everything inside was as still as a tomb.

He was prepared to cut the glass on the patio door, but it was unlocked. All he had to do was walk inside and close the door silently behind him.

In the family room, he sorted out the scents of the various people. Wilson, the son, his lover, the uncle, servants. Above all, Olivia. Her scent wafted around him, sending a dart of arousal through him. She had been in the room recently.

He was here to steal artifacts. Instead, he pictured himself going up the stairs and searching out her room. It was easy to imagine slipping into her bed and folding her close.

With a grimace he canceled the heated scene. What the hell was wrong with him?

His jaw clenched, he made his way down the hall to the art gallery, went past, and stepped into the closet that housed the control panel. The paper he'd employed on his last visit to blot up body oil showed him which keys were touched frequently.

Taking out a small computer designed by a very specialized electronics shop, he activated it and waited while it made connections to the keypad and simulated various combinations of punches. He didn't need to know the access code. The processor would figure it out for him. Still, this was always the part that made him the most nervous. He hated standing around while the computer did its work. In five minutes, his patience was rewarded. With a small electronic beep, the computer turned off the alarm on the cases holding the artifacts.

His night vision allowed him to work without switching

on the light. He had just unscrewed the glass panel on the side of a case when a noise from the doorway announced that he wasn't alone.

Whirling, he saw a figure standing in the darkness.

"Put your hands in the air," a cool voice said.

CHAPTER
FIVE

OLIVIA STOOD IN the gallery doorway, her heart blocking her throat as she kept the revolver in her hand trained on the shadowed form she knew was Sam Morgan.

Reaching for the wall switch, she turned on the light. He stood casually beside a display case, and as they regarded each other across ten feet of charged space, she knew he was trying to decide what to do: rush her and damn the consequences—or bide his time.

She tried to keep her expression neutral, but it was difficult, given the mixture of emotions roiling through her. Before the party, Sam Morgan's bio and picture had intrigued and attracted her. After their meeting, thoughts of him had filled her mind, both awake and in her dreams.

Still, she'd been sure she was prepared to see him again. As he casually studied her, she knew she had been a fool.

He spoke first, in a maddeningly controlled voice. "I take it you knew I was coming back."

She might have denied the obvious. Instead, she gave a small nod.

"Me, specifically? Or just some random thief?"

"You, specifically."

He tipped his head to one side, studying her. "How did you know this was the big night?"

"There are sensors installed under the rug," she answered, because it was easier to focus on small details than on the big picture.

"And your brother dreamed up an elaborate plan to trap me?"

She raised one shoulder. "You don't think I could lure you here by myself?"

A smile flickered on his well-shaped lips. "Not with pre-Columbian artifacts."

The wolfish way he was looking at her sent a shiver over her skin, and she silently cursed herself for reacting to him.

"So was your father in on it, too?" he asked.

She felt her facial muscles go rigid. "Dad's going to . . . hit the roof when he gets the news."

"The news about what, exactly?"

She was the one with the gun. She had the advantage, she told herself, as she moved out of the doorway and into the room. "The news that Colin and I have hired you for a job."

His eyes widened briefly before he could hide his surprise. "I hate to mention it," he said evenly, "but I haven't accepted. I don't even know the job specs." His gaze went pointedly to the gun. "Is that my reward if I decline?"

She licked her dry lips, watching him take in the small movement. He had picked a very bad night for his invasion, but she'd simply have to make the best of it and hope that nothing went wrong. "I can turn you over to the police. But I don't want to do that. I'd rather have you on our side."

"That's an interesting suggestion," he said, and she had the distinct feeling he wasn't afraid of her or the gun or the cops. "What's in it for me?" he added.

"The thrill of pulling off the biggest heist of your life," she answered, giving him the line she'd rehearsed. Even to her own ears, it sounded stilted.

"You mean, I walk away with a lot of money?"

"Not from the job, exactly."

"Then what?" he pressed.

"If we get back the family jewels, then I'm sure Dad will pay you a handsome sum."

His calm façade cracked open. "The hell he will!" he spat. "I wouldn't take his money if he stuffed it in his mouth and crawled over broken glass to hand it to me."

"I believe you said the wrong thing, my dear." Colin's maddeningly rational voice came from over her left shoulder.

She fought a mixture of relief and annoyance as her brother stepped into the room. She'd told him she could handle this, knowing he was probably going to butt in, anyway. As her gaze flicked to him, she saw from his expression that there had been an unfortunate development upstairs.

"What?" she asked.

He gave a small shake of his head, and all she could do was hope everything was under control.

When he spoke, he addressed her, not Morgan. "Daddy's money means nothing to him—unless he steals it. He thinks he's Robin Hood, with a modern twist. His mission is to screw the nasty bastards who rape the land, then give the loot to the environmentalists."

She'd argued that couldn't be Morgan's primary motive, but the sudden hard look in his eyes told her that Colin had him nailed.

Her brother moved farther into the room and sat down

in the easy chair in the corner. His health had been a little better recently. Maybe Brice's magic ceremonies had done some good. Or maybe it had been the herbal concoctions Brice kept whipping up in the blender and making Colin drink. Still, she knew her brother needed to conserve his strength.

Morgan addressed his next comment to Colin. "Let's cut to the chase. Stop playing the grand puppeteer, and tell me what's really going on."

Her brother spread his hands. "We're not playing anything. A thief of your caliber seemed like the perfect solution to our problem. But given the nature of your profession, we didn't think we could call you up on the phone and ask you to steal something for us."

"You've got that right." Morgan shifted his weight from one foot to the other. "Okay. What's so insanely valuable that you hatched this elaborate plot to get me here?"

Considering the stakes, Olivia thought Colin sounded surprisingly calm as he replied, "Something . . . important to our family. We want it back."

"Your sister just called it the 'family jewels.'" Morgan cocked an eyebrow. "I assume she didn't mean it in the usual sense. So what is it?"

"A valuable artifact," Olivia elaborated.

"So how did you decide I was the guy to come to your rescue? I'm not exactly a knight on a white horse."

"Colin is a computer genius," she answered.

Morgan cocked an inquisitive eyebrow at her brother. "Congratulations. Um . . . pardon my rudeness, but so what?"

"Olivia exaggerates my talents," Colin clarified. "I know how to tease facts out of the Web. I know how to calculate probabilities and make correlations, and to put information from one source together with completely different data. We went looking for a master thief. I saw a pattern of difficult robberies, and I began assembling known facts. They led me to you. So we made sure you knew about Daddy's prized collection."

Morgan waited a few beats before saying, "Well, if *you* figured all that out, maybe the police are about to scoop me up."

"I doubt they have the resources to produce the kind of statistical probabilities I can generate," Colin answered, and she heard the touch of pride he couldn't conceal.

Morgan nodded and leaned casually against the display case, silently telling her that he wasn't worried. What did he know that they didn't?

"I think you'd better tell me more about your employment specifications. But first"—he cocked an eyebrow at her—"put down that gun, before somebody gets hurt."

In truth, the damn revolver had been weighing down her hand. After a quick glance at Colin, she set the weapon on the cabinet near the door, then cleared her throat. "The Woodlocks have been feuding with the Ethridge family for years," she said. "Luther Ethridge has stolen something important from us. It's heavily guarded, and we can't get it back without help."

"What is it?" Morgan demanded.

"A priceless ancient box that's been in the family for years," she answered.

Morgan studied her face, as though he knew very well she wasn't telling the whole truth. "A box. Uh-huh. What's in it?"

"Maybe nothing," Colin tossed out, his voice dismissive.

Olivia couldn't stop herself from shooting him a shocked look. "Don't say that!" She looked from her brother to Morgan. "It's something valuable—but not to anyone but us."

Right. Only a matter of life and death.

"Then why does this guy named Luther Ethridge think it's worth stealing—and keeping?"

"To hurt us," Colin answered for her. "It's a revenge thing."

Morgan folded his arms across his chest. "What did you do to him?"

"Our families have been . . . associated for decades. We've been more successful, and he can't stand that."

"That's a start. Now let's have the truth—not a bunch of crap that sounds like you lifted it from a bad spy movie." Morgan gave them both a disgusted look. "You're not hiring me to steal a box."

Colin spread his hands. "This isn't like any movie. It's more like a fairy tale."

"Ah. Well, then, I beg your pardon," Morgan answered, sarcasm coloring his voice.

Ignoring the editorial comment, Olivia added, "There's an ancient legend handed down through the years that we must keep the box safe or our family will . . . come to ruin."

Morgan studied her, and she felt naked under his gaze. "And you believe that?" he asked sharply.

"My father does. Luther does," she whispered. "And as long as they think it's true, it is. You studied my dad's environmental record. It was a lot better five years ago before Luther took away . . ." She stopped and started again. "Before Dad lost confidence in his own judgment, and his business started failing."

"So, now you're telling me I should save your family—for the sake of the spotted owl?"

"I can't tell you any more, not until I know I can trust you." Even as she uttered the phrase, Olivia silently admitted the lie. She could never tell him the truth. And even if she did, he wouldn't believe it.

But maybe she'd piqued his curiosity.

Colin began speaking again. "If you need another in-centive, there's always saving yourself. I've documented your criminal history. I could send the information to the cops."

She gave her brother a pitying look. Apparently he still thought he could operate on a logical level with this man. That was Colin—tied to logic and numbers and probabilities.

Morgan kept his gaze fixed on her. "Let's assume for the sake of argument that I buy into your grand scheme."

"Okay."

"First, you and I have to talk—alone. Otherwise, no deal."

She looked at Colin. "I guess you'd better clear out."

"I don't like that idea. He's dangerous."

She wanted to shout that she'd known that all along. Instead, she simply answered, "You said he's never killed anyone."

"Yet."

"If you want my cooperation, I get some private time with Olivia," Morgan reiterated.

Her brother's only response was to stand up and leave the room.

When he was gone, Morgan looked around. "Come outside, where it's less likely that someone is going to be listening in on the conversation."

"Are you implying the room is bugged?" she snapped.

"Now, why would I think a room with sensors under the rug might be bugged?"

She made a dismissive sound but did as he asked, leading him down the hall to the room where they'd first talked. He opened the door to the patio, then gestured for her to step outside.

She would have preferred to stay in the house, but she gave him a defiant look as she strolled onto the patio. The moon allowed her to see only a little in the darkness, and she concluded that his night vision must be better than hers when, as she shivered, he came up and put an arm around her shoulder.

She stiffened. "Don't."

"Why not?"

"You make me nervous," she admitted, hating the quaver in her own voice.

"But you want me to work . . . with you," he said.

"For me."

"I don't work *for* anyone."

Yet he was still here. Standing close, with his arm around her.

The cold air should have helped clear her brain, but it didn't. She had thought of him night after night. And she couldn't fool herself about his motives. Olivia knew he'd come back to the house where she lived because he wanted—no, needed—to be with her again. As much as she needed to be with him.

He made an angry sound.

"What?" she asked, alarm lacing her voice.

He took her by the shoulders and turned her to face him, staring down into her upturned face. "Maybe you picked the wrong guy. Maybe I'm too ruthless to deal with," he said, and she caught something unexpected below his words. He was as wary of her as she was of him.

That gave her the courage to insist, "You're not the wrong guy."

"You're sure you haven't made a bad mistake, luring me here?"

"It wasn't a mistake." She could hear the desperation in

her tone as she begged, "Please, can't we just make this simple. I need your help. I'll make it worth your while."

He laughed. "I'm afraid you've caught a tiger by the tail. Are you smart enough to realize that?"

"Yes," she whispered into the darkness.

"You mentioned fairy tales. Don't you remember that the man who saves the kingdom ends up with the king's daughter?"

Her mouth was almost too dry for speech. But she managed to say, "In this case, that's impossible."

He didn't answer with words, only stared at her mouth. For a charged moment, neither of them moved, but she was aware of the silent messages passing between them.

I want to kiss you.

I know. But you can't. I can't.

You can. Because I have to do this. Just this once . . .

Before she could back away, he lowered his head. As his lips touched down on hers, a conflagration crackled to life, heat blazing through her, startling and all-consuming in its intensity.

She was instantly ready for sex, and she made a small, shocked sound deep in her throat, because nothing in her experience had prepared her for the speed or intensity of her response. Until this moment, she'd been able to fool herself into thinking she could handle Sam Morgan. Now she didn't even know if she could handle herself.

His lips had looked so hard when they'd been talking in the gallery. But they weren't hard at all. They felt soft and yielding against hers, as though he was caught by the same wild sexual need that had swallowed her whole.

She forgot about how she and Colin had tricked him into coming here. Forgot about the desperate reason why they needed his help. Her only reality was the strong, intense man who held her in his arms. She felt her heart slamming against the inside of her chest as he gathered her into a possessive embrace. Or maybe it was his heartbeat she felt.

Every danger signal urged her to pull away. Some rational part of her mind was issuing warnings—demanding that she end the kiss before it was too late, insisting that she tear herself out of his arms and run away into the darkness.

Instead, she opened her mouth for him, begging him to deepen the kiss. He gladly accepted the invitation, angling his head for better contact, devouring her with his lips, his tongue, his teeth.

He tasted of dark, mysterious forests and ancient legends. He tasted of the magic that she had so desperately sought. She didn't know how it could be so, but without doubt, it was. With a gruff sound, he gathered her even closer, holding her firmly against his hard-muscled body, as though the intimate contact were as necessary to him as the air he breathed.

Suddenly a wind sprang up, disturbing the still night, shaking tree branches and whipping around them. When she swayed on her feet, his hands slipped to her hips, cradling her bottom and anchoring her more firmly against his erection, showing her in no uncertain terms that one simple kiss had made him ready to drive himself into her.

She answered with a small sound that might have begun as a protest. Instead, she knew it only revealed her own sharp and powerful needs. In the tiny corner of her mind that could still deal with concepts, she recognized him as the man ordained for her since the beginning of time. But the part of her that had to live in the world shoved the knowledge aside. She simply couldn't deal with such thoughts. Not now. Not ever.

Yet the sensations he was arousing inside her were too powerful to ignore. She wanted him. This instant. On the damp grass, if they couldn't make it to some place more comfortable in the next five seconds. And from the way he clung to her, swaying on unsteady legs, she gathered that the feeling was mutual. The knowledge gave her a sense of power.

In the next instant, that power, along with all else, was shattered by the sound of a gunshot cracking the night air.

CHAPTER
SIX

THE SOUND OF a gun firing was like a bolt of lightning lancing through Sam's brain. It had come from inside the house, but the shooter could come charging out the door at any minute.

"Get down!" In one swift motion, he pushed Olivia toward the shelter of the back wall. Following her to the ground, he covered her body with his, offering her what protection he could.

Instead of cooperating, she struggled against him.

"Stay down," he snapped. "Do you know who's shooting?" The thought of her in danger was like a garrote tightening around his throat, and he tried to hold onto her, even as a gust of wind seemed to be bent on tearing her away.

And she wasn't helping. "Let me up. I have to—"

Colin dashed onto the patio, breathing hard as his gaze darted around, finding them and instantly taking in Sam's protective position. "It's . . . Darwin," he said between gasps for air.

A blast of wind roared across the patio, as though punctuating the words.

"Where is he?" Sam demanded.

"He ran onto the sun porch and locked the door," Colin answered, pitching his voice above the roar of the wind.

"Upstairs?"

"Yes."

Sam helped Olivia to her feet, then guided her toward the overhang where the second story sheltered the patio.

She pushed her hair back, drawing Colin's attention, and Sam wondered if it was obvious what he and Olivia had been doing before the shot rang out.

But, hell, who cared? Compared to being shot at, it hardly mattered that he'd been about to ravage the fairy-tale princess.

Colin took a deep breath and seemed to gather his wits. "Darwin must have come down and found the gun in the gallery."

Olivia's skin had gone pale as bleached bone.

She opened her mouth, but Colin spoke first.

"I should have been thinking about him," her brother said. "I knew . . ." He trailed off when his sister shook her head.

"What the hell is going on?" Sam cut in. "Is anybody hurt?"

"Uncle Darwin's having mental problems," Olivia said, raising her voice above the moaning of the wind.

Before Sam could comment, another shot split the darkness, the bullet whizzing past his shoulder.

"I think you'd better call the cops," Sam growled as he herded Olivia and Colin through the door, fighting to close it as gusts of wind tried to tear it from his hands. Finally, he slammed it shut, and the noise level dropped abruptly.

"No police," Colin answered.

When Brice appeared in the family room, an anxious look passed between the two men.

"Are you all right?" Brice asked.

"Yes."

The discussion broke off abruptly when Wilson Woodlock came puffing into the room. He stopped short when he spotted a stranger in the middle of the family group.

"Who the fuck are you?" he demanded.

Olivia answered quickly. "He's Sam Morgan. You met him at the party. Remember?"

"What's he doing here—tonight?"

"He's going to help us."

"How? By taking Darwin off to the funny farm?" her father snapped.

"Of course not."

Sam stepped between father and daughter. "I understand your brother is holed up on the sun porch. Maybe you'd better make sure he stays there."

"Thurston is watching the door."

"Is he armed?" Sam asked.

"Yes."

"And what's he going to do if Darwin decides to come out? Shoot him?"

Wilson took the point. "Maybe I can talk Darwin into putting down his weapon. He might listen to me."

"That would be helpful," Sam muttered under his breath as the old man hurried off. He'd watched the house for weeks. It had seemed relatively normal, considering the massive wealth of the occupants. Who knew it was an insane asylum? Giving Colin a sideways glance, he suggested, "Maybe it's time to get some professional help for your psychotic uncle."

"He's not psychotic," Olivia broke in.

Instead of arguing with her, he said, "Okay, we'll discuss abnormal psych later. Tell me about the sunroom and the roof." He hadn't studied that area in detail because he hadn't planned to go anywhere near it. Stupid—and he knew better. He should have been thorough. "How do you get into the sunroom without going in through the hall? Are there windows? What else? What about a door to the roof?" Realizing he'd hit them with a lot of questions at once, he added, "Maybe you'd better draw me a diagram."

Colin sat down at the desk in the corner and pulled out a sheet of paper and a pencil. With great precision, he began drawing a picture. The room was rectangular, with long, wide windows. One door opened to the end of a hallway. French doors opened onto a roof deck.

"The door to the hallway is solid? I mean, all wood— with no glass?" Sam asked.

"Yes."

"And it's closed?"

"Yes."

Sam studied the layout, wondering if he could climb up without getting shot, particularly with the wind blowing. "Let me have a look at the wall," he said. "Maybe I can get up there."

Olivia put a hand on his arm. "What if he comes outside with the gun again?"

"You'll lose your draftee thief," he said dryly.

She looked torn. "You think you can get the gun away from him?" she asked.

"First things first." His gaze swung from Olivia to Colin and Brice. "Listen carefully. If I do this, I need to handle it my way. I want that door"—he pointed to the sun porch door on Colin's diagram—"to stay closed until I say it's okay to open it. Do you understand?"

"Yes," they all answered, but he wondered, anyway, if somebody would come bursting into the room at the wrong time. They'd get a nasty surprise if they did.

"I'd better go up," Olivia said and started for the door.

Sam grabbed her arm. "Be careful."

She turned and looked into his eyes. "I will," she answered, and he knew from her expression that there was a lot more she wanted to say to him. Personal things. But not in front of an audience. And not in the middle of a crisis.

When she had left the room, Sam turned to Colin. "Your uncle—a couple of years older than your father, five foot ten, a hundred and eighty pounds, practically bald, pasty complexion. Right?"

"Yes," Colin answered. "I'll probably end up looking like him—if I live that long."

"You're going to be all right," Brice said fiercely.

Sam wanted to ask what was wrong with Colin, but this wasn't the time to satisfy his curiosity. Gripping the handle of one French door, he held it tightly against the wind as he opened it and stepped outside. What was with this damned wind, anyway? He'd checked the weather reports—standard procedure for break-in nights. The forecast had been for clear skies with hardly a breeze. Yet as he wormed his way past a line of tall shrubs whose long branches were wildly thrashing, he thought a hurricane must have blown in out of nowhere.

He finally spotted the second-floor balcony. As he looked up, he saw a vine-covered drainpipe along the wall, but he had the feeling that neither the vine nor the pipe would hold his weight. He circled the other way around the house, stopping where he'd dropped his knapsack. Squatting, he pulled out the coiled rope and grappling hook he'd used to scale the wall encircling the estate. Olivia and her family might as well reap the benefits of his having come prepared.

The situation had a certain irony, he thought as he hurried back to the balcony, throwing an arm in front of his face to ward off a flapping branch. To get a view of the sunroom, he took a dozen steps away from the house. As far as he could see in the moonlight, the homicidal uncle had gone back inside—or he was lurking in the shadows, waiting for someone to attack him.

Hoping the latter wasn't the case, Sam judged the range. As he calculated the amount of swing he'd need for the rope, he asked himself why he was leaping into danger to help the Woodlock family. They'd given him the perfect opportunity to slip away. He could go over the wall, then call 911 and tell the police there was a crisis in progress at the millionaire's estate.

But he knew he wasn't going to do that. The choice he'd made to help had a lot to do with Olivia, but she wasn't the only reason. It seemed he'd stumbled into a nice little mystery, and his curiosity had gotten the better of him.

Let's hope curiosity doesn't kill the wolf. Compensating for the wind, he managed to connect with the metal railing, the hook clanging like a church bell. He tensed, then breathed out a sigh when no wild-eyed bald guy with a gun in his hand bent over the edge of the balcony to see what was going on.

In fact, the sound of furniture breaking somewhere above seemed to suggest that Uncle D was busy elsewhere.

Since success in his profession depended as much on his physical as his mental power, Sam kept himself in good shape. The climb to the second floor normally would have taken him less than a minute, but the wind kept blowing him back and forth as he clung to the rope. By the time he swung onto the tiled balcony surface, he was breathing hard.

He waited until his breathing had returned to normal,

then quietly crossed the eight-foot-wide balcony. Careful not to step into the light pouring from the open doorway, he looked through the window. He saw wicker furniture, a variety of flowering plants, and a hulking bald man standing with his back to the open French doors. Uncle Darwin, Sam presumed. He was wearing dark slacks and a dress shirt that was plastered to his body by perspiration. Waving the gun, he was shouting words Sam couldn't make out—doubtless, at someone on the other side of the hallway door.

As he watched through the window, he thought about the best way to take the guy down. He considered going in as a wolf, since that was his most natural fighting mode. But a wolf couldn't subdue a man without inflicting serious damage.

So he pushed the door open a crack, relieved that Darwin was still focused on whoever was in the hall. Obviously upset, he waved his arms and shouted, "If you won't join me in the good fight, go away! The demons of war are on us."

Demons? What the hell . . . ?

"Darwin, let me help you," came Wilson's voice, muffled by the closed door but sounding far calmer and more reasonable than he had downstairs.

"Help me how?"

"Let me in. Everything's going to be all right if you just put down the gun."

"How can you say that, you fool, you . . . you dupe of the Old Ones? We are doomed! The demons have stolen the breath of life! And now they are coming to finish us off!"

"No. Darwin, listen to me. You're sick. There are no demons."

"What's wrong with you? Can't you feel their hot breath on your face? On your neck?"

"Darwin, let me in. You'll feel better if you take your medicine."

"You lie! The demons have corrupted your thoughts! They have put false images in your mind!"

"Please, don't do this."

The conversation between the brothers was fascinating. Darwin was obviously delusional, but something—an intuitive feeling he couldn't define—made Sam wonder if there was some grain of truth in the old man's ravings. He wanted to keep listening, but when Darwin pointed the gun at the door, Sam acted swiftly.

Sprinting across the room, he leaped onto Uncle Darwin's back, intending to grab the gun and bring him down.

The weapon discharged, the bullet hitting the floor. And a shout came from the other side of the door. "What's going on?"

When the door rattled, Sam yelled, "It's okay. Stay back."

He didn't have time or breath for more conversation. Hoping Wilson was smart enough to remain where he was, Sam banged Darwin's gun hand against the floor. But old Uncle D was stronger than he looked. Or perhaps he had the ferocity of the insane. Regardless, he wouldn't let go of the weapon, even when Sam banged his hand repeatedly against the floor.

Darwin had a hundred pounds on him, and before Sam could stop him, the lunatic wrenched away, rolled over, and pointed the gun at his attacker.

Instinct took over. The ancient chant came to Sam's lips without conscious thought.

"Taranis, Epona, Cerridwen," he growled, fighting danger in the way his ancestors had fought since they had emerged from the forests of ancient Britain. He was still fully dressed, but he felt himself changing, felt the gray

hair sprout on his face and hands, felt his features reform themselves.

His vision blurred as the world around him changed in shape and texture. But Darwin Woodlock was very close, and Sam had no trouble seeing the look of utter horror suffusing the man's features.

CHAPTER
SEVEN

DARWIN MADE A low, anguished sound, part fear and part pain, then scuttled across the floor like a crab looking for a hiding place. As if tuned to his fear, the wind still raging outside strengthened even more, rattling the windows as it howled. Dropping the gun, he cradled his arms over his head.

The wolf had served his purpose and was of no further use to Sam. He broke off the chant in mid-syllable. The pain was terrible as he stopped in the early stages of transformation. He could barely think. Barely breathe. Barely keep a scream of agony locked in his throat. When the door burst open, all he could do was look up stupidly at the figure charging into the room.

"The demon. The demon," Darwin shouted, pointing toward Sam.

A muscular man who looked like a bodyguard or a

bouncer gave him a hurried glance, and Sam braced for some kind of violent reaction. But he assumed he must have returned to acceptable human parameters because the newcomer hurtled past, heading for Darwin, with Wilson following more slowly behind him.

The bodyguard dropped to his knees beside the old man. In his hand was a hypodermic needle. He looked back at Wilson, clearly asking for permission.

"Give me a moment," Wilson answered, then took a step closer to his brother and hunkered down beside the bodyguard. They looked like they were getting ready to pray for Uncle D's salvation.

"Darwin, you're all right. Everything's all right," Wilson soothed.

The man on the floor fixed his eyes on Sam and shrank back against the wall. "He's a demon! With wolf's teeth and claws! Kill him! Kill him!"

Sam winced.

"No, we're not going to kill him. Everything's under control now."

"Get him away from me!" He kicked out at the bodyguard.

Wilson gave a short, frustrated sigh. "We'd better do him."

They worked as an efficient team, probably because they'd done this before. Wilson grasped his brother's shoulders, and the other man plunged the needle into a pudgy arm. Uncle D struggled and screamed, then went still.

A third guy came in. He, Wilson, and the bodyguard picked up Darwin and lugged him out.

Sam climbed to his feet. All attention was focused elsewhere, which gave him the opportunity to slip out of the room and down a set of back stairs. Outside, he dragged in lungfuls of the night air, trying to clear his head. Some part of his mind noted the utter calm around him. The wind had died, leaving the night air still and cool.

So what about Darwin? He'd seen enough to know there was something pretty strange about Sam Morgan. With luck, nobody would believe him. After all, he'd already been babbling about demons.

Sam sighed. He'd jumped right in and tried to subdue the mental patient. Now that he was thinking a little more clearly, he wondered why he was still here.

Olivia and Colin had set a trap for him—baited with pre-Columbian artifacts. He'd told himself he was coming to steal them. So . . . why not take them now, while everybody was busy dealing with Uncle D?

Because he didn't really want the damn little figurines enough to bother. He'd come because he couldn't stay away from Olivia, and he had made a serious mistake. Without giving himself time for a big mental debate, he walked outside and picked up his pack. Then he took off across the lawn, climbed the wall, and headed for the grove of trees where he'd changed from man to wolf. He hesitated for a moment, then decided not to risk another transformation tonight. He picked his way up the hill, which took twice as long on two legs as it would have on four.

TWO hours after he'd arrived at the estate, he was in his Lexus and on his way home.

It wasn't a long trip. He lived in the mountains south of Lompoc, on a ranch that he'd purchased from a dedicated old environmentalist who wanted any potential buyer to sign a contract saying he wouldn't subdivide the property. The conditions suited Sam just fine. The whole point of buying a ranch was to make sure he didn't have any neighbors besides deer and coyotes.

He'd lived in the ranch house for a couple of years, while he'd constructed the dwelling he wanted, bringing in skilled tradesmen for the jobs he couldn't do himself. The new house was built into the side of a hill, with a window wall overlooking the valley and an interior courtyard lit by a skylight. It was a wolf's den, basically. But that was what he loved about it. It was wonderful to step into his lair and lock out the world. The den wasn't a trap. He had an escape hatch, if he needed it—a tunnel in the back that led to an exit on the other side of the hill.

By the time he pulled into the parking area, he was emotionally and physically exhausted. Not too exhausted, however, to realize he'd made a miraculous escape. He'd been damned lucky to get away alive and unharmed.

The darkened house was a blur around him as he strode to the bedroom and threw himself onto the king-sized bed.

He went to sleep almost at once and, soon afterward, began to dream. In his dream, he was a wolf, running through the hills, reveling in his freedom beneath the moon and stars shining down from a velvet dome of sky.

A tantalizing scent blew toward him on the wind, but he turned away from it to hunt game. He brought down a mule deer and filled his belly with fresh meat, then drank from a stream that rushed down the mountain in the rainy season.

He trotted on, traveling farther and faster than whatever would be possible except in a dream. Still, the scent he'd sniffed on the wind followed him, pulling at him. All at once, he recognized it—the tantalizing woman scent of Olivia Woodlock. It wrapped itself around him, calling him. And finally there was no way he could deny his need for her.

In the dream, he turned toward home, racing now, an impossible blur of motion in the darkness. His steps were sure and steady until he reached the bluff above his home. There, he faltered to a stop, looking at the magnificent sight that awaited him on his patio: Olivia Woodlock, dressed in a white silk shirt and slacks. He had fled her, but she had followed him home, because the two of them were bound together by invisible cords.

She sensed him, as he had sensed her. Raising her head, she met his gaze, her eyes asking him silently to make love with her.

The cords between them tightened as he walked down the hill.

Take off your clothes. Let me see you. The wolf couldn't speak, of course. But he knew she heard him in her mind when she smiled, then began to unbutton her blouse.

He came eagerly to her, his eyes never leaving her as she opened the garment, then tossed it onto the flagstones. She'd worn nothing beneath it, and he watched transfixed as she lifted her beautiful breasts in her hands, offering them to him.

Stroke your fingers over the tips. Make them hard.

She did as he asked, giving him a smoldering look that made his blood run hot and fast in his veins.

He stood ten paces from her as she pulled off her slacks. Again she was wearing nothing underneath. Naked, she faced him, so that he could take in every detail of her body. The high breasts, the inward curve of her waist. Her flat belly and sensually rounded hips. The tantalizing dark triangle of hair covering her mound.

Suddenly, the patio table and chairs were replaced by a wide bed, and she lay down upon it, her gaze still locked on his. He climbed onto the mattress and pressed his flank against hers. She reached for him, circling his neck with her arms, kissing his ruff, the side of his face, his muzzle.

He moved his head so that he stroked his face against her breasts, then circled them with his tongue, taking them delicately between his wolf's teeth.

She made soft, aroused sounds that incited him further, her body writhing as he kissed and licked his way down to the hot, swollen core of her, lapping up her luscious nectar as he gave her pleasure.

"Please . . . please, don't make me wait," she cried.

Then, suddenly, he was a man, aching and trembling with white-hot need for her. His body covered hers, and he plunged his hard cock into her, claiming her, making her his. His hips moved in a frantic rhythm that she met thrust for thrust, excitement and need and sheer, unadulterated pleasure swirling around them until the very air turned white with it, and all that existed was that hot, wet, throbbing place where their bodies joined.

He felt the signs of impending climax only seconds before it took hold of him. He gave himself up to it entirely, crying out as it washed through him and out of him and into her, leaving him weak and shaking and replete. . . .

Sam blinked awake and knew immediately that he was alone in his own bed. The sheets were tangled around him, and his body was slick with sweat and the sticky evidence of ejaculation.

"Christ . . ."

He couldn't remember the last time he'd had a wet dream. Hell, he'd never had one like it. He had left the Woodlock estate last night, convinced that he had put the whole insane family behind him. But the dream had made a liar of him. He had brought Olivia with him—to his bed.

"Christ," he said again, shaken to the core.

He had never invited a woman to his home. Nor had he ever come to a woman in wolf form, although he had fantasized about it. But none of those fantasies had been as arousing or vivid—or as real—as the one his subconscious had just conjured. What struck him most about it, though, wasn't the almost blinding sexual excitement he'd experienced.

More telling was that Olivia had accepted him for what he was.

"Oh, sure. Right."

He climbed out of bed to stand on unsteady legs. Cursing again, he strode down the hall and stood staring out the front windows at the brown hills. It was late afternoon. He had slept for hours.

He clenched his hands at his sides, struggling for calm. When he felt more in control, he thawed a steak from the freezer and brought the meat outside to the patio, to his normal table and chairs, not the bed where he and Olivia had ravaged each other.

It had been a dream. Just a dream. Just a very male response to a very attractive woman.

He sat eating the meat, looking out at the scraggly vegetation on the hills, the live oaks, and the clumps of pampas grass he'd planted along the creek, struggling to keep his mind in neutral.

Later he tried to work. But he couldn't keep his attention on any of the jobs he had started planning. As the sun dipped low, he left the house and walked over the hill, into the brown landscape. When he was certain no other human being could see him, he took off his clothing and laid it on the ground. Then he raised his face to the wind and began the chant he had started in the Woodlock sunroom.

This time it wasn't an emergency. This time he was doing something he wanted—needed—for himself.

"Taranis, Epona, Cerridwen," he said in a clear, loud voice that carried across the hillside. He repeated the phrase, then went on to the next. *"Ga. Feart. Cleas. Duais. Aithriocht. Go gcumhdai is dtreorai na deithe thu."*

The transformation didn't come without penalty. There was always pain, like needles stabbing into his brain, into his muscles. But the ancient words helped free him from the bonds of his human shape.

He was a creature of the natural world now. A wolf. His life was easy. Uncomplicated. But as he leaped into the dry grass and started off across the mountains the way he had in the dream, he knew in his heart that he was trying to outrun kismet.

His father had told him years ago that this would happen to him around the age of thirty. Every man in his family was destined to find his mate—the one woman who would complete him. And he would be helpless to resist her.

He had been away from his family for so long that he had stopped believing the old myth—until he had felt someone's eyes drilling into his back. There, standing in a house he'd planned to burglarize, he had turned around and found himself facing Olivia Woodlock.

The daughter of a man he despised.

She couldn't be his mate. He wouldn't let it be true. He would take control of his life. He would break the ancient magic and find another woman. Someone who shared his values. Someone who hadn't been raised like an exotic flower in a temperature-controlled hothouse.

He was safe here, in his own realm. He had saved himself by coming home. The dream was just a fantasy. Nothing to worry about.

Of course, there were other things he might consider a tad worrisome. Olivia and Colin knew he was a master thief, and they could send the cops after him—if they even knew where he lived. Which he doubted, because he had kept his home a secret from the world.

If they sicced the law on him, he was pretty sure their "evidence" wouldn't hold up in court. But they could certainly add a harassment factor to his life.

Still, he didn't think they would do it, if only because he could harass them right back—starting with a report to the Environmental Protection Agency detailing the Woodlock record in Oregon and ending with a visit from Uncle Darwin's "demon."

LUTHER Ethridge stood in his tasteful beige and brown living room, looking out over the lights of the city.

He was one step closer to his goal, and the thought made his lips curve in a satisfied smile. Too bad his toxic parents hadn't lived long enough to see his triumph. They had been in awe of old Abner Woodlock—Wilson's father. They'd sent their son to the tony prep school where the Woodlock sons had gone for generations. And when they'd paid his college tuition, they'd told him he was preparing for a career with the Woodlocks.

But Luther had had other plans for himself. When he'd gotten tired of arguing with his parents about his future, he'd broken off contact with them.

He'd taken the money that had come to him on his eighteenth birthday and started a business, delivering fast food to the dorm rooms of the students at U.C. San Diego. He'd made money and invested in several other businesses, always improving his financial position. And when his big opportunity to buy dot-com stock had come along, he'd jumped into the world of Web enterprise—but had had sense enough to get out before the bubble burst.

Today he was doing a lot better than any of the Woodlocks. And he had ensured that he would do better still.

The report of Darwin Woodlock going on a psychotic rampage warmed his heart. "Old man, you'll be dead soon," he said into the darkness beyond the window. "And if you're in shit shape, Wilson can't be far behind. Or Colin."

A prickle of uneasiness nipped at him when he put Olivia into the picture. But she would come to her senses. Or he would force her to see that he was her only choice. Either way, he'd have her.

Of course, he did still wonder who the wild card in the mix had been that night. Some guy named Morgan had been meeting with Olivia and Colin and had helped subdue the wigged-out old man. Luther's informant didn't know what Morgan had been doing there or even how he'd arrived. Or, for that matter, how he'd left. In the confusion after Darwin's outburst, Morgan had somehow slipped away.

But that had been three weeks ago, and as far as Luther could see, nothing of note had resulted from Morgan's brief appearance on the scene. As a precaution, he had told his informant to keep an eye out for the man, but his intuition told him that nothing would come of it. Nothing was going to spoil his project. If it took a little more time, well, he was an expert at waiting. That was one of the lessons drummed into him at Dickensen Prep.

A smile flickered on his thin lips. It was amazing what you could pick up at a top prep school, along with math and English. He'd discovered that even if it took six months or a year or two years, he could find a way to get even with each of the boys who had tormented and humiliated him. He had cultivated the art of making elaborate plans. And he had learned that you could often get what you wanted by paying someone else to do the dirty work.

Like when poor Sid Howard had come down with that nasty case of food poisoning, after a smidgen of shit had gotten onto those chocolate chip cookies his mom had sent him.

Or when Ryan Underwood had gotten expelled after someone had alerted his teacher that he'd bought a term paper from a "scholastic service." That one had been easy because a lot of the boys had hated smug, cheating Ryan.

But the victories at Dickensen had been schoolboy stuff. Now he was playing for the highest possible stakes.

He had no doubt that his plans would eventually come to fruition. Until they did . . . well, he would continue to entertain himself with the reluctant houseguest who had moved in a few months ago. In fact, he'd pay a visit this very evening.

But first, he thought he might go down to the security vault. Not because there was a problem. He just liked to admire his treasure.

The security was state of the art, updated every few years. The basement alarm system was on at all times, except when he was in personal attendance in the secure area.

Luther punched in the code on the keypad, then opened the heavy door, and started down the steps. Anybody who disarmed the lock and came down here thinking he was safe was in for a nasty surprise. Before he reached the bottom of the stairs, Luther stopped and opened another panel on the wall. Inside was a second keypad into which he pressed another code.

A click told him that the automatic weapon emplacement at the bottom of the stairs had also been disarmed. Still, he never passed it without a slight shiver running through him. It was cold in the windowless chamber because, for security reasons, the heating system did not run down to this level. Nor did the plumbing.

There was no furniture. Only a tasteful Oriental rug warmed the floor in front of the vault. The whole enclosure, including the vault, had been blasted out of the solid rock of the mountain. There were no windows or doors besides the one he had come through.

The natural stone walls called to mind a dungeon, as did the vault door, which had been specially made of reinforced steel. Like a bank vault, you could unlock the door manually, the old-fashioned way. But unless it was done with the remote control scanner, the outer chamber would flood with knockout gas.

He punched in the scanner code, then waited for the click to signal that the door had opened.

As always, his chest tightened painfully as he turned the handle on the door and stepped over the threshold. The room beyond was like a vault but with a very high ceiling so no one could reach the spy camera high above. Inside there was one piece of furniture: an ornate antique table about four feet square, carved from a single block of mahogany.

Sitting in the middle of the table was an even more ornate box. It, too, was made from a solid block, although this one was semiprecious stone—white jade barely tinged with green. A stylized flower was carved into the middle of the lid, with the roots spreading from the base of its stem in all directions, over the top and down the sides. The hinges were also carved from the jade and so was the catch.

Luther stared at the box for a moment, then crossed to the table and lifted the lid. His breath caught, as it always did, as he looked down into crimson liquid shimmering in the bottom of the box. He estimated there had been three inches of the precious substance when he'd stolen the Woodlock family legacy. It now appeared more like two. Some of the fluid had evaporated even with the lid closed, even in the climate-controlled atmosphere of the locked room.

Luther swore softly under his breath. He hadn't expected the elixir to evaporate. But each time he checked it, he saw less liquid. Which meant that he had less time than he had assumed he would.

But that wasn't going to be a problem, he assured himself. He was going to bring about a resolution within the next few weeks.

He stared at the shimmering red elixir, wondering if the amount would make a difference to him—personally. Maybe less was actually better where he was concerned. He kept his hands at his sides, willing himself not to reach out. He had done it before and been very sorry. Still, he kept coming back, hoping something had changed. Intellectually, he knew it hadn't, but for a moment, desire and need overcame rational thought, and he simply could not prevent his hand from reaching into the box, almost as if someone else were moving his muscles.

The instant his finger touched the surface of the glistening liquid, he came to his senses, screaming. It was like sticking his flesh inside a furnace filled with molten glass. He yanked his hand back and staggered to the wall. There, he slumped, cradling his hand and breathing hard, cursing himself and the Woodlocks and the whole damned universe.

THE wolf trotted over the crest of the hill and stopped short. It was early in the morning, and he was going home to his lair to sleep off the night's hunt.

But as he looked down toward the parking area in front of his house, he saw a car that didn't belong there. Next to his Lexus sat a sporty little silver Jaguar. As if sensing she was no longer alone, Olivia opened the car door and climbed gracefully out, stretching her arms over her head and shaking her rich golden brown hair over her shoulders.

Finding her there was so much like his dream that for an instant he felt disoriented, as though he wasn't certain if what he was seeing was real. It helped him to put things into perspective. She wasn't wearing the same white blouse and slacks she'd worn in his dream. Her no-nonsense denim skirt and long-sleeved blue sweater weren't designed with seduction in mind.

It did appear, though, that she was alone, unless someone was hiding on the floor of the car, which was highly
unlikely, given its size.

Sam watched her, his heart pounding hard and fast.
Every deep breath of the mountain air he dragged in was
filled with her scent, carried on the early morning breeze.
And he had to wonder how the hell he had managed to
keep on living these past few weeks as though nothing cat-
aclysmic had happened to him.

She stood back, looking at the unique house he'd designed for himself, then walked to the front entrance and
knocked on the door. Of course, she got no answer. After a
minute, she knocked again, and when no response was forth-
coming, she cupped her hands to the window beside the door
and looked in at his warm and cozy den.

A couple of seconds later, she turned away from the
window and stood staring out across the hillside, her arms
wrapped around her shoulders.

Over the past weeks when he was awake and rational, he
had told himself he was better off without her. He had told
himself she couldn't be the werewolf's mate. He had even
convinced himself that he believed it. But as he stood
struggling to draw breath into his lungs, utterly mesmer-
ized by the sight of her, he couldn't remember any of his
reasoning.

She hadn't spotted him. He still had a choice. He could
still turn and fade into the mountain landscape.

Right, a choice. Stop kidding yourself.

Yet even if he had run headlong into what his father had
claimed was his fate—and he still wasn't entirely ready to
acknowledge that he had—what was her excuse? Why was
she here? She must have gone to considerable trouble to
track him down. He never listed his home address on any
written communications. In fact, only an unnamed gravel

track leading into the mountains marked his ranch. He picked up his mail at a post office box in Lompoc. So she'd had to do some serious sleuthing to find him.

No, not her. Her brother. Colin Woodlock, whatever else he might be, seemed to be a persistent bastard, and Sam realized he must have sent Olivia looking for the master thief. After all, she was the one who'd do a better job of making their pitch. He sighed, then opted for honesty. He didn't care why she was here. He was simply delighted to see her. In fact, if he were a normal man, he would have pulled out all the stops and set about courting her.

Courting? If his vocal cords could have formed the sound, he would have laughed.

He couldn't picture his parents doing anything so mundane. He had always assumed that when his father had known his mother was the one woman for him, he had carried her off to a cabin in the woods and fucked her eyeballs out until there was no way she could deny the bond that had formed between them. Then he'd broken the news that he was a werewolf. He didn't doubt that the shocking revelation had completely freaked her out.

Olivia was a lot more sophisticated and more complicated than his mother. But would that make it more or less likely that she would lose it when she learned the truth about him?

When.

He had progressed from if to when.

Walking at a steady but unrushed pace, he started down the hill, wondering if he were moving of his own volition or being drawn by the invisible cords he had first sensed in his dreams, the cords that connected his soul to hers. He might have admired the fanciful imagery, if his pulse hadn't been pounding so hard in his ears that all he heard was the roaring of his own blood.

When she raised her head, he stopped. He knew from the sudden tension in her shoulders that she had seen him moving through the brown grass.

If life were like his dreams, this was the place where she would hold out her arms to him.

Instead, she took a careful step toward her car, reached for the door handle, and opened the door. Yet she didn't climb into the car. Maybe, deep in her heart, she knew the truth, too.

Forcing himself to walk slowly, wanting very much not to frighten her, he descended through the scrubby grass and brush to the edge of the parking area. But he came no closer. From twenty feet away, he stood looking at her, every cell of his attention focused on her.

As the wind ruffled the fur on his back and played with the strands of her hair, he felt as though the currents of air were pulling them together. Dream images mixed with reality. Olivia naked. Holding out her arms. Gathering the wolf to her.

He wasn't sure how long they stood in front of the house, gazes locked in mutual fascination. But finally some inner voice told him it was enough—they'd gone as far as they should go. For now.

He moved one leg, then another. Not toward her, but away. The movement released him from his trance, and he turned quickly. Circling around to the back of the house, he headed into the hills again.

CHAPTER
EIGHT

THE WOLF HAD disappeared. Or maybe it had been a dog, but she didn't think so. Either way, with the animal gone, Olivia suddenly felt as though her legs had turned to limp ropes. Stumbling to the patio, she flattened her hand against the top of the table, then sat down heavily in one of the comfortable chairs.

There were two chairs, one on either side of the table. With part of her mind, she wondered who might have sat here with Sam Morgan. Or did he have the two merely for symmetry? As isolated as he was—and as hard as it had been to find out where he lived—she wondered if anyone besides him had ever seen the place.

But those were only stray thoughts weaving in and out of the whirlpool of information in her brain.

When the dog or wolf or whatever it was had come toward her, she had been terrified. But he'd stopped far enough away that her fear had ebbed slightly—enough to keep her from jumping into her car and slamming the door. The beast had simply stood there, staring at her with intelligent eyes, as though he knew very well what was going through her mind. At the same time, she had felt a connection to him that she was at a loss to explain. It was as if she knew him. As if she could trust him. Impossible notions. She had never laid eyes on the animal before.

While she was still trying to figure out what had happened, a flicker of movement at the top of the hill caught her attention.

Her head jerked up, and she prepared to meet *canis lupus—familiaris* or not—again.

Instead, she saw a man. Sam. He was dressed in sweatpants, a T-shirt, and running shoes. Obviously he had been out for an early morning run.

Relieved, she watched him descend the hill. He came toward her just the way the animal had come—slowly, as though he were afraid she might jump up and leave. The comparison between the animal and the man was so strong that her throat tightened, and for just a second she felt as if she were experiencing the supernatural.

Clenching her hands, she forced herself to look as if her nerves weren't screaming.

She and Sam regarded each other across fifteen feet of charged space. When he remained silent, she cleared her throat.

"Your dog scared me," she said.

"He's a wolf," Sam answered promptly, his gaze unnerving, as though he expected her to object.

"He belongs to you?"

He hesitated for a moment, then finally said, "As much as a wolf can belong to a man. He's part of my early warning system."

"He seemed intelligent."

"He is."

She wanted to ask more about the wolf, but she sensed that the subject made him uncomfortable. Actually, there was nothing comfortable about this whole reunion.

He shoved his hands into his pockets. "I notice you didn't sic the police on me."

"I never intended to."

"That's not what you said."

She kept her eyes focused on his face. "At the time, I didn't think I had a choice. I was taking Colin's advice."

"So you follow your brother's lead?" he said, making it sound like an insult.

She raised her chin. "I had the idea of looking for a master thief. He came up with several candidates, and I picked you."

"Oh yeah? So you started off thinking you would use someone."

"I wouldn't call it that."

"You mean you don't want to call it that."

She sighed. "Okay. Make it sound as bad as you like. We were desperate. We still are."

She wanted to look away. Instead, she kept her chin up and her gaze fixed on him as he slowly crossed the patio and lowered himself into the chair across from hers.

"I told you, I don't work for anyone but myself," he said.

She ignored his statement and went on. "We still need your help." She paused and licked her lips. "And I realize you need to know why I'm desperate."

He leaned back in his chair and stretched out his legs, but she knew he wasn't relaxed.

Before she lost her nerve, she said, "There's a genetic problem in my family. Colin, my dad, and my uncle are all sick from it."

That got his attention. "What is it?"

"It doesn't have a name. Call it Woodlocks' Disease. I don't know anybody else who has it."

He was still listening with unnerving attention, and she had to look down at her hands as she said the next part. She hoped he would think she was only embarrassed about revealing intimate family details. "It causes various symptoms. You had a nice demonstration of what it's done to Uncle Darwin—attacked his brain. It affects Colin's muscles and, I guess, his nervous system. He doesn't talk much about it to me. But it kills me to see him fall down the stairs or trip for no apparent reason or drop things."

She took her bottom lip between her teeth, wondering if she'd made any real dent in the harsh assumptions he'd made about her family.

She raised her gaze once more to find him still watching her with unblinking intensity.

"Your dad seemed in pretty good shape," he said. "At the party—and then when your uncle wigged out."

His almost casual tone made her want to scream at him. She wanted to ask how he'd like seeing the members of his family slowly die.

Instead, she spoke calmly. "I know you don't think much of my father. I feel like anything I say will be wrong. But maybe telling you things I shouldn't will make a difference."

He answered with a small shrug.

"I'm speaking in strictest confidence. Dad is a lot sicker than he looks, but he takes drugs to keep himself going. I mean stimulants. Medications he can get from a doctor who's willing to treat his symptoms. And sometimes cocaine. The drugs keep him functioning. But he knows they will shorten his life. He's made that trade-off because he can't stand to be weak and sick."

Sam's expression gave no hint of his reaction. He simply went on staring at her.

Quickly, she added, "My dad is rich, as you know. The disease has plagued our family off and on for generations. This . . . this is the first time so many of the men have it at the same time. So Dad hired a researcher to work on a cure. Dr. Regario did find something that seemed to help. He called it Astravor."

Sam's eyebrow quirked upward briefly. "Weird name. So that's what's in the box?"

"Yes."

"If you had the sickness for years, why are you just now developing a cure?"

Olivia realized she hadn't thought that through very well. Damn! She hoped she didn't look like she was lying when she said, "We had a folk remedy. Modern medicine is obviously better. But we never broke the tradition of using the ancient box.

"And before you ask—the folk remedy doesn't seem to be very effective anymore. Or maybe it never was. Or maybe the sickness has mutated . . . But the Astravor was a godsend for us. I guess the doctor made up some combination of syllables for the name. Or it's a foreign word," she said carefully, then hurried on. "Dr. Regario was in a fatal car accident. When we went to his lab, we found all of the doctor's notes had disappeared. We think Luther Ethridge took them when he stole the Astravor."

"All that because he hates your family?"

Olivia sucked in a steadying breath, then let it out in a rush. "There are several factors. I think his parents urged him to be like us. They even sent him to the school Dad and Uncle Darwin had attended. He was a social outcast there. It was a miserable experience for him. I think that's part of the reason he hates us."

"Part?"

"He wanted to unite the families. He wanted his sister to marry Colin."

"Who flat out refused."

"Yes." She swallowed hard. "And he wanted to marry me. I couldn't stand the idea of his laying a hand on me."

She kept her gaze steady on him. "The bottom line is that if we can't get what my dad refers to as 'the elixir' back, he and Colin and Uncle Darwin will die."

There was more to it than that, of course. But she had revealed enough about their personal tragedy.

Sam's gaze turned inward. "Can you strike a deal with Ethridge?" he asked. "He's proved that he can bring you to your knees. Maybe now he's willing to take your money."

Olivia shook her head. "We tried that. He's not interested in money. He's already very rich."

"And you're not lying about this . . . this elixir?" Sam asked bluntly, his gaze still trained unwaveringly on her face.

"No!" she insisted, holding that piercing gaze, knowing he couldn't possibly detect any lie in either her tone or expression, because it was the truth she spoke. "It's a matter of life and death for us."

"And this, uh, family disease . . . you're not talking about something that's . . . catching?"

"No," she said, fudging the truth a bit. At least, it wasn't "catching" in the literal sense.

CHAPTER
NINE

SAM STUDIED THE woman sitting across from him. She certainly looked as if she had run out of options and was willing to throw herself on his mercy. Her eyes were huge and impossibly green. They would have been beautiful except that the dark circles below them spoiled the effect. The marks were like purple bruises on skin that was otherwise so pale it was almost transparent. In the bright sunlight, he could see fine lines at the corners of her eyes that he hadn't noticed before.

The last time they'd talked about what she wanted him to steal, she'd given him a cock-and-bull story about an old box. She was still lying—or, at least, holding back. Oh, he believed her about the men in her family being sick. But there was something else . . . something she wasn't saying.

"What's Dr. Regario's first name?" he asked.

"Henry," she answered promptly.

He'd check that out later. Meanwhile, he wanted to leap

out of his chair, take her by the arms, and tell her she had to trust him if she wanted his help. He wanted to ask if her uncle's ravings about demons had any basis in truth. Was her family really haunted by malevolent creatures?

Sam knew all too well that there were things ordinary mortals dismissed as myth and fairy tale that were, in fact, as real as the sunshine beating down on them from above. Still, he didn't want his own experience—his very existence—to cloud his vision of the obvious. A genetic defect that was so rare as to be unique to one family sounded pretty far-fetched. Even his own genetic anomaly wasn't *that* uncommon. There were werewolves other than those in his immediate family—or so he'd been taught as a child. He hadn't met any of them besides his father and brothers because of an unfortunate werewolf trait: all of them were Alpha males. Once they reached adulthood, they fought for dominance, which was why he'd moved out of his father's house as soon as he'd been old enough to get a job working for a landscape company.

As he took in Olivia's shuttered expression, he could see he wasn't going to get any closer to the truth by grilling her further about the so-called Woodlocks' Disease.

Besides, grilling her was the last thing he wanted to do. He ached to hold her and tell her that everything would be fine, to fold her close and stroke her soothingly. . . . Well, okay, more than stroke, and quite a lot more than soothingly.

For a moment he was caught up in the vivid memories from his dreams. As he sat across from her, he pictured her falling into his arms, begging for his help. And he imagined telling her that they'd talk about it—after they made love.

Instead, he came back to the truth buried beneath his wild, erotic fantasies. This woman was his mate. She didn't know it yet, but these were the first moments of their future together. He wasn't going to start off by dragging her, either by physical force or coercion, into his bed.

So he sat where he was, struggling to hold his carnal impulses in check while he pretended they were discussing his terms of employment, since she still apparently thought she'd come up here to hire him for a job.

"Let's back up to the way your father runs his business," he said. "It's unacceptable from an environmental standpoint. If I agree to help your family, I want him to sign a statement saying that he'll discontinue all practices that are poisoning the water and the land."

She stood up and walked to the edge of the patio, her restlessness proclaiming her tension. When she turned to face him, her face was grim. "He won't."

"If he wants my help, he will."

"He doesn't think he needs your help. Colin and I have to change his mind. So starting off with an ultimatum will just scotch this whole deal."

"What do you suggest?"

"Colin and I will work on the company's environmental practices."

"Who runs the company?"

"Dad has been relying on managers. We'll meet with them."

He wanted to push for more, but he was a realist. He nodded and watched some of the tension ease out of her shoulders.

Lifting her chin, she said, "We need something from you, too."

He waited while she seemed to screw up the courage to continue.

Finally, in a rush, she said, "We need you to be at the estate, so we can be on top of everything you're doing."

"I always work alone," he shot back.

She shook her head. "We have to be in on your plans."

"I don't like the 'we' concept. I'll deal with one person—you," he countered, then watched color creep into her pale face.

"Why me?" she asked in a thin voice.

He stood, facing her squarely. "Who else would you suggest? Certainly not your father. And not Colin. Not your uncle. And not that guy Thurston—the one who's probably the head of your father's security detail."

She blinked, as though she were surprised he'd picked up on the goon's function around the estate.

He waited for her answer, his breath shallow. "Okay," she finally said.

"Good." He couldn't stop himself from pushing her a little farther. "And your mom's not in the picture because she left your father fifteen years ago?"

Her head jerked toward him. "How do you know that?"

"I research everything about places I plan to rob."

"And why was that particular piece of information helpful?" she demanded.

"It established how many people live in your house."

He saw her lips compress into a grim line. "We don't need to talk about my family."

"I disagree. If I'm going to live with you, I need to know what kind of atmosphere I'm stepping into. Are there any other surprises like Uncle Darwin?"

"No."

Even as she answered the question, his mind was streaking off in another direction.

"So you want me to live with you."

"Not *me*. Us."

He let it slide. "What am I supposed to be doing at your estate?"

"You could be working for my father."

He laughed. "Nobody will buy it that I'm working for your old man. We need something more believable."

"Like what?"

"Like I've moved onto the estate because you and I are getting married."

Her dumbstruck expression wasn't particularly flattering.

"What? You can't bear the idea of getting hitched to a thief?"

"It's not that." She flapped a hand in a searching gesture. "I just . . . I'm not sure . . ."

But he'd reached his limit on calm discussion.

"I am," he said, rising to his feet and circling the table. "And we'd better be able to convince anybody watching us," he added, as he pulled her out of her chair and into his arms, "that we're comfortable with each . . . other." He spoke the last word an instant before his lips covered hers.

He had kissed her once before, and the meeting of his mouth with hers had torn through his body like a smoldering forest fire bursting into flames. He was prepared for something similar. Or perhaps he wanted to prove to himself that he could handle his response, that he could manage his lust until the time was right for them to make love.

Either way, he'd been a fool.

Control evaporated like water escaping a steam valve. He made a sound that was half gasp, half growl as his lips brushed hers, then all at once his mouth was locked to hers, the essence of her making his head spin. She tasted of warmth and spice and some indefinable quality he had craved all his life without knowing it—until the night he'd kissed her on her patio. It had taken hold of him then, worked its way into every fiber of his being, and he knew as surely as he knew his own real name that he'd never again be satisfied without it.

He could tell himself any damn lie he wanted—like he was conducting a private test of his self-control. The experiment was over before it had begun. He was caught in a trap of his own making.

Helpless to do anything else, he went on kissing her with lips and teeth and tongue. The small sounds she made in her throat gripped him like iron bands, binding him to her even more tightly. Her hands moved restlessly up and down his back and over his shoulders before she twined her arms around his neck and tangled her fingers in his hair.

"Yes," he growled into her mouth. "Yes."

Reaching downward, he slid his hands under her bottom and pulled her against him, nestling his aching cock against her belly, his hips rotating slowly, rhythmically, increasing the pleasure and the pain. They were standing outside, under the sparkling dome of the blue sky, but that didn't stop him from slipping his hand under her knit top to cover her breast. Through the silky fabric of her bra, it felt soft and at the same time heavy in his hand, and the hardened tip pressing into his palm stabbed at his nerve endings.

"Oh!" she cried out as he rubbed his hand back and forth, torturing himself with the feel of that hard bud and imagining it inside his mouth.

Imagining wasn't enough. Not nearly enough.

With both hands, he dragged her top and her bra up, freeing her breasts, then held the quivering mounds in his hands. They fit perfectly, neither too big nor small, exactly as if they'd been made just for him to hold. And they had—again, the truth hammered home. Taking the pebbled nipples between his thumbs and fingertips, he pulled and twisted gently, hearing her breath accelerate.

When he tore his mouth from hers and lowered his head

to swirl his tongue around one taut nipple, she went absolutely still. And when he drew it into his mouth and sucked, she made a low, sobbing sound, her hands cradling the back of his head, holding him against her.

The need for her was like a fire in his blood. Now. The wolf would claim his mate now, in the morning sunlight.

But not in the scrubby grass that would scratch her tender flesh.

He picked her up and set her on the table with her legs dangling, then pushed her skirt up and out of the way. Her panties were a flimsy barrier. He ripped out the crotch, exposing her most intimate flesh to his questing fingers. She was wet and swollen for him, and she made low, pleading sounds as he stroked her slick folds. Her woman's scent wafted toward him like musky perfume, fueling his need.

He wanted to taste her. But as he bent his knees, anticipating that delicious goal, far above them a jet plane screeched through the sky, splitting the silence of the hillside. He could have ignored it—could have ignored anything at that point, short of World War Three—but the noise clearly shocked her, brought her back to the real world. He saw her eyes blink open in alarm, watched her stiffen.

Scrambling off the table, she struggled to put her clothing back into place.

He could have reached for her and stopped her frantic efforts. Instead he dug his nails into his palms and did nothing. He absolutely was not going to force her in any way.

She spoke in a high quavering voice as she reached under her shirt to rehook her bra. "You . . . you made me forget myself."

"And that's a bad thing?"

"Yes. I have to remember why we can't do this."

"And why is that? You want me. You know damn well I want you."

She dragged in a shaky breath. "But I can't trade sex for your cooperation."

He shook his head. "You're not."

"Then what am I doing?"

"Admitting that there's a lot more between us than a business deal."

Again she paused to draw a breath. When she looked at him, her eyes were haunted. "Sam, what I feel for you frightens me."

"Why?" he asked softly.

She hesitated, seeming to debate what answer to give him. Finally she settled on, "Because being a Woodlock comes with obligations. You think of my family as . . . well, as out for whatever we can get. I was raised to believe that I had a responsibility to the Woodlocks."

"Like what?"

"Like marriage as a way of cementing an alliance with another powerful clan."

His reaction was swift and angry. "That's medieval!"

"Yes," she agreed in a tight voice.

"With Luther Ethridge?"

"No! And we're going to change the subject now."

He watched her breath turn shallow as she waited for his answer. He knew she was asking him to play a very dangerous game. If he wanted to come out of it in one piece, he had to make her lay more of the Woodlock cards on the table. But right now he had the luxury of time.

"All right," he agreed. "Let's talk about what the scenario will be when I get to your place."

"What do you mean?"

"Well, for starters, if I'm your fiancé, how did we meet? And, uh, what do I do for a living?"

She blinked. "So . . . what do you do for a living?"

"I manage my investments. Anyone who checks into my

background will find I have more than enough legitimate resources to account for my lifestyle. But, of course, I'm not as rich as the Woodlocks appear to be. So maybe I'm a gold digger who wants to marry the tycoon's daughter for her money."

He'd spoken off the top of his head. Now he paused to collect his thoughts. "Yeah, I met you at some of the charity events you attend, and I ingratiated myself to you. I've made a point of going to other events where you would be present. But mostly we've been carrying on our courtship by phone and E-mail. The high point was those two visits to your house—the first time at the party and the second, when I came at night to see you and got caught in that flap with your uncle."

"You came up with all that in the last five seconds?" she asked.

"I'm a quick study," he answered, unwilling to admit that his fantasies had suddenly turned into reality. Before she could ask another question, he fired off one of his own. "What computer do you use for E-mail?"

"We have a wireless network in the house. My laptop is hooked up to it."

"Is it password protected?"

"No."

"Too bad. Because if anyone has been checking up on you, they'd see that we haven't been sending messages."

"Who would do that?"

He shrugged. "Your father, for all I know."

"He's too busy for that."

"Good. Does your maid snoop?"

"Irene? Of course not!"

"How many maids do you have?"

"Until my family got sick we had day staff come in. But now it's more convenient to have live-in help."

"Okay. But I'd like to have a trail of correspondence. I can manipulate the date on my computer so that if anybody goes back and checks your E-mail, he'll see that we've been writing to each other."

"What were we writing?"

"Love letters."

She tipped her head to one side in a skeptical look. "You're going to manufacture a bunch of love letters, just like that?"

He hesitated fractionally. "No, I'm going to copy some posts from a blog site I came across—and alter the contents so it looks more personal." He was not going to tell her that he'd already written her love letters, when the pressure of his feelings for her had clamored for release.

Instead, he said, "I've got a lot of things to do in the short term. So perhaps I'd better agree to meet you at your house three days from now."

Her eyes widened. "Three days! We need to get started right away."

"You waited this long for me to come and claim my bride. I'm afraid you're going to have to wait a little longer."

CHAPTER
TEN

THE WOMAN IN the high tower room looked through the barred window at the lights of the city spread below her. It was a beautiful view. A rich man's view. But she took no pleasure in it.

To keep her hands from trembling, she clasped them in front of her. She was in a hell of a fix, and she had no clue how to get out of it.

My name is Barbara Andres. She made the proclamation in her head because she didn't dare utter the words aloud. The room was bugged, and she had been punished in the past for daring to speak her own name. Standing with her back to the room, she raised one hand and gently touched her face. The skin felt smooth. Her nose was small and straight. But it wasn't the nose she had been born with. A Mexican doctor had changed the shape—and more. He had carved new lines into her features. Now that the scars had healed, she looked so much like another woman that the change took her breath away. She looked whole and healthy. Because no one could see the mental scars.

She fought to keep them hidden, because that was the safest course.

Turning, she glanced at the clock. It was after six, and her captor would unlock the door and come in all too soon. He would test her on her lessons, and if she failed the test, he would punish her.

First she turned to the DVD player and played the disk again. It showed several people. But the focus was on a young woman who looked a lot like she now looked.

She watched the woman smile. Holding up a mirror, she imitated that smile. After watching the woman walk, Barbara took a trip across her room, gliding with the same elegant motion. Next, she got out the sheets of paper she was supposed to memorize by that evening. The questions today were all about food.

She sat at the small desk beside her bed and laid the paper in front of her. Covering the right side of it with one hand, she murmured the answers. "My favorite breakfast food is scones with blackberry jam because the cook used to fix them when I was little. My second favorite jam is strawberry. A long time ago, my mother would take me and my brother to a farm, where we picked our own berries. We loved to pick them. And we loved to help Momma make jam."

She gave another quick glance at the paper and went on. "I like my steak medium-well. I like sweet potatoes with orange and spices, never marshmallows. I like lobster bisque and onion soup with lots of cheese on top."

She paused and took a breath. "I hate eggplant, snails, and coconut cream pie. I love chocolate mint ice cream. When I was a little girl, I always asked for a chocolate birthday cake."

She glanced down and saw the word "nuts."

"Oh, right. I love pecans, but I hate walnuts. And I joke that peanuts are for elephants."

She wanted to shout to the hidden microphones that she couldn't be someone else. It was stupid. Impossible. But she remembered what her captor had done to her when she'd refused.

I'm Barbara, Barbara Andres, she silently insisted, but this time she couldn't repress a small shudder. She was trapped in this nightmare. He had said he would let her go when she had done what he asked. But she didn't believe it. She had to get herself out of this trap. If she was given a chance to escape, she had to take it—even if she risked her life to do it. Because fulfilling her role was a death sentence. She knew too much about him to be allowed to live when he had finished with her.

Fear made her chest tighten. Willing herself to steadiness, she wiped her sweaty palm on her slacks. Then her eyes darted to the clock on the bedside table. She didn't have much time left before he arrived. She'd better make sure she had memorized the list of facts. Grimly, she went back to the paper. Yet, as she paced alongside the queen-sized bed with its damask spread, the thought of seeing her captor this evening set her heart to pounding and made it almost impossible to concentrate. Memorizing facts from another woman's life was bad enough. But not as bad as the rest of it. The way he treated her. The way he touched her. The way he wanted her to act with him.

She thought of slapping his face and of the satisfaction that would give her. Then she thought of what he did to her when he was angry, and a sick feeling rose in her throat.

With renewed determination, she sat down once more at the desk and applied herself to memorizing the list.

CHAPTER
ELEVEN

OLIVIA TRIED TO project an appearance of calm as she waited nervously in the living room. She paced to the front window several times before forcing herself to sit on the burgundy-colored sofa that she hated.

In fact, she hated the whole room. Once it had welcomed her with light, delicate colors. But after Momma had walked away from the family, Dad had gone on a rampage, wiping out every trace of her presence. He'd brought in a trash bin for her clothing and anything else that was personal. Well, not her fine jewelry, of course. She'd taken a lot of the good pieces with her. What she'd left was in a safe in one of the guest bedrooms.

After pitching out Momma's things, Daddy had hired a professional decorator to redo the house—starting with the master bedroom, which was now dark and masculine.

Before the trash company had picked up the bin, Olivia had risked her father's wrath and secretly climbed inside.

Rooting through the mess, she'd taken out a few precious things. A beaded evening bag that had always fascinated her. A Mardi Gras mask with the blue and green feathers. A gold pen and pencil set that she and Colin had given Momma one year for a birthday present. The ivory cup she'd used in the bathroom.

Olivia squeezed her eyes shut, trying to force the painful memories back into the locked corner of her psyche where they usually resided. They'd popped out because she was nervous about seeing Sam again, after the mind-blowing encounter on his patio. And after the letters he'd sent. Eighteen of them had appeared in her E-mail files, in groups of three or four, spaced out as though they had arrived over the past six months. She'd read—and reread—every word. They were very personal. Too personal to be copies of anything. Besides that, the words sounded so much like him that, as she read them, she heard his voice echoing in her head.

He'd started by establishing a history for the two of them.

"It was great to meet you at the Paper Products Expo. I enjoyed our talk about the spotted owl. . . ."

Despite herself, that had made her smile. He'd managed to work the environment into the letter.

"I would love to see you again, but I do understand that your family duties keep you busy. You mentioned the dinner being given by the California Business Association in Santa Barbara on the fifteenth. I'm looking forward to meeting up with you there. . . ."

And so the early letters had gone on—merely friendly in tone, a man who didn't want to be too forward with a woman he'd recently met. But as the supposed months of their relationship progressed, the tone changed, and he began to sound more like a lover than a friend.

She could almost believe that she was reading the history of a developing romance. One of the last letters in particular had burned itself into her brain.

"I miss you so much. I will be counting the hours until I can hold you in my arms again. Your kisses were so sweet the other night. You taste like a field of flowers or the pure water of a stream high in the mountains. And your body is like no other woman's. I can't stop thinking about the feel of your breasts in my hands, of your nipples beaded against my palms, telling me that you want me as much as I want you."

She made a sound low in her throat. They had done those things together—and more—only a few days ago. She remembered it all in vivid detail. And so must he, if he could write about it in such explicit detail. He sounded too poetic for a thief—not that she knew how a thief should sound. But she did know that Sam's words had the power to make her burn with arousal.

And he was going to be living in this house. He'd be here in the morning when she woke up and at night when she went to bed. And she had no idea how on earth she was going to cope with having him so close.

She shook her head, wishing she could shake off the restless frustration she felt thinking about Sam Morgan and their kiss . . . and his hands on her bare skin, his fingers rubbing her nipples, stroking the inside of . . .

Ruthlessly, she quashed the heat rising in her belly by turning her mind to a relationship gone wrong—her parents. Had they ever loved each other? Had there been kindness and tenderness and passion between them once, even though theirs had been an arranged marriage, like the one her father wanted for her?

She couldn't ask her father about his love life any more than she could ask about his destructive business practices.

She'd told Sam those practices had started after Luther had stolen the elixir and the family fortune had gone downhill. In truth, she didn't even know if that was true.

The sound of tires on the driveway made her head whip around. Hurrying to the window, she saw the car that had been parked in front of Sam's house.

He was here.

Swiftly, she crossed the living room and the front hall and threw open the door. As he lifted a suitcase from the trunk of his car, she had a moment to admire his dark good looks. He had been devastating in a tuxedo and drop-dead sexy in his burglar outfit. Today his mahogany-colored hair was cut to a conventional business length, and he had dressed neatly in a black golf shirt and gray slacks. The perfect outfit for meeting his fiancé's father, she thought.

Closing the trunk, he picked up his bag and turned toward the door. When he saw her in the doorway, a smile of such warmth and intimacy spread across his face that it was easy to believe he had come to stay for no other purpose than to see the woman he loved.

She barely had time for an answering smile before he surged across the driveway and pulled her into his embrace. He held her as though he planned to never let her go. Although that should alarm her, she could do little more than cling to him. He was so solid and warm and strong. But she had to keep remembering that trusting him completely was too dangerous to risk.

"Olivia, I missed you," he said in a voice meant to carry inside the front hall.

"Yes."

They were playing the parts he'd dreamed up for them, she told herself as he lowered his mouth to hers.

She had lain in bed at night, hot and wanting and anticipating the heat of this kiss. The heat of his hands on all the intimate places he had touched before. But the contact was over almost as soon as his lips touched down. Before she had time to melt against him, he was putting his hand on her shoulders and setting her away from him. Despite all the warnings to herself, she couldn't hold back a spurt of disappointment.

"Let me feast my eyes on you," he said, then added tenderly, "You look fantastic."

It had to be a lie, of course. She knew her worry and uncertainty were etching themselves into her face.

He stroked the corner of her mouth with his thumb. "But I do detect a little stress."

"Well, I was anxious for you to get here," she managed.

"Mmm, me, too."

She looked up and saw their butler and maid hovering in the doorway. "Jefferies, Irene, this is my fiancé, Sam Morgan," she said, hoping they would attribute the quaver in her voice to engagement jitters. "He was here a few weeks ago. And he'll be staying with us for a while."

"I've gotten the room next to yours ready, the way you asked me to do," Irene answered.

"Thank you." She turned to Jefferies. "Would you see to it that his things are put there, please?"

"Of course."

In fact, she would have put Sam down the hall from her room, but he had suggested in an E-mail that it should look as if she wanted him close by. She had seen the logic in that—and also the danger. The closer he was, the more tempted she would be.

"Nice to meet you," Sam told Irene and Jefferies, then he took Olivia's hand. "Let's go for a walk."

"All right."

He guided her around the house and into the back garden, confidently leading the way as if he had been there many times before. Probably he had. Before the night in the gallery, she'd sensed him—watching the house, watching her.

They walked down a path that ended in a little arbor where bright purple bougainvillea climbed up a white trellis.

His demeanor in front of Jefferies and Irene had been confident, assured of his position, but her sideways glances told her that the farther from the house they walked, the more uncertain he seemed to be.

"What?" she murmured, suddenly afraid he was going to tell her that he'd changed his mind about getting involved in her family's problems. When he reached into the pocket of his slacks and pulled out a small black velvet box, her eyes widened in shock and she felt suddenly light-headed.

With a hand that wasn't quite steady, he held it out to her.

"Sam?"

"Open it," he whispered.

Her heart was thumping as she took it from him and lifted the lid. Inside was a square-cut diamond, at least two carats, set in white gold with baguettes on either side of it.

When she drew in a sharp breath, he spoke quickly. "Don't worry, I paid cash for it."

"I . . . I can't accept this," she stammered. Seeing the ring overwhelmed and confused her. Sam Morgan was a hard case. A man who lived on the edge. Was he letting her see his softer side? Or was this some kind of trick to make her drop her guard?

When he spoke, his voice gave no clue to his real intentions. "Of course you can accept it. We're engaged."

"But . . ."

He lifted the box from her grasp, took out the ring and cupped her icy hand in his while he slid the ring onto her finger.

Her pulse pounded even harder as she stared down at the token of his invented love for her. The ring fit perfectly. But it felt all wrong on her hand. He had no business acting as if this were a real engagement. Yet what was he supposed to do? She had agreed to the charade because she couldn't think of a better reason for him to be living with her family. Suddenly, she was trapped into making it look plausible.

When she stole a glance at him, the anxious look on his face made her heart ache.

Questions bubbled inside her, but all she could manage was, "Sam?"

His Adam's apple bobbed.

Determined to find out what was really going on, she raised her arms to his neck. This time when they kissed, it didn't end before it got started. And she couldn't stop thinking of where else his mouth had been on her body.

Remembered intimacy fed into the kiss. At the same time, she was caught in a moment that was real and passionate and brimming with unspoken emotions. He opened his mouth, drinking her in as his arms drew her close, holding her against the hard length of his body. She wanted more. So much more. Not just for this moment, though, but for the whole of their lives. Things she couldn't have, she frantically tried to remind herself. But it was impossible to hang on to her doubts as his hands skimmed up and down her ribs and the sides of her breasts, arousing her through her bra and silk blouse.

She spoke his name with her mouth against his, then passed beyond speech as his tongue stroked inside of her lips. Her tongue glided against his, sending vibrations throughout her body. She knew he felt her response as he drew her deeper into the shadows of the private bower.

"I missed you," he growled.

"Yes."

When his hand cupped her breast and his fingers skimmed over the nipple, she felt the heat of his touch.

"Lord, Olivia. Let me . . ."

"Yes." Again, she gave him the only answer that made sense.

They were fast progressing to more frantic activities when the sound of someone clearing his throat made them both go rigid.

In alarm she looked around and found Colin standing eight feet away, just outside the arbor, watching them.

"How long have you been there?" she demanded at the same time Sam muttered a curse and turned to hide her body with his as he lowered his hand to her waist.

"Not long."

"You could have given us some privacy."

"Yeah, well, congratulations on your engagement," he said, his tone somewhat wry.

"Thank you," Sam answered, sounding a lot less flustered than she was certain he must feel.

"Father has been eager to see you," Colin said to him.

"Give me a minute." He stayed facing her, and she knew he was trying to will away his erection.

She couldn't help thinking that her own arousal was probably equally obvious, and she smothered the impulse to look down at her nipples. They ached, and she knew they were probably standing out against the thin fabric of her blouse.

Three days ago, on the way back from Lompoc, she'd thrown her torn panties away in the ladies' room of a rest stop. After arriving home, she'd showered and changed her clothes before seeking out her brother. But she knew she hadn't been able to hide her emotional state then. Colin had known that something heated and personal had taken place at Sam's house. Today he could see the evidence for himself.

Colin confirmed her assumption with his next words. "So, this is a little more than a business relationship."

"Yeah, it is," Sam answered. "Do you want to make something of that?"

"I'm not my father. I want my sister to be happy."

"I appreciate your pragmatic attitude," Sam answered.

She kept her expression as neutral as possible—and shifted her attention away from herself, as she did so often.

Hoping she didn't look obvious, she gave Colin a quick inspection. He'd been spending the afternoons in bed for the past few days, and she would have suggested that he conserve his strength now. But she knew he wanted to be in on the meeting, to show that they were in this together.

"Your father knows I'm coming?" Sam asked.

"We figured we'd better make him part of the plan."

"How did he take it?"

"With the predictable explosion."

CHAPTER
TWELVE

SAM STROVE TO keep his face impassive as they walked back through the garden.

"The ring is a nice touch," Colin said.

"It adds verisimilitude," he answered evenly. The ring had started as an expensive impulse. Then he'd decided he liked the idea of putting his brand on Olivia.

As they crossed the lawn a jagged bolt of lightning slashed horizontally through the clouds billowing over the house. Looking up, he was surprised to see how dark the sky had grown. It had been perfectly clear when he'd arrived.

Sam watched Colin and Olivia exchange nervous glances.

"Better get inside," Colin muttered.

They all walked quickly to the terrace, and Sam couldn't help feeling that the weather was pushing him toward the coming confrontation.

Inside, Colin led the way toward the home office complex, then knocked on a closed door.

"Come in," a gruff voice called out.

They stepped into a room that was a movie set designer's idea of a man's retreat, with dark wood wainscoting, a matching desk as big as New Jersey, and Leroy Neiman horse-race paintings on the walls, along with photos of Wilson Woodlock shaking hands with a dozen notable men.

The patriarch of the Woodlock clan sat in the power position, in a high-backed leather chair behind the wide desk.

At first Wilson ignored them while he scratched some notations on the papers in front of him.

As they all stood waiting, Sam ordered himself to stay cool, but he couldn't stop his stomach from knotting. Deliberately, he used the time to size up the enemy. Woodlock might want to project the appearance of power, but the tightness around his mouth gave away his tension. Finally he looked up, his gaze flickering over his son and daughter before fixing on Sam.

"So, you're a thief," he said, getting right to the point.

Sam slipped a hand into his pocket. "Yes. And a very good one."

"You fit right in at my party several months ago. You looked and sounded as if you came from a good family. Yet there's no record of you before you appeared out of nowhere in California eight years ago."

"I value my privacy."

"Who were you before you were Sam Morgan?"

He kept his gaze steady. "You don't expect me to answer that question, do you?"

"Not really," Woodlock conceded. "I guess the most important thing about you is that my children think you can get into Luther Ethridge's fortress and steal back the . . . medicine that's going to save our lives."

"That's right." Without being invited, Sam walked to one of the guest chairs and sat down. After a moment's hesitation, Olivia took the chair next to him. Colin retreated to the easy chair in the corner.

Woodlock glared at Sam. "I don't like a stranger knowing . . . sensitive family business."

"I'm sure you don't," Sam answered quietly. "But what alternative do you have?"

"I always have alternatives," Woodlock shot back. His gaze jumped to his daughter—where it lingered.

In less than a heartbeat, the man's condescending expression hardened and a red stain spread rapidly across his face. Jesus, was he going to have a stroke right there in front of them all?

"What the hell is that?" Wilson demanded.

Olivia looked startled. "What?"

"On your finger! What the hell is that on your finger? Let me have a better look."

She held up her hand, keeping her voice even as she answered the sharp question. "My engagement ring. It's lovely, isn't it?"

"Don't get smart with me. That ring is carrying your charade one step too far. I forbid you to wear the accursed thing."

"Not a good idea," Sam interjected as calmly as he could, considering his pulse was now pounding in his temples.

"That's not your call," Woodlock snapped. "Or did you suggest this whole farce thinking you could use it to persuade my daughter to marry you?"

The man's perception rattled him a little. Still, Sam kept his tone even as he replied, "Olivia and I are supposed to be getting married. You're a rich man. It would look very strange if your daughter were engaged to someone who couldn't afford to give her an impressive ring."

Woodlock shifted in his seat. "Did you buy it or steal it?"

"Bought it. Do you want to see the receipt and the appraisal?"

"No!" He fixed Sam with a menacing glare. "I expect results—in the thievery department—from you!"

"You'll get them," he promised, projecting confidence when he didn't even know the specs of the job.

"It would be a good idea if we all had dinner together," Colin said from the corner of the room, and Sam realized he had forgotten all about him.

"I'll be working late," Wilson snapped.

"I think we need to establish a friendly tone for Sam's stay here," Colin added.

"You go ahead and do that for me," his father muttered. "And now, I need to get back to business."

"Thank you for giving us so much of your time," Sam said as he stood.

Woodlock's eyes narrowed. "Are you being sarcastic?"

"I wouldn't dream of it." Turning, he walked toward the door, followed by Olivia and Colin.

In the hall, Colin said, "If he kicks you out, we'll have to go to Plan B."

"I wasn't aware there was a Plan B," Sam said, suddenly wary.

"There isn't. But I'll think of something," Colin replied with a twisted smile.

Despite his tension, Sam laughed. "I guess you didn't inherit your old man's rigidity."

"I prefer to alter my opinions—and my plans—to fit the facts."

"Good," Sam answered, thinking that under other circumstances he and Colin could have been friends. "I liked the way you kept out of the conversation."

"I used to be in Dad's face all the time. It wasted energy, his and mine."

"Smart decision."

The butler approached them in the front hall. "Will the family be eating in the dining room?"

Colin answered, "We're going up to get a little better acquainted. Send something light up in a couple of hours—for me, Olivia, Sam, and Brice."

"Would you like some of cook's quesadillas?"

Not exactly wolf food, Sam thought. "I'd like steak—or burgers, if it isn't too much trouble," he said.

"Certainly, sir."

Olivia gave him a look that suggested she didn't like having him make requests of her staff. But she only nodded to the butler.

WILSON sat behind his desk, his shoulders rigid, eyes fixed on the papers that he'd picked up when he'd made it clear to the conspirators that the interview was over. The text was a blur before his eyes.

He had sent his children and the interloper away because he couldn't stand the sight of Sam Morgan. But the three of them were out there talking about him. Making plans. Scheming. And Brice would be in on it, too. Let's not forget his son's sycophantic lover.

Some part of his mind recognized the thoughts as paranoid. His children were doing what they thought was right. But he didn't have to like it. He just had to let them think he was going along with them.

"Sam Morgan," he muttered. He didn't like the name. It was too short. Too common. A name the man had made up, and he couldn't even pick something distinctive.

He didn't like working with a common thief. Corporate

theft was one thing. This was completely different.

He didn't like having Morgan living under his Spanish tile roof. And he didn't like the sexual energy sparking back and forth between the man and his daughter. There was something dangerous going on there. Something more than a business arrangement, and he was going to find out exactly what.

But the big question was—did he get rid of Morgan now or later?

He leaned back, smiling, allowing himself the pleasure of considering some delicious choices.

WHEN Sam and the others reached the upper floor, they found Brice standing in the hall, looking anxious. "How did it go?"

"He didn't kick me out—yet," Sam answered.

Brice nodded his approval, but it was clear most of his attention was focused on Colin. "Okay, you made it to the meeting. But you haven't been so great for the past few days. You need to rest," he said.

"I'm fine!"

Brice flicked a glance at Sam again. "He shouldn't be involved in this!"

Sam put a hand on Brice's arm. "Let's go into the computer room," he said, just as a nearby door opened.

A burly man in a white coat stepped out. Beyond him, another man dressed in burgundy pajamas was sitting on a bed. It was Uncle Darwin, his round face cradled in his hands and his sparse hair sticking up in tufts. As he looked up and stared at Sam, recognition bloomed in his eyes.

Horror contorted his face, and he reared back. "The devil," he screamed. "The wolf devil! He wants to drag me to hell! Get him away! Away!"

The attendant swore and bolted back into the room. After throwing a quick look at Sam, he knelt beside the patient. "Calm down. It's all right. Everything's all right."

"No! He's the devil! The devil, I tell you! Come here in the shape of a wolf!" Outside, thunder rumbled, punctuating his words.

"Oh, great," Sam muttered.

The attendant gave them an apologetic look and shut the door. But Uncle Darwin's voice continued to reverberate through the hall.

Sam stood where he was, until Olivia took his arm and steered him down the hall.

"Sorry," she said.

"Is he worse?" Sam asked.

"No worse physically. But he keeps talking about you."

"Should I be flattered?"

"Apparently you made an impression on him."

Sam could have told her why but didn't. All in good time.

He followed her into the computer room which was as much upstairs lounge area as work space. When they were all inside, he closed the door, then turned to face them. "I hope you haven't been talking openly about your burglary plans. The fewer people who know about this, the better."

"Only in the privacy of our bedroom," Brice answered.

Colin chose to make a point. "You're in on our little conspiracy because we need your expertise. Brice is in on it because he and I are a couple. You can consider that anything I know, he knows."

"Okay. But my comment about keeping this close to our vests wasn't just a random crack. The more people who know our plans, the more likely they are to fail."

"There's no one here but family and trusted servants," Colin answered.

"I hope so."

Olivia glanced at Sam, then started to sit in one of the easy chairs. He steered her toward the sofa.

"I . . ."

"You want to sit with your fiancé, so anybody who happens in here can see how happy we are," he finished for her, linking his fingers with hers and feeling a slight tremor go through her hand.

"You were fantastic with your father," he murmured.

"I've had practice," she said, detaching herself.

He could have insisted on the contact, but he gave her the space she was asking for. And gave himself space, too. Just sitting next to her was arousing enough. Touching her was a big distraction.

Colin cleared his throat, then went back to Brice's original question. "I need to be in on this meeting," he said to his partner. "Sam's doing this for me. The least I can do is support him."

"I thought you agreed that Olivia was going to work with Morgan," Brice said.

"Call me Sam. I'm going to be one of the family, after all."

Brice nodded. "Okay."

Sam turned to Colin. "Are you up to briefing me on Ethridge's home and security?"

"Yes." Crossing to the computer, he sat down and tapped a key. A screen saver sprang to life. It was a view of Michelangelo's David in the Academy art gallery in Florence. With another key stroke, he replaced the picture with a directory. "I have exterior and interior shots of the Ethridge house. I have the architect's plans, specs from the security company that Ethridge hired, and interviews with some former employees. And I have several pictures of Ethridge."

"That's pretty thorough."

"We're trying to give you as much information as possible."

"Where does he keep the . . . elixir?"

"In a basement vault. I'll tell you what I know about the security."

"Have you been able to talk to anyone who works there now?"

"He has no live-in help. Various people come in during the day. If one of his people talked to us, that person's life wouldn't be worth much."

The way he said it made the hairs on the back of Sam's neck prickle. His gaze fixed on Colin, he asked, "You have proof that he's killed somebody?"

CHAPTER
THIRTEEN

COLIN SLOWLY TURNED toward Sam. After casting a quick glance at his sister, he said, "Yes, as a matter of fact."

Sam fought to keep his voice even. "Who?"

"A couple of young women he stalked."

Olivia made a strangled sound. Apparently she hadn't heard about this part of Colin's research.

Sam clasped her hand as he asked, "And the police didn't arrest him?"

"They didn't have enough evidence to link him to the victims. There were no bodies."

"But you know he killed them?"

"I don't need the same standards of proof as a court of law. I deal in probabilities. And I know two women who got mixed up with him disappeared."

"You have names?"

"Yes. Alana Holz and Barbara Andres. Alana was a ditz-brain health club instructor who went missing on a camping trip in the mountains. Barbara was a graduate student, a woman with no family and no boyfriend. Ethridge was careful to make sure he didn't create a pattern—and careful to make it appear that he couldn't possibly be involved."

Sam fixed Colin with a dark look. "You knew this, but you withheld the information until you'd roped me into working with you."

"I didn't rope you in." Colin's gaze shot briefly to Olivia, then back to him. "You made the decision on your own."

Olivia's brother knew why he was here, all right. Sam gave her hand a gentle squeeze, and when she returned the pressure, he felt his throat tighten.

The family illness, whatever the hell it was, weighed heavily on her. If he could ease that burden and make a difference in the way Woodlock Industries was run, it would be worth a few risks. But he'd be damned if he was going to get himself killed *only* to save the male Woodlocks.

"Okay, show me the house," he said.

Colin brought up a picture of a castle, a forbidding pile of stone clinging to the side of a mountain.

"Hmph. The hall of the mountain troll," Sam muttered.

"Yeah," Colin agreed, zooming in on the front. "Notice how the door is recessed, so an invader can be trapped and killed before he gets inside."

He switched to the rear elevation, where the building presented a sheer wall.

There were several more exterior views, then some interior shots.

"How did you get them?" Sam asked.

"We bribed workmen with large enough sums to make them willing to risk their lives. Here's the stairway leading to the vault."

Sam leaned forward to inspect the photo. "I assume there's only one way down there?"

"As far as we know."

"Maybe we can tunnel under the structure," he murmured.

"You're kidding, right?"

"Right."

"I'll show you what we have from one of the security companies."

"He has more than one?"

"He's switched several times."

"Because he wants to make sure that we can't get the elixir back," Olivia interjected.

"How did he get it in the first place?"

Olivia and Colin both went tense. She was the one who finally spoke. "My dad thought, since it was of no use to anyone but us, nobody was going to steal it."

"So he just left it lying around?" Sam asked, astonished.

"Of course not!" she said, indignant. "It was locked up. But he should have beefed up his security precautions."

Sam saw plainly in both Olivia's and Colin's expressions—hers, chagrin hiding behind indignation; his, carefully blank—that there was more to the story. He also saw that he wasn't going to get it out of them. Not yet, anyway.

With an inward sigh, he said, "Okay, tell me about the security companies he's used. Who are they?"

They spent the next two hours focusing on the recovery operation, mostly going over information Colin had collected. After a short break for dinner, delivered by Irene, they went back to work. But it wasn't long before it was clear that Colin needed to rest.

"Print out everything you have for me, including the pictures of Ethridge," Sam suggested. "I can go over some of this stuff on paper. Then we'll talk again."

"Yeah," Colin agreed. "But it will take a while."

"I'll handle that," Brice said, then turned to Sam. "You can come back and get it later."

"Thanks." He inclined his head toward Olivia. "Why don't you show me my room?"

"Okay."

He gave her a closer inspection. She looked worn out, too. He rather hoped it was because she'd spent the last few nights tossing in bed, thinking about him as he'd been thinking about her.

She led him down the hall to a spacious room with a view of the back garden. He would have liked to fall with her onto the large, comfortable bed, but he had work to do that required privacy.

"I don't know about you," he said to her, "but I'm beat. I think I'll take a nap."

She looked a little surprised—but also, he noted ruefully, relieved. "Sure. I'll, uh . . . well, come and find me later, if you want." And before he could change his mind, she stepped into the hall and closed the door, leaving him alone.

Sighing, Sam opened his overnight bag and took out what looked like a travel alarm clock, but was really a high-tech device designed to detect hidden cameras and microphones. With the "clock" in hand, he walked around the room, checking the antique furnishings, the knickknacks, the spectacular Oriental rug, and the marble tiles in the bathroom. He hated to think that his hosts would bug him, but he wouldn't put it past them.

He didn't find a camera, but he unearthed a small microphone in the base of a ceramic lamp. His lips quirked as he thought about who might have put it there. Wilson Woodlock, wanting to know if his daughter was being screwed by a thief? Colin, being obsessively thorough in obtaining every last fact he could learn about the burglar he'd hired? Or could it have been Olivia—and what would her motive have been? He didn't know and didn't want to think about it.

One thing was certain. If he destroyed the damn thing, whoever had planted it would know he'd searched the room. He decided to leave it where he'd found it and make sure nobody heard anything interesting from it.

He looked around the opulent room, wondering what it would have been like to grow up in a house where the bedspreads and drapes were real silk and the bed and cabinet pieces were English antiques. Sam Morgan didn't belong here. But for the time being he was trapped.

He considered lying down with his shoes on, just to show the maid how uncouth he was. Instead he slipped the shoes off, pulled the pillows from under the spread and lay down, intending to relax for twenty minutes.

When his eyes blinked open and he looked at the clock on the bedside table, he saw that two hours had passed.

Well, at least the printing should be finished. After using the bathroom and washing his hands and face, he went back to the computer room. No one was there, but papers were stacked beside the printer. On top was a sealed envelope. Inside, a typed message said: "I need to talk to you. And I don't feel comfortable doing it in the house. Could you meet me outside? If you go out the patio door and walk straight back, you'll see a dead tree near the back wall. I'll be out there at seven, and I'll wait for you."

The signature, Olivia, was scrawled across the bottom.

So, did that mean she knew about the bug in his room? Or was she just being cautious?

He glanced at his watch and saw that it was already a little after seven. Quickly he grabbed a light jacket from his duffel bag, pulling it on to ward off the chilly Southern California evening as he headed downstairs.

He saw no one as he hurried through the family room,

then out the French doors into inky darkness. As he crossed the patio, he breathed in the night air. It smelled of rain and damp earth. Somewhere not far overhead he heard a bat's wings flap.

As he started across the grass, a chilly wind riffled his hair. The temperature had dropped a few degrees, and several steps farther on, he felt splatters of light rain hit him.

He wanted to call to Olivia, but ingrained caution kept him silent as he continued across the lawn. The bare trunk and branches of the tree loomed in the darkness.

Suddenly, he saw blue denim fabric flapping on the other side of the trunk. It looked like the skirt she'd worn when she came to his house.

"Olivia?"

She didn't answer, and a sudden spurt of panic made him hurry forward, his eyes fixed on the patch of fabric.

"Olivia, are you all right?"

As he rushed toward her, the smell of damp earth intensified. But, fixed on his goal and worried, he didn't note it as a warning and, so, was totally unprepared when the ground disappeared beneath his feet.

CHAPTER
FOURTEEN

BY THE TIME Sam realized what had happened, he was plunging downward into an open shaft of some sort.

"Shit," he cursed as he tried to stop his fall, arms and legs bashing against jagged rocks.

Frantically he grabbed at them, scrambling for purchase. When his left foot collided with something solid, he instinctively stiffened his leg to keep it there while grabbing with both hands for another anchor. His left hand pulled away a chunk of rock, but his right found a crevice. The broken-edged surface was slimy with something that smelled of mold and algae and mud. But his fingers gripped it, and he flattened himself against the wall, checking his descent.

Heart pounding, he clung precariously to his perch and tried not to do anything that might cause him to lose his hold on the slippery surface beneath his right hand and left foot. For several muscle-straining minutes, he remained perfectly still, feeling dampness wafting upward, toward him.

In the darkness, he could see nothing beyond the rough surface, a few inches from his face, that could have been either rock or brick.

Cautiously he shifted his right foot, gently probing the surface until he found another rocky protrusion that might serve as a second foothold. The instant he attempted to put any weight on it, though, it crumbled. A few seconds later, he heard a series of splashes, telling him that the chunks had landed in water.

Great. He'd fallen into the shaft of an old well. And from its eroded condition, he guessed the walls had been damaged in an earthquake. Lucky for him. For as painful as those sharp-toothed walls had been during his fall, if they were smooth, he'd be treading water right now. Now that he was in here, he remembered noting an old well on the Woodlock property. It had been securely covered. But how recently? Had someone removed the cover and planted Olivia's skirt as a lure? Then left him the note?

He'd deal with that later. Right now he had to figure out how to get out of here.

Another careful search with his right foot located a fairly large crevice, and when he tested it, it held. He performed the same operation with his left hand but found no other spot for it but the one his right hand was occupying. To relieve his burning muscles, he very slowly switched hands.

Then, being careful not to follow the pieces of the wall down the shaft, he tilted his head back and looked upward. He could see the wide circle of the well mouth and a patch of cloud-covered sky. He judged he was down only about six or seven feet, but without more light, he couldn't see any other footholds that would bear his weight—if there even were any.

He was contemplating the possibility of having to remain in his current strained and very unstable position until daylight when a high, urgent voice floated toward him from above.

"Sam?"

"Olivia?" His voice boomed upward, echoing off the walls of the well that surrounded him.

"Sam, where are you?"

"In a damn well."

"Oh, Lord, are you all right?"

"At the moment."

Her head appeared over the rim. "Oh, Lord," she said again. "What happened to the cover?"

"You tell me," he growled.

"I . . . I don't know."

"Yeah, well, I'd like to get out of here. The shaft's too wide for me to reach from one side to the other, but I could shimmy my way up. Do you have a rope?"

"I . . . Hang on a sec."

It was more like twenty seconds before something dark came dangling down toward him. Cautiously, Sam reached out and grabbed what he realized instantly was the leg of a pair of jeans. He gave her high marks for quick thinking and inventiveness, but he knew she'd never be able to support his weight.

"Can you tie the other end on something up there?" he asked.

"There's nothing close . . . wait. Maybe this will . . ." He heard her moving around, and a minute later, she looked over the rim again. "I tied a knot in the leg, then wedged it into a crack in the bricks."

He pulled carefully, and the connection felt solid. It would do—as long as the wall didn't crumble away from the knot. Supporting some of his weight on the pants leg, he braced his feet against the wall. When that didn't bring a pile of bricks down on his head, he let the makeshift rope take all his weight and began to inch upward.

It was slippery going in the old shaft. He'd climbed only about two feet when a section of brick gave way under his foot and plunged into the water below.

Above him, Olivia gasped. "Sam! Are you okay?"

"Yeah," he clipped out, unable to spare more breath for explanations.

She must have realized that talking was a bad idea, because she kept quiet, even when he slipped again, cursing loudly. Still, he kept moving upward, and as he approached the top, he could hear her breath sawing in and out of her lungs—like his. He realized then that she didn't just have the pants leg wedged between the bricks. She was holding onto it—insurance against the possibility of the wall disintegrating.

About fifteen inches from the rim, the pants leg began to rip. Olivia screamed as he fell back, one leg dangling into space.

Sam lashed out with an arm and caught the rim of the well. Pain shot through his hand, but he hung on because it was the only option.

Teeth gritted, he let go of the pants leg, transferring his other hand to the rim, then began hauling himself up and over it.

When Olivia leaned into the opening, his heart leaped into his throat as he imagined the lip of the well crumbling under her weight. "Get back!"

Ignoring the warning, she reached under his arms and tugged him toward her. With her help, he was able to pull himself over the edge. Flopping onto the damp ground, he lay panting.

Olivia crouched over him, her breath as labored as his. "Sam . . . Sam . . ." she gasped. "Are you all right?"

"Yes," he answered automatically. As he looked up at her, he saw she was half naked and shivering. He reached for her, pulling her down so that she sprawled on top of his body.

She melted against him, and he clasped her fervently. In the process of almost getting killed, he had found out something important. She cared about him—a lot, it seemed. Enough to risk her own safety.

"Thank you," he whispered.

She wrapped her arms around him and hung on. "I was so scared."

With a growl low in his throat, he caught the back of her head, bringing her mouth down to his in a wild, desperate kiss that had him instantly hard and aching. He wanted her with a fury that frightened him. And she returned the kiss with the same mindless need.

The near-death experience made him reach out for life on the most basic level. And life had become Olivia.

He gathered her against himself, his mouth ravaging hers. His hands roamed over her body, moving her so that her cleft cradled his rigid cock, then cupping her bottom to increase the pressure for both of them. When she moaned and squirmed against him, his hands dove under her blouse, stroking across the silky flesh of her back.

There was no doubt in his mind what they would do next. He would tear off her clothing and his, then roll on top of her, and plunge his aching cock deep inside her. He would finally slake the hot lust that had consumed him since the night they had first met.

But even as those tempting images danced in his mind,

even as he fumbled for the catch at the back of her bra, he recognized that she was shivering in his arms. And he knew he couldn't make love to her here. He had to get her out of the wind . . . Christ, and the rain. It hadn't even registered in his brain that the few splattering drops he'd felt earlier had now turned into a steady drizzle.

Pulling his hands from under her blouse, he shifted to his side, then gathered her up and helped her to her feet. "You're cold," he said, his voice gritty.

She blinked, then murmured, "No. I'm hot."

He allowed himself the luxury of a laugh. "We both are. But we can't make love out here." Or now, he realized as intellect began to conquer emotion.

Someone had tried and failed to kill him. How soon would they try again?

He pulled off his jacket and wrapped it around her legs like a skirt, tying the arms at her waist, keeping her close as he led her to the side yard, avoiding the direct route to the house.

"Doesn't that damn well have a top?" he asked.

Olivia looked back over her shoulder into the darkness. "It should. Sam, I was . . . so scared you were going to . . . to fall to the bottom. . . ."

"I know. But it's all right now," he said, his arm tightening around her waist in a gentle squeeze as he steered her onto the patio. "Where can we talk—where it'll be private?" he asked. "I mean, not my room," he clarified. "There's a hidden microphone in there."

Olivia stared at him, genuinely astonished. "What?" she breathed.

"Someone put a bug in my lamp. And I don't mean a grasshopper."

She felt a frown flicker across her brow. "How . . . how do you know?"

"I don't take my surroundings for granted. Did Colin feel that he needed to keep tabs on me?"

"No!" she objected immediately.

"What about your father?"

She took her lower lip between her teeth, not quite so certain. "I . . . I don't know."

"We can't stay out here. Where can we talk?" he asked again.

She thought for a moment before leading him to the left side of the yard, to the glass-enclosed pavilion that housed the swimming pool. Rain drummed on the glass roof. But inside, the air was warm and heavy with the odor of chlorine. After switching on a small lamp in the bar area, she turned to face him.

He shut the door behind them, keeping his gaze on her, and she wondered if she looked as frightened and fragile as she felt.

Unable to look him in the eye, she studied the azure water of the pool, trying to find her equilibrium. It amazed her that she had almost made love with Sam out there on the lawn. She had been terrified for him. When he had pulled her on top of him, the only thought in her mind had been getting as close to him as she could. She would have let him do anything he wanted. But he was the one who had stopped. Now he was deliberately keeping several feet of space between them as he studied her face. Pulling a sheet of paper from his pocket, he unfolded it and thrust it toward her.

After scanning the type, she raised her head and finally looked into his eyes. "Do you think I wrote that?"

"No," he answered, his voice harsh and grating. "I figured out you didn't, but not until after I ended up on my way down to Hades."

"The signature looks a little like mine. But it's not."

"Yeah, well, if we go back out there, we'll find some fabric attached to the tree. I thought it was your skirt. Somebody went to a lot of trouble to take the top off the well, then lure me out there—so I'd fall into the shaft and drown, if I didn't break my neck on the way down."

She sucked in a sharp breath but didn't contradict him.

"How did you know where I was?" he demanded.

"I . . . I was standing at the window. I saw you and wondered where you were going."

"Lucky for me."

He took her by the shoulders, his fingers digging through her sweater. "Who wants me dead?"

"I don't know."

He sighed. "Okay. We can go over the list of suspects later. Pack some clothes. You and I are going somewhere safe."

"What?" she managed.

His voice turned low and dangerous. "Don't you get it? I've been at your house for less than ten hours, and somebody's already trying to get me out of the picture. If I stay, they're going to make another attempt. And another. I'm not going to play sitting duck. And if you want to keep working with me, you're going with me."

"Where?"

"I'm not going to talk about that while we're still on Woodlock property."

"I can't just leave," she objected.

"I'm clearing out. You can come with me or stay here."

It sounded as if he were offering her a choice, but she had already discarded the illusion of choice.

She raised her chin. "Are you trying to get me off alone so you can . . . have me?"

"I wouldn't put it in those terms."

"What terms would you use?" she asked in a shaky

voice, knowing what she wanted to hear, yet at the same time dreading it.

"I'd call it making love. And you wouldn't have stopped me out there on the lawn—would you?"

She swallowed. "No."

"At least you're being honest about that."

She ignored a twinge of guilt and plowed on. "But now I'm thinking straight again. And we both know . . . intimacy . . . is more likely if we're off somewhere by ourselves."

He gave her a crooked grin. "If you say so."

She knit her hands together in front of her. "I was trying to avoid . . . getting involved with you . . . sexually."

"Why?"

"Because we have to stick to business."

"Oh, yeah?" He crossed the space between them and pulled her to him, leaning down to nuzzle his lips against her neck, her jawline, and she knew he felt her instant response. "We're already involved sexually. We just haven't taken the final step. Yet."

His words and the feel of his body against hers sent heat leaping between them. A familiar heat that only he could generate. "I should be afraid of you," she whispered.

"Why?"

"You're a violent man. I didn't really know what I was getting into when I hired you."

"Yeah, I can be violent. But I would never hurt you, Olivia. I swear it, on my life."

"I think I know that, too," she answered, marveling that they were speaking so frankly, yet not quite frankly enough. "But you might hurt my father. Or my brother."

"Only if I found out they'd done something . . . underhanded to me."

"We're all working together."

"You and Colin. But not necessarily your father."

"He wouldn't try to kill you." Even as she mouthed the protest, she couldn't be completely sure. And she knew he sensed her uncertainty.

"Unfortunately, I can't take your word for that."

"Doesn't it create a problem for you—wanting me and hating my father?" She asked the question that neither one of them had addressed until now.

"Yes," he said with a catch in his voice. "But we're getting off track. Let's go."

"I have to let Colin know we're leaving."

"No. We're not talking to him or anyone else right now. We're simply disappearing," he said, making it clear that he was setting the rules. Stepping back, he gave her a critical look. "Put on my jacket. It's big. It will hide the fact that you're walking around with your butt hanging out." Before she could object, he untied the jacket from her waist and handed it back to her. Feeling trapped, she shrugged into it and let him usher her out of the pool enclosure and toward the house. Unfortunately, almost as soon as they stepped inside, they ran into Jefferies.

"Miss Olivia! What happened?" he asked, his gaze taking in her appearance.

"We had a little run-in with the well," Sam answered, watching the man's face.

To Olivia's relief, he looked shocked and confused. "The well? What . . . ? Oh! You mean that old well the previous owners used before the waterlines were laid?"

"Yes."

"We're just going to clean up," Sam said brusquely, and without further explanation, he took Olivia's arm and urged her toward the stairs.

They quickly headed up to her room. Once inside, he

closed the door behind them. "Pack a few things," he said tersely.

She didn't want to leave the safety of the house. Except it had suddenly ceased to be a refuge.

"I'm going to get my stuff," he said, then left the room.

As soon as he was out of the room, she started scribbling a hasty note. But he came back in less than a minute and snatched the message out of her hand and read it.

"Dear Colin, Sam says he and I have to leave. I've agreed. I'll talk to you later."

He might have crumpled it up, but he allowed her to write a few more lines. "Ask him to see if he can find out who took the cover off the well."

"Okay."

She wrote that down, then packed. On their way out, she slipped the note under Colin and Brice's door.

Fifteen minutes after they'd gone upstairs, they were in his car and heading for Route 101.

"Now are you going to tell me where we're going?" she asked.

"Actually, not until I make sure that there isn't a bug in the car. Or a transponder, with someone sitting on the receiver end, tracking our movements."

"That sounds kind of paranoid."

He grunted. "Do you blame me?"

"I guess not."

"We're going south?"

"Yes. We might as well end up a little closer to Ethridge's house. I'll decide where, after we put some distance between us and your place."

She slid him a sideways glance. His face was set in harsh lines. She wanted to reach out and make physical contact with him, but she kept her hands locked in her lap. He was such a study in contradictions. He could be tender, angry, sexy.

Somehow, without even realizing it was happening, she had formed a strong emotional bond with this man. Of all the times in her life when she'd been frightened—and there had been more than a few of them—one of the worst was finding Sam dangling by his fingernails in the well.

After several miles of silence, he said, "Tell me about the people who live in the house. Is there anyone besides the ones I've met—your father, Colin, Brice, Darwin, Jefferies, Irene, Thurston."

"Mrs. Leon, our cook, comes in during the day. We have several trained attendants taking care of Uncle Darwin now. Ralph Patrick." She thought for a moment. "George Swift. Will Murphy."

"And everyone knew your fiancé was going to be staying with you."

"Yes. Well, maybe not the part-time staff."

"Which ones of them were at the house today?"

"We had a four-man crew from Arbor Gardening Service."

"Oh, great. Four more suspects." He turned his head toward her. "Maybe someone asked them to remove the cover from the well."

"Why would anyone want to do that?"

"I don't know. But someone arranged for it to disappear. Or maybe a big wind blew it off?" he muttered. "And then one of your skirts blew off the clothesline you don't have and got stuck on the back of the tree trunk."

He was watching her from the corner of his eye. Deliberately she tried to relax her grip on her own hands. "Obviously, someone did it," she whispered.

He took an exit off the freeway and drove into Carpinteria. When he found an all-night gas station with a car wash, he drove into one of the stalls.

"What are you doing?" she asked.

"Looking for transponders and bugs."

He got out, inspected the undercarriage of the car, then the bumpers, before going over the interior thoroughly. When he found nothing, he drove them through the car wash, then gassed up, and headed back to the freeway.

"I'm sorry," she said as they merged onto the road.

"About what, exactly?" he asked cautiously.

"About putting you in danger."

"You did that the minute you asked me to steal back that Astravor stuff from Luther Ethridge."

"Yes. But you chose to be a thief. That's the main thing I knew about you. And I . . . I didn't know I was going to get . . . involved with you." She had used the word "sexual" before. Now she gulped and said, "Emotionally, I mean."

His gaze shot to her before he focused on the road again. "Would you like to elaborate on that a little bit?"

She hesitated, then drew a steadying breath and spoke the truth. "I don't know you very well. I shouldn't care what happens to you. But I do. I care a lot."

He reached over and laid his palm gently against her cheek. She drew comfort from the contact, but that didn't stop her from wondering how far she could trust him.

LUTHER was waiting by the phone. When it rang, he snatched up the receiver.

"Where have you been?" he demanded.

"Busy. I can't get away anytime I want, you know."

He did know, but he wasn't going to give an inch.

"The fiancé arrived this afternoon," his informant said.

Luther bit back a snarl. The very idea that Olivia could be seeing anyone made his blood boil. Who the hell was Sam Morgan? And how had she met him, anyway?

He'd done a great deal of research on the man, picking up every scrap of information available. Morgan seemed to be wealthy, although he could be living beyond his means. Which might mean he was after Olivia for her fortune.

Morgan spent money generously on liberal causes—and also gave some bucks to conservative ones. He liked his privacy. There wasn't much on record about him. Most interesting of all, he had little history. Eight years ago, it appeared as if the well-built, dark-haired man had simply blinked into existence. Before that, there were no credit card bills for Sam Morgan, California resident. No medical, dental or school records. No mortgage loans or apartment rentals.

The earliest information Luther could find about Morgan showed he had lived in a cheap apartment in Isla Vista near the University of California, Santa Barbara, and that he had worked as a golf caddy. He'd moved several times since then, always to better digs. Five years ago he'd bought a home in Ojai. Then a ranch near Lompoc. It looked as if he'd connected with Olivia at some of the charity functions they'd both attended.

Luther clenched his fingers around the receiver. Olivia belonged to him. And he wasn't going to allow some mystery fiancé to get in the way.

"What about the well?" he demanded.

"He took the bait."

"And?"

"He fell in."

Luther's thin lips curved into a smile. "Good."

His informant waited a beat before delivering the bad news. "And somehow he got himself out."

"Fuck! How?"

"I don't know. They came back to the house together after stopping in at the pool house. Unfortunately, I don't have a bug in there."

"She was outside—with him?"

"Yes."

He swore again. "Why?"

"I don't know."

"Then what?" Luther demanded.

"Then he hustled her upstairs, and they both packed."

"What are you saying?"

"They've left."

"Jesus Christ! Where did they go?"

"I don't know."

"Find out! Damn you. Find out."

"If I can, I will."

Luther shouted obscenities into the phone. The informant waited through the barrage, then asked for further instructions.

"Do your damn job," Luther snarled, then slammed down the receiver.

Seething, he paced back and forth in his office, his blood pounding in his temples. Images of Olivia in another man's arms filled his mind until he thought his head would explode with fury. He couldn't stand it, couldn't bear to think about it. Yet he couldn't think about anything else.

But he had to. If he didn't keep a clear head, everything he'd worked and planned for would be lost. And he wouldn't be able to bear that, either.

He needed to get himself back under control. Find something else to focus on for a while. Not exercise—that would engage his body but not his mind. He needed something mentally distracting. But something soothing and pleasant . . .

A visit to the woman upstairs.

He stopped pacing, and gradually, as he considered his guest, who would do anything he asked because she had no other choice, he began to feel calmer. She really was quite lovely.

And as he pictured her familiar face, he couldn't stop a little fantasy from playing in his head. What if she were eager to see him? What if his loving wife were waiting for him upstairs? What would that be like?

Deeply buried needs stirred inside him.

He clenched his fists, willing away the tender feelings.

The desire for intimate human contact was only a weakness. He had learned long ago that he could trust no one but himself. Love no one but himself. No matter how much he might long to let down his guard, he could never do it again. He had done that once at school. He'd thought he could trust his secret fears and longings with another kid who was as miserable as he was at Dickensen Prep. He'd thought Teddy Branson was his friend. But the little snot had gone running to the bigger boys. He'd used his new knowledge as a way to curry favor, and he made things a whole lot worse for Luther Ethridge.

He made a low sound that was part pain and part anger. He'd trusted Teddy with his most private thoughts. And that had been a big mistake. He'd made the mistake one more time in his life. Maybe he was a slow learner. But he'd let himself be vulnerable again, this time with a woman. He'd been willing to give her the world. And she'd flat out rejected him.

Well, never again. He'd grown stronger for it. Too strong for anyone to hurt him.

A few minutes later, with a smile on his face, Luther headed upstairs to spend some quality time with his unwillingly cooperative houseguest.

* * *

IN her prison, Barbara heard the sound she feared most—
the sound of gas hissing into the room.

Her fingers clutched at the neck of her robe, echoing the
sick dread that clutched her throat.

Her gaze darted to the wall, to the metal stems of the
gas jets. She had tried to twist them off or stuff them up
with washcloths, but to no avail. He had only increased the
pressure, blowing away her makeshift barriers.

As she stared in terror at those shiny protrusions, she
dragged in a lungful of clear air, then held her breath, even
though she knew it would do no good. When her lungs felt
like they were going to burst, she would be forced to gasp
in a choking breath.

He had done this before—too many times. The bastard.
And she had no defense against him.

The vapor filled the room, filled her mind with swirling
clouds, and made her body heavy. She swayed on her feet,
then dropped to her knees. With the last of her strength, she
lowered herself to the carpet.

She wanted to close her eyes. But it was too hard to
work the muscles. She wanted to scream for help, but she
knew that no one would hear her. So she lay on the rug, unable to fight the sick, scared feeling that made her limbs
tremble.

The trembling increased when she heard the pump that
evacuated the vapor from the room and made it safe for
Ethridge to come in. The gas had made her groggy. It had
done its work. And now he was coming in to claim her. She
longed to lash out at the man who held her captive. But all
she could do was lie there, waiting for him with her pulse
pounding.

Then he was in the room, looking down at her. Bending,

he hauled her up and tossed her onto the bed, where she bounced like a rag doll.

"It's useless to defy me, Olivia," he said in an even voice, putting special emphasis on the name.

She wanted to scream that she wasn't Olivia. But he had hired a plastic surgeon to change her face, and he had turned her into a woman named Olivia Woodlock. A woman he wanted. A woman he apparently couldn't have. So he had created a substitute.

He stood above her, watching her as he slowly took off his clothing. She saw his hairless chest and his muscular arms. And as he sat beside her on the bed, she saw his disgusting penis, red and swollen, jutting toward her.

A smile played on his lips as he opened the buttons of the robe. It was the only garment he allowed her to wear. He spread the placket apart, baring the front of her body for his inspection. And there was nothing she could do about it, because the gas had made it impossible to move.

But not impossible to feel.

She wanted to scream at him to stop as he tenderly began to stroke her. First the column of her neck, then her breasts. She was helpless to prevent his touch. He delicately circled her nipples, creating the illusion of arousal as he made them pucker.

"I love the way you get excited for me, Olivia," he murmured.

She wanted to shout at him. She wanted to tell him he was mistaken. She wasn't excited—only disgusted. But speech was beyond her.

He squeezed her nipples too hard, knowing there was no need for gentleness. He opened the drawer of her bedside table and took out lotion, pouring it on his fingers before slipping them inside her vagina, pretending he had made her wet.

"How do you want it tonight, sweet Olivia," he asked in a silky voice as he fondled her. "How many times can you come?"

None, she silently cried out.

She ached to tell him she wasn't Olivia and that all she wanted was for him to leave her alone. Instead she said a silent prayer that he would finish with her quickly and leave her alone. And that he wouldn't hurt her too much.

CHAPTER
FIFTEEN

AS THEY DROVE into the night, Olivia slouched, sound asleep, in her seat, her head resting against the window. Sam knew she must be both emotionally and physically exhausted, so he let her be. But he kept glancing at her, admiring the shape of her lips or the way her dark lashes lay like raven's wings against her cheek. She was beautiful, although she looked fragile, too.

Was she the reason someone had gone after him? Did someone opposed to their engagement want him out of the way?

Or was the attack designed to keep the Woodlocks from getting back their magic elixir? If that were the case, the person who'd tried to kill him had to be someone who knew why Olivia had hired him.

He decided against turning off the highway again until he knew that he was too tired to keep driving with any degree of safety.

As he approached Tarzana, he took a secondary road, heading into the mountains. He'd stayed at the Burroughs Motel a few times, but he didn't want to go where he was known. He drove to another place he'd seen before—the Rustic Lodge. Each room was a separate cabin, and the wooded grounds backed onto a state park, the ideal place for a wolf to roam.

Olivia's eyes blinked open when he cut the engine. Sitting up, she peered at the unfamiliar scenery. "Where are we?"

"A little east of Tarzana. I'll get us a room."

"With two beds."

"If they have any left."

He woke a clerk who had nodded off and signed in, using an alternate identity that he'd kept up over the past few years. Sam Lucien.

After ushering Olivia into cabin fifteen—with two double beds—he went to get their luggage. When he returned to the room, she was in the bathroom. As she came out, her gaze found him.

"You wouldn't try anything I didn't want you to do—correct?"

"Correct," he answered. It was the truth, as far as it went, although he was sure that if he started kissing her, he could bring her around to his point of view pretty quickly. But he wasn't going to try anything now. She looked too washed out. When they made love for the first time, he wanted it to be as good for both of them as he could make it.

Turning her back to him, she pulled off her jeans. Still wearing the T-shirt, bra, and panties she'd put on earlier that evening, she climbed into one of the beds and rearranged the pillows before snuggling down.

He was tempted almost beyond endurance by the need to strip off his clothes, climb into bed with her, and take her in his arms. He grew hard as he stood looking at her.

Before she could open her eyes and see his state of arousal, he turned away.

In the bathroom, he took a cold shower, then pulled on clean briefs and a T-shirt.

When he crossed the room again, he could tell from her even breathing that she'd fallen asleep. Either she was too exhausted to keep her eyes open or she trusted him enough to let herself go—or both.

He thought about going outside, changing to wolf form and running through the park. But he was tired, too. So he slipped into the other bed.

He woke early, as soon as he heard her stirring. When he opened his eyes, she was looking across at him.

Unable to stop himself, he climbed out of bed and slipped under the covers beside her. He felt her body stiffen, but he only slung his arm around her and stroked his hands through her wonderful hair as he cradled her head against his shoulder. He wanted her with a force that shook him. He knew he was going to make love with her soon. But maybe he was savoring the anticipation as much as the act. That was a new experience for him. Bending his head, he kissed the tender place where her hair met her temple.

"How are you this morning?" he asked.

She stirred against him. "Wondering why I let you convince me to leave home.

"It's safer."

She turned her head and looked at him. "That depends on your point of view."

"The point of view of my not getting killed," he answered immediately.

"There's that."

He kept stroking her hair. "I took all the papers that Colin printed out. I'll study the material he's got on the

Ethridge house. Then I should drive down to La Jolla and have a look around."

"I'm going with you."

"I don't want you near the place."

She sat up and looked at him. "I mean, when you break in, I'm going with you."

"The hell you are. It's too dangerous."

"I know it's dangerous. But . . ." She stopped and sucked in a breath. "I'm the one who knows what the elixir looks like."

He sat up and returned her direct look. "You can tell me about it."

She kept her gaze steady. "No."

As they glared at each other, his mind scrambled for a good way to keep her out of danger. "Taking you could be the thing that sinks the mission."

"Why?"

"Because I work alone. Because you could be more of a liability than a help."

"I have to go." The fierceness in her voice told him that he wasn't going to argue her out of it. Not this morning.

"I won't take you along unless I know your capacities," he said, keeping his voice even.

"What does that mean—exactly?"

Thinking fast, he said, "We go on another job first."

"As in rob someone else?" she clarified.

"Jackpot."

"I'm not going to participate in anything like that."

"Then we're not going to Luther Ethridge's."

She swallowed hard. "Who were you planning to rob?" she asked.

He thought over the next project he'd been scouting out. He liked to do a lot of research, contemplate his subject for months before going in. "A man named Harold Reese," he finally said. "He's got mining operations all over the west. His father was responsible for giving hundreds of miners radiation-related diseases and asbestosis. Instead of paying their medical bills and compensating their families, he spent millions fighting their claims. Harold has continued in the same pattern." He climbed out of bed, pulled his duffel bag to the top of the dresser, extracted a folder he'd brought with him, and tossed it on the bed.

Before she could continue the conversation, he picked up the duffel bag again and carried it and clean clothing into the bathroom. He kept his expression calm until the door was closed. Then he clenched his teeth so hard he could have bitten through an iron bar. He wanted to stamp back into the bedroom and give Olivia hell. He'd never conjured up pictures of the woman who might be his mate. But in a million years, it wouldn't have been rich Miss Olivia Woodlock. Who was it—F. Scott Fitzgerald?—who had said "the very rich are different from you and me"? Fitzgerald had been right. And now Sam was stuck with one of them. A modern princess who insisted on getting her way.

He hadn't thought he could fall for a woman like Olivia. He hadn't thought he'd be forced to cooperate with her. He couldn't even be sure if he could trust her. And now he was wondering about his motives for leaving her estate so quickly. Sure, he wanted to keep his hide intact. But hadn't he been secretly relieved by the excuse to decamp because he didn't feel comfortable living in a house where he fell over servants every time he turned around?

When he came out, Olivia was sitting up in bed reading the dossier on Reese like she was studying for an exam.

"Well?" he asked, struggling to keep any hint of temper out of his voice.

"He sounds like a person who doesn't care about anything besides himself and his money."

"Right."

"But he's just a side issue."

"Not for me."

They glared at each other.

"I'm hungry," he finally said. "There's a fast-food restaurant up the road where we can buy breakfast. I know it's not what Jefferies would serve in the dining room. But you can get pancakes or some kind of breakfast sandwich."

"What are you getting?"

"A couple of sausage sandwiches."

"I'll have pancakes," she said.

Leaving Olivia alone in the cabin, Sam climbed into his car, drove to the restaurant, and pulled into the drive-in line.

OLIVIA stared at the closed door, then at the phone sitting on a table in the cabin. She had only moments to make a decision. As she pictured Colin's worried face, she chose loyalty to her family.

Picking up the receiver, she dialed her brother's private number. He answered on the first ring.

"Where in the hell are you?"

The curse and Colin's tone of voice told her he was worried out of his mind.

"I can't tell you, but I don't want you to worry," she tried to reassure him.

"Come home!" he demanded.

"I can't."

"Why did you leave?"

"Because somebody tried to kill Sam. Was it you?"

"How could you even ask a question like that?"

"Because you've lost control of the situation. And you hate that. Maybe you even hate him."

"Stop trying to analyze me."

She sighed. "Colin, I have to get off. I just called to tell you I'm okay."

"No! Wait! He's taking you on a job—right?"

She sucked in a sharp breath. "What are you talking about?"

"You told him you wanted to go to Ethridge's with him. He said he wouldn't take you unless you proved you were up to the challenge. Now he's going to drag you on a burglary."

"How do you know?"

He answered with a sardonic laugh. "I'm the boy genius, remember. Who are you going to rob?"

"You know I can't tell you that!"

"Then tell me the town where you'll be."

"Why?"

"So I can check the news to make sure you're not in jail."

"Carmel." Her head jerked up. "He's back. Got to go."

Before he could ask any more questions, she hung up, then stood and looked at her reflection in the dresser mirror, trying to wipe away the trapped, guilty look. When she couldn't manage it, she went into the bathroom and splashed cold water on her face.

SAM walked into the cabin. For a panicked moment, he thought Olivia had fled. Then he heard the toilet flush.

When she came out of the bathroom, he studied her expression. After setting down the sacks of food, he said, "I guess it's not safe to leave you alone. Who did you call?"

Instead of denying it, she asked, "How do you know I called anyone?"

"It's plastered all over your face."

"I was hoping it wouldn't show."

"Well, either you called Colin, or you called the cops to come arrest me."

Taking a shallow breath, she let it out and said, "I knew Colin would be worried. I only wanted to reassure him."

He gave her a long look, then walked to the bathroom, collected his toiletries, and packed them in his duffel bag. "We're leaving."

"Why?"

"We're not safe here."

"I didn't tell Colin where we were."

"But somebody could trace the call." He went on quickly, "You trust Jefferies with your life? Or Thurston? Or that maid? Or the men taking care of your uncle?"

"I . . ." She stopped, probably because no one had put it in those terms.

"You've got five minutes to get your stuff together."

"I haven't showered."

"Take two minutes for that."

Apparently she felt guilty enough to do what he asked without arguing.

He had planned to stay put for several days, relaxing and studying the Ethridge material. Instead, once they'd stowed their gear in the car, he drove to the office and settled the bill.

In the car, he fished into one of the fast-food bags, pulled out a cup of water, and took a small sip as he headed onto the highway.

"Why are we going north?" she asked.

"Because Reese's house is our next stop. When we're through there, we'll go back to La Jolla."

Her head swiveled toward him. "You're not just testing my resolve?"

"No. I'm going to find out how you react under stress—and how well you think when you're under pressure." He set the water in the cup holder and glanced at her. "Well, I guess I know how you react. You call your brother."

She sank down into her seat and turned her head away, watching the scenery.

"Eat your breakfast."

"I'm not hungry."

"Too bad. You put me in charge of this operation. And Master Sergeant Morgan says you're going to take care of yourself and eat."

"Why aren't you a general?"

"I didn't go to college. I can't be a commissioned officer."

Sighing, she fished a pancake out of her bag and nibbled on the edge.

"Hand me a sandwich. And take off the top layer of bread," he said.

"You're on the Atkins diet?"

"The what?"

"Low-carbs. You know."

"Yeah. That."

Neither of them ate much as he drove.

"It's not fair to say I call my brother because I'm under stress," she finally said.

"He called you?"

"You know he didn't. But Colin and I are close." She sighed. "We grew up in difficult circumstances."

"Such as?"

"When I was little, my parents didn't have a lot of time for us. Dad was at work most of the time. Or that's what he said. Momma had a lot of obligations—parties, charity committees."

He let her keep talking. He'd thought she'd grown up getting anything and everything she wanted. He had a sinking feeling his assumptions had been dead wrong.

"My mother hated having so much to do outside of the

house, but my dad wanted her to have a public presence. Or maybe he wanted to keep her busy. If anyone raised us, it was Jefferies. When he was busy, Colin and I turned to each other."

When she didn't continue, he cast her a quick glance. "Go on. I'm listening."

She gave him a look that said she wasn't worried about his listening but about his feelings about the Woodlocks. "Our family life built up to a big crisis. My mother realized Dad wasn't working every minute—he was sleeping with a lot of women." She swallowed hard. "She told Dad he had to change, or she was getting a divorce. He refused to live his life any differently. I don't know if it was a matter of principle for him or . . . or if he didn't really love her. Maybe he just married her because she was beautiful and smart, and he wanted beautiful and smart children."

"You're both of those," he said, softly.

"You think I was stupid to call Colin."

"You haven't been in this situation before." He reached over to take her hand and give it a squeeze.

"No, I haven't," she replied.

A sideways glance told him she was staring at his hand covering hers. He kept the contact until a curve in the road required both hands on the wheel.

"What about your parents?" she said suddenly.

He felt a sharp pang of homesickness. "They have a strange marriage—but it's solid."

"They're both still alive?"

"Yes. I check up on them from time to time."

"Could you elaborate on the 'strange' part?"

"My dad insists on ruling the roost. But he and Mom want to be together," he said, keeping it brief. The knowledge that he would eventually have to spill everything made his stomach knot.

He wondered if his anxiety showed when she spoke again. Her voice had softened—a gentle, sympathetic sound, as if she actually cared. "Do you go home for visits?" she asked.

"No. They think I'm dead."

She drew in a sharp breath. "Dead? Why?"

He hadn't planned to tell her so much so soon, but he heard himself saying, "I left home when the members of a biker gang pinned a murder on me." After spitting out the confession, he spared her a quick look to see how she was taking that.

She was focused on his face, and he found it difficult to breathe while he waited for her verdict. "You didn't kill the person," she said, making it more of a statement than a question.

"No. But I cut my losses and split." He made a self-deprecating sound. "You come from money. My dad didn't make enough as an auto mechanic to support his wife and kids. So he supplemented his income by burglarizing houses." He managed a sharp laugh. "That's how I picked my profession—family tradition."

She tipped her head to one side. "I get the feeling he wasn't as methodical as you are."

"No. But before I left home, I wasn't the same guy, either. Back then, I was running wild—out of control, you might say."

"Tell me about the murder," she asked softly.

"There was a fight in a bar, and one guy ended up dead. Maybe one of his friends used the excuse to do him. But none of them was going to take the rap. They thought I was unconscious and agreed to pin it on me."

"You were hurt?"

"Yes."

"How did you get away?"

"They took a lot of guys to the hospital. It was mass confusion. Then a bunch of victims came in from a big car crash. The emergency room physician thought I was dead. Or maybe I *was* dead—and God gave me another chance." He laughed. "Maybe God decided to let me come back as Super Thief because he let me slip out of the morgue."

She gave a quiet snort.

"Anyway, I'm here."

"So you made up a new identity," she concluded.

"Yes."

"With your background, how did you learn to . . . fit in with the rich and famous?"

"You mean, how did I acquire some polish?" he clarified.

"Yes."

"First, I got a job as a caddy at a tony golf club. I studied the men . . ."

"And you furthered your education in the women's beds."

His head snapped toward her, then back to the road as a truck approached. "How do you know?"

"You're sexy and very appealing. And you're pragmatic."

"And I learned from a whole string of women who were older than me how to be a good lover," he added. She might as well know the whole ugly truth.

They were both silent for several moments.

"Married women?" she finally asked.

"No. Divorcées and widows."

"Did they pay you?" she whispered.

"For sex?"

She gave a small nod.

"Some of them wanted to. I was too proud for that." He sighed. "I've always had principles. Sort of." He'd let them buy him a few presents. Not many, though. "And I was already supplementing my income with some B and E."

They fell silent again.

"How did you get to be an environmental Robin Hood?" she finally asked.

"I've always had a love of nature. That was something positive my father taught us."

"Aren't you lonely? I mean, don't you miss your family?"

"Enough about me," he said brusquely. "What sports do you play?"

"Why?"

"I'm trying to assess your burglarly skills."

She hesitated for a moment, then launched into a recitation. "I took gymnastics when I was a kid. I was on my school's swim team. I'm a good tennis player. I've been rock climbing a few times. And my Girl Scout troop went on a lot of camping trips that involved hiking, backpacking, canoeing, sailing, and skiing. I've tried to keep up with some of them now and then, especially skiing, which I enjoy a lot."

"Impressive."

"Thank you."

"What about guns? Can you really shoot? Or was that revolver in the gallery just for show."

"I can shoot."

"That was on the curriculum at Miss Worthington's?"

"No. My father wanted to be sure both Colin and I could defend ourselves."

"He couldn't eat dinner with you, but he had time to teach you to shoot?"

"No. Thurston's predecessor had that job."

"Okay. We'll stop somewhere it's safe to engage in a little target practice."

"You have a gun with you?"

"A Sig." He turned and looked at her. "Target practice is one thing. Have you ever shot a man?"

"Of course not. Have you?"

"No."

"But you think you could kill?"

"Yes." The violence of the wolf was part of him. If he were cornered or provoked, he didn't even have to question that he would be capable of killing.

"I guess I saw that in you."

"What else did you see?" he asked, not certain he wanted to hear the answer.

"You're a man who rarely tells the truth," she said, the insight too close to home.

"Truth is an occupational hazard for me," he tossed back.

"But you've made it clear you want a relationship with me. What are you going to base it on—mutual lust?"

"That's a good start." He hoped the flip response disguised his growing tension.

"But it's not enough. You're going to have to trust me."

"Or what?"

"Or I walk away from you when this is over."

He didn't argue. Let her think she had the option. He knew she was only kidding herself—or engaging in wishful thinking. At least, that was what he wanted to believe.

CHAPTER
SIXTEEN

SAM DROVE TO a vacant ranch near his home. He'd thought about buying it, so he'd inspected the property.

Kids had set up a target range in the shelter of a hill. He had no trouble picking up pop and beer bottles lying around on the ground.

After setting up some targets, he handed her the Sig Sauer that he kept in a locked box under the front seat and watched her check it out.

He didn't have to tell her what to do. She took the gun in a two-handed grip and fired at the first bottle, shattering it. Then she went on to the rest, missing only one.

He felt a surge of pride. His woman could defend herself.

His woman. It felt startlingly good to think of her in those terms.

"Okay, we know you can shoot," he said in a thick voice.

She gave him a surprised look, probably wondering

why he was getting all choked up about guns. "I told you," she murmured.

He made his tone businesslike. "Tonight when we stop, you can read more on Harold Reese."

"I'll do some more as soon as we get back on the road."

When they were finished with target practice, they headed back to the car. There Sam dug the folder out of his luggage again and handed it to Olivia. She scanned the pages as they drove north, or maybe she was only pretending to read so she could put some distance between them. He mostly kept his eyes on the road. But every so often he cast glances at her.

They were going to be spending another night together. And he could make love with her. That's what he ached to do. If she was any other woman, he'd reach for her the moment they were alone in the motel bedroom. But he had a feeling he was going to let her escape again.

WHEN they pulled off the highway, Olivia raised her head and blinked, aware of their surroundings for the first time in several hours. Not far away she could hear surf pounding against sand.

"Where are we?"

"Pismo Beach."

"I've never been here. But I always thought the name sounded funny."

"It's a variation of the Chumash Indian word for tar. *Pismu.* They got it from a nearby canyon and used it to seal their canoes."

"You looked that up?"

"Yeah."

"I never heard of a Chumash Indian."

"That's because they were wiped out by the Spaniards. Not in wars. They caught our diseases and died."

"Sad. And infuriating," she murmured.

"They were here a long time. Nine thousand years. And the white man swept them off the face of the earth in a few decades. Just another example of the benefits of civilization."

Taking in her gloomy expression, he lightened his tone. "I won't blame the disaster on Woodlock Industries."

That won him a little smile. "Thanks."

"The white man's town started as a seaport, then got into tourism. They still have some motels right on the ocean. It's a nice environment."

"Do you know every nature-oriented place to stay up and down the California coast?"

"I know a lot of them," he allowed as he pulled in at a motel with a VACANCY sign. "Wait here while I get us a room."

"Two beds," she said automatically.

Several minutes later, he emerged with a key. Their room was around the back, less than eighty yards from the shoreline. The place was smaller than the cabin where they'd spent the previous night, and he watched her looking around nervously. Well, too bad. She'd have to earn his trust before he let her have her own space.

COLIN was using his laptop. Dressed in jeans and a sweatshirt to keep his arms warm, he sat propped up in bed. The table lamp was turned low, as he checked some of the Web community where he lurked. You never knew when Out of the Closet or the American Philatelic Exchange was going to come up with something interesting. And if he was scanning messages, he didn't have to worry about Olivia.

A movement from the doorway had him glancing up.

"You should be sleeping," Brice said.

"I'm resting."

"You're restless."

Colin took off his glasses and rubbed the bridge of his nose. "Yeah."

"Since you're not sleeping, anyway, come down to the family chapel."

"To pray for the favor of gods?" Colin asked.

"Yes. And we wouldn't want to forget the goddesses."

Colin swung his legs over the side of the bed. Brice offered his hand, and he let the other man pull him to his feet. It wasn't something he allowed many people to see, but in the privacy of his bedroom, he didn't have to worry about family or servants evaluating his lack of muscle tone.

Brice pulled him close, and he rested his head on his partner's shoulder. They stood embracing for a long moment. When Brice stroked his hand down his back, then over his butt, Colin felt a surge of regret.

"Sorry I haven't been thinking much about making love lately," he murmured.

"You will, when you're feeling better." Brice found his hand and squeezed hard. "Come see what I've set up in the chapel."

They walked hand in hand down the hall, then stepped into the magical realm of flickering candlelight, soft textures, and carefully selected icons. Colin lowered himself to the carpet and gathered a comfortable pile of pillows to lean on, then studied the arrangement of talismans, which were now lying on a square of the highest quality Thai silk.

As Brice settled opposite him, Colin picked up the Indonesian male figure with the huge penis and testicles, turning it one way and then the other for a good view of the outsized equipment. "Are you praying to get me well enough for some fun?"

Brice laughed. "That's one reason for including him. But also, he projects a sense of power."

"Yeah. Like her." He picked up the Aztec fertility goddess and held her in his other hand, then put both statues down.

There were new objects on the scarf, including a small carved totem pole and a four-leaf clover encased in plastic.

Colin touched the clover and raised an eyebrow.

"I go by instinct. There's no point in excluding something because it's too modern."

Colin nodded, then pick up a small gray-green jade figure of a wolf. "I understand the symbolism of the clover. What's this for?"

Brice gave him a direct look. "It felt . . . important."

Colin nodded. He'd always paid attention to his partner's hunches. Brice's mystical side was one of the things that had attracted him in the first place.

Brice cleared his throat. "Have you been listening to Uncle Darwin lately?"

"He's so loud, you can't miss him."

"He was talking about demons. Now that includes wolves. One wolf in particular. Sam Morgan."

"Yeah."

"So . . . did he see something we haven't?"

"How?"

"Sam was in the sunroom with your uncle for a few minutes before Thurston broke in. I've tried to talk to Uncle D about that. When he's calm enough to hold a conversation, he says he saw Morgan turn into a wolf. Well, not completely. He was half wolf and half man."

Colin shivered. Still, he felt compelled to offer a counterargument. "We both know that since Darwin's mind started turning to oatmeal, he's seen plenty of things that weren't there."

Brice gave a small nod.

"But you think there could be something to it this time?" Colin pressed.

"Maybe." Brice cleared his throat, shifted against the pillows. "Do you believe in werewolves?"

"More than most people would, I guess." But even as he said it, he felt a spark of alarm igniting in his gut. They were talking about the guy who had spirited his sister away from the safety of the estate. "Damn," Colin muttered.

"What?"

"If it wasn't for me, she would never have met him. I got them together—for criminal purposes."

"You didn't know he was dangerous."

"I should have seen . . . something."

"Maybe I'm way off base."

"I hope so," he whispered, his mind going down some interesting pathways. Before he could get too far, Brice hit him with another zinger.

"Do you think perhaps we should talk about the weather?" he asked.

"You mean the thunderstorms that come out of no-where?"

"Yeah. Those. And the windstorms."

SAM lay in the bed next to Olivia's, his nerves too taut for sleep. The blood ran hot and fierce through his veins, and he gathered up a fistful of sheet to keep from rising out of bed and going to her. He'd been with her all day, repressing his need for her. In the darkened motel room, he felt on the brink of madness.

Yet he understood that taking the final step would change

his life forever, and not only because of who he was. Olivia Woodlock was no ordinary woman. She was a member of the powerful Woodlock family. More than that, there was a quality about her that he couldn't name that had something to do with presence or . . . maybe power. Given time, he'd figure it out. Given time, he'd uncover all her secrets.

He turned his head on the pillow and looked toward her. He knew she was no more relaxed than he was, but exhaustion had apparently kicked in because she was asleep.

Good. He could leave the confines of the room for a while and run along the beach.

Climbing quietly out of bed, he padded barefoot across the room and carefully opened the door. Then he slipped into the night, closing the door behind him.

He was the only person out and about so early in the morning. Once on the beach, he headed for the darkness under a clump of palm trees. After checking the area to make absolutely sure he was alone, he pulled off his T-shirt and sweatpants and said the chant.

The change started with the familiar pain and ended with the sense of freedom that always suffused the wolf spirit within him. Raising his head, he drank in the night air, catching the familiar scent of deer not far away. He needed to hunt. Needed to run wild and sing the song of the wolf. But he didn't want to return to the motel room, to Olivia, with deer blood in his mouth. So he raced down the beach, drinking in the salt air, listening to the crash of the surf. Stopping to dash into the waves and cavort as only an animal could.

An hour later, he turned and retraced his steps, toward the motel, hoping the wolf had calmed him enough to slip back into bed and get a few hours of sleep.

* * *

IT was four in the morning by the clock on the nightstand when Olivia's eyes snapped open. Something had awakened her. Swiveling her head toward the other bed, she didn't see Sam. And he wasn't in the bathroom either.

Panic gripped her at the thought that he might have left her. She had hired the man because he was a skilled burglar. In the beginning, she had told herself that his profession meant she was better than he was. But she had never really believed that. She believed it less every moment she spent with him.

He had overcome a childhood she could only imagine. He had made his own life. And he had a moral code that was as strict as it was unconventional.

She felt a surge of relief when she saw his duffel bag. He must have waited until she was sleeping, then climbed out of bed and gone for a walk. Probably to get away from her—because proximity and sexual frustration were driving them both crazy.

Wide awake now, she was too keyed up to lie in bed, wondering when he was coming back. Instead, she crossed to the door, opened it, and made sure it wouldn't lock behind her. Then she stepped outside. It was still dark, but several overhead lights illuminated the motel grounds.

Standing by the door, she scanned the area, then took a few steps toward the ocean. Her body went rigid when she spotted something moving along the beach. Too low to the ground to be a person. Had to be an animal—a dog or . . .

A wolf.

She had seen a wolf less than a week ago. Sam's wolf. He hadn't brought the animal with them, and it was simply impossible that the animal could have followed them and kept up.

But what was a wolf doing loping along a beach on the crowded California coast?

All this ran through her mind in an instant, the same instant in which she drew in a startled breath. Clearly hearing her, the animal raised its head and pinned her with a glowing yellow gaze. As he regarded her, she felt a shiver stir the hairs on the back of her neck and travel down her spine.

He was coming for her. She knew it. She should dash back into the motel and lock the door. But Sam was outside. She couldn't lock him out—not with a wolf on the prowl.

How the devil had the creature gotten here? Was he even real? Or was she caught in the grip of a dream brought on by worry and stress and, yes, sexual frustration?

She scraped her bare foot a couple of inches against the edge of the concrete strip, feeling it firm and solid and rough against her flesh. But that proved nothing. She could make any rules she wanted in a dream.

While she was trying to work her way back to reality, the wolf faded into the shadows under a clump of palm trees. And she was left with her pulse pounding in her temples.

Released from indecision, she started to back up—until another dart of movement grabbed her attention, and her heart leaped into her throat.

Then she saw it was Sam, running across the sand, wearing only a pair of sweatpants. His chest was bare and so were his feet.

"Sam, thank God!"

"Is something wrong?" he asked in a careful voice.

"I saw a wolf! He was here!"

"Forget about the wolf," he said, his voice low and thick.

As he came toward her, she felt the same panic she had felt moments earlier when she'd seen the yellow-eyed creature approaching her.

Sam fought to think logically, his head spinning. The one thing he knew was that he had to make Olivia forget about the animal she had seen outside the motel room.

Closing the distance between them, he folded her into his arms and lowered his mouth to hers. Fierce emotions roiled through him. She clung to his shoulders, anchoring herself to him, returning his kiss with a passion that turned his blood molten. When he finally broke the kiss, they were both breathing in great gasps.

Her vulnerability showed in her eyes as she looked up at him. "This time you're not going to stop, are you?" she asked.

"No."

"Thank God."

His gaze burned down into hers. "You wanted separate beds."

She swept her hand down his back, stopping at his buttocks, pulling him more tightly against herself. "I was afraid."

"And now?"

"I can't fight the pull. The power. The . . . oh, Lord, Sam, I can't help it. I just want you so much." Lowering her head, she pressed her lips against his shoulder.

The feel of her form molded against his sent waves of arousal crashing through him. Hardly able to catch his breath, he held her cradled against him, feeling the world tip and sway beneath his feet. She spoke of power and fear and desire. And yet it was more than any of that. Much more. Deep down he had feared the potency of this moment. Maybe that was why he had drawn back every time. But finally he knew that he had no choice.

No choice at all.

She was the one who stirred. "We'd better go in."

"Yes."

Locking his fingers with hers, he led her back to the room, feeling her hand tremble, and he silently vowed that he would wipe away her fear and replace it with ecstasy. His and hers.

The moment they were inside, he slammed the door closed with his foot, then fumbled behind him to snap the lock before bending to ravage her mouth again as he dragged her T-shirt up and pushed her bra out of the way so that he could take her breasts in his hands. When he circled her nipples, then caught them between thumbs and forefingers, he heard a sob break from her lips.

"Sam. Oh, Sam," was all she managed as he skimmed her panties down her legs, then stroked his hands along the strong line of her back, over her bare bottom and between her thighs, his own hands shaking all the while.

She was hot and wet and aroused, moving restlessly against him. He had almost made love with her outside his house. Then he'd nearly taken her on the lawn beside the well. He was grateful that he had waited until they were in a bedroom, where he could love her with some finesse. Wanting a horizontal surface under them, he swept back the covers on the nearest bed and laid her down.

Never taking his eyes off her, he tugged down his sweatpants, then kicked them away. Naked and on fire, he turned on one of the bedside lamps, then swept his gaze over her. She lay with her arms stiffly at her sides, and the look of raw nerves on her face made his heart ache.

"You look so beautiful—and so vulnerable. But I would never hurt you."

She swallowed. "I know. But standing over me like that, you are a little intimidating. Well, not just intimidating. Magnificent," she added.

He gave her a crooked grin. "Concentrate on the second part, and I'll work on being a little more, uh . . . approachable."

In truth, the flames lapping at him made it difficult to

think. But he knew tonight would set the tone for the rest of their lives together, so he moved slowly as he came down beside her and gathered her into his arms, awed by the feel of her naked body against his.

She stroked her hand over his shoulder, through his hair. "Sam, I have to tell you something."

He reached to touch his thumb to her cheek, then trace the curve of her lips. "You want to tell me what you like when you make love?"

"I . . . want to tell you that I haven't had much experience doing this."

The little tremble in her words made him go very still. "How much experience, exactly?"

Her breath hitched. "None."

CHAPTER
SEVENTEEN

FOR AN INSTANT, the world stood still around him as the single word she'd spoken, and its implications, filtered into his brain.

His voice, when he finally managed to speak, was little more than a raspy whisper. "You're a virgin?"

She buried her face against his shoulder and nodded. "I told you I wasn't into casual sex. I didn't . . . well, it just never felt . . . right."

He lifted her face with a finger beneath her chin, then bent forward to kiss her cheek. "And it does with me?"

"You know it does."

Yes, he did. And maybe he should feel energized, he thought, as his fingers stroked, barely moving over the silky skin of her shoulder. Like those terrorist martyrs who thought they were going to heaven with eighty-seven virgins, or whatever the number was. If you took a virgin to bed, she didn't have anyone to compare you to and, so, wouldn't know how badly you'd failed if you didn't satisfy her. Only that wasn't the way he was thinking about it at all.

He had wanted her since the night he had first met her. No, not just wanted. He hadn't thought of another woman since, and he'd never thought of any woman the way he'd thought about her. Yet he felt nearly overwhelmed with the responsibility she had just handed him.

"I guess I've given you something to worry about."

He nuzzled his lips against the tender place where her cheek met her hair. "Yeah. A little," he admitted. Well, a lot, actually.

Her fingers played nervously across his chest, winnowing into his thick dark hair. They found one nipple and drew a circle around it, sending a cascade of reaction through his body.

"You've got that part right," he whispered.

"I figured if it felt good to me, it would feel good to you, too," she answered. He saw her cheeks redden. "And . . . uh . . . in the interest of full disclosure, I should admit that I know what an orgasm feels like."

"Oh, yeah?" He watched her color deepen. "I appreciate your sharing that with me," he added, thinking about what he wasn't yet ready to disclose.

This time, when he kissed her, it was a tender exploration, his lips moving against hers, his tongue stroking the sensitive tissue just inside her lips, then playing with the edges of her teeth. His mouth moved to her jawline, then the curve of her ear, making a leisurely tour that traveled to her collarbone and back to her mouth.

"Thank you for trusting me," he murmured, knowing she still wasn't entirely sure about him. He planned to do everything he could to wipe the uncertainty out of her mind, once and for all.

He set himself to fueling her pleasure as he brought his

attention to her breasts, his fingers plucking at one peaked nipple while he drew its mate into his mouth, swirling his tongue around the crest, then taking it delicately between his teeth. He was rewarded by the small sounds of wanting she made.

He was so hard he thought he might self-destruct, but he was determined to keep his focus on her. Then her hand slipped between them, finding his cock and closing around him.

His indrawn breath brought an answering murmur of satisfaction from her.

"I guess we can't call you a . . . shy virgin," he managed.

"I want to be an active participant."

For a few moments, he let himself enjoy her caresses, tentative at first but incredibly talented—indeed, almost uncanny in how she seemed to know exactly what felt good to him. Then, when he couldn't take any more, he lifted her hand and brought her fingers to his mouth for a quick kiss.

"Better stop. I'm already so turned on, I could come in about a minute flat. And I want this to last awhile. But turn-about is fair play, don't you think?"

His hand slid down her body, paused to play with the dark curls at the top of her legs, then delved lower between the slick folds of her sex, taking one long stroke and then another, barely dipping inside her before traveling upward to her clit. She made a sound low in her throat, then showed him what she liked, covering his fingers with hers, increasing the pressure of his touch as she rocked her hips against his hand.

He leaned to stroke his tongue around the curve of her ear, then whispered, "Do you want me to make you come, love?"

"Yes. But not this way."

He had never wanted a woman more in his life. And at

the same time, he hesitated to take the next step. "I don't want to hurt you."

"Maybe you can't avoid it." Again she reached for his erection, sensuously stroking her fingers up and down his shaft, wringing a sharp exclamation from him.

"Open your legs for me," he gasped, gathering her to him, moving against her but not trying to penetrate her yet. He was so close to the edge that he knew if he put even the first inch of his cock inside her, it would all be over. She was slick and wet, and he slid his shaft back and forth, stroking her as he had with his hand. Determined to make her first time something she remembered with pleasure, he kept up the sweet torture and listened to her breath come faster and faster as she climbed toward climax.

"God, yes. Come for me. Show me how good it feels," he crooned. When she cried out in pleasure and her body shuddered in his arms, he felt a surge of triumph. She clung to him as the spasms shook her, and he kept stroking until he felt her settling down to earth.

Then, changing the angle of his thrusts, he warned her, "Now, love," and plunged into her. He did it fast, in one decisive stroke, while she was limp and relaxed with the force of her orgasm. Still, she made a strangled sound and dug her nails into his shoulders as he broke through the barrier of her virginity.

"Olivia . . . Oh, love . . . I'm sorry," he gasped. But he was caught in a whirlwind of need, his hips moving, his cock stroking in and out of her, and he came quickly—as he knew he would.

He collapsed on top of her, his breath coming in great gasps. Raising his head, he looked down, his eyes meeting hers. "Are you okay?" he asked urgently.

She reached to kiss his cheek, then she stroked back a lock of damp hair from his forehead. "More than okay."

Staying inside her, he rolled to his side, holding her in his arms, kissing and caressing her, keeping her with him as he began to build her pleasure—and his—again.

She clung to him, returning his kisses, trailing her fingers over his back and shoulders and down to his buttocks, pressing him into her as they rocked together, caught again in their spiraling need.

"Good, that's so good," she whispered.

"God, yes."

He felt the exquisite pleasure of her inner muscles contracting around his penis as he brought them both back to full arousal. This time he made the pleasure last, barely moving inside her until she was thrashing against him, silently begging for release.

He slipped his hand between them, finding her clit, stroking with his hand as he moved in and out of her—holding back until she convulsed in his arms, moaning. While the aftershocks of her climax still rippled over him, he let go and poured himself into her.

As his heart rate came back to normal, he felt her stir against him.

"I didn't know how wonderful that would be," she whispered against his neck. "It's not just physical release. It's so much more."

"Only with you, love."

Her breath caught. "You're telling me the truth?"

"Oh, yeah. I've never felt anything like that," he answered, because it was the truth.

He held her for a few more minutes, then slipped out of bed and went into the bathroom. It was past dawn, and by the light from the window, he could see her blood on his body. He used a washcloth to clean himself, then warmed another cloth under the faucet and wrung it out.

Her gaze fixed on him when he came back to bed with the cloth and a towel.

"What are you planning?"

"A little TLC," he answered as he eased onto the bed and gently moved her legs apart so he could clean her inner thighs and her still-wet and swollen folds.

"I should be embarrassed."

"Nothing we can do together is ever going to be embarrassing," he said, meaning it.

When he had washed the blood from her body and dried her with the towel, he came back to bed and gathered her in his arms.

"I was afraid of you," she whispered. "I never knew you could be so gentle."

"You make me gentle," he answered, meaning that, too. "I just wish it could always be true."

He had been balanced on a knife blade of sexual obsession for days—weeks. Finally he could relax, holding her in his arms as he slept.

When he opened his eyes hours later, he found her studying him.

"Second thoughts?" he asked, hearing his own tension.

"Of course."

"You belong to me now."

"In the caveman sense?" she asked, the edge in her voice warning him that the statement had been a bit too aggressive. So he struggled to frame his feelings differently.

"No. You said you weren't into casual sex. That wasn't casual for either one of us."

"What was it for you, exactly?"

He wanted to duck away from her penetrating gaze. Instead, he held it with his own as he told her the stark truth. "It was the most important night of my life."

Her eyes widened a little. "Why?" she breathed.

"Because I knew that if we made love, we would be . . ." He stopped and fumbled for words. "Making a commitment."

The look in her eyes told him she didn't want to think in those terms.

He had to stifle the sudden urge to let the caveman take over. Before he could say something else he regretted, he rolled out of bed and got out clean clothing, then ducked into the shower.

Later, while she dressed, he walked down to the beach, raising his face to the salt wind. He had to tell her about the wolf—soon. But not yet. Not until he was sure she wouldn't run from him. Because he had to keep her with him now. Whether she understood it yet or not, she was the wolf's mate.

When she was showered and dressed, he took her to one of the restaurants in town for an enormous breakfast.

She ordered coffee. He got his standard herbal tea.

"You don't drink coffee?" she asked.

"No. Or liquor. And I don't smoke, either." He laughed. "I'm into clean living."

She glanced over her shoulder to make sure they were alone. "Except for your profession."

"Yeah."

"So, are you going to let me off the hook with that Mr. R?" she asked as she forked into a huge stack of pancakes.

"I will, if you agree to stay home when I visit Mr. E."

"That's not negotiable," she answered.

"Then neither is Mr. R."

They sat looking at each other across the Formica table. Had his mother ever defied his father like this? He didn't think so.

But Olivia Woodlock was her own woman. And he'd sure as hell better remember that.

FROM his mountaintop haven, Luther Ethridge sat in a comfortable chair by the window, looking out at the magnificent view spread out below him.

It was early in the morning, and as he watched fluffy white clouds drifting across the blue sky, he felt like a king surveying his domain. He was rich enough to be a king. And when he had the Woodlocks begging for mercy, his satisfaction would be complete.

It was easy to imagine what that would be like, because he was already well along in the process.

His mind went into a little fantasy about the woman in his tower room. The woman who looked so much like Olivia that even he couldn't tell the difference. Jesus, that gas he pumped into the room was wonderful. He could do any damn thing with her that he wanted. Just thinking about what he was going to do next made him hard as a rock.

Leaning back in the chair, he unzipped the fly of his slacks and reached inside, stroking his fingers against his enormous boner.

Then the phone rang.

"Fuck."

He didn't want to be interrupted. He wanted to enjoy his fantasy. Then he looked at the number on the Caller ID and a new surge of excitement coursed through his veins.

Snatching up the phone, he demanded, "What do you have for me?"

"I think I know where Olivia and the fiancé are going."

"You think?"

"She didn't say. But Colin has been trying to track them. I know from what he's been doing on the computer."

"You got into his files?"

"He left some notes beside the machine. I copied down the important information." The voice on the other end of the line began reeling out facts.

"Not so fast. Let me write it down." He jumped up, forgot his pants were unzipped, and had to pull himself back together as he wedged the phone between his ear and his shoulder, then grabbed a notepad from the drawer in the drum table beside the sofa.

"Okay. Give it to me slowly," he ordered.

"I don't have much time," the person on the other end of the line complained.

"That's your problem, not mine." He took down the information. It didn't make a lot of sense, but his informant had never been wrong.

"How's Colin's health?" he asked when he had the gist of the material.

"His energy level is dropping. He's spending more time in bed."

"Good."

"I have to go. Sorry."

The connection went dead.

"Shit!" Luther stared at the receiver, longing to dial back and demand some explanations. Instead, he settled for staring at his notes as his mind formulated new plans.

SAM sat in an Adirondack chair, looking longingly at the woods. He would have liked to strip off his clothing, transform, and run free. But until he told Olivia his secret, he had to keep the wolf in check.

She opened the door and cooking smells wafted from the kitchen. They were in a rental house in Monterey—a short-term lease. The real estate agent didn't know it was for less than a week—since he'd paid for a month.

"I have the salad and the potatoes done," she said.

"Then let me put the steaks on."

They'd been sharing the simple cooking duties because he wanted it that way. He wasn't going to make her do all the work, the way his father had done with his mother. And he'd make sure they got someone in during the day to help with the kids.

Hell, who was he kidding? He was picturing married life in terms of his parents. In a tiny house stuffed full of scrappy little boys. Would a woman who had been raised like Olivia stand for less than a mansion staffed by a butler, a maid, and a full-time nanny?

Well, that wouldn't be possible when the daddy was a werewolf! He'd have to make that damn clear.

He took a deep breath. He was getting way ahead of himself—he hoped. The first night they'd made love, he'd been too overwhelmed by need even to think about birth control—another sign that she was his true mate. Because he'd never forgotten about that little detail with the women in his past. Since then, however, he'd gotten a supply of condoms. He hoped to hell it wasn't a case of locking the zoo cage after the tiger had escaped.

As he laid the steaks on the grill, he thought about why they were on the Monterey peninsula. He'd been excited about the Reese job months ago. The guy had some stunning old German snuffboxes and some Chinese jade pieces from the Chang Dynasty. Scooping them up had totally lost its appeal, because it clashed with his need to keep Olivia safe. But he couldn't let her off the hook if she was going to Ethridge's with him.

He took his steak off the grill, then cooked hers a few minutes longer.

When he stepped into the dining room, she raised her

head and gave him a direct look. "How about tonight?"

He knew immediately that she wasn't talking about making love, which they'd done every night since Pismo Beach.

"Unless you've changed your mind," she added.

"I haven't changed my mind," he clipped out.

"Then we'll eat quickly so we can get some sleep before we have to leave."

SAM woke Olivia at two in the morning, then watched her eyes blink open and focus on him. She looked fragile. Worn out. Because he'd been keeping her up for hours every night. Every night but this one. And during the days, he'd been testing her physical abilities.

"We don't have to go now," he muttered.

She climbed out of bed, wavering a little as she headed toward the bathroom. "I want to get it over with." When they met in the front hall a few minutes later, she seemed okay. He gave her last-minute instructions as they drove to Carmel, to a side road off the beach. Leaving her in the car, he made a final reconnaissance trip to the Reese house. He knew the owner was in Europe, but he carefully checked the exterior, including the hookup to the security system. The setup looked perfect. There were a few lights on around the grounds, but the lot was large and well-screened by trees. Still, he waited for almost half an hour, making sure everything looked okay.

It did. But he couldn't banish the tight feeling in his chest. Because he hated this whole deal, he told himself. He'd rather be home in bed making love with his mate.

She jumped when he leaned down toward her car window. "What are you trying to do, scare me into wimping out?"

"It's a plan."

Ignoring the comment, she asked, "Are we all set?"

"Unfortunately."

At least he was gratified to see a flash of pure nerves on her face as she stepped onto the gravel road surface.

Shrugging into his pack, he adjusted it for comfort, then turned and started up the coast, listening for the sound of her running shoes crunching behind him.

He would have preferred to go in as a wolf. But since he hadn't dredged up the courage to break the bad news to Olivia, he led her up the coast, glad that the darkness hid his grim expression.

Silently he willed her to back out. He longed to hear her say that she'd changed her mind about starting a career as a burglar. But she followed him to the back of the house, which had been built before underground utilities.

He put on climbing spikes, went up the electric pole, and disconnected the system at the power source, so that the security company would think the electricity was off.

Then he came back down.

Next he walked to a small double-hung window in back and jiggled the top part until it came free of the lock.

"I'm ready," Olivia said.

Since Reese was out of town, they had agreed that she would go in first, then come around and unlock the back door for him. He didn't like that much. But it was part of the test he'd told himself it was important to administer.

Making his hands into a step, he hoisted her up. She slithered inside, then disappeared.

Quickly he walked to the back door. He was always calm and methodical on a job. But his heart was drumming inside his chest, and his hands squeezed into fists as he waited for her to let him in.

It was taking too long. Where in the hell was she?

He dragged in a thankful breath as he saw her pull aside the curtains, then reach to unlock the door.

"Where were you?" he growled.

Her eyes were large and round. "Come in, and I'll tell you," she whispered.

The look on her face made him hesitate. Something was wrong, but he didn't know what.

Then a voice behind her cut through the pounding of his pulse in his ears.

"Drop your pack. Raise your hands and come inside, or I'll drill a very messy hole in Miss Woodlock's back."

CHAPTER
EIGHTEEN

SILENTLY, SAM RAISED his hands and stepped inside the darkened house. Standing directly behind Olivia was a hard-bitten man with stringy hair sticking below a baseball cap. He had a gun in his hand.

The gunman's expression was something between smirking and grim. "Thanks for finally showing up," he gloated.

Sam kept his voice steady as he worked his way through the implications. "You're not Reese."

"This isn't about Reese."

"Then what?"

"That's for me to know. And you to find out." He stepped back, then gestured with his gun. "This way."

Olivia kept her hopeful gaze on Sam. For the moment he was clean out of options.

Their captor led them down the hall, then into a small room that had apparently been prepared for their arrival. It was empty except for several pairs of handcuffs on the floor.

The gunman turned to Sam first. "Sit down. With your hands behind your back."

Sam sat.

The man turned to Olivia. "Cuff him," he ordered. "Wrists and ankles."

She gave Sam a miserable look, and he tried to tell her with his eyes that he'd get them out of this. At least he hoped to hell he would.

After she'd done as their captor ordered, he made her slip the cuffs onto her own ankles before he snapped them closed and secured her wrists. She was cuffed with her hands in front. Which could be an advantage. But he wasn't going to ask her to take any chances. "Back soon," the gunman said, sounding pleased with himself as he slammed the door.

The moment they were alone, sitting on the floor in the almost pitch-black room, Sam leaned forward.

"Did he hurt you?" he asked urgently.

"No."

He heard the edge of tears in her voice, and he wanted to scoot across the floor and comfort her. That would have to wait until later.

"He knew who we were. He was waiting for us," he said in a grim voice.

"I know," she agreed, sounding miserable.

Confronting his worst fear, he demanded, "Did you tell anyone where we were going?"

"No. I swear I didn't." She stopped and swallowed. "Well, after Colin guessed you'd be testing me, I told him what city we were going to."

"Shit! And Mr. Computer figured out the rest. Then he ratted us out."

"No!"

"Okay. We don't have time to argue about it. The main point is that we walked into a trap. And when that guy comes back, things are going to get worse."

"What are we going to do?" she asked, and he heard the fear in her voice.

So much for hoping he could break the news to her gently. The only saving grace was the darkness; she wouldn't be able to see a hellova lot of anything.

He took a deep breath and let it out in a rush. "You remember that wolf you saw at my place—and the one you saw at the motel?"

"Yes," she answered in a shaky voice.

"Same wolf. He's going to get us out of here."

A couple of seconds of silence passed.

"How . . . what do you mean?" she whispered.

Ignoring the question, he plowed on. "We don't have much time, so listen closely. The wolf can't talk. And when he's here, I won't be. I'm going to get out of my cuffs. I can't get you free until later. Move as far into the corner as you can. *The wolf will not hurt you,*" he said, punching out the words. "But it could get a little dangerous in here when our captor comes back with his gun. So stay out of the action."

He pressed his ear against the wall. "He's out there, talking on the phone. Someone's coming to get . . . you."

"Get me? What about you?"

"Apparently, I'm expendable."

"Oh, my God," she breathed.

"I'm not going to let any of it happen," he said, praying it was true. "So let me do what I have to—and stay out of the way. Now, move!"

His night vision was good enough for him to see her scooting across the floor. He did the same, moving as far away from Olivia as possible. The knowledge of what came next made his stomach curdle, but he knew it was their only chance.

Thankful again that the darkness would hide him, he began chanting.

"Taranis, Epona, Cerridwen."

"Sam? What is that?" she cried out, her voice high and edgy.

Ignoring her, he repeated, *"Taranis, Epona, Cerridwen."*

"Sam. You're scaring me."

"Ga. Feart. Cleas. Duais. Aithriocht. Go gcumhdai is dtreorai na deithe thu."

Long ago, his father had been with him when he spoke the chant for the first time in a clearing in the woods. Later, he and Dad had changed together a few times. No one else had ever heard him say the words of transformation. But he stopped thinking about either the past or the present danger as he felt the change take him, contorting his body, transmuting skin and bone into a different shape. The cuffs had bound the man's hands, and their position would have been agony for the wolf. But even as he changed, he yanked his front paws from the metal bracelets. When they were free, he used his teeth to hold the other set of cuffs steady as he pulled his back paws from them.

He was still hampered by his clothing, but long ago, he had practiced undressing post-transformation. He tugged at the sweatpants with his teeth, pulling them down and over his legs, ripping the fabric in his haste.

"Sam?" Olivia's voice quivered in the darkness. "Sam?"

He stayed away from her, working feverishly to get himself ready. But he ran out of time when he heard footsteps returning.

Quickly he yanked his paws from the sweatpant legs. He was still wearing the T-shirt, which now hung on his lean wolf's body. But it didn't restrict his movements.

Footsteps stopped outside the room. Flattened against the wall behind the door, he tensed as the lock clicked. Then the door opened. The guy had set a battery-powered light on the floor. The first thing Sam saw in the shaft of light was a hand holding a gun. He sprang, sinking his teeth into flesh and bone.

The gun discharged. The man screamed. And so did Olivia.

Sam felt his insides twist, but he couldn't let go of the man to see if she was all right—or neither of them would get out of this mess.

Their captor went on bellowing as Sam crunched down on his hand. When the gun finally dropped, Sam sprang forward and knocked the man to the floor. The baseball cap flew off the man's head as he went down. The violence of the wolf was on Sam. He wanted to rip out their captor's throat. The guy was scum. But he stopped himself from making the kill. Olivia had already seen enough for one night.

The last thing he wanted to do was leave her alone with their captor. But when he pawed at the guy, he didn't move.

Unwilling to make eye contact with Olivia, Sam dashed into the hall. As he moved, he was already saying the chant again in his head, hurrying through the words. The transformation seemed to take forever. But he knew it was less than a minute before he was a man again—naked except for his black T-shirt.

Ignoring the strange picture he must make, he sprinted back into the room.

Olivia was sitting with her back to the wall, looking dazed.

"Are you all right?" he asked urgently.

She stared at him, and the wounded look in her eyes nearly destroyed him. Slowly, he came closer. She was very pale and still. Worse, blood had plastered her shirt sleeve to her arm.

"Shit. Your arm. You're hit."

Following his gaze, she looked down at her arm, her eyes widening into a look of horror.

He bent, inspecting the wound.

"It's not bad. It's not bad," he tried to reassure her.

She gave a small nod, but her face said that she didn't believe him.

He ached to gather her close. But they couldn't stay here.

Quickly, he turned back to examine their former captor, who lay unmoving on the floor, his body limp and his jaw slack. Sam checked to make sure the man was breathing, then riffled through his pockets and found the key to the cuffs.

When he swung toward Olivia again, she hadn't moved a centimeter and still looked as if she were in shock. His heart was pounding as he freed her hands and feet, then spared the time to pull on the pants and shoes he'd discarded, ignoring the rips up and down the pant legs where the wolf's teeth had bitten through the fabric.

After grabbing the gun, he carefully helped Olivia to her feet.

"Can you walk?"

"Yes."

She moved slowly, and they were barely out of the house when he saw headlights cutting through the darkness, coming up the long drive.

"Shit!" he muttered again, pulling her into the shrubbery as the lights approached. "We've got to split."

Stuffing the gun into the pocket of his sweatpants, he picked her up and slung her over his shoulder like a sack of rice, then ran back the way they'd come.

"Don't," she protested, her voice weak.

"We have to get the hell out of here."

Without sparing any more energy on explanations, he headed for the beach, keeping in the shadows as much as possible as he made for where he'd parked the car.

By the time he reached their sheltered parking spot, he was breathing hard.

Trying not to sound like a wounded elk, he opened the passenger door and set Olivia in the front seat, then turned and ripped away the sleeve of her shirt.

She made a small sound as he used the flashlight in the glove compartment to examine the wound. As far as he could see, the bullet had cut across the skin of her arm, and the wound had already stopped bleeding.

Glad that he had parked facing the highway, he looked toward the Reese house. When he saw no traffic, he pulled out and headed in the opposite direction, deliberately keeping below the speed limit when he wanted to floor the accelerator.

He didn't want to get stopped for speeding, but at the same time, he kept picturing a car full of thugs coming after them. He watched the rearview mirror as much as he watched the road ahead. When he was sure nobody was behind them, he headed toward the house they'd rented.

She had seen the wolf in action. And they needed to talk about it—despite the fact that he would have liked to avoid the topic for the next hundred years. Luckily, it would have to wait, since he had other urgent business.

"I want some straight answers from you. Did you tell Colin where we're staying?"

"No!"

He sighed. "Okay."

"You think I'd lie about something like that?"

"I hope not."

"Right, like you wouldn't lie about that damn wolf," she tossed at him.

He wanted to look away, but he kept his gaze steady. "I haven't lied to you except by omission—not telling you all there is to tell. As we both know, you're guilty of the same thing. Trust doesn't seem to come easy for either one of us."

She dropped her gaze, a frown flickering over her brow.

He turned back to the road. He knew it wasn't the best time for hard questions, but he also knew he had to ask, "Do you want me to take you home?"

From the corner of his eye, he saw her head jerk toward him. "And leave me there?" she asked as he pulled into the driveway of their rental.

His mouth was so dry that he could only nod.

Centuries passed before she whispered, "No."

Because you know it's dangerous, or because you want to stay with me? He couldn't make himself ask the question. For now, it was enough that she wasn't running away.

"I'd better take care of your arm," he muttered.

Opening her door, he scooped her up again, hugging her against his chest as he carried her into the house and into the bathroom.

Neither of them spoke, and he could feel his heart thumping as he bent his head and brushed his lips against her. She didn't respond in any way, and she remained silent while he set her on the toilet, then ran warm water in the sink.

He cleaned the wound in her arm, then inspected it carefully, giving it his full attention. Looking up, he found her watching him, and his heart leaped into his throat at the soft, tender look in her beautiful eyes. He'd expected anger—and revulsion. "I'm sorry," she whispered.

"For what?"

"Making you take me there."

"It was my idea," he muttered.

She sighed. "We both know why."

"We'll talk about that later," he answered, then moved to catch her as she lost her balance and slipped to the side.

"You need to lie down." When she seemed steadier, he fumbled in the medicine cabinet, finding alcohol. He would have preferred something she wouldn't feel, but it was the only antiseptic they had. He slopped some onto a hand towel, the fumes almost choking him. "This is going to sting."

When she winced, he clenched his teeth. She endured the procedure silently. Then he tore open a sterile gauze pad, covered the wound with it, and wrapped more gauze around her arm to hold it on.

"Let's get you to bed," he said, kneeling to pull off her shoes and socks before carrying her to the bedroom.

He should leave her alone. She needed to sleep. But he stayed beside the bed. Swallowing hard, he asked, "Can I lie in bed with you?"

Again, centuries passed before she gave another small nod, looking as if it took her last grain of strength to do it.

His movements were jerky as he crossed to the dresser, found a clean pair of sweatpants and pulled them on. Then he dragged off his T-shirt and climbed in beside her.

Taking her gently in his arms, he cradled her against himself, stroking her hair and grazing his lips against the side of her face. And when she stayed in his arms, he allowed himself a spurt of hope.

She had seen the wolf attack a man, and she was still here.

As he held her, he mentally went over the list of people living at the Woodlock estate—starting with her brother and his boyfriend. Were they trying to help? Had they hatched a plan to get Colin's sister out of the clutches of the nasty burglar?

Or was there a more sinister explanation?

He had no way of knowing and no proof of any theory.

He tried to stay awake, because he wanted to be there if Olivia needed him. But the events of the very long day had left him exhausted. His eyes closed, and despite his raw nerves, he slept.

HIS face a mask of anger, Luther Ethridge paced back and forth across the length of his elegant living room.

He had been so close. So close. And now . . .

He'd been gleefully anticipating a cheerful call from the men he'd hired to kill Sam Morgan and bring Olivia to him. But it had gone completely wrong.

Nobody had known exactly when Olivia and Morgan would show up at the Reese house. So it seemed that only one of the thugs—a man he knew as John Smith—had been on the scene when Morgan and Olivia arrived. He'd had complete confidence in the team he'd hired. Well, he'd been confident that the men wanted to do the job and collect their pay.

But somehow they had screwed up. It sounded like Smith had gone off the deep end. He was babbling about being attacked by an animal with teeth and claws that leaped out of the empty storage room where he'd locked Olivia and Morgan.

It was ludicrous, of course. There was no other entrance to the room besides the locked door, and no animal could have gotten in there. Obviously, the man was handing him some load of bullshit to cover his own mistake. Maybe he'd been drunk—or high. Or maybe he'd scrambled his brain when he hit his head fighting with Morgan.

Smith's cohorts didn't know. They claimed they'd been in town picking up food—at three in the morning. *Damned unlikely,* Luther thought. Still, there were all-night stores, so he couldn't prove they were lying. Regardless of where they'd been, they had told Smith they'd come straight back when he called them to say he'd apprehended the would-be burglars. But the captives were gone when they arrived, and Smith was staggering around babbling nonsense.

The other men had found a trail of footprints—human, not animal—on the beach. One set, not far from the house. Luther guessed that Morgan had to have been carrying Olivia. But why? Was she hurt? Or sick? His chest tightened at the thought.

He'd plotted everything out so carefully, but one thing after another was going wrong. Swiping a hand angrily through his hair, he acknowledged that he'd probably never know the truth of what had happened at the Reese house.

But dammit! He needed to know what the devil was going on up there in Carmel. And right now, it looked like there was no way of getting reliable information.

"Fuck!" He hated hired help who failed. He could easily arrange for their punishment. But that left the problem of Olivia.

Again he couldn't hold back a curse. He wanted badly to know what had happened to her and if she was all right.

Maybe Morgan would take her back to the Woodlock estate. Then his informant could give him an update.

SOMETIME later, Sam's eyes snapped open.

Enough light filtered in around the curtains for him to get a good look at Olivia. What he saw made fear leap inside him.

Her eyes were closed. Her skin was clammy, and sweat had broken out on her forehead. Her head moved back and forth on the pillow, and her arms struck out at him.

"Olivia. Wake up. Olivia." He shook her shoulders, and she moaned, but it took several moments before her eyes opened and focused on him.

He braced for her to shrink away from the wolf locked inside him. But she stayed where she was, her breathing ragged.

He swallowed hard. "What? What were you dreaming?"

"It's . . . all my fault," she cried out.

"What?"

"Ethridge . . ." She broke off, moaned again.

"How?" he asked urgently.

"Ethridge. He was . . ."

He gathered her close, rocking her in his arms.

"Sam . . ." The pressure of her hand against his chest made him shift his grip. Looking down at her, he saw her face was contorted. Her lips were working, but it took several seconds before she managed to speak again. "He was . . . holding it out to me. Teasing . . . me. But he wouldn't let me have it. And I was getting so sick. So sick."

"It's okay. I won't let him get you. It's okay."

"No. You don't understand." She gulped, then started to cough. When she raised her head, her face was bleak with tension and sadness. "I lied to you."

CHAPTER
NINETEEN

A CURSE SPRANG from Sam's suddenly dry lips. "Christ! What the hell did you lie about? Is your father going to show up here? Or are you communicating with Ethridge? Is that it? You've been cluing him in all the time."

Her face turned frantic. "No! Not that . . . never him!"

"Then what?"

She swallowed and squeezed her eyes closed, as though she couldn't stand to face him.

Her skin was as pale and fragile-looking as skim milk. And a pulse was beating at her throat.

"What did you lie about?" he growled, making an effort not to shout. Before she could answer, she gasped and pressed her palm to her forehead. Then a moan of agony contorted her features.

He went from anger to fear in a heartbeat. "Olivia, love? What?" Self-reproach clawed at his throat.

He wanted to reach for her, but holding her might block off her oxygen. So he kept his hands at his sides.

Her whole body jerked and began to shake. From her throat came a low, anguished sound of pain that raised the hairs on the back of his neck.

Against his will, his mind flashed back to the night that her uncle had gone berserk and started shooting at anyone in sight. He had sounded a lot like Olivia did now.

"What is it. What's wrong?"

She tried to answer, but she could only gasp for breath, her eyes wide with terror.

He couldn't sit there doing nothing. Gathering her up, he carried her into the bathroom. When he'd been a little boy, he'd had breathing problems a few times. And his mother had filled the bathroom with steam.

He did that now, setting her on the toilet seat while he turned on the hot water in the shower full blast.

Then he lifted her up again, taking the seat and gathering her onto his lap, cradling her against his chest as he stroked her damp hair.

The water heated, the room turned hot and steamy. Maybe it helped. He didn't know. But as he stroked her hair and shoulders, feeling tremors wrack her body, he knew that if he could have taken them into his own body and spared her, he would have done it.

Through a swirl of steam, he watched her open her eyes and tip her head toward him. He watched her trying to get control of herself.

"You . . . have to . . . call Colin . . . or . . . my father," she gasped out.

He had been prepared for disaster. But not that. Her plea was the last thing he wanted to hear. Managing not to shout, he said, "You know I can't do that. Let me get you to the hospital."

The suggestion made fear leap in her eyes. "No! Doctors don't . . . know"—she stopped, dragged in a breath, and let it out—"die . . . in hospital."

His own terror made him grip her shoulders. This time he couldn't keep his voice steady when he demanded, "What do you mean? What the hell is going on? You have to tell me!"

"I have . . . it."

"What?"

"Like . . . Colin . . . my uncle. My family . . ."

He felt as though a knife blade had sliced through his chest. "Jesus. No. Why the hell didn't you tell me?"

"First time . . . I . . . like this." She tried to say more. Her lips moved, but no sound came out. Then her body went limp against his chest.

His heart blocked his windpipe as he felt the pulse in her neck. It was thready, and her breath came in gasps.

"Olivia, what is it? What's wrong? Jesus Christ, tell me!"

But she didn't answer. And when he tipped her head up again, he saw that she had slipped into unconsciousness. He gathered her to him, thinking that he would carry her to the car and take her to the nearest emergency room. She looked like she'd die if he kept her here. But she had said she would die if he did the logical thing. Could her warning possibly be true? Or was she delirious—like her uncle?

He tried to force that idea out of his head. But it came bouncing back. She had told him to call Colin. And he was sure Colin was responsible for their getting caught at Harold Reese's house.

He stroked Olivia's damp hair again, willing her to wake up and tell him what the hell to do for her. But she lay against his chest, still as death, and terror constricted his throat and chest.

He felt as if his own life were in the balance as he stared down at her. Standing, he turned off the shower, then carried her back to the bedroom and laid her back on the sheet. After grabbing his cell phone from the dresser, he eased back onto the bed, clasping Olivia's hand as he dialed the number that he knew from his research was Colin's private line. It rang once, twice, three times.

To his everlasting horror, Brice answered.

"Hello."

Sam almost stabbed the OFF button, but then he looked over at Olivia's pale face and he knew he had to continue with what he'd started.

"This is Morgan," he said tersely. "Let me speak to Colin."

"Where are you?"

"Let me speak to Colin."

"I can't do that."

Unable to control his anger, he shouted, "Well, this is a matter of life and death, you jerk."

There was a long pause before the other man said, "Just a minute."

Sam waited with his heart pounding while the boyfriend went away. The longer they stayed on the line, the more likely it was that someone could trace the call. Was Brice setting up a trace? Sam clenched and unclenched his hand around the phone, wanting to hang up. But he couldn't.

COLIN snatched up the phone. "Morgan? What the hell is going on? What have you done to Olivia? Where are you?"

"Never mind where I am. I have to talk to you alone. Get your boyfriend out of there."

"Brice and I . . ."

Sam cut him off before he could finish. "Somebody just

tried to kill me—at the Reese house. And that's your fucking fault, isn't it?"

Sick horror constricted Colin's throat. "How can you say that?" he managed.

"You figured out where we were going. And if you didn't turn us in, somebody else did. But that's not what I have to talk about now. Olivia just collapsed."

"No!"

Ignoring the exclamation, Sam plowed ahead. "Before she went unconscious, she said she has the same sickness you do. I need to talk to you about that. Now!"

He sounded like he was at the edge of his control.

Colin put his hand over the phone, and looked at Brice. "Give me a minute," he murmured.

Brice must have seen the agony on his face. After a short hesitation, he stepped out of the room.

"Okay. I'm alone," he said.

"I can't stay on the phone long—in case somebody is tracing this call."

"They're not!"

"How the hell do you know? Somebody there arranged for an armed reception at the Reese house. Who knows what kind of technology they're using."

"Let me talk to Olivia," Colin demanded.

"You can't. She's unconscious."

"Oh, Christ!"

"Shut up and listen," Sam snapped. "I need information. Before she passed out, she said that if I took her to the hospital, it would kill her. Is that right?"

"Yes," Colin managed to answer.

"Why?"

He struggled to keep his voice from shaking as he thought about his sister lying in bed, sick and unconscious. "Because we don't respond the way the doctors expect.

Her blood pressure and her heart rate will be low. They'll give her stimulants. And that will kill her. As far as we can figure out, that's what happened to my Uncle Randolph."

"You lying bastard. Your damn father takes stimulants."

"Now. But not in the early stages. This is the first attack?"

"As far as I know."

"She could have been hiding the symptoms."

"Wonderful," Sam snapped.

"Was she injured?"

"Yes. A tough guy with a gun was waiting for us. When I was trying to get us out of there, she got shot."

Colin gasped. "How bad is it?"

"The bullet grazed her arm. I treated the wound and put her to bed. She was having a nightmare. When, I woke her up . . . she started shaking—and babbling."

"She should be all right in a few hours. Or . . . she won't be," Colin heard himself answer.

"What the hell does that mean?"

"The first time . . . it can go either way."

"I'm taking her to the hospital."

"Don't do it," Colin shouted. Struggling to sound coherent, he cleared his throat. "Bring her home where we can take care of her. We've had experience with this."

"How many of you are sick?"

He gulped in air and let it out in a rush. "All of us. When we reach our late twenties."

"So it's not just the men."

"Of course not!"

"You want me to bring her home—so somebody there can make sure she doesn't recover?"

"She'll be better off here. You have to trust us," he pleaded.

Morgan answered with a bitter laugh. "Trust you? I can't trust any of you—including Olivia. Since one of the last things she said was that she lied to me. If you're not the one who blew us out of the water, then put your energy into finding out who did."

"How?"

"Oh, for Christ's sake! You're the computer genius. Figure it out." Morgan sighed, then spoke more calmly. "No. Wait, we'll have to do it together. Set a trap. I'll e-mail you later. Just tell me what to do for Olivia now."

"Keep her warm."

"With blankets?"

"Yes."

"What else?"

"That's all you can do."

"Oh, that's just great." Morgan slammed down the phone, and Colin replaced the receiver, then lowered his head into his hands.

He'd thought he'd known what he was doing. Now he wondered what the hell he had set in motion.

SAM wanted to scream in frustration. Was that really all he could do for his mate? Keep her warm? He wanted to call the brother back and drag out every fact that Colin could dredge up about the family illness and the elixir, Astravor, that saved their lives. This was the time to do it, while Colin was still grappling with the shock of his sister's attack.

But Sam couldn't take the chance that he would lead the bad guys straight to them. And he needed to focus on Olivia.

Razor wire twisted in his gut as he looked at her, lying on the bed, so still and lifeless.

He found the pulse in her throat, counted the beats. Forty. Her heart was beating slowly. At least Colin had told him the truth about that.

After pulling the comforter up to her chin, he got off the bed, took the spare blanket from the top shelf of the closet, and folded it in half before placing it over her.

As he stared down at her, he clenched and unclenched his fists. Her brother had been through this. Other people in the family had been through it, too. Some of them had died.

"Not you, love. Not you," he whispered. "I need you to live. Olivia, do that for me. Get well. Please, get well."

He didn't know if he believed in God. But that hadn't stopped him from praying once—long ago, the night before his dad was going to take him out to the woods so he could change to wolf form the first time.

Four of his six older brothers had died trying to get through that damn change. Only Ross and Adam had survived. He'd been scared shitless and worked hard not to show it.

He was scared shitless now.

"Please, God, don't let her die," he begged. "You can save her. She's a good woman. Brave. Loyal to her family. She didn't ask for this. Please save her."

The prayer sounded hollow—coming from a man like Sam Morgan. But it was the best he could do.

CHAPTER
TWENTY

THE NECK OF Sam's T-shirt felt like it was strangling him. He pulled at the knit band, but it retracted back into place. Finally, when he couldn't stand the constricted feeling, he pulled the shirt over his head and tossed it away.

It helped. But not enough. His wild nature clamored for open space. He needed to run through the woods, howling his fear and his anger. But there was no way he could leave Olivia. He had to be here when she woke up. He had to be here if she needed him.

The concept was a strange one to him. Had anyone ever needed him?

Like all kids, he'd been dependent on his parents when he was little. His mother had nurtured him, shielded him from the wrath of the Big Bad Wolf, as his brother Ross had called their dad.

But his father had done the one essential job bred into his genes. He had taught his sons the ancient ritual and coached them through the first awful transformation from man to wolf. Some had lived. Others had died.

Johnny Marshall had needed his father then. But nobody had ever needed the man he had become—Sam Morgan.

Well, he thought with a start, that wasn't exactly true. Olivia had needed him to break into Luther Ethridge's house. She'd said it was to save her family. Now he was pretty sure it was to save herself as well. But she hadn't told him that. She'd hidden that part from him.

He wanted to pick up the lamp and hurl it across the room. If she'd just confided that she had the family illness, he would have played this differently. He certainly wouldn't have fucked her brains out every night—and worked her hard every day.

He wanted to blame the whole mess on her. But he recognized the self-protective impulse. She had kept her secrets. He had kept his.

She knew the worst about him. He still didn't know what else she was hiding from him. Somehow he stopped himself from pounding his fists against the wall. He ached to do something that would help his mate. But all he could do was keep her warm, for God's sake.

Getting up, he returned with first aid supplies. Carefully he took the bandage off her arm and examined the wound. It looked like it was healing normally, so he put on a fresh gauze pad.

As he finished, he felt her stir.

Her eyes stayed closed, but her lips moved. Bending over, he heard her whisper his name. "Sam."

"Right here, love. Did I hurt you?"

"No."

He couldn't stop himself from pulling aside the covers so he could slip underneath and take her in his arms.

She moved her head against his naked shoulder. "Yes . . . hold me."

He stroked his lips against her cheek and the tender place beside her ear.

"Have to . . . sleep . . . sorry," she murmured without opening her eyes, and he fought a fresh spurt of panic as she drifted off again. But unlike earlier, her respiration seemed normal. And when he laid his hand over her heart, he felt the strong steady beat. Counting, he found it was up to sixty.

All of which proved that she was going to recover, didn't it? He wanted that to be true so badly that he could barely breathe. But he didn't know the progress of the attack. His fingers itched to pick up the phone and call Colin. If her brother wasn't the one who had betrayed them, he was probably suffering—waiting for news. But every contact with the Woodlock mansion was taking a big risk. So he kept one arm firmly around Olivia and gathered up a fistful of sheet with the other.

Again, the waiting was agony. The next time she stirred, she looked more like herself. And he fought a mixture of relief and nerves.

She ducked her head and eased away from him.

"Got to go . . . to the bathroom," she said.

"Probably a good sign," he answered. When he would have scooped her into his arms, she shook her head. "Let me walk."

"Okay," he agreed, but kept his arm around her as she made her slow way down the hall, leaning against him. She stepped into the bathroom and shut the door, and he propped his shoulder against the wall, waiting for her to emerge.

After he'd helped her back into bed, he asked, "Do you want some food?"

She thought for a minute. "The proverbial tea and toast."

"Okay."

He knew they were both postponing a frank conversation as he went into the kitchen, started the kettle and toasted wheat bread, then added a little butter and blackberry jam.

He put a mug of sweetened tea and the plate of toast on a tray for her, then added a mug of cranberry tea for himself.

When he came back to the bedroom, he saw she'd combed her hair and changed into a fresh T-shirt.

"I'd say you shouldn't be up. But I have no idea what I should be advising," he said.

"The way we do it is to see what we can manage," she murmured.

He set the tray on the bedside table near her, then took his own mug. "How do you feel?"

She considered the answer. "Weak. But I'm recovering."

"How long before you get sick again?" he asked, unable to keep the harshness out of his voice.

"I don't know," she said in a low voice.

He muttered a curse under his breath.

She watched him set down his mug on the nightstand, then said in a conversational tone, "I thought maybe you didn't drink alcohol or tea because you were a straight arrow. Now I guess it's a werewolf trait."

He was glad he hadn't taken a sip of the hot liquid, because he might have choked. "Yeah, our sense of smell and taste are too acute. And we overreact to drugs," he managed, then plumped up the pillows before sitting down beside her.

She took a bite of toast and washed it down with tea before saying, "I would have appreciated knowing your . . . special talent before you seduced me."

His hands clenched on his mug. "Like I would have appreciated knowing you had the family illness before I dragged you on a risky mission. Why the hell didn't you tell me?"

"Because I knew you wouldn't take me," she shot back, then looked down at the bandage on her arm. "I think I would have avoided the attack, if I hadn't gotten shot."

"Your brother asked if you'd been injured."

"You talked to Colin?"

"Yes."

He saw alarm flash in her eyes. "What else did he say?"

"What else are you hiding?" he shot back.

"Nothing!"

He regarded her carefully. "I know that look. You're avoiding something. Some crucial fact I need to know to keep your butt out of the wringer!"

When she didn't deny it, his anger flared again. He wanted to ask her about the dream she'd had just before she'd gotten really sick. She'd woken up saying this was all her fault. What was she talking about? He wanted to know, but he was going to have to wait on that.

Instead he said, "Colin said you could have died if I'd taken you to the hospital. I was scared enough to do it. I would have, if I hadn't talked to him."

"I'm sorry," she whispered, then leaned back against the pillows and closed her eyes. "This is wearing me out."

"Or you're using it as an excuse not to continue the conversation."

"That, too," she admitted in a small voice.

He sighed. "I'll let you rest. For now."

She sank down lower against the pillows. Seconds later, she was sleeping.

Gently, he took the plate off her lap and set it on the table.

Because he was still afraid to leave Olivia alone, he brought his laptop computer into the bedroom and booted up. For a long moment he stared at the screen. Then he connected to the phone line and opened a Web browser. There was something that didn't add up. Something that he had meant to check out and had never gotten around to. He might not be as good a researcher as Colin Woodlock. But he was pretty proficient. When he put Dr. Henry Regario into several search engines, he came up with no one who could have produced the elixir that Olivia had told him about.

He brooded about that for a while. Then he opened the E-mail he rarely used.

After deleting the accumulated junk, he looked over toward his mate. She was still sleeping, so he typed in an address from memory. An address he had looked up but never used. Rmarsh@asl.com.

Simply staring at his brother's name made him feel lightheaded. When he'd run away from that hospital morgue in Baltimore, he'd let his family think he was dead. Now there was a reason to contact them. He needed a better understanding of what the future held for him and Olivia.

Yet what the hell was he going to say? Ross was five years older—a big gap in their ages when they'd been young. Ross had always been a real straight arrow. He'd gone to the University of Maryland, worked two jobs, and basically bought into solid citizenship, at least as solid as a man could be who turned into a wolf at night and roamed the woods, probably helping to thin the deer population.

That image gave him the courage to write:

"I guess if you're at the computer, you're sitting down. I know that eight years ago you thought Johnny Marshall's body got lost in the shuffle after that bar fight. That's what he wanted you and everybody else to think. He woke up in the hospital and remembered the bikers from the bar talking about how they were going to pin a murder rap on him. So he decided it was dumb to stick around and try to defend himself when a dozen witnesses were going to say he did it. Being the sophisticated guy you remember, he stole a car and got the hell out of Dodge. On the way to California, where he lives now, he changed his name—to Sam Morgan. That's me."

He stopped and read the message, made a few changes, and considered his next words. Ross might revert to the violence of the werewolf when he was alone in the woods. But when he was a man, he was a private detective, which probably meant he was in favor of law and order. The minute he found out his youngest brother wasn't dead, he was going to do some checking up on him. And probably he'd come to the conclusion that his sources of income weren't entirely legal. Would he rat on him? Or would he be glad to hear that his kid brother wasn't dead after all?

He thought about pressing the DELETE button. Then he reminded himself why he was taking this step and went on:

"After I got out of Baltimore, I decided it was better just to live my own life, considering how well the Marshall guys get along. But I need to find out some things. I've checked up on you. I know you married a doctor who's a genetics specialist. Did she figure out anything that would give your children a better chance at survival?"

He broke off again, because his chest had tightened painfully. Before he could change his mind, he sighed the message, "Your brother, Sam Morgan."

After clicking the SEND button, he looked up and saw Olivia was awake and watching him warily. "What are you doing? E-mailing Luther Ethridge?" she asked in a shaky voice.

"Of course not! What makes you think so?"

"The look on your face."

"Which is?"

"Tense. Guilty. You look like a kid taking the loose change your dad left on the dresser."

He sighed. "I was e-mailing my brother."

"The one you haven't talked to in eight years?"

"Yeah."

"Why?"

He scrubbed a hand over his face. "I need advice."

"About what?"

He had a split second to come up with an answer. He settled for a half-truth. "Married life."

He saw her complexion go a shade paler. "Who said I was going to marry you?"

"Will you?" he asked, because he had been thinking about it for weeks.

"I don't know. Don't you think you should have told me the truth about the wolf before we got locked in that storage room?"

"Yes. You know why I didn't. But the way you found out doesn't change anything between us."

Her eyes narrowed. "I wouldn't count on it."

He kept his own gaze steady. "One thing about the sexually mature young werewolf—he can have any woman he wants."

"That's pretty arrogant."

"Yeah, but it's true. Until the happy-go-lucky werewolf hits his thirties, and he meets the woman who is going to be his mate. When that happens, the two of them bond." He swallowed. "The moment I met you, I knew you were that woman. I tried to fight the attraction because I didn't like the idea of being tied to anyone, especially the daughter of Wilson Woodlock."

She raised her chin. "I don't like the idea either. And I'm not going to be your ordained mate because you think it's written in the stars."

CHAPTER
TWENTY-ONE

SAM ACHED TO set her straight. Instead, he dragged in a breath and let it out, before forcing himself to say, "Okay. One thing at a time. Stay with me until I get the elixir—the Astravor—that will keep you alive. Then you can walk away from me if you want."

Her face contorted. "You're not playing fair."

"What do you suggest? Or did you give up the idea of my helping you?"

She looked down at her hands, then back up at him. "No. I didn't give that up. I knew instantly that you were the right person for the job." She clamped her fingers together. "And that was way before I knew your special talents."

She had given him the opening to say, "Well, that's something we have to talk about. I mean, you've got your secrets, and I have mine. I'd appreciate it if you kept the wolf to yourself."

"What do I tell my family about how you got me free?"

"It was dark. I'm Houdini. And I don't give away my secret methods."

She licked her lips. "Okay."

He eyed her cold toast. "You need to eat. At least, I think you do. I don't know much about your family illness, Woodlocks' Disease."

She looked relieved at the change of subject. "Yes. I'm hungry."

He went back to the kitchen, brought more toast and tea. And a small glass of orange juice, in case she could handle that. He also made a quick roast beef sandwich for himself because he had gone without food for hours.

The few minutes he was away gave them both time to cool off.

"Thank you," she said politely when he returned with the food. He delivered hers to the bed, then sat back down at the desk, turning his chair so he could look at her. They both ate in silence for several minutes, and he didn't push her to talk because he wanted to judge how she was feeling.

When she had finished the toast and taken several sips of tea, she asked, "What did Colin tell you about the family sickness?"

"Not much. It was a short conversation since somebody at your house told the guy waiting at Reese's that we were coming. So who is the stool pigeon working for? Your father?" he pressed.

Her head jerked up. The look of fear that flashed in her eyes told him that he'd hit a nerve.

"Why him?" she asked in a shaky voice.

"He wants you back, and he's got plenty of money to spend. He could have arranged for a reception committee. And I think he's ruthless enough to want me eliminated if he thought that was the best thing for you."

"I know you have a low opinion of him. But I can't believe he'd have you murdered."

He sighed. "Let's put that aside and go back to Woodlocks' Disease. You told me a little about it. I need to know more."

She swallowed and looked away, and he wondered if her next words would be truth or fiction.

"Nobody develops symptoms until after age twenty-six or so. Then the elixir keeps it in check. It's worse for some of us than for others. I thought . . ." She stopped and huffed out a breath. "I didn't get sick right away. And I thought I would be okay for a while longer." She made a snorting sound. "Maybe I was counting on how healthy I'd always been. Dad and Colin would rather die than exercise. I always made the gym part of my life."

"You're better now. But for how long?" he asked, digging relentlessly for information.

"I don't know." She kept her gaze steady. "I've survived the first full-blown attack. It can be fatal."

"Colin told me that. It scared me shitless."

"Oh, Sam. I . . . I'm so sorry I did that to you." She held out her arm, and he went to her, folding her close. "I can be okay for weeks or months," she whispered. "But sooner or later, I'll get sick again. And there's no way of knowing what it will do to me. It could attack my body. My brain." Raising her head, she looked at him. "How would you deal with that?"

"I'm going to get you that elixir. And I understand why you didn't tell me. Believe me, I know about family secrets. The Marshalls had a lot to hide."

"Marshall—was that your name?"

"Yes. You're the only person in the world who knows that Johnny Marshall is Sam Morgan, at least until Ross gets my E-mail. I'm being honest with you," he said, thinking that he had no choice. And he didn't want to give her one, either. "Get used to being honest with me."

"I am."

He gave her a narrow-eyed look. "Then let's talk about Astravor. You said a researcher developed it, a Dr. Regario."

"Yes," she said carefully.

"That's a lie, isn't it?" he said quietly.

He watched her expression turn uncertain. "How do you know?" she asked.

"In the first place, you're not talking about it like it's a new discovery. It sounds like it's been around for generations—like it's that 'folk remedy' you mentioned. Only it was always effective. And in the second place, I looked up Dr. Henry Regario. He didn't work for your father, did he?"

"No," she finally whispered.

"Why did you lie about that?"

"Colin and I thought it sounded more plausible than telling you that Astravor has been part of my family heritage back into ancient times." She swallowed. "The legend is that a pagan goddess gave it to us to save us from an enemy. My ancestor accepted the bargain. And that tied him and his descendants to the Astravor for all time. I mean, how many people are going to believe that?"

He laughed. "A man with an ancestor who asked the Druid gods for special powers and doomed himself and his descendants to be werewolves."

"I didn't know that at the time."

"You do now."

"Yes."

"So what else are you hiding about Astravor?"

She swallowed but said nothing.

"Can I assume you're not concealing something that would be dangerous to me?"

"Yes," she whispered.

"Maybe when we get the elixir back, you'll trust me."

"Sam . . ."

"Did the goddess give your ancestor the Astravor to fight demons?"

She blanched. "Why do you ask?"

"Because the first time I met Darwin, he was raving about them."

She gave a small nod. "Yes. That's part of the legend. I never took it literally until Luther Ethridge stole the Astravor. Then I started wondering if it was a metaphor for the enemies of my family."

"Yeah," he agreed, sensing he had pushed her as far as he could on the subject of Astravor for now. Clearing his throat, he asked, "Are you feeling well enough to travel?"

"Yes."

"And well enough to help me set a trap for the spy at the estate?"

She firmed her lips. "Yes."

"And you'd stake your life on it not being Colin or Brice?"

"Yes!"

Could he trust that? Not completely. But he answered, "Okay. First, I want you to get dressed. I want to see if you're steady on your feet."

"I am," she said again, then eased away from him and got out of bed. He watched her rummaging in her suitcase for clean clothing, watched her head for the bathroom. While she was gone, he sent an E-mail to Colin.

ALONE in the bathroom, Olivia leaned toward the mirror and inspected her face. She had been feeling sick off and on for the past few months. But she'd tried to ignore that.

It hadn't done her any good. The illness had grabbed

her by the throat anyway. And that wasn't her only problem. Sam had told her she was going to be a werewolf's wife! How did you prepare yourself for that? Or did you run? If you did, would it do you any good?

When she came out, she saw Sam was lying comfortably on the bed. Well, he looked comfortable with the pillows bolstered, his hands stacked behind his head. But he couldn't hide his tension from her.

Watching her carefully, he said, "Last time Colin and I talked, it was on his personal line. I've just e-mailed him and gotten an answer. And he's erased the messages. I told him you'd call in a little while. He's agreed that this time we'll use the house line, keep him on the phone for a while, and hope that our spy is listening in." He went on to give her instructions, then handed her the phone.

Olivia looked from the small instrument back to Sam. "Thank you for trusting me," she whispered, then sat down in the chair by the window.

He stood in the doorway, watching her—making her nervous, if she was honest.

Without looking at him, she made the call. Jefferies answered, and her stomach clenched. It could be him. He could be the traitor. She didn't want it to be him. She didn't want it to be anyone in the house.

"Can I speak to Colin?" she said.

"Miss Olivia. We've been so worried about you. Where are you?"

"I can't talk about that now. I need to speak to my brother."

"Of course. I didn't mean to overstep."

"I know you didn't."

He was away for several moments. Then Colin came on the line. "Olivia?"

"Yes."

"Thank God. How are you?"

"Okay," she said around the lump that had formed in her throat. "I have to tell you some things. Important information."

"What?"

"I can't do it over the phone." She stopped and took a breath. "Sam is out. If he comes back, I'll have to hang up right away." She wanted to add, you know that's a lie, don't you? But she could only think it.

"What would he do if he caught you?" Colin asked.

She raised her head and looked at Sam. "Beat me within an inch of my life."

"The bastard," Colin said. "I take it he's treating you pretty badly."

"Yes," she answered, knowing that he understood she was putting on a show for whoever might be listening. "I'm going to try and get away from him. He has to sleep sometime. If I can get home, I'll drive straight through. I'll meet you at the old well out back—where we had that earlier incident. You know where I mean?"

"Yes."

"Where are you?"

"I'd rather not say. But I'll do my best to be home by midnight. If I can't make it by then, wait for me." She paused. "And keep it secret. I feel like such a fool for going off with him. I don't want everybody there to think I'm a fool."

"They won't!"

"Promise you'll come alone, so we can work out some kind of story. Like we did when we were kids, getting around Dad."

"I'll be alone."

She looked up and saw Sam scribbling something on a piece of notepaper which he handed to her. Quickly she read the message and nodded. "Repeat back to me where we're meeting."

"We're meeting at the old well. Out back. At midnight. Or later, if you can't make it by then."

"Yes. Thanks. I love you."

"Love you. Be careful, Olivia."

"I will."

She hung up and glanced at Sam. "How was I?"

"Perfect. Anybody listening would think you hate me."

The look on his face made her heart squeeze. "I don't," she whispered.

"But you're not entirely sure how you feel," he said in a gritty voice.

He had told her to be honest. The best she could say was, "I'm still confused." Maybe it was the safest answer.

WHILE Olivia got some sleep, Sam took the computer into the den. He might go days without checking his E-mail, because there wasn't anyone he wanted to communicate with. Now he connected to the phone line again and opened his mailbox.

When he saw a message from Rmarsh@asl.com, he sat staring at the subject line for several moments. It said, "Thank you for contacting me."

Wondering exactly why Ross welcomed the contact, he pushed the ENTER button and watched the message flash on the screen.

"Sam, I'm so glad to hear from you. I've been hoping and praying for years that I would. I investigated the bar murder. I knew you didn't do it. But I couldn't be sure the cops would believe me."

With a feeling of unreality, Sam stared at the words. Ross had believed in him all those years ago.

"I also investigated the hospital morgue. I knew there was a chance you'd slipped away. But I knew you didn't want to be found. So whenever I talked about you or even thought about you, I acted like you were dead. Because that was my only option."

He rocked back in the deck chair, stunned by what he was reading.

"Sam, I'm so thankful you pressed the SEND button. And I have a pretty good idea why. You're thirty. And I'd guess that you've met your lifemate. If so, I have some good news for you. As you know, my wife Megan is a doctor with a specialty in genetics. She's been able to figure out that we have an extra chromosome that's responsible for our . . . special qualities. It's sex-linked, which is why only male children survived. But she's been able to overcome that. She and I have a son and a daughter, if you can believe that. Adam, who runs a private nature park in Georgia, is married and has a son. And Megan thinks she has the hormone problem figured out—so that none of our sons will have to face the risks we did when they reach puberty. She thinks we can make sure they make it through the change."

Stunned, Sam had to stop reading again and simply focus on his breathing. Then he went back to the text.

"So I'm here to give you any help you need in that department. I know you're probably blown away by the information I've just given you. And there's so much

more I want to say. But the bottom line is that Adam
and I are friends. And we've even made contact with
our cousin, Grant Marshall. I know you're thinking
about the way we used to fight with Dad. But if you understand how to work it, you can control the impulse to
dominate. I guess the big point is that the guy who's on
his home turf gets to call the shots. I'm telling you so
you'll consider coming back for a visit—with your
mate. I won't give away your secret. But I know Mom
would be thrilled to see you. And so would Dad, for
about twenty minutes. No, maybe longer. We're slowly
bringing him into the twenty-first century.

"So now the ball is back in your court. Your brother,
Ross."

Blinking back the moisture in his eyes, Sam reread the
E-mail, then read it again, then pressed REPLY.

His hands weren't quite steady as he typed:

"Thanks for getting back to me so fast. Yes, I'm blown
away. And relieved. And I'll contact you again after I've
absorbed some of that."

After sending the message, he sat staring at the computer screen. He'd just gotten more than he bargained for.
The part about the children was a shock. A good shock. But
there was still the problem of his profession.

Or did Ross already know his brother was a thief? Was
he keeping silent on that point because he wanted to establish better communications first?

THREE hours later, he woke Olivia. In the dimly lit room,
he slid her a quick look. They had gone into the Reese

project feeling uneasy about each other. Their relationship still wasn't exactly on what he'd call normal footing. Yet something had changed.

Together, they packed efficiently, got in the car, and left Monterey. She dozed on the way down the coast, then woke as they approached the northern suburbs of Santa Barbara.

Watching her stretch, he asked, "How are you feeling?"

"Not bad. You can drop me off, then park the car nearby so it won't take too long for you to get into the backyard." She rummaged in her purse and pulled out a key ring. "There's a door in the front wall—about twenty feet to the left of the driveway. It's covered by ivy, and most people have forgotten about it. Nobody would be expecting me to come in that way."

"I don't like us getting separated. And I don't like using you as bait."

"I know. But it's the best way."

They rode in silence for another ten minutes, before he cleared his throat and managed to relate the news, "My brother sent back a message."

"I'll bet he was happy to hear from you," she said instantly.

"Yeah." Sam's hands tightened on the wheel. "When we were teenagers, we all had to face . . . the first time we changed."

"I guess it was frightening," she said in a strained voice that made him think she might have some understanding of what it was like.

"A lot of us didn't make it. I mean . . . some of my older brothers died in the process."

Her gaze shot to him. "It's dangerous?"

"Yes. But Ross married a doctor who specializes in genetics. She thinks she has a solution."

"Good."

He wanted to add "for our children." But he couldn't go quite that far. So he said, "Another thing my parents had to face. In our family, the only children born alive were boys."

When she sucked in a sharp breath, he went on quickly. "But Ross's wife has solved that problem, too. They have a daughter and a son." He glanced at her to see how she'd taken the information.

"Will the daughter be . . . like you?"

"I don't know. I don't think so."

They had arrived in Montecito. He stopped down the road from the estate and put the car into park. When she turned toward the door, he dragged her back and wrapped her in his arms.

"If I didn't think I'd scare off the traitor, I'd be there with you," he said.

"I know, but I'll be fine," Olivia answered. The reassurance was as much for herself as for him.

With one hand, Sam reached toward the glove compartment, opened the latch, and got out the gun she'd practiced with and a set of handcuffs that he also carried with him. "Take these. If you catch the spy before I get there, get Colin to cuff him."

She eyed the gun. "Why didn't you bring that to the Reese house?" she asked.

He laughed. "Habit. A wolf doesn't need a gun. And a burglar who gets caught with a weapon is in a lot more trouble than one who's unarmed."

"So taking me to target practice was just one of your ploys to get me to back off."

"Pretty much, yeah," he admitted.

"Thanks for leveling with me."

He cupped his hand over her shoulder. "Olivia, everything between us is on the level—as far as I'm concerned."

She looked down at the weapon, hefting its weight in her hand, wishing she could say the same thing to him. But that was still impossible.

After slipping the gun into the compartment in the door, she hugged him tightly. "You be careful."

"I will."

She gave him one more fierce embrace, then took the gun, and got out.

WHEN Olivia disappeared from sight, Sam felt a surge of panic. He had come up with this plan to trap the spy. But now that they were in the middle of it, he had to force himself not to go after her.

With his jaw clenched, he drove to the next cross street, then to the end of the block.

Quickly he got out and retrieved his small pack from the back. After methodically checking the contents, he hooked the pack over one shoulder and headed for the grove of pine trees where he'd changed before. Hanging the pack on a low branch, he took off his clothing, feeling the cold wind whip against his body. It was uncomfortable, but it also helped sharpen his senses as he said the ancient chant that changed him from man to wolf.

After dropping to all fours, he sniffed the wind before wiggling into the pack that dangled low enough for him to reach easily. Then, because he knew Olivia was feeling alone and scared, he raised his head and howled—calling out to his mate.

THE hair on the back of Olivia's neck prickled as she heard the sound of a wolf howl. There was only one wolf around here. At least she hoped so.

"Sam," she whispered, knowing that he was calling to her, telling her that he would be there soon.

Quietly she opened the door in the wall and slipped inside. For a long moment, she stared into the darkness beyond the glow of the floodlights. Then she stiffened her knees and walked around the house, holding the gun down beside her right leg.

The moon came out from behind a cloud, turning the garden into a place of magic. She had always thought of it like that. The Woodlocks' magic realm.

Tonight the silvery light and the smell of the flowers enveloped her like a familiar caress. Still, she felt goose bumps pepper her arms as she crossed the open space between the house and the well.

It was impossible to shake off the notion that somebody was standing in the shadow of a tree or bush, watching her progress as she walked toward the wall at the back of the property.

She kept her pace steady, struggling not to show the lingering effects of her recent illness. She knew how hard Colin worked not to let the family curse interfere with his life. If he could do that, so could she, particularly since he was probably watching her.

In fact, he was already at the spot where they had agreed to meet, leaning against a tree.

When she softly called his name, he raised his head, and she speeded up, rushing toward him.

"Thank God, you're all right," he whispered. "I've been worried about you."

"I'm fine."

He lowered his voice to a whisper. "Sam said you were sick."

She swallowed. "I thought I was going to escape the family curse. I guess not."

"I was hoping you would."

"We'll fix it!" she said, then stopped suddenly as the sound of leaves crackling told her that someone had followed her from the direction of the house.

The spy.

Whirling, she strained her eyes into the shadows beyond the moonlight. When she saw Brice coming out of the darkness, a grim look on his face, her heart leaped into her throat.

Oh, God. Not Brice.

CHAPTER
TWENTY-TWO

OLIVIA FOUGHT FOR breath. She was so unprepared to see Colin's partner that she didn't know what to do. Raise the gun? What?

"We were worried about you. Are you all right?" he asked in a tense voice.

"Yes," she managed.

Colin stepped forward, looking as sick and conflicted as she felt. "What the hell are you doing here?" he demanded.

Olivia's head swung toward him, aching with sorrow for her brother.

Brice raised his chin and addressed himself to Colin. "We're in this together, in case you've forgotten. I knew something was going on. Something to do with Olivia and Sam, and I wasn't going to let you deal with it alone."

Lord, was he telling the truth? Or was he an excellent liar? Either way, he had just thrown a wild card into this rendezvous.

"There are some things I have to deal with on my own, family things," Colin snapped.

As she turned toward her brother, the feeling of being watched from the shadows made the hairs on the back of her neck straighten.

Someone or something was edging closer to the three of them, concealed by a screen of shrubbery.

The wolf? He had said he would change back before they confronted the spy. But everything was happening too fast now.

Brice moved, dashing into the bushes, pulling someone out into the moonlight. Again Olivia couldn't stifle a feeling of disorientation. It was Irene Speller, the maid who had helped Jefferies run their household for the past five years.

Brice stayed close to the woman. Colin stared at her, looking as shocked as Olivia felt. "Irene? What . . . what are you doing here?" he demanded.

"I was out for a walk," the maid answered, with just a hint of nerves in her voice. "I'm sorry if I intruded."

Colin wedged his fists on his hips. "I don't think so— not at this time of night. Not when I've been tripping over you every time I turn around. You were in the hall when I came out of my room after I was talking to Olivia. You were spying on me. Why?"

"No," she said, but she couldn't quite hold her voice steady.

"You'd better stay right here until we sort this out," Olivia said as she raised the gun, pointing it at the maid.

Irene glanced at the weapon, then took a step back.

"Stop right there," Olivia warned.

The maid raised her chin. "Or what?"

"Or . . . I'll shoot you," Olivia answered.

"You don't have the guts." Irene turned and ran, heading for the house.

"Don't shoot," Brice shouted. Tearing after Irene, he caught her in a football tackle, bringing her down on the grass.

Olivia and Colin rushed forward. Brice kept his hand on the maid's arm, pulling her to her feet.

"Why do you want to hurt us?" Colin whispered.

"I don't!"

"Stop lying," Colin ordered.

"I'm not," Irene insisted, but her eyes darted nervously to the side.

Brice shook her. "Talk!"

"Get your hands off me," she shrieked, apparently cracking under the stress.

Olivia stepped forward. "I know you're scared. Let us help you."

"Oh yeah. Sure. You're just like everybody else in your filthy rich family." Fear and anger must have given the woman strength because she wrenched away from Brice, leaping at Olivia, who screamed as Irene knocked her to the ground and tried to snatch the weapon away.

THE wolf had reached the exterior of the garden wall when he heard Olivia scream.

Oh, Lord, no! He had sent his mate into danger. And now she was in trouble.

He wanted to howl in anger. Instead, he crouched down and sprang upward, making it to the top of the wall in one bound. Pausing only an instant to catch his balance, he plunged down the other side and bounded forward, spotting the maid named Irene on top of Olivia.

The wolf sprinted forward and leaped onto the woman's back, making her screech in terror as he yanked her away and tossed her like a dirty rag onto the grass.

He could hurt her badly. The wolf part of him ached to leave some tooth or claw marks on her.

But someone was shouting at him. It was Olivia. "Don't, S—" She started to say his name and changed her mind. "Don't! Please, don't!"

Raising his head, he saw the pleading look in her eyes and the stunned expressions on the faces of the two men.

OLIVIA pushed herself up. Leaving the gun where it had fallen on the ground, she pulled out the handcuffs that Sam had given her and knelt beside the maid, cuffing her wrists behind her back, the way Sam had been secured at the Reese house only days before.

When she was finished, Olivia scrambled over to the wolf, throwing her arm over his back as she looked up to face her brother and Brice.

The two men both stared at her as though struggling to take in what they were seeing.

Olivia gave them a fierce look. "My new guard dog," she clipped out, hoping that her voice and her expression conveyed that she wasn't going to go into any more explanations in front of the woman who had been spying on them for months—maybe years.

"Let's get Irene back to the house," Brice suggested.

"No, I want to know what she was doing here," Olivia answered. She hadn't been able to shoot an unarmed woman in cold blood. But Irene wasn't going to escape anytime soon. And she was pretty sure Sam would want to press their advantage right now. When she turned toward the wolf for confirmation, he gave her a small nod, then pawed at the woman, who whimpered, the fight gone out of her now.

Olivia found the gun and handed it to Brice. "Keep her covered. But don't shoot her unless you have to."

Brice moved closer to Irene, keeping the weapon trained on her. "Unlike you, I will kill her if I have to," he muttered.

The wolf stayed where he was, standing guard.

Olivia yanked Irene to a sitting position. Part of her was standing back, watching in amazement as she grabbed the maid's hair and tipped her head up. "I'll have my dog tear you to pieces," she said, "unless you tell me who you're working for."

"Please. Let me go," Irene begged, her eyes fixed on the "dog."

"Tell me why you informed someone where Sam Morgan and I were going."

The wolf growled and bared his teeth, and the maid shrank back. When the animal took a step toward her, she moaned, looking like she might have a heart attack on the spot. "Please, get him away from me."

"Who are you working for?" Olivia snapped, giving the maid's head a shake.

When she refused to speak, the wolf took her shoulder in his teeth. Olivia could see he was acting with restraint, but Irene didn't know that.

She moaned. "No. Don't! Make him stop."

"I will, if you tell me who paid you to spy on us," Olivia answered, then held her breath as she waited for the worst.

"Luther Ethridge," Irene whispered.

A wave of relief washed over Olivia. Not her father! At least it wasn't her father who had tried to kill Sam. Still, the confirmation that a trusted household member had been feeding information to Ethridge made something inside Olivia go sick and cold. "You work for us," she said. "How could you work for him, too?"

When Irene raised her head, her eyes were cold. "Do you have any idea what it's like to work for Wilson Woodlock?" she spat out. "He wants value for money! That means he wants you to work eighteen hours a day, seven days a week. And he wants to pay you shit. Just think of all the staffers who have quit because they couldn't take it! I was going to leave a couple of years ago. Then Ethridge made me a very nice offer. And I decided to collect double pay. More than double."

Olivia sucked in a shaky breath, hardly knowing what to say. She raised her eyes to Colin, and he looked as sick as she felt.

"We'll take her inside," Brice said, "then figure out what to do."

"Yes," Olivia agreed. When she turned her head, the wolf had faded back into the shadows.

She tugged on Irene's arm, pulling her erect. "Come on."

As they crossed the lawn, Sam joined them, dressed in a different shirt and pants than he'd been wearing earlier, and she realized they must have been in the small pack he'd had strapped to his back.

The whole group stopped in their tracks, shrinking back from him.

Olivia looked at Colin and Brice, giving a small shake of her head when Brice opened his mouth.

"It looks like you missed the excitement," she said to Sam.

Sam gave her an approving look, noting the relieved expressions on the men's faces. He didn't know if they bought her explanation. But he'd bet they wanted to believe it.

Moving next to Olivia, he slung an arm around her shoulder, the way she had embraced the wolf. "I gather you did fine without me. I'm sorry I wasn't here to help."

When they were almost to the house, Wilson Woodlock stepped out onto the terrace, his hair uncombed and his white shirt only partially buttoned.

"What the hell is going on?" he demanded.

"Your maid has been feeding information to Luther Ethridge," Sam answered.

Woodlock's gaze riveted to Irene. "I don't believe it!"

"We just set a trap for her, and she walked into it," Olivia added. "Then she confessed."

"But you can't prove anything," Irene pointed out, speaking for the first time since the interrogation.

"You told us you were working for Luther Ethridge," Colin clipped out.

"I lied."

Colin snorted. "Now that we have you in custody, I can prove you didn't."

Irene glared at him.

Ignoring her, Colin addressed the group. "What are we going to do with her?"

"Get her out of here! Turn her over to the cops," Brice bit out.

Woodlock's head whipped toward him. "We don't deal with the police," he snapped.

For once, he and Sam were on the same side.

"But that doesn't solve the problem. We can't keep her prisoner," Olivia pointed out.

"I think we can, until we discuss some other matters," Woodlock answered. "Bring her inside."

Brice and Sam each took one of the woman's arms and marched her into the house. They halted in the family room while Woodlock considered their next move. Finally, he led her to an interior bathroom that had a bar lock on the door. Sam unsnapped the cuffs before ushering her inside.

As the door lock clicked, Irene started to whimper.

Sam took Olivia's arm and led her away. "How come you have a bar on the outside of a bathroom door?"

"We actually did have a dog for a few years before

Daddy got tired of having him mess up the furniture. He got locked in here for punishment," Olivia answered.

"Charming," Sam murmured, then took a good look at her. "You need to sit down." When she didn't argue, he put his arm around her and guided her back to the family room, where she dropped heavily onto the sofa.

He followed her down, clasping her hand in his. "Are you all right?"

"Well, it's been a strenuous evening," she answered, moving closer to him.

He wanted to order her upstairs to rest. But he'd already figured out that she didn't take orders real well.

He looked up to see the rest of the group watching them. Before anyone could make a comment, Thurston came around the corner.

"Irene's locked in the bathroom crying. What's going on?"

"We had a little problem," Sam answered. "But it's under control."

Woodlock was breathing heavily. After slowly crossing the room, he dropped into one of the recliners.

Brice and Colin sat down on the other sofa. Thurston remained standing in the doorway.

Sam studied the crowd. As far as he was concerned, the fewer people who knew his personal business, the better. But there were a lot of questions floating around now. They had to at least cover the basics, but he didn't know how much each of these people knew.

He looked at Thurston. "You're in charge of security here?"

"Yes."

"Well, you'll want to know that Irene Speller has been feeding information to Luther Ethridge."

Thurston's head swiveled toward Woodlock. "Is that true?"

Woodlock sighed. "It appears so," he answered.

"You knew that Olivia and I were on a . . . secret mission?" Sam asked, feeling as if he'd slipped into the spy mode.

Thurston nodded.

"Olivia spoke to Colin, and he figured out where we were going. Irene snooped around and got our exact location, then told Ethridge. A hired gun was waiting for us."

"Sam got us out of there," Olivia jumped in. "Otherwise, he'd be dead. And I assume I'd be on my way to Ethridge's house." As she said that last part, she glanced at her father.

Colin made a strangled exclamation. "I am so sorry," he said, giving Olivia and Sam an apologetic look. "I started figuring the odds on where you'd go—and came up with your most likely target. With ninety-seven percent probability."

"Yes," Olivia whispered.

"Luckily, we made it back here alive," Sam added, pausing to let the observation sink in. It had been touch and go. "And now we know what happened. But it's been a long day, and Olivia and I need to sleep. We can talk later about what to do with Irene."

He stood, tugging on her hand. "Come on."

Without looking at anyone else in the room, he led her into the hall before she could object. But he was aware that Colin was following them up the stairs.

Sam opened the bedroom door and waited for Olivia to go inside, then turned to face her brother. "I take it you have some concerns?"

"You've convinced me it's better not to speak in the hall."

"Yes."

They stepped into the room Sam had used on his last visit to the house. Crossing the carpet, Sam picked up the lamp where he'd found the bug, removed it, and crushed it between his fingers.

"What was that?" Colin demanded.

"A microphone. I'd like to assume Irene left it in here. But I can't be sure."

"Good Lord!"

"I'll check the rest of the house later."

Crossing the rug, he propped his hips against the dresser. Although he was pretty sure he knew what Colin wanted to talk about, he looked at the other man questioningly.

Colin cleared his throat. "First, I want to thank you for getting my sister out of a bad situation—and taking care of her when she got sick."

"You know damn well I'm going to take care of her." Sam shifted his weight against the dresser, then looked up as Olivia stepped through the connecting bathroom.

"You're supposed to be lying down," Sam said.

"I know. But I saw Colin follow us, and I have an excellent idea of what's on his mind." When she crossed to Sam's side and slipped her arm around his waist, he dared to let out the breath he hadn't known he was holding.

Colin looked from Olivia to Sam. "Dad may be too sick to ask the right questions, but I have to."

Sam struggled to keep his expression neutral. "Okay."

"Darwin has been babbling about wolves for weeks. Not just wolves . . ." He stopped and swallowed. "Wolves and—you."

Olivia tightened her grip on Sam. "And what did you make of that?" she asked.

"Brice thought the connection between you and the wolf was . . . an interesting possibility. You know I've always been open-minded. In public I'm willing to go along with your guard dog story. But in private, I'd say that we got a pretty good demonstration tonight of what an intelligent wolf can do."

Turning his head, Sam watched Olivia give her brother a fierce look. "He heard me scream. So he came leaping over the wall to rescue me."

"So you're admitting that was him—and you knew it."

Olivia glared at him. "Of course I know!"

"When did you find out?"

"The night Ethridge's goons caught us at the Reese house. That's how he saved us!"

Colin winced.

"I'd appreciate it if you don't say anything to Dad about his special abilities. He's got enough to worry about. Deal?" she asked.

Again Sam held his breath, waiting for the answer.

Colin's full attention was on his sister. "You have to admit that it's a little unsettling knowing your sister is involved with a werewolf, but I'll bow to your judgment," he finally said.

Once again, Sam was able to breathe. "I appreciate it."

"The two of you have had a pretty traumatic couple of days," Colin muttered.

"Yeah."

"So get some sleep. We can talk again in the morning."

When Colin had gone, Sam turned to Olivia. "Thanks for getting him off my back."

"It was the least I could do—after everything you've done for me."

She walked through the bathroom to her own bedroom, and he listened to the sounds of her getting ready for bed. He waited until she was quiet before using the bathroom and taking a quick shower. Then there was nothing to do besides lie down in the guest room and stare at the shadows on the ceiling.

Until Olivia, relationships had been easy—and pleasant—for him. If he'd said the words, he could have married several different super-rich women. But he had never met "the one" until Olivia. Now he had no clue about how to get her to feel committed.

He lay awake for a long time, aching to climb into her bed and make her moan with ecstasy. But she needed to get her strength back. So he stayed where he was and finally closed his eyes.

His sleep was marred by nightmares. In his dreams he'd be holding Olivia in his arms. Then someone would snatch her away from him. Sometimes it was Wilson Woodlock who shouted that he would never let a werewolf fuck his daughter. Sometimes it was Colin who protested that it was his duty to protect his sister. And sometimes it was another man: Luther Ethridge, whom he recognized from the pictures he'd seen.

Sam shook off the dream, then couldn't stop himself from tiptoeing to the door of Olivia's room to see if she was safe in her bed. She was there. Breathing slowly and evenly, so he returned to his room and fell into his sweat-drenched bed.

He woke again before dawn, instantly alert, knowing something was wrong downstairs.

Leaping out of bed and pulling on the sweatpants he'd draped over the chair, he headed for the stairs.

CHAPTER
TWENTY-THREE

SAM REACHED THE first floor, then followed the sound of raised voices.

Thurston was standing in the front hall, struggling with Uncle Darwin. He was dressed in pajamas and a robe. His gray hair was wild, and he was muttering curses.

The security chief was obviously trying not to harm a family member and was consequently taking a beating from the man's large flailing fists.

"Need some help?" Sam asked, pretty sure that the mere sound of his voice would affect the outcome of the altercation.

He had guessed right. Darwin whirled. Wide-eyed, he cowered back against the man he had been fighting only moments before. "You! Get away from me," he wailed.

Thurston was able to grab the older man's arms and hold them behind his back.

Darwin kept his gaze fixed on Sam. "It's him. It's the wolf demon. Get him away from me."

"I won't hurt you," Sam soothed, moving slowly forward.

Darwin began to whimper.

Sam pulled Darwin's belt free of his robe. "Turn him around," he said to Thurston, who apparently agreed with the strategy.

As Darwin shivered and buried his face against the security man's shoulder, Sam tied his hands, listening to the sound of more footsteps.

Aware that they now had an audience, he raised his head. Colin, Olivia, and Brice were ranged along the upper balcony, looking down with expressions ranging from nervous to alarmed. Jefferies had come around the other way and was in back of Thurston and Darwin, his face a study in perplexity. And Wilson Woodlock was on the stairs, his complexion red with anger.

"What is the meaning of this?" he bellowed. "What's all this uproar? Take your hands off Darwin."

"I can't do that, sir," Thurston answered quickly. "I came down and found Mr. Darwin wandering around. I also found the door to the bathroom unlocked. It looks like he helped the prisoner escape."

"Christ!" Sam shouldered his way past Thurston and Darwin. When he came to the open bathroom door, he cursed again.

Hurrying back, he gave Thurston a sharp look. "Wasn't Darwin confined to his room?"

"Yes," the security man answered smartly.

"Doesn't he have round-the-clock attendants?"

"The man who was supposed to be here this evening didn't show up."

"And somebody took advantage of that to let him out," Sam said.

"Or he got loose on his own," Wilson countered.

"How likely is that?" Sam snapped.

"Impossible," Thurston muttered in a voice that didn't carry very far.

"The main point is that Irene got away," Sam answered. "How long has she been gone?" he asked Thurston.

"Hard to say," the security chief answered. "I found Mr. Darwin about ten minutes ago. But I don't know how long he was down here."

"On the off chance that Irene is still in the neighborhood, we'd better look for her," Sam said, heading for the backyard as Wilson ushered Darwin upstairs. In the shadows, he tore off his clothes and changed once more.

He'd picked up the maid's scent in the bathroom. Rounding the house, he caught it again at the front door, then followed down the driveway—where it stopped abruptly. Obviously she'd gotten into a vehicle. Had someone been waiting for her? Or had she called someone to pick her up?

When he returned, human once more, the other men had gone out to search in cars and on foot.

"Well?" Olivia said as he joined her in the family room.

"She got into a vehicle at the end of the drive."

"You're sure?"

"Unfortunately, yes. Her trail ends abruptly."

The others drifted back, reporting they had found nothing.

"Three guesses where she's gone," Sam muttered as they assembled in the family room an hour later.

LUTHER Ethridge sat in the easy chair in his comfortable den, a snifter of brandy in his hand.

A lesser man might need the alcohol to steady his nerves. Luther was simply having an afternoon drink after a little bit of an exertion. He'd just thrown Irene Speller's body into the deep well that had originally supplied his mountaintop property with water. Despite his anger, he liked the irony. Irene had taken the cover off the old well on the Woodlock property, then lured Sam Morgan outside.

Sam had escaped the trap. Now Irene was the one in the well.

She'd arrived in a cab that morning—following the instructions he'd given her long ago. "If you get into trouble at the Woodlock house, come to me. Take a cab if you have to. I'll pay for it."

Unfortunately, she didn't know who had helped her escape. They'd unlocked the door and run away. He'd gotten all the information he could out of her, then terminated her with extreme prejudice, as the spooks liked to say—at least in spy novels.

Her story had been unsettling. A big dog had figured in the scenario. Was it the same dog that had leaped out at Mr. Smith in the Reese house? That couldn't be a coincidence. But what did it mean?

That Sam Morgan seemed to have a very well-trained dog or dogs at his disposal? Or that he had strong hypnotic powers? Maybe that was it. He made you think you were being attacked by an animal, which allowed him to get the drop on you.

Luther didn't much like that hypothesis. But either it was true or the beast was real. Which made Sam Morgan a continuing problem and one he wouldn't tolerate.

SAM spent the morning checking the estate for hidden microphones, paying particular attention to the computer room. He found listening devices in Colin and Brice's room—much to Olivia's brother's chagrin. And one in the dining room.

By noon, Sam felt like he had to get out of the Wood-lock Asylum, so he hunted up Olivia.

"I'll be out for the rest of the day," he informed her.

"Where are you going?"

"I'd like to tell you. But under the circumstances, it's probably better to just say I'll be back around six."

She answered with a quick nod, and the look of uncertainty on her face tore at him. So he pulled her close, to reassure her—and because he needed to hold her for just a moment before leaving.

Then he drove back to his own house to collect some more of his clothing and check his mail. The moment he was in his own place, he felt more at ease. Just being confined at the Woodlock estate set his nerves on edge.

On some deep, instinctive level, he knew he didn't belong there. Or he didn't want to be there. And he wasn't sure what he was going to do about it. Olivia was his mate. But she was tied to her family in a way he couldn't even understand. When he thought about how they were going to work out the details of their lives together, he came up against a blank wall.

Now that he was away from the Woodlock home again, he wanted to stay away. And that was as disturbing as anything else. But he knew he had to go back. Olivia was sick and in danger. And he belonged at her side.

So, around five, he started back.

When he stepped into the front hall, he saw a padded manila envelope sitting on the ornate side table. It hadn't been delivered by the U.S. Post Office.

There was no stamp. Only the words "Sam Morgan, Personal and Confidential," written in bold black marker on the front.

Sam's hands were suddenly damp. He wiped them on the legs of his jeans, but he didn't pick the envelope up. Instead he went to find Jefferies.

"When did that package arrive?" he asked.

"Just an hour ago. A messenger delivered it to the front entrance."

"Did you ask who hired him?"

"He works for a delivery company that the Woodlocks have used in the past."

"So somebody in the family could have sent me this package?"

"Yes, sir."

"Okay. Thanks."

Sam's heart was pounding as he returned to the hall, picked up the envelope, and sniffed it carefully. If it contained any explosives, he couldn't smell them—and he was pretty sure he wouldn't miss something like that.

He wanted to plunge the envelope, into a bucket of water, just to be on the safe side. Instead, he went into the kitchen and set it on the counter. Then, using a sharp knife to slit the wrong end, he spread the sides of the cut apart before reaching inside and extracting a plastic DVD case.

A bright orange note stuck to the case said: "Dear Sam, here's something for your viewing enjoyment."

He held the case in his hand, pretty sure that he wasn't going to enjoy it. He'd seen a DVD player in the family room. But he didn't want an audience. So he carried it to his room, set his laptop on the desk, and booted the computer.

After inserting the disk in the player in the side of the machine, he leaned back in the padded desk chair to watch.

The image that flickered on the screen made his whole body go rigid. It was Olivia. She was lying naked on a bed in a room he didn't recognize. A very opulent room.

He didn't want to see any more of the DVD. But his

hand refused to obey when he ordered himself to turn it off.

Gripping the arms of the desk chair, he kept staring at the computer screen.

The image was sharp. Olivia's face looked so familiar that he could barely breathe.

Her eyes were closed, and as he watched, they flickered open and looked toward the camera. The expression on her face was dreamy as she moved her head on the pillow.

Then a man stepped smartly into the scene. Like the woman on the bed, he was naked. His shoulders were broad. His hips lean. He obviously took care of his body. It was tall and hard.

Turning, he favored the camera with a satisfied grin.

Sam felt sickness rise in his throat. He recognized the man from the pictures he'd seen. It was Luther Ethridge. And his erect dick was standing out from his body like a flagpole. He stroked his erection slowly, as if displaying himself for the viewer.

Then he turned back to Olivia, and the camera angle changed so that the view was from the other side of the room, giving Sam a clear picture of both Ethridge and Olivia.

He said something Sam couldn't hear. But the sound didn't matter. It was the images on the screen that made bile rise in Sam's throat.

Ethridge sat down beside Olivia, leaning forward as he stroked her face, her neck, and down to her breasts, lifting and shaping them in his hands before taking her nipples between his thumbs and fingers, pulling and twisting them—hard.

Olivia made a sound that was lost on the tape. Had he hurt her? Or did she like it rough? He didn't want to watch any more of this home movie. But he couldn't drag his eyes away as Ethridge leaned down to take one nipple between his teeth, biting down on one as he used his fingers on the other one.

Sam wanted to gag when he saw one of Luther's hands slide down Olivia's body, separating her legs, sliding into the folds of her sex. As he caressed her, she moaned. From pleasure? Or pain?

He kept stroking—one hand playing with her breast, the other at her vulva. Then the view was partially blocked, and he couldn't tell if the bastard had brought her to climax.

He tasted blood in his mouth. A familiar taste for a werewolf. Only he knew that he had bitten into his own lip as he'd watched the man and woman on the bed.

The man on the DVD must know the effect he was having on the viewer. He looked directly at the camera, grinning again. Then he shoved Olivia's legs wider, his hands working her clit, his fingers dipping into her vagina to slather moisture on himself. Then he covered her body with his and plunged his swollen dick into her, pulling far enough out with his first few strokes so Sam could see exactly what he was doing.

When he climaxed, he turned his face toward the camera again, silently shouting out his triumph.

A gasp from the doorway told Sam that he wasn't alone. Looking up, he saw Olivia watching the picture, a hand pressed to her mouth, her features contorted into a mask of horror as she watched herself being fucked on the screen.

CHAPTER
TWENTY-FOUR

THROUGH A RED haze of anger, Sam watched Olivia—the real woman, not the image on the screen. In a voice that sounded surprisingly calm to his own ears, he said, "I know that wasn't shot anytime in the past few days, since you've been cozied up with me. How did you manage to convince me you were a virgin?"

"I was a virgin. Until we made love."

"Oh, right. So how do you explain that?" His arm shot out as he gestured toward the computer screen.

Her gaze swung back to the damning image. He was amazed she could keep her tone level as she asked, "Where did you get that fascinating piece of trash?"

"Special messenger," he spit out. "A surprise from your ex-boyfriend. Maybe you'd like to finally stop the god-damn lying, and tell me what's really going on."

She closed the door, then crossed the room, and laid her

hands on his shoulders, making him flinch. Making him want to smack her across the face.

He knew she felt the violence in him, but she spoke with only a small quaver. "Luther Ethridge has never been my boyfriend. And that woman is not me."

"I wish to holy hell you were telling the truth," he said through parched lips.

He wanted to run from the room before he hurt her. He wanted to flee from all the lying and the pretending that filled this house. He had sensed there was something very wrong here. Now he knew what it was. He could have broken Olivia's hold on his shoulders. He was stronger than she was. But her slender grasp kept him where he was.

"You've lied to me from the first. I knew you were still lying about something. Now we both know what's really going on."

Her hands were trembling now. They should be!

Yet her next words sounded strangely calm. "That woman isn't me," she said again. "Try and be objective. Go back to some part where you can get a good look at the person lying on the bed. Freeze the image, and you'll see what I mean."

"Why not? You missed most of the show, didn't you? We might as well enjoy the whole thing together," he growled.

She lifted her hands away from him. With jerky movements, he clicked back to the first track where she was lying on the bed alone. Then he froze the picture on the screen.

Olivia was moving around behind him. He heard the door lock click. When he looked up, she was standing with a deadened expression on her face as she took off her clothing.

"What the hell are you doing, trying to get me to fuck you and forget about Ethridge?"

"No."

She had already kicked off her shoes, skirt, and panties. As he watched, she tossed her blouse onto the floor, then her bra.

Naked, she walked over to the bed in Sam's room. After arranging the pillows the way they were on the screen, she raised her head toward him, and he saw that all the color had drained from her face. Then, staring straight ahead, she lay down on the bed with her arms at her sides.

As though she were delivering a seminar paper, she said, "I know you were too upset to look for important details. But what you saw in that video is some kind of trick. Look at the screen and look at me. Her face is a lot like mine, I'll give you that. Almost identical. But it's not my body. Not at all. Her hips are narrower and her thighs are smaller. Her breasts are bigger. Her hands are all wrong. And so are her feet, for that matter. Look at the body parts—if you can still think rationally. Do that for me," she added in a voice that suddenly dropped to a whisper.

If she could lie there naked when she knew he wanted to rip out her throat, he could do as she asked. It was easiest to start with the hands. He looked at the screen, then back at Olivia's hands. He drew in a breath as he saw that they were narrower than those of the woman on the video, with longer fingers. Next he looked at her feet. Then back at the screen. They were different, too. Olivia's toes were longer and her entire foot was shorter.

His heart was pounding as he dragged his gaze a little higher up the frozen image. Now that she'd forced him from emotion to logic, he saw a lot of differences.

When he finally lifted his gaze to her face, he saw that

her eyes were large and staring, and tears were slipping silently down her cheeks.

With a low sound in his throat, he sprang out of the chair, surged to her side.

"Oh, Christ. I am so sorry, love. So sorry."

OLIVIA had lain very still, forcing herself not to clench her fists or cover her body with the sheet. Now that Sam was beside her, she lost control. Suddenly it was impossible to stop a sob, then another, from wracking her body. She had held herself together long enough to prove that the woman in the video wasn't her. But his words were somehow too much. When he reached for her, she tried to roll away, but he wouldn't let her go. Stretching out beside her on the bed, he gathered her close, rocking and stroking her body and whispering urgently to her.

"I'm sorry. So sorry, love," he repeated over and over. Lifting her hand to his lips he kissed her palm, her fingers. "I never should have doubted you. I couldn't stop myself from reacting the way he wanted me to react. Forgive me for that. Please forgive me."

She nodded against his shoulder, trying to stop crying because she hated letting him see her weak and helpless. But now that she had started sobbing, it was so hard to gain control again. And she knew it wasn't just because Sam had doubted her. She had been through so much in the past few weeks. Then the video and his reaction had been like an anvil falling on her, delivering a crushing blow.

But finally, finally she conquered the tears.

When Sam reached for a tissue on the bedside table and handed it to her, she blew her nose, then tipped her face toward him.

"You know that woman isn't me?" she asked, needing to hear him say it.

He must have understood, because his Adam's apple bobbed. Then he said, "I know that woman isn't you."

"I don't know how he did it. I just know it's some kind of very nasty trick. You said he sent the DVD to you?"

"Yes. By messenger," he repeated.

"So I guess Irene ran to him and talked about what happened last night. She must have told him you and I were close, and he wanted to drive a wedge between us."

"And he would have. I would have walked away from you, if you hadn't brought me back to my senses," Sam admitted in a gritty voice.

Her eyes questioned his. "All the things you've been proclaiming about a werewolf and his mate. Now you're saying you could walk away from me?"

He swallowed hard. "I didn't think so. But I was sure you had betrayed me. I was angry and wounded enough to run away. I don't know what would have happened after that."

She was cold now, icy cold. When she started shivering, he pulled the covers aside for her. As she slipped under, he got up and pulled off his jeans and shoes, then climbed in beside her.

She needed the warmth of his body, but it wasn't enough to stop the shivering.

"I think I got a little taste of how a rape victim feels," she whispered.

"Oh, Lord, Olivia. I am so sorry. I should have turned the damn thing off. But I had to keep watching."

"So did I."

"How much did you see?"

"Enough to almost throw up." She stopped and knit her fingers with his, holding on tight. "You went out. You were gone for a long time, and I was waiting for you to come home. When I heard you come in, I needed to be with you. So I came up here—and got treated to the horrible picture on the screen."

He played his fingers through her hair, gathered her close.

Trying to hold her voice steady, she said what she should have admitted out loud a long time ago. "Sam, this is all my fault."

"Of course it's not."

He said that now. He hadn't heard her story yet. "Let me get this off my chest . . . finally."

She could feel his muscles stiffen, but he said nothing.

To moisten her dry throat, she swallowed. "When Luther Ethridge turned thirty, he threw himself a big party to celebrate his birthday and the millions he'd made. We were invited, and my father said we had to go. I could tell he was proud of Luther. His family and the Ethridges had been close. We all got together a few times a year. So we knew each other. And I knew that Luther . . . liked me. But he always gave me the creeps."

Sam stroked his hand up and down her arm.

"Dad had let him think it might work out, if he made himself worthy of me. And now I think he had decided Luther had done well enough for himself."

"Jesus."

She wanted to look away, but she kept her gaze steady. "Luther had always been . . . diffident . . . with me. But my father's reaction must have given him the message that things had changed. He got me off in one of the private rooms of his house. Not the castle where he lives now. He hadn't bought that yet."

"What did he do to you?" Sam growled.

"Not much. I mean, he started talking about how he had

always admired me. And how he thought we would make a good team. He kept telling me his plans for the future. His plans for *us*. And then he tried to kiss me. Only I was grossed out . . . and scared spitless. I panicked and shoved him away. Then I ran out of the room." She closed her eyes, then opened them again. "And after that, he was cold and angry. And I knew . . . I knew . . ."

"How old were you when that happened?"

"Seventeen."

"And he was . . ."

"Thirty."

"Jesus! He was a grown man. And you were in high school. You think the incident was your fault?"

"It was—to his way of thinking. He wanted me to love him. Or at least respect him and acknowledge we were a good match. And when I rejected him so dramatically, he found another way to get me—to get us."

"The sick bastard. You were a kid and he was an adult." Sam's gaze bored into hers. "And you've carried that guilt around all these years?"

"Yes," she whispered.

"You're not responsible for Luther Ethridge's delusions. Don't ever think that."

"I should have told you sooner. But I felt like it was a deep dark secret I needed to keep. I didn't even tell my father the details."

"It never should have happened. *You were not responsible*," he said, punching out the words. "And stop letting your father make you think otherwise."

She took in his tone, his expression, his reassuring touch. She had felt guilty for so long. And alone, even in the midst of her family. Her father had been furious that she'd rejected Ethridge. Now, miraculously, Sam had helped her sort out reality and guilt.

When she reached for him, he lowered his mouth to hers for a quick, savage kiss that meant more to her than she could ever tell him in words.

As he raised his head, she looked into his eyes. "I need you to make love with me."

"You were just sick. I . . ."

She reversed their positions and gazed down at him. "I need to tell you I love you."

He looked stunned. "I thought I would never hear you say that."

"I've been thinking it, but I've been afraid to say the words out loud. Now I'm afraid not to. I want you to know that I would never betray you. Never. Not with Luther Ethridge or anyone else."

"I know that! I should never have doubted you."

She went on, because she had to finish. "I belong with you. Only you."

"Olivia. Olivia. I think I knew you were the woman meant for me before we ever met."

"It was the same for me. As soon as Colin told me about you, I asked for every scrap of information I could get on you. There wasn't much. When you came to the party, I had to get close to you—even though I had told myself I'd keep my distance."

He made a rough sound. "That night, when I first saw you, it felt like the earth dropped out from under my feet. I'd been intrigued by you. But your pictures didn't do you justice. You are so, so beautiful."

She flushed. "I'm not."

"Of course you are! And so much more. But I didn't want to be in love with Wilson Woodlock's daughter. Then I stopped kidding myself. I knew there was no fighting what I felt for you."

"Yes. Oh, yes." She lowered her mouth for a deep, hot kiss, a kiss that left them both panting.

Coming back for more, she drank from him, trying to tell him how much she needed him, how much she loved him.

"I love you," he said, thrilling her with the words as he gathered her to him, taking and giving, just as she did.

The kiss flared from hot to white hot, igniting a depth of feeling she had only imagined before. With a low growl, he angled his head, his mouth greedy and soothing at the same time as he gathered her to him, urging her body to his.

Finally she understood what it meant to be the werewolf's mate. Powerful and weak at the same time. And she surrendered to that knowledge, because her only hope of survival lay in clinging to this man. And everything that had come before was only preparation for this vivid, golden moment in time—this moment when their lives together really began.

Surrender was sweet. So was conquering.

She shivered as his tongue took possession of her mouth, then felt him tremble in turn as she returned the pleasure.

She knew why the images on the screen had cut him like a dull saw blade. He had made a commitment to her long before she had the courage to do the same. She had been afraid of the ultimate intimacy. Not just giving him her body. But her heart and soul.

Tonight she silently offered him everything she had the power to bestow. "I need you naked," she murmured. "I need to feel your skin against mine. All of you."

"God, yes!" He eased away long enough to tear off the rest of his clothing before wrapping her in his arms, and she sighed as she absorbed the rough feel of his hairy chest against her breasts, his lean hips pressed to hers, his erection nestled in the cradle at the top of her legs.

He lowered his mouth to hers again, nibbling and sipping by turns as his hands stroked up and down her back and buttocks, rocking her against him, increasing their pleasure.

When he pulled back, she reached for him.

"Lie still," he growled, moving his lips against her cheek as he spoke.

She did as he asked. And he kissed her mouth again. Then slid his lips to her chin, her neck, her collarbone, then lower.

He paused at her breasts, stiffening his tongue and flicking it at her nipples, then drawing each in turn into his mouth, wringing low whimpers from her.

She wanted more. And he knew that. He took one pebble-hard tip between his fingers, playing with it as he kissed his way down her body, pausing to dip his tongue into her navel. She was so hot and wanting that when he gently ran his hands up her inner thighs, she arched her hips, begging for more intimate contact.

He looked up and smiled at her.

"Sam. Please."

"You are so beautiful. So ready for me," he murmured, then lowered his head and made an exploratory foray with his tongue, stroking upward, ending by circling her clit.

He had kissed her intimately before. But he had never brought her to climax this way. Now when he slipped two fingers inside her and stroked them in and out, she knew his intentions.

She closed her eyes, focusing on the sensation of his lips and tongue on her, his fingers adding to her pleasure with their erotic rhythm. In seconds, she was helpless to stop her hips from rising and falling in tune with the sweet torture.

She reached down to tangle her fingers in his dark hair. She was close to orgasm, very close. And when he added a sucking pressure on her clit, her movements turned frantic as she strove for release. She came then, in a wave of ecstasy that lifted her up and over the sun, suspended above the earth.

When he felt the aftershocks subside, he withdrew his fingers and lifted his head.

"Sam, Sam," she cried out, holding out her arms.

"Olivia." He slid up and over her body, covering her, kissing her mouth as he plunged his penis inside her. Then he began to move with the same frantic rhythm that had driven her.

He was her mate, and she wanted to give him pleasure, every way she could. She angled her hips so he could drive deep into her, her hands stroked over his back, down to his buttocks, urging him closer. He moved with her—in her—hard and fast. Then he shouted out his satisfaction as his body went rigid and he poured himself into her.

"My love. My only love," he whispered, turning his face to nuzzle her ear.

"Stay with me," she murmured.

"Yes. Straighten your legs."

She did, and he hugged her close, rolling to his side, taking her with him. Still joined to her, he kissed her deeply, as he swept his hands up and down her back in long, luxurious strokes. And she felt the wonderful sensation of his penis hardening inside her again.

"I read some books about sex," she murmured as her hands played with the curve of his buttocks.

"Oh yeah? What did you learn?" he asked, amusement in his voice.

"That most men can't get hard this fast after climaxing."

"A werewolf has special . . . gifts. To please his mate. And himself." He moved his hips, just enough to demonstrate.

She closed her eyes, drifting on the sweet sensations of arousal. Then, as he nibbled at her ear, an erotic but shocking idea made her inner muscles tighten around him.

"Nice," he murmured.

"I thought of something."

"Um?"

"Something that's not in any books I read." She gulped in a breath, then let it out before asking, "Does a werewolf ever come to his mate when he's a wolf?" she whispered.

Sam went very still. Then his Adam's apple bobbed. "How would you feel about that?"

"Turned on."

She felt him grow harder inside her. "You want to do that with me?"

"I want to do everything with you," she answered, her own blood running hotter.

"Up at my ranch. Out in the hills," he said, his voice thick. "Me tracking you. Following your wonderful scent. Catching you."

"When?" she asked in a breathy whisper. He stroked his lips against her cheek. "Not until we get the elixir back." He slid his mouth to hers, found the hardened crests of her breasts with one hand, making her moan as he brought her to climax again.

Finally, exhausted, she slept, more content than she had ever been in her life.

WHEN she woke, she knew instantly that Sam was not in the bed with her. Then, in the darkened room, she saw the glow from the computer screen—and went rigid.

He must have heard her stir. "I'm e-mailing my brother," he said in a low voice.

"Oh."

"I've progressed from hiding my identity to telling him

a little about our problems. He's offered to help us. Would you object to that?"

"No," she said instantly. "Because I trust your judgment."

"But you were worried I might be looking at that DVD again."

"Yes," she admitted.

"I might, if I thought it would give me insight into Luther Ethridge. Would that upset you?"

"Yes. But I think I can handle it." As she spoke, she got out of bed, turned on a lamp, and found the clothing she'd discarded. When she'd pulled on her skirt and shirt she crossed to Sam, reached for his hand, and held on tightly.

"How are you?" he asked.

"Good."

Sam swiveled around to study her. "You don't exactly look relaxed. Are you really okay with my hooking up with Ross?"

"Yes." She cleared her throat. Then before she lost her nerve, she said in a rush, "We have to talk to Colin about the DVD. If anyone can figure out how Ethridge pulled off that video, it's him."

He nodded. "But you hate the idea."

"Yes."

CHAPTER
TWENTY-FIVE

"MAYBE COLIN DOESN'T need to actually see the DVD," Sam offered.

"The moment you tell him, he'll insist. He'll want to try and figure out the technology. And he can't do that sitting behind a screen, having you describe the action."

Despite the situation, that image made Sam laugh.

"It's not funny," she murmured.

"Actually it's a good reminder that we need to keep our life as normal as possible."

This time, she was the one who laughed. "Normal! A tree hugger werewolf and the daughter of an environmental rapist."

"If you put it that way, I see the problem. But you know what I mean. Like . . . when was the last time you ate?"

"This morning."

"Same here. So let's get some food," he said, glad that

he could make the suggestion for both of them instead of mentioning his real concern: her health.

"Okay. I guess I can manage a bowl of lobster bisque."

"You have lobster bisque on tap?"

"No. But I've liked it ever since I was a kid. So I have packs from a gourmet Web site in the freezer."

"Then lobster bisque it is," he said, thinking she'd just jolted him back to the real world Woodlock-style. When he'd been a kid, his favorite food had been a McDonald's hamburger.

While she heated her soup, he thawed a steak in the microwave.

She'd eaten half her soup when Colin walked in. As the brother eyed his cold steak, Sam forced himself not to drape his arm around his plate.

"Raw flesh?" Colin asked.

"Yeah, steak tartare. Like in the best restaurants," he answered. Then, seeing that the blood had drained from Olivia's face, he abruptly shifted the focus from himself.

"I can handle talking to your brother," he said. "You don't even have to be involved."

"I can't just put it off on you," she answered, her voice strained, her eyes haunted.

"What are you talking about?" Colin asked.

"Let's discuss it in private," Sam answered.

The three of them went up to the computer room.

When they had settled on the sofa, Colin closed the door and asked, "So what was on the DVD?"

"A personalized sex show," Sam answered.

"What the hell is that supposed to mean?"

"To be blunt, a woman is lying naked on a bed. Ethridge comes into the bedroom—also naked—fondles her, then screws her."

Colin's features were suffused with tension. "And why do you think he sent that particular video clip to you? He wants you to marvel at his virility?"

"Maybe. But I think he had another motive as well, since the woman on the bed looks almost exactly like Olivia."

Sam watched Colin whirl on his sister, his face flushed and his body rigid. "Did you go to him? Let him fuck you? And then he didn't let you have the Astravor anyway? Is that what this is about?"

"No!"

"I want to see the video," Colin demanded.

"You don't need to," Sam heard himself saying. "Not to verify the woman's identity. Or rather her non-identity. It's not your sister. I can guarantee that."

Colin stood with his hands on his hips as he glared down at Olivia. "She could have done it—for the wrong reasons."

Olivia glared back at Colin. "You're worse than Sam!"

"Why?"

"Because you're supposed to be logical. Use your famous probability method. You can be one hundred percent certain that Ethridge wouldn't have needed to try and capture me in Carmel if I'd been with him. All he'd have to do was offer me the Astravor again."

After several tense seconds, her brother dropped into the computer chair and Olivia continued, "Ethridge wasn't counting on someone like Sam coming along to rescue us. And I think that one purpose of the DVD was to make everyone think he's 'got' me. It worked with you—and you haven't even seen it."

Colin looked abashed. Taking off his glasses, he polished them on his shirttail.

"You're not the only one who jumped to the wrong conclusion," Sam admitted stiffly. "I thought she had been playing mind games with me all along. Then she made me see that the woman wasn't her. I mean, the face is very close to hers. But not the individual body parts."

Colin blew out air. "I'm sorry. I guess you're right. He wanted us to react, and I did."

Sam looked over at Olivia. She was sitting with her lower lip between her teeth. When their eyes met, she said, "It's more than that. I think the home movie represents his fantasy of getting even. Of doing whatever he wants with me. Somehow he put all that on a DVD." She pressed herself close to Sam as she gazed across at her brother. "I'd rather be dead than let that man touch me. But I could only make that decision for myself. Refusing Ethridge has meant condemning the rest of my family. In the end, I have always felt I was going to have to give in."

As Sam clasped his mate more firmly, he was thinking that he understood this whole mess better. But not completely. "I've been getting this chronicle in bits and pieces. I think this might be a good time for the whole saga, whatever it is," he said quietly, but with steel in his voice.

OLIVIA kept her focus on her brother. "Colin?" she murmured.

He glared at her. "If you're asking me to give you permission, you're not going to get it."

"Sam has let us in on his deep dark family secret."

"Not because he wanted to," her brother shot back. "Because a wolf came bounding into the backyard—and we all knew it was him."

"He heard me scream," Olivia reminded him. "And he risked everything to save me. So I think we need to tell him that the elixir does more than simply keep us alive."

"We only tell a husband or wife after we're married," Colin said. "Maybe never."

"Are you saying you haven't told Brice everything?" Olivia asked carefully.

His expression revealed that he had.

"Well, Sam and I are as 'married' as you and Brice. We can go down to the courthouse and get a license, if that will make you feel better. But we're having a crisis now."

The silence in the room lengthened. Finally Colin gave her a small nod.

She answered with a grateful look, yet she couldn't help glancing anxiously at the door, imagining her father suddenly swooping down with fire in his eyes.

He didn't magically appear, and she knew that he was too sick now to be making decisions for the family.

Moving so she could look Sam in the eye, she cleared her throat. "I told you about the family illness. I told you that we have a genetic problem. An illness that's peculiar to us. If we don't take the elixir, starting in our mid-twenties, we gradually—and painfully—die. But that's only part of the truth." She paused for a gulp of air, then went on.

"In your family, you and your brothers have the ability to change your form. In our family, the elixir gives us special powers, too. Powers we hide from the world—just as you do."

She watched Sam's eyes widen as he took that in. "Shape-shifting? Are you telling me that you're like me?"

She had locked his hand in a death grip and didn't seem to be able to let go.

"No. It would have been a lot easier to tell you that!" She sighed. "Just to make things confusing, we have a grab bag of psychic powers. It's not exactly the same with each of us. Just like the illness doesn't run the same course in each of us. My father could see into the future. Which, as you can imagine, was a big help in building the Woodlock financial empire. That's why he's so frustrated now. And it's why the business has been in trouble since Ethridge stole the Astravor."

"Yeah, I can imagine," Sam muttered. "But if what you're telling me is true, how did your father let Ethridge steal the stuff? I'd like to know exactly how he let that happen."

"Liquor impaired his psychic abilities," Colin snapped. "And he was arrogant enough to think the security here was good enough." He clenched his teeth before relaxing his jaw and going on. "Then he was in an automobile accident and ended up in intensive care with a concussion. Probably Ethridge was responsible because while we were all at the hospital, he broke into the house and took the elixir."

"So it wasn't Dr. Regario whose car crashed. It was your father's car," Sam clarified.

"Yes."

"And suddenly Ethridge had all of you by the short hairs."

"Yes. Without the elixir, our psychic talents faded away, along with our health," Colin added.

"What talents, exactly?"

"My uncle who died could move objects without touching them. It was more of a party trick than anything else," Colin answered.

"Did you get some doses of the elixir?" Sam asked.

"Yes." Colin laughed. "I could . . . um . . . put my hand through walls. Maybe if I'd gotten more of the stuff, I could have walked through them. But I think I'm not destined to be the most powerful member of the family when it comes to psychic talents. I think it's because my brain is too straightforward and logical for the supernatural. Uncle Darwin was more down to earth. Or maybe that's the wrong way to put it. When he was angry, he could summon a thunderstorm. Or a hailstorm, if he was really pissed off. I think he hasn't completely lost that power. I think he's still affecting the weather around here, maybe because he's the oldest, and he got the most elixir."

Sam nodded again, taking it in.

Olivia was still holding on to him tightly, still desperately needing the contact. "So that's our big secret," she murmured. "To be guarded at all costs. Is it freaking you out?"

He pulled her close to his side. "It might, if I didn't have my own strange family history."

Clearing his throat, he asked, "I guess you don't know what you can do because you never got the elixir."

"Right," she said in a small voice.

Colin jumped back into the conversation. "But once every few generations, one of us comes along who has multiple talents. We're hoping it's Olivia."

"Which is why I have to go with you when you get the Astravor," she said. "I may need to take a dose of the stuff, then use whatever power it gives me to fight Ethridge."

"If it's such a big secret, how does he know what the Astravor really does?"

"Because, like I told you, young people in his family often married into our family." She sighed. "It was a big honor, which is part of the reason he wanted me. Like his cousin who married Uncle Randolph."

"What happened to her?"

"She's in seclusion somewhere," Olivia murmured. "Under Luther's protection."

"Did they have any children?"

"No. It's always worked out that only one line is fertile.

There aren't many of us. Maybe because the Astravor can only support a limited number of people."

She watched Sam take it all in, seeing wheels turning in his head. He might not have the benefit of a college education, but he was a very intelligent man. "Let's get back to you," he suggested. "What you're not saying is that going in to steal the Astravor and trying to use it all in one fell swoop could be dangerous, right? Because you're going to use psychic abilities that you haven't tested and you don't know how to control?"

SAM saw a host of emotions flicker on Olivia's features. She was so used to playing fast and loose with the truth that this interview must be pretty difficult for her. But finally she looked at him and sighed. "Yes," she admitted.

"And I get to put you in that position?"

"I'm sorry. Yes."

He had known the answer, but he couldn't hold back his reaction. "Shit!"

"I don't like it any better than you do," she insisted, tightening her grip on his hand.

"I have another question. Why did you need me? Ethridge was going to give you the stuff anyway—right? You could let him do it, then zap him."

"I don't know for sure that I can zap him, as you put it. Also, he understands that allowing me to develop my powers would be dangerous to him. I think he was only planning to let me have a little of the elixir, just enough to keep me alive. Not enough for me to work any . . . psychic tricks."

"Giving her only a small amount could ultimately kill her anyway," Colin added.

"Nice guy," Sam muttered. After a few moments of

thought, he came to a decision. "I'm going to take Ross up on his offer."

"Who is Ross?" Colin asked.

"My brother. It looks like you're going to get two wolves for the price of one."

"You approve?" Colin asked his sister.

"If we're going up against Ethridge, I think we need all the help we can get," she answered. "We know he's ready to use any dirty trick he can think of. We should have the same privileges."

Sam could see that Colin didn't like the idea of inviting another werewolf into the sheep pen. Probably there were a lot of things he didn't like. Maybe he'd wanted the special powers that turned up every generation or so. He'd lost the lottery, and he was forced to root for his sister. That couldn't be easy for him. So—was he on Olivia's side only until they got the elixir? Then was he going to stab her in the back? Sam didn't want to think so, but he wasn't going to relax his guard, either.

"My brother Ross and I have been in touch by E-mail," he said. "But I haven't seen him since I left home eight years ago." He looked at Olivia. "You need to get some rest."

"I'm fine."

"No, you're not. You need to do everything you can to guard your health."

He watched her stop fighting him, stop struggling with her own pride. "Okay. I'll go lie down."

"I'll be up in a minute," he told her, walking her to the door. "I want to finish that steak."

When she had left the room, Colin said, "You're not really hungry, are you?"

"No. We need to talk about that DVD."

"Yes."

"Olivia hates the idea of your seeing it. And I certainly understand why. I hope you'll be gentlemanly enough to skip the nasty part. The beginning gives you the best view of the woman. I want you to tell me if the image is computer-generated. Or did he find some woman who looks like Olivia's twin?"

"I think I can do that."

"I'll meet you in the computer room."

Sam hurried up the steps and ducked into his bedroom. Quickly he removed the DVD, put it in the case, then carried it down the hall. Colin was waiting for him.

He sat down, slid the disk into the slot, and began to play it. When the image of the woman flashed on the screen, he swore, then swore again as a naked Ethridge stepped into the picture. "That bastard. I understand why he enjoyed sending this to you."

"Yes," Sam said through his teeth.

"Well, now that I've talked to you, I think I can keep my cool. I told Brice I would be busy. You go get some rest. I'll get back to you when I know something."

Sam scuffed his shoe against the rug. "You were sick. How are you feeling?"

"I'm in remission. Or whatever you call it. Keep your fingers crossed."

"I will." His gaze bored into the back of Colin's neck. "What about Olivia?"

Her brother turned to him. "There is no way to predict the course of this damn disease. Which is why we need to get that elixir."

Sam fought not to clench his teeth. "Okay. If I'm sleeping when you finish with the DVD, wake me up."

When he came back to his room, Olivia was in his bed under the covers, dressed in a T-shirt, but he could tell from the rhythm of her breathing that she was awake.

She lay very still while he pulled off his shirt and pants and climbed into bed. When he was beside her, she found his hand and knit her fingers with his, then whispered, "There weren't many times when I defied my father. But I felt a terrible urgency about not hooking up with Ethridge." In the darkness her breath hitched. "I think now that I was waiting for you."

His heart swelled. "I'm thankful you did," he answered, gathering her to him.

She snuggled down beside him, her body warming his.

He was relieved when he felt her drift into sleep. But he lay awake, staring into the darkness. He had found his mate. But nothing with her was ever going to be simple. Before he'd met her, he had thought of her as a spoiled rich princess. Then he'd found out she had problems he hadn't even dreamed of. When he'd come to live with her, he'd realized the difference in their backgrounds was going to make things difficult. Tonight she had let him in on the big family secret, and everything had shifted under his feet again.

Suddenly, it was hard to catch his breath. Olivia had called him because she needed him. In some ways she was dependent on him now. She needed the elixir to live. But when she got it, would their relationship change in ways he couldn't handle?

He just wanted everything to be normal. Well, as normal as a werewolf's life could be. But he was pretty sure he'd have to be prepared for the unexpected again.

Finally, he slept. Some time later, a sharp rap at the door made his eyes snap open. Glancing at the bedside clock, he saw that it was six in the morning.

Quickly he slipped from under the covers and reached for the sweatpants he'd draped over the back of a chair.

When his head swung toward Olivia, he saw that her eyes were open.

"Go back to sleep," he said, then strode toward the door.

A rumpled-looking Colin was standing in the hall, a mixture of triumph and disgust on his face.

CHAPTER
TWENTY-SIX

SAM STUDIED COLIN'S expression. "I guess you figured it out," he said.

"I think so."

"And you don't like what you found."

"Exactly," Colin answered, but now he was looking past Sam and into the room.

Turning, Sam watched Olivia climb out of bed. She was wearing shorts under her T-shirt, the outfit telling him that she'd been prepared all along to sit in on any upcoming information sessions—and he'd be wasting his breath by objecting.

He expected her to follow him down the hall. When she didn't, he felt his chest tighten. He knew she had hidden an oxygen tank in the dressing room. He knew she was sneaking breaths from it. But he wasn't going to say anything until she did.

Her color looked better when she joined him in the computer room.

Colin strode to the sideboard and filled his mug from a quarter-empty glass coffeepot.

The idea of someone dumping that much caffeine into his body made Sam wince. But he made no comment as Colin took a sip and hunched toward the computer screen.

"Did you look at the video?" Olivia demanded.

He took off his glasses and wiped them on his shirttail, then put them back on his face. "For about five seconds. I know it's not you."

"Is it a real person—or a computer projection?" Sam asked.

"Real."

Olivia made a low, anguished sound. "How do you know?"

"Ethridge isn't shooting *The Lord of the Rings*. His capacity for special effects is limited."

"If she's a real person, tell me who she is," Olivia demanded.

To Sam's surprise, Colin answered. "With 99 percent probability, a woman named Barbara Andres."

"Wait—didn't you tell us she was dead?" Sam asked.

Colin glanced at Olivia, then back to Sam. "That's what I thought. I told you two women who knew him disappeared. Apparently, with the first one, he was practicing his hunting skills—and his ability to foil the police. He killed Alana Holtz. I think he kidnapped Barbara and held her captive. She was a graduate student at UCSD with her own apartment in San Diego. Her parents died and left her enough money to live on while she went to school. No siblings. And it looks like she didn't have many social contacts. She spent a lot of time in chat rooms, which is where he picked her up. So she wouldn't be missed by too many people. She disappeared five months ago."

"He's had her for that long?" Olivia breathed. "Oh Lord, I wonder if she's still sane."

"I hope so," Sam muttered. "What about her apartment?"

"The rent's still being paid," Colin answered. "For all I know, Ethridge has the refrigerator stocked with groceries and then has them cleaned out again."

Colin worked the mouse, and a picture flashed onto the screen. It was a woman with delicate features, large green eyes, and golden brown hair.

"That's her?" Sam asked, studying her face. She was Olivia's type, but that was as far as the resemblance went. "What did he do to change her face?"

"Well, let's look at the records of the Tomaso Clinic in Tijuana." Colin brought up another file. It was a medical form, showing a photograph of the woman named Barbara Andres, only now she was listed just by a number—597.

Colin scrolled through the file. It detailed what had been done to her, complete with before and after pictures.

Sam stared at the transformation, then at Olivia. Her jaw had literally dropped as she looked at the woman who had gone from family resemblance to twin.

"I wouldn't believe it unless I'd seen it," Sam muttered. "How did you get these pictures?"

"I hacked my way into the clinic records," Colin said.

"But how did you get to the clinic in the first place?" Sam asked.

"Digging! And some luck. I've been sifting through every scrap of information I had on Ethridge—then looked for more. Four hours ago, I found a record of a prescription for pain medication for Luther Ethridge, written by a Doctor Hernando Tomaso and filled in Tijuana. Then I asked myself, what was Ethridge doing down there? Buying recreational drugs? Or something else? When I found out that Dr. Tomaso was a plastic surgeon, I figured that perhaps he'd done some work on Ethridge."

"Did he?"

"Oh yeah. Ethridge has had his eyelids lifted. His chin liposuctioned. His penis lengthened."

"How the hell do you do that?" Sam asked.

"The top of the shaft is apparently inside the body. It can be dropped down."

Sam winced. "Sounds painful."

"I wouldn't want to do it. But with him, image is important. I've just given you the highlights."

"How do we get from Ethridge's plastic surgery to Barbara?" Sam asked.

"Well, from Ethridge's correspondence with Tomaso, I assume he's got something on the doctor. And he used the leverage to get his cooperation to operate on Barbara Andres."

"All that's interesting," Olivia snapped. "But we need to get that woman out of there as soon as possible! I told Sam I felt like a rape victim. She *is* one."

"Let's look at the house plans again," Sam suggested. "And see if we can figure out where she is."

The conversation was interrupted by a loud voice from the doorway. "What the hell are you all talking about? What is this, some kind of conspiracy?" They all jerked around to see Wilson Woodlock, dressed in a rumpled silk robe, glaring at them.

Sam had never seen him looking so sick. His complexion was gray and moist. His eyes were red-rimmed, and he was swaying on his feet. In the past few days, his condition had obviously gone downhill quickly. The implications for

Olivia made his throat tighten. Then he told himself that she was younger and stronger, and she hadn't put herself on a course of powerful self-medication.

Woodlock raised his hand. The sick old man was holding a gun. It swung unsteadily toward Sam.

God, another crazy Woodlock with a weapon. *I guess this is what they do when they've had magic powers, and now they can't use them.*

Colin's voice cut through the sudden silence in the room. "Put that down," he said, speaking slowly and deliberately. When he took a step forward, the weapon swung toward him.

"Stay where you are, you worthless piece of shit."

The color rose in Colin's face, but he stopped in his tracks.

"That's right," Woodlock said. He propped his shoulder against the doorjamb, apparently too sick to stand on his own.

"Please, Dad. You're not well. You need to lie down," Olivia whispered.

Her father answered by pointing the gun toward her, and Sam's heart leaped into his throat.

Woodlock was breathing heavily. "I'm tired of this farce. I want Morgan out of here. I want you to do your duty." He dragged in air and let it out in a rush. "Can't you see I'm going to die? And it's your fault. Call Ethridge. Tell him that you'll give yourself to him."

"She already has," Sam said, making his voice low and angry, hoping he sounded convincing, because he wanted this to end without any violence—to Woodlock or anyone else in the room.

The old man focused on him with narrowed eyes. "If you expect me to believe that, you've got the brains of a jackass. We both know she hates Ethridge. She said she'd never marry him. That's why we're in deep shit."

Sam didn't bother to point out that Olivia wasn't the one who had let the elixir slip from her grasp. Instead, he said in a grating voice, "But little Miss Goody Goody decided you were right after all. So she went to him. I can show you."

"How?"

"Ethridge sent us a tape to prove it," Sam answered, knowing he had everyone's full attention. "That's why we're up so early."

"You're lying," Woodlock gasped.

"I wish I were. Have a look for yourself."

Wondering if he was going to end up with a bullet in his back, Sam crossed to the computer and brought up the directory.

"Don't," Olivia shouted, still trying to protect the damn image on the DVD.

But it was too late. Sam switched to the DVD drive and began to play the video that Ethridge had sent the day before.

Woodlock's eyes riveted to the screen as he saw a woman he thought was his daughter lying naked on the bed. Then Ethridge entered the scene. As he sat down beside the woman and began to touch her, tears glistened again in Olivia's eyes.

"He doesn't have to see that," she moaned. The old man spared her a glance, then swung back to the screen. As he focused on the man-woman action, Sam moved slowly and cautiously behind him.

"Get down," he shouted to the group as he wrested the weapon away from the sick man. Thurston darted in from the doorway and helped subdue his employer.

Woodlock sobbed in frustration, then turned to the security man, screaming. "Do your duty. Arrest them! Arrest them!"

Sam held his breath, wondering what would happen next.

"Sorry, sir, I can't do that."

"You work for me," Woodlock sobbed out.

"I work for the family. And I have to take your best interests to heart."

Olivia had stepped in front of the computer screen. Still blocking the image, she turned off the picture, then joined Colin at her father's side.

"I'd love to tell the bastard how we just used the DVD he sent me," Sam growled. "Maybe I'll get a chance."

WILSON lay in bed, listening to the voices in the hall. The door was open, and he could hear his daughter talking to Jefferies.

"How is he?" she asked.

"He's calmed down," the butler said.

"Is he sedated?"

"He was. He's due for another dose."

"Don't give it to him yet."

"Why?"

"I need to talk to him."

Jefferies stuck his head into the room, then disappeared again. "I wouldn't recommend it. He's very unpredictable at the moment."

Wilson wanted to bellow, "You're fired." But he didn't waste the energy. This was his chance to escape. If he could just get out of the damn bed.

Olivia was blathering again. "I understand. But I need to speak to him about something important."

Yes, send her in. I'll give her some important advice.

"He may not be able to help you."

"Jefferies, you've been with us a long time."

"Yes."

"So you know how vital it is that we get the elixir back."

Yeah. He knows it keeps them alive. He doesn't know it gives them magic powers. Nobody except people in the family knows about the powers.

"If you need to speak to your father about it, I'll come in with you."

Wilson waited, every muscle in his body tensing.

"No. I have to be alone with him."

When Olivia stepped into the room without Jefferies, Wilson let out the breath he was holding.

He lay with his eyes closed, a light blanket over him. He could feel the perspiration making his cotton pajamas stick to his body.

He longed to surge off the bed and give his daughter the shock of her life. He found he couldn't muster the energy. But when she bent over him, he was able to shoot out a hand and grasp her wrist.

She gasped, and he opened his eyes in satisfaction. He could still frighten his little girl. And he could still demand obedience.

"Why aren't you with Luther?"

She looked him in the eye and said, "I will be soon."

"That's a lie."

"Believe what you want."

"You're a . . . disobedient daughter," he said, his voice hoarse.

"No. I'm trying to save your life," she corrected him.

"You're . . . selfish. Go back to Ethridge." He pulled himself up, glaring at her, then felt confused for a moment before his thoughts cleared. "What . . . are you doing here?" he asked, hating the way the question came out as a quaver.

But he kept his fingers clamped on her arm, knowing he was inflicting pain. "Dad, please listen. Ethridge wants me. But he doesn't want you or Colin. You're a danger to him. Do you really think he'll give the Astravor to anyone besides me? Do you really think he'll give me enough to tap into my psychic abilities?"

He felt a moment of uncertainty. Then his lips firmed. "You can . . . force him."

"Tell me how! Tell me how to use the Astravor. How to use it to fight him."

His mind drifted back to his young manhood. "You don't have much control at first. You have to wait for it to develop."

"I'm only going to get one chance," she whispered. "Help me. Tell me how. What did you do when you used it?"

Memories crowded in on him. Good memories. He had been powerful, and his lips curled into a smile.

"You feel like a god," he murmured. "It's wonderful. Better than any drug." He looked at her urgently. "But it's not free. It comes with responsibility."

"I know that," she whispered.

"You know nothing! You must learn to control it. That takes practice. It doesn't work all at once."

"Yes, but if you had to learn fast—how would you do it?" she asked.

He had used up all his energy. His lids drifted closed.

He felt her hand grasping his shoulder, shaking him. "Dad, please. Tell me what talents I can expect?"

He mustered the resources to look at her again. He had been angry with her. But he felt pride, too. "You may have . . . strong powers. . . . Nobody has had . . . the great power in generations."

"Maybe it's gone. Maybe that's why."

He was speaking to her, but to himself also. "Get it back for us. One way or another, get it back. Let it into your mind," he whispered. "Let it fill you. Then take control. You have to . . . fight the fear."

"How?"

He felt himself falling, falling into darkness. And he knew that he didn't have much time left.

CHAPTER
TWENTY-SEVEN

SAM PACED BACK and forth in the family room, trying not to keep his gaze fixed on Olivia. It was only thirty-six hours after Woodlock had come at them with murder in his eyes. Now, he was locked in his bedroom, like his brother. A very visible sign that things were going rapidly downhill at the mansion.

But the two elder Woodlock men weren't Sam's primary concern. Fear such as he had never known in his life threatened to steal his sanity. The possibility of Olivia ending up like her father or her uncle clawed at his gut.

He tried to focus on his plans for going into Ethridge's house. One thing he knew; they sure as hell better do it right. But he kept losing his train of thought because he was listening for the sound of the doorbell as he paced back and forth. Even so, when he heard the chimes, he literally jumped a few inches off the carpet.

Olivia stood and moved quickly to his side. He took her hand as much to steady himself as to reassure her.

Striding into the front hall, he threw the door open and stared at the tall, dark-haired man standing under the front balcony's overhang. Suddenly he felt like a kid again, the kid who had fled Baltimore because it was the only way out of the mess he was in.

Ross Marshall stepped forward, set down his duffel bag in the hall, and caught him in a bear hug.

"Sam," he said in a gritty voice. "I'll have to get used to calling you Sam."

The black sheep of the Marshall family clung to his brother for a long moment. His flesh and blood. He had thought he would never see this man again. But as soon as Ross learned what was happening in California, he'd started making arrangements to get on a plane and come out here to help.

Stepping back, Ross looked him up and down. "You've grown up," he said, his voice edged with emotion.

Sam swallowed around the lump in his throat. "I hope so."

Ross's gaze swung to Olivia. "And you've found . . . "

"A mate," she answered for him. "We just have to get through this rough patch before we can settle down."

Ross nodded.

"Thank you for coming to help us," she said.

"I'm glad to be here. I was afraid I'd never see . . . Sam again. Just tell me what you need."

"Thank you," she answered, holding out her arms. Ross gave her a hug, then stepped back.

"My brother, Colin, and his partner, Brice, are anxious to meet you," she said. "But I'm sure you want some private time with Sam."

As she walked upstairs, Sam stiffened. He wasn't sure

if he wanted to be alone with another adult male were-wolf, given the stories he'd heard, the father-son brawls he'd witnessed, and his own violent tendencies.

To buy himself some time, he said, "Let's go up to the computer room."

Ross followed him up the stairs and down the hall.

After Sam had closed the door, his brother lowered himself into an easy chair; Sam was too restless to sit.

Ross raised his head. "The first thing I want you to know is that you're in charge. I'll make suggestions, if I have something to contribute, but you call the shots."

Sam answered with a tight nod.

"Getting along takes a little practice. But it's worth it. The way Adam and Grant and I handle it, the guy on his own turf is the leader," he said, restating his previous assurance.

Sam thought about it for a few seconds and decided the idea had merit. "Okay," he said. "Makes sense."

"So what do you need?" Ross asked.

"Is breaking and entering against your code of ethics?"

Ross laughed. "Are you trying to start off this reunion by getting me into a moral argument?"

"Maybe I am," Sam admitted.

"Well, the way most PIs operate, breaking and entering is part of the job description. And other stuff I won't brag about in public. But I'm ready to do what it takes to bring down Luther Ethridge. Or, to put it another way, it's against my code of ethics for the bastard to withhold the medicine my brother's mate needs to live. And holding an innocent woman captive against her will is also against my code of ethics. So I think we're on the same page."

"Good," Sam answered. He had longed to see Ross, but he hoped they could take the relationship in easy steps. "Let me get the others," he said.

"Right," Ross answered, probably because he understood the need to take the personal stuff slowly.

Sam walked back into the hall where he found Olivia looking anxiously in his direction. "Is everything okay?" she asked.

"Yes. Go get the rest of the troops."

She hurried to Colin's bedroom.

Five minutes later, Colin, Brice, Olivia, Sam, Ross, and Thurston were assembled in the computer room. Olivia made the introductions, and Ross shook hands with the others.

Sam had filled him in on everyone's background—and who knew who their special talents. They were still keeping that secret in the family. In fact, while Thurston and Jefferies knew the elixir was imperative to the family's health, they didn't know it gave the Woodlocks special abilities.

When they had all taken a seat, Ross turned to Sam. "Why don't you tell us what you have planned."

Sam fought the impulse to clasp his hands together in his lap. He wasn't used to sharing his private business—or used to public speaking. He had made a virtue of being self-sufficient. But he'd learned enough about Luther Ethridge to know that he couldn't go up against the man without help. And he was counting on the assembled group to give him any assistance they could.

After clearing his throat, he began. "We have two missions to accomplish at the Ethridge castle: to rescue Barbara Andres and to take back the elixir that Luther Ethridge is holding hostage. I think the best way would be to do both at once."

"What kind of time frame are you looking at?" Ross asked.

"As soon as possible," Olivia answered, then looked embarrassed to have jumped in.

He turned his head toward her. "I know you're in a hurry," he said, keeping his voice even so that he wouldn't broadcast his fears to everyone in the room. "But we have to proceed carefully. We're dealing with a man who is absolutely ruthless. A man who won't hesitate to kill Barbara—or us—if he thinks he's cornered. So let me outline what I have in mind."

CHAPTER
TWENTY-EIGHT

A CLOUD DRIFTED across the gibbous moon, and the night turned inky black. In silence, two wolves trotted up the lower slopes of the mountain.

Despite the dangerous circumstances, this was a strange and marvelous occasion, Sam thought. He'd never dreamed of having his brother with him out here among the scrubby Southern California vegetation and rocky landscape. But Ross was right beside him, and he had to fight to keep his vision from swimming when he thought about the implications.

This might be the first time two werewolves had worked together in all the years since their misguided ancestor had asked for powers no man should possess.

The thought that they might learn to cooperate on a long-term basis made his throat tighten. But first, he had to live through the next hour. So for now, it was enough that they hunted together.

Sam looked up at the solid walls towering above them like man-made cliffs. Ethridge had constructed a fortress, a medieval castle designed to repel an invading army. With modern additions, like the video cameras scanning the immediate area.

Sam pawed the ground, and they both took a step back, well out of what they assumed was the range of the cameras. If Ethridge was watching he would see only two wolves. But there was no point in attracting his interest.

Since the meeting three days ago, they'd kept watch on the road to his property, and he hadn't stepped out of his castle. So he was certainly in there, protected by the booby traps Colin had uncovered.

The camera scanned the grounds. The only alarms appeared to be on the doors and windows, and Sam already had a plan to deal with them and the other security devices.

Beside him Ross made a low sound, and Sam turned his head. They had talked before they had changed from man to wolf. Now they could only convey the simplest ideas.

They had both seen a light go on in the tower room high above them, but there was no way to know if Ross had picked up the detail that Sam saw: the grillwork that he'd noted in the video. No other window had the same protection. So, unless Ethridge had moved his captive for some reason, that was the room in which they'd seen Barbara Andres on the DVD. Sam switched his gaze back to the sheer walls. They were built of rough stones which offered some opportunity for foot and handholds. At least for a man.

He wanted to say, "What do you think? Should we do it tonight?" But he couldn't speak. He could only take his brother's nod for silent agreement with his thoughts.

They were obviously operating on the same wavelength

because they both turned and started down the hill to where Olivia was supposed to be waiting in an SUV screened by brush.

Only she wasn't inside the vehicle. She was standing in the darkness, looking up the hill.

He had to repress a growl. He'd told her specifically to stay out of sight until they gave the all clear. But she hadn't followed orders, which was typical. Although he wanted to give her a lecture, he wouldn't do that. Not when he had watched her stumble on the stairs. Or when he had seen her secretly going into her closet to take a hit from her oxygen tank.

Ross disappeared into the bushes.

Sam lingered for a moment, his gaze sweeping over Olivia, assessing her fitness for the evening's activity, before he joined his brother.

Ross was already pulling on his shirt when Sam made the transformation from wolf to man.

"What do you think?" he asked.

"There's no wind. I'd say this is as good a night as any. And we have surprise on our side," Ross answered.

"I hope," Sam muttered. He knew that no matter how carefully they planned, this was the most dangerous job he had ever attempted. He was sure they were going to encounter some surprises. He just prayed they weren't fatal surprises. When they were both dressed in black sweats, they returned to Olivia, who was wearing a similar outfit.

"You didn't spot any extra security?" she asked anxiously.

"No. Only what we were expecting."

"Then you're going ahead with Plan A?"

Sam sighed. "Yes," he confirmed, then gave her a hard look. "You're not going to try anything foolish on your own, right? Because this operation only works if the timing is right."

"I know that," she answered coolly. Yet he saw from the rigid lines of her profile that she wasn't as calm as she sounded. Worse, she was as likely to make her own decisions as follow orders.

She was her own woman, and always would be, werewolf's mate or not.

But she was getting sicker faster than anyone had anticipated. She needed the elixir.

Turning toward the SUV, Sam helped Ross get out the backpacks with the equipment they needed, plus the long roll of canvas Colin had provided.

Then he got one more thing from the back of the SUV.

Olivia eyed the small oxygen tank. "What's that for?"

"For you."

"I don't need it."

"Let's not waste our breath arguing. We're going to climb up a hill that will have us all puffing. You haven't got the strength we have."

She nodded fractionally, and they started up the hill, moving more slowly than before.

Sam carried the oxygen, then made Olivia stop and take several breaths of it.

They paused four more times until they reached the spot where they'd stopped before; then they stepped out of camera range again. At least it was out of range, if Colin was right. And his judgment was critical to their success.

Sam set down his pack. Then he got out the pieces of tent poles he'd brought along and snapped them together to make uprights. While Ross and Olivia attached the six-and-a-half-foot high canvas to the uprights, Sam stretched out on the ground, making his profile as low as possible as he hammered in spikes with hollow tops, then set the poles into the holders.

The side of the canvas facing them was blank. On the

other side was a computer-generated landscape that mimicked the scene from the windows—based on Colin's computer projection of what the view should be.

After making sure the canvas screen was stable, Sam looked at Ross and Olivia. She nodded tightly.

Behind the screen of the canvas, he retrieved the rope from his pack. During the past two days, he had practiced this maneuver, using several abandoned warehouses as a substitute for Ethridge's tower. He'd kept at it until he could hit the high window on the first try.

Now that he was faced with the real thing, he found that it was harder to work on a slope rather than a level area. Judging the range, he swung the rope, and held his breath as it sailed upward into the air—toward the window. The grappling hook attached to the end hit the window grill with a clank. But the connectors failed to catch, and the rope fell toward the ground.

LUTHER Ethridge sat up in bed. He'd been restless all evening. Before settling down, he'd thumbed through several decorating magazines, collecting ideas for when he redid the living room. Now something outside had awakened him.

Without turning on the light, he got out of bed and looked out the back window. The moon was behind a cloud, and the view toward the city looked as peaceful as ever. Had some animal come tramping across his property? He knew there were deer in the hills and smaller animals.

He saw nothing, but the unsettled feeling wouldn't go away. So he pulled on his pants and a shirt, thinking he could go down to the kitchen. He'd laid in a nice supply of lobster bisque. He served it to his guest almost every evening, because he liked to watch her eating it. But he'd developed a taste for it himself. He could get a packet out of the freezer, heat it in the microwave, and eat it while he took a look at the view from the TV monitor screens in the den.

SAM held back a curse.

He and the others stared up at the window. When a face appeared, he caught his breath.

It took a frantic second for him to register that it wasn't Ethridge. It was the woman, and she looked out over the landscape.

They couldn't shout to her. They couldn't tell her they had come to spring her.

All Sam could do was stand there with his heart pounding as she tried to figure out what had hit the grill over the window. Finally she stepped away.

His jaw tight, Sam tried again. This time, the hook caught. Almost immediately, the woman was back and staring down.

Sam wished he could see the expression on her face. But they were too far away to judge her emotions.

"She's not going to warn him," Ross whispered. "If she's smart, she'll get the idea."

Sam hoped it was true, as he watched his brother step around the canvas and sprint to the wall.

LUTHER tore the top off the plastic bag, then poured the contents into one of the large, wide-mouthed mugs that he liked to use.

Selecting some imported French crackers to go with the soup, he placed the small meal on a tray and carried it across the hall. After setting the tray on the Chinese inlaid end table, he opened the walnut doors that covered the surveillance monitors.

Sometimes he didn't look at the tapes for days at a time. Now he felt the compulsion to make sure all was right with his world.

Settling on the leather couch, he took a sip of soup, then activated the six screens. They showed various views around the interior of the castle and outside. But because there were twelve security cameras, the view varied unless he chose to focus on one scene.

As he looked up from another sip of soup, he saw a flash of movement on the upper right hand screen.

A little jolt sizzled along his nerve endings. Quickly he brought back the scene. It was a view of the rear of the castle, but as he leaned forward and stared at the screen, all he could see was the peaceful view of the valley below his wall.

For a long moment, his gaze stayed riveted to the screen, searching for something that shouldn't be there.

Then, because he saw nothing, he pressed the replay button and went back about forty minutes. Watching the picture closely, he ran the tape forward again.

When another shadow flickered on the monitor, he stopped and ran the tape slowly forward, then froze the frame.

What he saw made goose bumps pop up on his arms. Two large gray animals. German shepherds. Or wolves. Like his man at the Reese house had been babbling about. And Irene. Now they had appeared on his property.

He tried and failed to draw in a deep breath.

What the hell was going on?

He started the tape again, expecting them to approach the house. Instead they both took a step back, out of camera range, and he was left with a heavy feeling in his chest.

For a long time he sat paralyzed, his gaze riveted to the screen. Then he began slowly searching the tape again.

SAM looked across the fifteen feet that now separated him from Ross. His brother hugged the side of the stone wall where the camera couldn't pick him up. At least, that's what they were praying was true. If Ethridge figured someone was going in to rescue his prisoner, Ross would be left dangling from a rope, twisting in the wind.

But that wasn't the most dangerous job. Sam and Olivia were the ones going in the front door—then down to the vault. But the timing had to work with split-second precision.

Sam wanted to make sure his brother would be all right. But he needed to be in position for the next phase of the operation. So he and Olivia moved back down the hill, then circled around the house.

They had studied the security system. Sam was sure that all the elements on the stairs and in the vault area would be armed. But he knew from experience that few people kept the front door alarm on when they were in the house—since remembering to turn it off when opening the door was a major inconvenience. Was Ethridge paranoid enough to have the alarm on while he was in the house? Sam expected to find out pretty quickly.

BARBARA'S heart was thumping so hard that she thought it might bang its way through the wall of her chest. As she looked down from the tower room, she saw a man climbing up a rope. What should she do now? Was this some elaborate test that Ethridge was pulling on her? He'd come up with nasty surprises before. And he could do it again.

She glanced over her shoulder at the signal bell near the bed. Almost against her will, she took several steps toward the bed. She could use the bell to call her captor. If he had arranged this surprise and she didn't alert him, he would be angry, and he would hurt her.

On the other hand, what if what she had been praying for had happened? What if against all odds, someone had figured out she was here, and they had come to rescue her?

But then, why hadn't they simply called the police?

Her mind spun in so many different directions that she wavered on her feet.

Should she press the bell? Go to the window? What?

A man's head appeared over the sill. And she gasped.

He looked at her. Then he silently pulled something from the pack on his back. It was a sign with letters printed from a computer—in large type:

I AM A FRIEND.
I WILL GET YOU OUT OF HERE.

It could still be a trick. She couldn't take the sign at face value.

In terror, she watched as he got out a socket wrench and began to work on what must be the fastenings of the grillwork. Backing away, she took a step toward the buzzer.

CHAPTER
TWENTY-NINE

A SUDDEN VIBRATION made Sam jump. Then he realized it was the silent buzzer on his phone. Looking at the number on the screen, he saw Ross was signaling him to get ready.

He glanced at Olivia and caught the look of stark terror in her eyes.

"Ross?" she mouthed.

He gave her a tight nod. He'd thought about pulling a fast one on her. Letting her think she was going in with him, then giving her knockout gas or something at the last minute.

He wanted her outside. Out of danger. He could go in, get the damn magic potion and bring it to her.

Ross already had spirited the woman named Barbara Andres out of the tower room. And the two of them were down the hill by the car. So no matter how this came out, his brother was out of danger. Ross had volunteered for this job. But he had a wife and family back home in Maryland, and Sam was glad he was almost out of the action.

He would keep Andres safe until they had the elixir and were in the clear.

Inside the house, the phone rang. And Sam hoped to hell the call wasn't someone selling home equity loans.

LUTHER picked up on the first ring.

"Hello?"

"Is this Luther Ethridge?"

"Yes. How did you get my number?"

"I found it hidden in Irene Speller's room."

"Who the hell is this?" Luther demanded.

"Eric Thurston. As you probably know, I work in the Woodlock household."

"What is this, some kind of trick?" Luther snapped.

"No. I'm applying for a job."

"As what?"

"I want to take over where Irene left off. She did a lousy job of informing you of what's going on at the Woodlock household. I can do better. And I can prove it."

"I'm listening," Luther said cautiously. This could be a trick, but he wasn't going to hang up without trying to find out what the man really wanted.

"The Woodlocks are planning a raid on your stronghold."

"I'm ready for them."

"Not ready for what they have in mind. Sending that DVD to Morgan was a mistake. He and Colin figured out that you're holding a woman named Barbara Andres in your tower room. They're coming there tonight to get her out."

"I don't believe you," he shouted. Yet this man knew some inconvenient facts. Like his prisoner's name.

"It may already be too late. Check your security camera."

Luther looked up at the screen that would show Barbara's room. At present, it held a view of the front hall, and he quickly switched the picture. The room was empty. Or maybe this was some kind of trick. Maybe Barbara was hiding.

"Is the grillwork gone from the window?" Thurston asked.

Luther's gaze shot to the window. "Fuck!"

Slamming down the phone, he dashed for the stairs, taking them two at a time as he headed for the tower room.

SAM strained his ears. From inside the house he heard a loud curse, followed by feet pounding up the stairs.

As soon as the racing footsteps were out of earshot, Sam sprinted forward, a set of picks in his hand. The camera was still on, of course. But presumably Ethridge was too busy to be watching it. And when he stepped into the tower bedroom, he'd have a nasty surprise. Barbara would be gone, and a booby trap would go off in his face.

At least, Sam was praying there were no screwups in the tower.

By hacking into the security company computer, Colin had gotten the specifications for the front door lock, and Sam had practiced working on a similar model, just as he'd practiced with the rope. He was good at this part of his profession, and he had the lock open in under a minute. Olivia was right in back of him.

When she tried to rush through the opening, he blocked her way.

"Wait," he whispered. Before crossing the threshold, he

took the Sig from his pack and held it in a two-handed grip, then stepped inside. The front hall was empty. But, as he looked into the room to the right, he could see six monitor screens glowing in the darkness.

That was a little worrisome. Apparently, even before the phone call, Ethridge had suspected something was up. Or maybe that's how he relaxed when he couldn't sleep. The mug of something on the end table confirmed the latter theory.

Sam took in the details in an instant, then ushered Olivia into the hall. They both knew where to find the stairs to the vault. And they both knew the security precautions.

LUTHER reached the top of the tower landing, two flights above the main floor, and skidded to a stop. The door to Barbara's room was still closed. But Thurston—if it was Thurston—had said someone had come in through the window. Luther's first impulse was to unlock the door and rush into the room. But now that he was here, he was thinking that might not be such a wonderful idea.

What if someone had taken his prisoner and left a little surprise in the room? Or what if Thurston was lying? But for what reason?

Luther paced back and forth on the landing, trying to figure out what to do.

Usually he referred to the woman inside as Olivia. Tonight he used her real name. "Barbara?" he called out. "Barbara, are you in there?"

There was no answer.

"When I come in, I'm going to punish you," he growled, thinking of the things he was going to do to her. She didn't have long to live anyway. Soon he would have the real Olivia. Then he wouldn't need Barbara.

* * *

SAM watched Olivia hoist her own weapon, then got out the oil-sensitive paper he'd used at her house. After determining which numbers on the keypad had been pushed on a regular basis, he attached the computer and asked for the correct sequence of numbers to push.

Time seemed to stand still as he waited for the computer to finish its calculation. He had to force himself not to tap his foot as each red number appeared in the horizontal bar on the screen.

When the sequence of numbers was finally displayed, he felt goose bumps rise on his skin. The OFF button was number one. Then four digits followed—1027. It was a birthday. Not Ethridge's but Olivia's.

Her face had turned pale as she stared at the numbers. Sam took a deep breath, then pressed the five keys. The red light winked off and the green came on. But the security system at the top of the stairs wasn't the only thing they had to worry about.

Ethridge had a special surprise for anyone who got this far and didn't punch in an additional code two steps from the bottom—a hail of bullets to the midsection.

The mechanism was triggered by a photoelectric cell, not by pressure on the stair treads. Which meant that Sam could lie on the steps and slide down. At least he hoped that was going to work—because he couldn't punch in the combination until he performed the decoding procedure.

"Stay back until I give you the all clear," he whispered to Olivia. She gripped his arm, and he turned back to her. "Are you okay?"

"Yes. Be careful."

He nodded, grabbed his pack, and gave it a push. It slid down the steps and bounced at the bottom. So was that because of its small size? Or because of the low profile? He guessed he'd find out in another minute.

Fear made Olivia's heart pound as she watched Sam working his way toward the bottom of the steps, his body as flat as he could get it against the stairs. She was feeling light-headed from terror, but she knew that wasn't the only reason. Another attack was coming on. She could sense its steely fingers closing around her throat.

She needed to lie down. She needed to catch her breath. But there was no time for that.

Hold it together. Just hold it together, she chanted inside her head.

But what if she couldn't hold out until she reached the Astravor? What if she fainted?

When her legs threatened to give out, she sat down on the floor at the top of the steps and breathed from the oxygen tank Sam had set there. Her eyes never left him as he slithered down the steps. He had said this would work. And she had desperately wanted to believe him when they had been making their plans. But what if something went wrong now?

What if Ethridge came charging down the stairs to the first floor?

If he did, she'd shoot him, she thought, even as most of her attention was focused on Sam.

Oh God, let him be all right. Let him be all right.

It seemed to take forever, but he finally made it to the bottom of the steps, where the rug softened his landing.

Taking the computer from his pack, he pressed close to the wall as he reached up the stairs again to attach the cables to the second keypad. Then he began the procedure that he'd used before.

As she watched, her vision blurred, and she took another hit of oxygen.

Again, centuries passed while Sam got the combination. Finally, he looked up at her, and gave the thumbs up. Still, they had agreed that she wouldn't walk down the stairs, just in case there was some additional secret to disarming the guns. She looked at the oxygen tank. She didn't want Sam to think she was in trouble, but the time for saving face was over. So she clasped the small tank in one hand and tucked her gun into her belt, then did what he had, sprawled on the steps and pushed herself downward. It wasn't elegant, but she had gravity on her side. And if it kept her from getting shot, that was fine with her.

She reached the bottom of the stairs, and it felt like she had descended into an old mine tunnel. It was cold down here. And the walls were hewn from solid rock. But what looked like a priceless Oriental rug underfoot helped ward off the chill.

"Over to the wall," Sam ordered, and they both pressed their shoulders against the chilly stone. She wanted to sit down on the rug, but she forced herself to keep standing.

There was one more door to unlock. The vault. Sam got out a different piece of equipment, something that would help him pinpoint the combination as he began to slowly turn the knob.

Olivia turned toward the stairs, gun in hand, guarding their back. It was almost over. Just a few more moments, and they would be inside.

Sam turned the knob, stopping on some number she couldn't see. Then he gradually turned it the other way. On the fourth turn, the combination clicked.

But at the same time, an alarm bell began to ring in their ears, and a hissing noise told her that some kind of gas was flooding the room.

* * *

UP in the tower, Luther was still trying to figure out what to do when he heard the alarm. He had been thinking that going into Barbara's room was a bad idea. Now he knew it was.

"Son of a bitch," he growled. Someone was down in the vault. Someone who had come up with an elaborate plan to trick him—and gotten past the machine gun emplacement.

But they had wasted their energy. Because he'd trapped them like rats in a flooded sewer pipe.

He bolted down two flights of steps to the second level of the house, grabbed an Uzi from one of the wall cases, pulled on a gas mask, and pounded down the stairs to the first floor.

OLIVIA saw Sam's look of horror as the gas flooded the room outside the vault. They had gotten all this way and finally run into a trap that Colin hadn't figured out.

Suddenly, she was very glad she'd brought the oxygen tank. Lifting it to her nose, she took a hit. Then handed it to Sam, who did the same.

His eyes fierce, he pulled the door a few inches open.

Olivia slipped inside. Sam followed, then slammed the barrier closed behind them.

The door had cut off the gas, and she dared to take a gulp of air. But now, as she looked around, she saw that they were closed inside a small metal room. And as she listened in dread, she heard the dial spin on the heavy door.

Luther was out there, undoubtedly wearing a gas mask. And he had trapped them in the vault.

She turned to Sam and terror leaped inside her chest as she saw him sag against the wall.

"Sam!"

"The gas," he wheezed.

She had breathed some, too, and her head felt muzzy. But she knew that chemicals affected him more strongly than they would a normal man. To her dismay, Sam slowly slid down the wall until he was lying limply on the floor.

CHAPTER
THIRTY

SETTING DOWN THE gun, Olivia knelt beside Sam. He was breathing, and his pulse felt strong. But he was unresponsive when she called his name. When she dug her fingers into his arm, the reaction was the same.

The oxygen tank lay beside him. She gave him a whiff, and he made a groaning sound. But that was his only response.

"Sam, wake up," she ordered, shaking him, desperation making her movements sharp and rough. He had gotten her down here. And she needed him beside her, but she couldn't wake him.

She dragged in a deep breath, then imagined the walls closing in around her and the air thickening. All at once, a frightening thought wormed its way into her brain.

The sensation of the air turning viscous wasn't her imagination. They were in an unventilated vault. At least she thought so. And eventually they would suffocate.

Her head jerked up, and she made a quick inspection of the room. When she saw a camera perched near the top of the high wall, she struggled to hold back a moan.

A camera! Ethridge was watching them. He didn't have to take a chance on getting shot. All he had to do was wait for them to use up the air in here.

The camera was too high for her to reach. Turning her back to the device, she grabbed the oxygen tank and checked the gauge. It was less than half full, and they would certainly need it later. With a shaky hand, she made sure the valve was off.

Could Sam hear her? She wanted to explain that she was going to get the elixir. But she didn't know if Ethridge could eavesdrop if she spoke.

She was on her own, she realized with a sick feeling in her chest. In a way, she had understood that all along. But she had counted on Sam's moral support.

Now she had no choice but to fulfill her destiny, whatever that would be.

First she gave Sam one more hit of oxygen. Then she leaned down and kissed his cheek.

"I love you," she whispered. Then she looked at the camera and said it louder. "I love him. I belong to him—heart and soul. No matter what you do to us, we belong to each other. And, in case you don't know it, you brought us together."

After taking a little more oxygen, she propped the tank against Sam's chest in case he woke up and needed it, then she pushed herself to a standing position.

She was light-headed now. Shaking on her feet. Squaring her shoulders, she struggled to remain erect as she walked toward the box that sat on the ornate table.

It felt like the camera was boring into the back of her head. With a harsh sound in her throat, she fought to put it out of her mind. She had to focus on the task at hand. And she couldn't let Luther Ethridge interfere.

Before Sam had walked into her life, she'd felt doomed. He had given her hope that she could command her own destiny.

Yet now that she was here, she still feared the ultimate test.

Her father had warned her to go slowly with the elixir. But she had no time left. No time at all.

Lifting the lid of the box, she felt her throat constrict as she stared into the blood red liquid shimmering inside like something alive. It could be poison. Or the wine of life. Or, she thought with a shudder, this might not even be the real thing. She had never seen the elixir. Ethridge might have secreted it somewhere else and set out this stuff as a decoy to lure her into a trap.

Lord, what if that were true?

It didn't matter. She had to try. How long should she stay in contact with it? Maybe someone who'd never had it before and who was sick should start slowly. Or maybe not. On a deep breath, she plunged her fingers into the viscous fluid.

Immediately, she felt a flow of energy into her body. The sickness vanished as though someone had lifted a heavy, wet cloak from her shoulders, and she realized for the first time how ill she had been—for months.

Suddenly, she was well, and she started to cry out in triumph. She had done it. She had gotten to the elixir and cured herself. But the jubilation was short-lived. In the next moment, her hand turned to ice. Hot ice that burned her flesh all the way to the bone. Then her muscles went rigid, and she toppled to the floor as her mind spun out of her control. Out of her body. Out of the universe, flashing across a dark field of stars. She had left the earth far behind. Left this plane of existence. And she knew with terrible certainty that there was no way to find her way back.

She tried to scream, but no sound came to her lips. She tried to breathe, but she had left her physical form too far behind. She had plunged her fingers into the elixir of life, but she was going to die because maybe she had taken too much, and now she had no idea how to control her reaction to the magic substance.

Time had no meaning. It seemed that centuries of agony flashed past in mere seconds. Olivia struggled to hold herself together. Yet she could sense her essence spreading thin, turning as insubstantial as vapor, molecule by molecule.

She would drift away into nothingness. But at least the pain would stop. Then, from far away she became aware of a voice. Someone was calling her name.

"Olivia, come back to me. *Olivia*."

It was Sam. The man she loved. Her mate. Calling out to her. But she couldn't respond.

Then something crushed her fingers. Flesh and bone. A hand. Sam's hand.

"Olivia. Don't you dare leave me, Olivia! We haven't come this far for you to cop out."

The anger and the agony in his voice sent a shock wave through her mind. A shock wave that rippled and clanged inside her head.

She felt the pain reverberate through her body. It helped to center her being. Helped her feel the cold floor of the vault under her hips and shoulders. But not her head. Because it was cradled in Sam's lap.

And somehow she fought her way back—toward the sound of his voice, toward the warmth of his flesh clasping hers. Toward her need to be with him—and his with her.

Slowly, slowly she felt her mind taking possession of her body again. Then she managed to draw a breath into her lungs, and knew Sam was giving her pure oxygen.

When her eyes blinked open, she saw him leaning over, staring down at her, his face drawn and anxious

"Thank God," he whispered. "How are you?"

"I don't know." She tried to push herself up, but he kept a gentle arm across her chest, keeping her head pillowed in his lap. Turning her head, she saw his gun was in his other hand.

"Rest. Don't use up air trying to explain where you went."

So he knew she had left her body. She gave a small nod.

"Talk about that later." He was blocking the camera with his body. Now he lowered his mouth to her ear and spoke in a whisper. "Bastard's out there. We have to assume he's listening."

"Yes," she mouthed. Then asked, "Why didn't he rush in here?"

"Coward."

She nodded, not wanting to use up their life's breath by talking. But there were things she needed to know.

"Call Ross?"

"Tried. Phone won't work from here."

She didn't waste her breath on a curse. "How do we get out of this?" she whispered.

He was silent for a long moment. "Did the elixir give you . . . special powers?"

"I . . . don't know."

They stared at each other.

"Tell him you'll cooperate," Sam mouthed.

"Never."

"Trick him."

"Too late, I think."

She knew he was scrambling for a plan. She tried to do the same. But something was distracting her. Voices in her head. Was she going crazy, like her uncle?"

Again, fear leaped inside her. Then pain stabbed through her skull.

"What?" Sam asked urgently. "Are you sick?"

"Let me listen," she whispered.

"To what?" he asked.

"Voices."

Sam answered with a curse.

"Real voices," she mouthed and pressed a finger to her lips.

ROSS looked at his watch for the hundredth time. "It's been over forty-five minutes. We should have heard from them." His phone was in his hand. He was waiting for Sam's call. But all he could hear was the insects buzzing around him, and he was starting to think that something had gone terribly wrong in Luther Ethridge's house.

Barbara distracted him with a question. "They couldn't get to the elixir?"

"How do you know about that?" he asked sharply.

"Ethridge used to talk to me about it. After he . . . after he gave me that damn gas." Her features grew fierce, and Ross put a hand on her arm.

"I know you've been through a horrible experience. More than most people could survive."

"I owe you a lot for getting me out of there. But I don't want your pity."

"Good. Because we don't have time for pity. I'm frankly thankful that you're not a basket case."

"I'm strong. Or I'd be dead."

"I think that's right."

Her hands clenched. "I want to kill the bastard. He . . ." Her words stopped abruptly, and her expression changed. It looked like she was listening to someone speaking. Only nobody else was here. "I know," she whispered. "It's not your fault. I never thought it was."

Ross stared at her, wondering if she'd finally flipped out. "What are you talking about?"

She stood without moving for several seconds, then raised her eyes to him. "Olivia. She's talking to me."

He looked around, confused. "Where? I don't see her. Are you saying they got away? How do you know?"

"She's talking in my head. She said she's sorry Ethridge held me captive. I didn't ever think it was her fault. I felt sorry for her. Because Luther wanted her. I was just a substitute." She stopped speaking again, and sucked in a sharp breath. "Oh, Lord . . ."

He gripped her arm. "What's wrong? Where is she?"

"In the vault. They're running out of air. And Ethridge is waiting outside."

Ross made a low, angry sound. "Tell her I'm coming."

"I'm coming with you!"

He gave her a long look. Was she in any shape to help them? Or was she going to be a loose cannon? He didn't know. But the determination in her eyes told him he'd have to tie her up to keep her away—and he didn't have time for that.

"BASTARDS. Fucking bastards."

Luther stared at the television monitor. Morgan had been unconscious. Then Olivia had gone for the elixir. It had hurt her. He'd heard her gasp, seen her face contort before she slipped to the floor. He'd waited a few minutes to make sure it was safe.

And just as he'd been about to go in, Morgan sat up, snatched up his weapon, and turned to face the door. He was still holding the gun. Now they were both awake again, thanks to that oxygen tank they had brought along. Otherwise the action would be all over.

"Fuck!" He wanted to fling open the door and charge in there. But it was too dangerous. They had a gun, and he could get hurt.

"ROSS and Barbara are coming," Olivia mouthed.

"Shit," Sam growled, then remembered to lower his voice. "Tell them to go back."

"I did. They won't."

"I want them safe!"

"I know."

"We have to get out of here." He looked from her to the door, then spoke in a whisper, "Colin said you might have multiple powers. You heard Ross and Barbara. Can you do anything else?"

"I don't know! My father said I couldn't do it all at once," she said, sounding scared.

He squeezed her hand in his, trying to give her his strength. "I can't unlock that door. But maybe you can. Like your uncle who could move objects with his mind."

"I can't just do it. Not without practice."

Leaning closer, he began talking rapidly in her ear.

LUTHER kept his eyes glued on the monitor. They were still conscious, but everything would change soon enough. All he had to do was wait for the air to fill with carbon dioxide.

Olivia was lying on the floor. Morgan was crouched over her, blocking his view of her face. They were talking. Even with the volume turned up, he couldn't hear what they were saying.

Making plans. Well, it wouldn't do them any good. He had them trapped. It was only a matter of time before they ran out of air. Even with that oxygen tank. It couldn't last forever.

Olivia sat up, and he tensed. She scooted back, leaning against the wall while Morgan gave her more oxygen. Then he took a hit himself. Good. Great. They'd just use up their supply faster.

The fucker helped her stand up. Now what? Were they planning something? What the hell could they do from inside the vault?

She swayed on her feet, then braced her shoulders against the wall, her face turned toward the door. And then something strange happened.

Morgan moved away from her and started taking off his clothing. Jesus, what was he going to do? Make love to her for the last time?

Luther reared back, letting out a bark of laughter.

In the next second, he felt his blood run cold, when Morgan, naked as a jaybird, started moving his arms with little flourishes, like he was going to perform an important magic ceremony. That got Luther's attention, all right. As he listened, the guy started saying some weird chant. Loud. Nonsense syllables, as far as Luther could tell.

IT had been a long time since Sam had felt so defenseless—standing naked in a vault with a TV camera focused on him. But he would do what he had to for Olivia. For both of them.

He saw her from the corner of his eye. She stood tall and straight, her vision focused on something he couldn't see. She had started discovering her powers. She'd been able to speak to Barbara. And now she had to try something else. Under terrible pressure, with pitifully little time to perfect any of her new skills, she was going to try and open the lock on the vault door. But Ethridge was out there, watching everything they were doing.

So he was going to pull Ethridge's attention away from Olivia by putting on a very dynamic show.

They had both taken another whiff of oxygen, but his lungs were already burning again. The air in the little room was getting soupy. They needed the damn door open.

Nude, exposed to Ethridge's gaze, he chanted the ancient words of transformation. This wasn't the way he wanted to give Olivia a firsthand view of the change. But he had no choice. So he kept speaking.

"*Taranis, Epona, Cerridwen,*" he repeated through parched lips. "*Ga. Feart. Cleas. Duais. Aithriocht. Go gcumhdai is dtreorai na deithe thu.*"

He had always said the words at deliberate speed. Not too quickly—or too slowly. Now he dragged out the syllables, dragged out the process, moving his hands in strange, meaningless gestures as he spoke, drawing attention to himself.

He kept his eyes away from the camera, but he would bet he had Ethridge's full attention. The guy had to wonder what the hell he was doing.

The first threads of transformation wound themselves around him. He wanted to hurry the process—the measured pace exaggerated the pain—but he forced himself to do it slowly, forced himself to give Olivia the chance she needed.

* * *

OLIVIA stood quietly on the other side of the room. She had made contact with Barbara. She had told her to stay away. But she knew that Ross and Ethridge's former captive were driving around the mountain—to the front of the house. She knew what Barbara wanted to do.

One part of her mind kept tabs on them—kept in contact with Barbara. But that was only a side issue. Most of her attention was focused on the door lock. She had watched Sam rely on burglar's skills to open the door. He had brought along tools to do it. She had no tools. She must employ the newfound powers of her mind. Untried powers.

She didn't really understand what process she was using. She only knew that failure was not an option. She had to free Sam because he had come here to save her life and ended up trapped like a rat in a hole. Free herself, so the love that had bloomed between them could grow and mature. And free her family from the curse of Luther Ethridge.

All those obligations weighed her down, even as they gave her the strength she needed to reach with her mind toward the door, toward the locking mechanism. Sam had told her how it worked. He had given her the combination. But she had to make the tumblers move. In the right sequence.

She thought of Brice's homemade magic ceremonies. She thought of his steadfast belief in magic. Even when the Woodlocks had lost their powers, Brice had kept the faith with his totems and his ceremonies. He had called on ancient gods. And his rituals had helped keep her hope alive, even when she had mocked him because she was afraid to let herself believe.

Locked in Ethridge's vault, she took her own leap of faith, because she had to rely on more than her own untested powers.

The legend said that long ago a powerful goddess had given the elixir to her family. As a teenager, she had tried to figure out who that might be. It could be Isis. Or Venus. Gaia. Frigga. Uma. She had studied all of them and others, looking for clues. Now she called their names in turn. Asking for their help. Desperate words spoken only in her mind.

From the corner of her eye, she could see her mate. See him changing with agonizing slowness. She knew the pain must be terrible. But he was doing what he had to do.

And so was she.

LUTHER couldn't take his eyes off the man standing isolated and naked—doing something strange.

The man.

No, not a man.

Luther's pulse pounded in his ears while he watched in horrified disbelief. He saw Sam Morgan's jaw elongate, his teeth sharpen, his body jerk as limbs and muscles transformed themselves into a different shape, a shape that no man should ever claim for his own.

"God, no. No."

Earlier this evening, he had seen two wolves outside, staring at his house. And here, before his very eyes, was a wolf dragging itself into existence. Gray hair formed along Morgan's flanks, covering his body in a thick, silver-tipped pelt. The color of his eyes glowed yellow.

And as Luther stared at the animal, at last he understood what had happened in that storage room in Carmel.

A gurgling sound rose in his throat. It changed to a scream when the door to the vault burst open as though a bomb had gone off inside. But there was no bomb. He could see through the open door that the wolf and Olivia were unhurt.

"Jesus, no."

All at once, he understood what had happened. While

he'd been focused on the man-wolf, Olivia had been using her power. The power she had gotten from the elixir. Late at night, Irene had heard the family talking about the Astravor. She'd told him that the powers wouldn't develop right away, even if she'd had no idea of what the term "power" meant.

Well, she had been wrong about that. And wrong about Morgan.

The wolf leaped through the door like an image in a 3-D horror movie. But this was no movie. It was real.

With a scream, Luther scrambled for the machine gun he'd laid on the floor. He would kill the wolf. And he would kill Olivia, too. She was dangerous. How had he ever thought he could control her?

What happened next seemed to take place in slow motion.

He raised the weapon, but a deep, menacing growl from behind made him stop.

He whirled to see the other wolf at the top of the steps. The two of them had him trapped.

Then Olivia's voice rang out from behind the new wolf.

"I'm up here. Not in the vault."

Two wolves. Two Olivias. Dressed in sweatpants and T-shirts—neither wearing Barbara's robe.

His hand closed convulsively on the trigger, sending a spray of bullets into the steps.

Olivia was behind him. The other Olivia.

"I'm here."

"No, here."

He raised the gun toward the stairs again. But the woman and the wolf had disappeared around the edge of the doorway.

"No. You're Barbara," he shouted.

"Wrong. I'm Barbara. In back of you," the woman in the vault called out.

"I opened the door for her, from the outside," the Olivia at the top of the stairs shouted. "With my mind."

His brain felt like it was spinning inside his head as he struggled to hold on to his sanity. He whirled again, intending to fire.

"Don't bother," the Olivia from the vault called to him, her voice cold and calm. "It's frozen."

Frantically, he pulled the trigger, but now it wouldn't move.

"No! No!" he screamed as the closer wolf leaped. Luther swung the gun like a club, and the wolf yelped. But still it landed heavily against his body, knocking him to the ground, jaws closing over his throat. Ripping through flesh and bone.

He tried to scream again, but the sound was only a gurgle of blood in his ruined throat.

He felt a terrible weight press down on his chest. Not the wolf—some massive outside force. And he knew Olivia was using her psychic power to aid the animal.

The last thing he saw was the image of two women standing over him. Olivia. And the twin he had made.

Which one was Olivia? He didn't know.

His lips moved. But no sound came out.

He wanted them to tell him which was which. But it was already too late. The light faded away. Faded to nothing.

CHAPTER
THIRTY-ONE

THE WOLF LIFTED his head, his mouth dripping with blood. Unable to face the women standing in back of him, he raced up the stairs and almost ran into the other wolf— Ross.

Together they turned the corner where a pile of clothing was waiting. Two pairs of sweatpants. Two T-shirts. Shoes.

Quickly, they both sped through the transformation. Once he had returned to human form, Sam picked up a silk pillow from the couch and wiped the blood from his mouth.

As he pulled on the sweatpants, he flashed his brother an angry look. "You said I was running the show. And I told you to stay away from the house after you got Barbara."

"I couldn't leave you to face Ethridge alone. If you want to make something of that, go ahead," Ross shot back.

For a charged moment, Sam thought they might leap on each other, the way he'd seen Ross and his father go at it.

Ross lowered his arms to his sides and bowed his head. "Hit me if it makes you feel better."

His brother's posture and his words brought Sam back to sanity. "No," he whispered. "What the hell am I thinking?"

"Knee-jerk wolf reaction," Ross answered. "I know I promised to stay out of it. But Olivia told Barbara what was happening. I wasn't in on that mental conversation, but when she told me you were trapped, I had to come back. And Barbara insisted on coming along to help."

"So she was working with Olivia just then?"

"Right. And I decided a wolf would add to the shock value."

"Um . . . what the hell did Barbara think about your changing in front of her?"

"I didn't do it in front of her." His brother gave Sam a direct look. "I tried to get Barbara to back off. But she wouldn't budge. She wanted to get Ethridge, at any cost. So I told her we had trained dogs working with us and not to be afraid of them. Then I left her at the top of the steps, ducked away, and changed. It was the best I could think of at the time. And I'm pretty sure Olivia told her the dogs were okay."

Sam nodded, thinking about continuing the conversation but knowing he was stalling. Instead of talking to Ross, he had to face Olivia.

When he reached the top of the stairs, she was at the bottom landing, looking upward, her expression riddled with anxiety.

They met in the middle of the staircase, and he was helpless to do anything but clasp her to him. His voice shook as he said, "You saw me kill."

She raised her head and met his troubled gaze. "You didn't do it alone. I stamped down on his lungs—with my mind."

He stared at her in shock. "You did?"

She gave him a fierce look. "I did. In the heat of the moment, I couldn't control my savage impulses any better than you could."

"I'm sorry," he murmured. "I know that's hard to deal with."

"It would be with anyone else. But not with Luther Ethridge. I know all the things he did to Barbara. I know what he was planning to do. He was going to kill Barbara on video, so my family would think I was dead."

"Christ!"

"Let me finish so I don't have to keep thinking about it. It gets worse. All along, he was going to hold me captive and let everyone else in my family die. He was only going to let me have a little of the elixir. But he was going to force me to have his children—who would be tied to me and tied to him."

"How do you know all that?"

"From his twisted mind. All in a rush of sick thoughts when the door burst open. He'd figured out he couldn't tame me, so he'd changed his plans. He was going to kill both of us."

Sam looked over her shoulder, seeing the woman who was Olivia's pseudo-twin sitting on the floor with her knees drawn up and her head resting on them. "What about Barbara and the wolves?"

Olivia kept her own voice low as she answered. "Well, I know Ross told her a story about trained dogs. But I decided it would be better if she just forgot about the whole animal thing. She just remembers you and me facing Ethridge—and her yelling down the steps."

"You have the power to alter her thoughts?" he asked carefully.

She dragged in a breath and let it out. "Not exactly. The

wolves frightened her. I was able to push them to the status of 'bad dream.' "

"How much can you do?"

"I don't know yet." She stepped back so she could meet his gaze. "Will you think I'm crazy if I tell you I felt the energy of half a dozen ancient goddesses flowing through me?"

"Not if that's what happened."

"Maybe it did. Or maybe I made it up. I don't honestly know."

He was aware of Ross helping Barbara to her feet, but he stayed beside Olivia as she went back into the vault to where the box of Astravor sat.

He watched her pull out a small knife that looked like it was part of the side of the container. Quickly she opened the lid, then cut her finger, letting some of her blood drip into the red liquid shimmering inside.

"What are you doing?" he asked in a hoarse voice, as the red drops mingled with the liquid in the box.

"Renewing the Astravor. Colin told me how to do it. I didn't have time before, but I have to do it now."

"Yes," he managed. The ceremony had made his throat constrict.

After closing the lid and replacing the knife, she picked up the box and cradled it tenderly in her arms.

"I have to get this back to my family," she said in a voice that was heavy with emotion yet at the same time filled with a strength he didn't recognize.

He had walked through fire to save his mate. The woman he loved. And now he wasn't sure he knew her anymore.

"We still have things to do," she said.

He should have been the one to point that out. But she had taken the lead.

Upstairs, she set the Astravor on a side table and used

his cell phone to call home and tell Colin that "the mission was a success."

"Thank God," he answered.

They kept the conversation short. When Olivia clicked off, Sam looked at Ross, who obviously wanted to say something.

"What?" he asked.

"We have to get rid of evidence."

"Yes," Olivia answered. "Tell us what to do."

"Start with fingerprints."

OLIVIA, Sam, and Ross retraced the path from the front door to the vault. After they had wiped away their presence and removed the silk pillow with Ethridge's blood, they joined Barbara in the tower room, where they did their best to remove the traces of her life there.

When a car pulled up in front, they all tensed.

"Who the hell is that?" Sam growled.

The door opened, and Thurston got out.

"What are you doing here?" Sam asked.

"I figured you could use some help about now." The security man swallowed. "And I'd like to be in on the end of this since Ethridge had a spy right under my nose."

"I understand," Olivia answered.

Thurston gave her a grateful look, then asked, "What about Irene's body?"

"She's in a well around back," Barbara answered.

"I don't want Ethridge's body there, too," Ross said.

As they all stood looking at the dead man lying on the small rug at the bottom of the stairs, Olivia said, "It's better if he just disappear."

"You stabbed him?" Barbara asked.

"Something like that," she murmured.

"We'll get rid of him," Ross said. "And let it be a missing person case."

Sam gave a sardonic laugh. "Convenient of him to bleed onto his own carpet. All we have to do is package him up and carry him away."

After rolling up Ethridge and wrapping the parcel in plastic, the three men carried it to the trunk of Ross's rental car.

When he'd closed the trunk, Ross gestured toward the hills. "Before I caught the plane out here, I did some research on local wildlife, which includes mountain lions. I'll take him up there, then meet you back at the Woodlock house."

"I'll go with you," Thurston said.

"And I will, too," Barbara added.

"You should get some rest," Ross told her.

"No. I need to go." She looked at the plastic-wrapped bundle. "I met Ethridge in a chat room. He was flattering and exciting. But he was scary, too. I should have run in the other direction."

"You couldn't know his twisted mind," Olivia told her. "He was very good at hiding his true self. Thank God you're free of him now."

"Thanks to you. But I need closure now."

"Yes," Olivia agreed, marveling at how coldly she could regard Luther Ethridge. But he had come close to consigning everyone in her family to a horrible death. Only Sam and Ross had prevented the ultimate disaster.

"We'll meet you back at the house," Ross said.

"And you'll stay with us as long as you want," Olivia told Barbara. "Let us help you get back on your feet."

"As long as I don't have to see another packet of lobster bisque."

"Why?"

"It's your favorite. He made me eat a lot of it."

Olivia swore under her breath. She would have continued the conversation, but Ross broke in.

"Let's finish this up," he clipped out, and she knew he was right.

Barbara climbed into the SUV. Thurston climbed into his own car.

Olivia watched Ross hesitate for a moment, then walk toward his brother.

Sam held out his arms, and they embraced.

"Sorry I got bent out of shape," Sam murmured.

"I understand. Believe me, I do."

"And I know I couldn't have done this without you. Thank you," he said, his voice gritty.

"I was glad I could be here, glad you contacted me," Ross answered.

Olivia stepped up and held out her arms, and Ross hugged her. "Thank you," she murmured. "Thank you so much."

"Family sticks together," he said, obviously trying to damp down his emotions.

He clasped her tighter, then stepped back. "We'll see you later."

Olivia stood beside Sam as the two cars drove away.

Now she was alone with her mate, and she knew that the two of them had to talk about what had happened and about the future. But she found she didn't know how to start such an important conversation, so she drove home with him, feeling the pressure of the silence between them.

It was a relief to step into the front hall where Colin and Brice were waiting.

"Dad's bad," her brother said. "I'd better give him the Astravor."

"Yes. Then you take a dose."

"No. Uncle D first, then me," Colin answered. She would have gone up with her brother, but she caught the look on Sam's face.

"You go on up. Sam and I need to talk about something."

Still, there was one more thing she had to do. Jefferies was hovering in the hall, and she stopped for a minute to receive his congratulations and personally thank him for everything he had done.

Then she turned to Sam. "Let's go out on the patio."

He nodded silently.

They stepped outside, and she carefully closed the door.

Finally she made herself ask the question that had been locked in her throat during the ride home. "Are you staying?"

ALL the way home, Sam had been dreading what they might say to each other. Now her question took him by surprise. Guilt made him ask, "Why do you think I wouldn't?"

"Since the vault . . . you've been . . . different."

"I'm sorry," he answered automatically, sorry that she had sensed the conflicts seething inside him. He didn't know exactly what he was feeling. And he didn't want to talk about it yet. Unfortunately, she was asking for answers from him.

Before he could speak, she did it for him. "You're having trouble dealing with a mate who . . . has changed . . ." she said.

"I'm sorry," he said again, feeling helpless and angry and—yes—frightened all at once.

"Don't be sorry. You saved my life."

He made a snorting sound. "I got you in there so that you could do the rest." He kept his gaze fixed on her, then forced himself to state the obvious. "You have amazing powers. You haven't even tapped into them all, I think."

"I wouldn't call them amazing."

"How would you put it?"

"That I have a heavy responsibility to carry."

He could only nod.

She kept her unwavering gaze fixed on him. "And you're worried about a couple of things. Like whether I still need you, since the crisis is over. And whether the powers I acquired will get in the way of our relationship."

"Are you reading my mind?" he asked sharply.

"No. I've been reading the expression on your face. I'm not walking around dipping into people's minds. It happened with Barbara because we were so tuned to each other, and we were in the middle of a crisis. Ethridge had done his best to turn her into Olivia Woodlock. That made her very open to me."

"Yeah, but what about with him?"

"That was a five billion megawatt blast of pure hatred hitting me between the eyes. Spewing out all the evil thoughts he'd ever had about me and my family."

"I felt it, too," he admitted. "But for me, it wasn't in words."

"You were lucky."

He raked a shaky hand through his hair, hearing the roughness in his voice as he spoke. "It's a little unnerving, being with a woman who can peek into your mind if she wants to."

"I know." She looked up at him. "I would never eavesdrop on you. Unless we wanted it. Or . . . in an emergency."

"I guess I'll have to take your word for that."

She stretched her arm toward him, then let it fall back. "We both did what we had to," she whispered.

"And you're not the same woman you were before you

took the Astravor," he said, knowing it sounded like an accusation.

"I'm still trying to figure out who I am," she said in a soft voice.

"And how I fit into your life now?" he asked bluntly. The pressure to say things that had been haunting him for weeks finally broke through his reluctance to speak frankly. "As a matter of fact, I never felt comfortable with the Woodlock family."

"Because we're so dysfunctional?"

He laughed. "No. That doesn't change the basic fact that you come from privilege. I come from . . . nothing. You went to the right schools. Took the right lessons while I was scraping together enough money to buy lunch in the school cafeteria."

"You think I care about that?" she asked.

"*I* care about it."

She wedged her hands on her hips. "So you can't handle a mate with a social position that makes you uncomfortable. And you can't handle a mate who has psychic powers that are greater than your own. Is that it?"

Her bluntness struck right at the core of the problem.

"I'm who I am," he muttered.

She kept her relentless focus on him. "I'd like an answer to my question—about us."

Sam ached to take her in his arms the way he had that first time out here on the patio. He ached to bring his mouth down on hers and feel the magic between them kindle again.

But his own inner doubts kept his feet rooted to the ground. "I can't answer you. Not yet."

When he didn't say anything more, she filled the silence. "Okay. I guess you're exhausted and confused, the way I am. We both need to rest." She sighed. "I feel like

I've used up a month's worth of psychic energy in a couple of minutes."

"But you don't know," he clarified.

"What do you want me to do about that? Make the whole thing go away?" she snapped.

When she said it, he knew it *was* what he wanted. But he wasn't going to admit that. Not when they were both so close to the edge.

He took a step back. "I need time to think."

She couldn't leave it at that. "You're walking away from me because your middle-class values won't let you imagine a mate who is your equal—or maybe more? Is that it?"

"Lower class. Make that lower-class values," he shot back.

Before she could say anything else, he turned away. Instead of walking through the house, he hurried around the vast structure. When he reached the driveway, he strode deliberately toward his car, all the time expecting some kind of mental bolt of energy from her. Some kind of angry denunciation. But he heard only the buzzing of blood in his own ears.

He started the car with jerky movements, then lurched out of the drive. He remembered the first time he'd come here. He remembered thinking that he'd changed a lot. He'd congratulated himself that he wasn't the angry, scared kid who had fled Baltimore. Apparently he'd been wrong. He was still Vic Marshall's son. He might have polished up his exterior, but inside he was Johnny Marshall. And that kid couldn't deal with Olivia Woodlock. Not when she had powers beyond his imagining, powers that could bring him to his knees with the touch of her mind.

He tightened his hands on the wheel, knowing he had to get away, even when the ache in his heart felt as though it might kill him. He'd said he had to think even when he knew he was fleeing the unknown. The question was—could he ever come back?

OLIVIA felt as though someone had cut through the wall of her chest with a dull knife and pierced her heart. Too shaky to stand, on her own, she reached back and braced herself against the balustrade.

She had been afraid of what she felt for Sam Morgan. She'd fought her attraction to him. Then, at the Reese house, he'd given her an excellent reason to run away from him. But the wolf had made no difference to her feelings. She'd fallen in love with him. And there was nothing she could do about it.

She'd thought the two of them would spend the rest of their lives together. Then, this evening, when she'd dipped her fingers into the Astravor, everything had changed.

She was still Olivia Woodlock, the woman who loved Sam Morgan. Yet she was more, and she couldn't lie about that—to herself or to Sam. As if lying to him would do any good.

Deep down, she had been afraid of what would happen when she claimed her family heritage. Now she had come into her powers and lost her mate.

She had taken the risk of loving, and she was left with ashes.

"Sam," she whispered. "Sam, don't turn away from me."

He couldn't hear her, and she wanted to reach out to him with her mind. Maybe she still had enough psychic energy left to do that. She didn't know. But she understood that it would be the worst thing she could do.

She looked toward the house. Probably Colin had given

her father the Astravor. But she couldn't face either one of them now. She didn't want to hear anyone tell her she'd made a mess of her life. Tears stung her eyes as she pushed herself upright. Stepping off the patio, she walked into the garden, not even sure where she was headed. The cold air raised goose bumps on her skin, and she wrapped her arms around her shoulders, rubbing.

"It's too bad I'm not carrying your child," she whispered into the darkness. "You'd have to stick with me then."

Even as she said the words, she denied them. She didn't want Sam on those terms. She wanted him with her because he loved her, because the two of them could make a life together. Because she was his mate and he was hers.

And if he never returned?

She would have to find a way to live alone.

Without Sam, she would have no children. And that would be so sad. There were other things she could do with her life, though, starting with reforming Woodlock Industries. But that would be a hollow existence.

"Come back. Just come back, and we'll work it out," she whispered into the darkness.

Only silence met her.

WILSON lay in the rumpled bed where he'd been confined for days. His heart was racing. He wanted to leap up. But he stayed where he was, his voice deliberately calm. "If you have the Astravor, then Ethridge must be dead."

"Yes."

"What happened?"

"I don't know for sure," Colin answered. "I wasn't there."

"But you know Olivia fought him," Wilson insisted.

"I think so," Colin admitted.

They were both silent for several moments, both lost in their own thoughts. He had taken the magic elixir a few minutes ago, and everything had changed.

"Are you feeling better?" Colin finally asked.

"Yes. Thank you. But I've been sick for a long time, and I need to rest," he lied.

"I understand," his son, the wimp, answered. He'd been raised to be the head of family. But he was willing to give that honor to his sister.

Wilson made his voice low and wispy. "Let me sleep for a while."

"Yes. Of course. I'll go take care of Uncle D. Then I'll come back and see how you're doing."

Colin finally cleared out, and Wilson sat up. The moment his fingers had dipped into the Astravor, he'd felt a surge of energy, wiping away the sick feeling that had hung over him for so long. He was himself again. Back in control.

The horrible muzzy feeling was gone from his mind, and he understood what his children had been doing. Going behind his back. Defying him.

Well, they had gotten away with it while he was sick. But he was better now. And it was time to test his psychic power—the power to see the future.

With a burst of joy, he called the old skill to him. There was a moment of fear when he felt nothing. Then the flickering of awareness crept into his mind.

A picture formed in his thoughts, gray and indistinct. But he knew how to bring up the color, sharpen the focus.

Cherished abilities came back. With a satisfying jolt of pleasure, the image was *there*. But as he stared into the future, the pleasure evaporated in a surge of fear and anger.

"No!" He wouldn't have it! Not after everything he'd been through. Not when he'd worked so hard to secure the future he wanted for his children and grandchildren.

He pushed himself out of bed, then cursed because it took a moment to get his balance.

When he was steady on his feet, he strode toward the door, knowing he was going to have to act quickly if he was going to have any chance at all of setting things right.

SAM sped north, feeling worse the farther he got from Montecito. He was doing the unthinkable. Leaving his mate.

Olivia.

And not Olivia. Because the woman he had left standing on the patio wasn't the woman he had first met at Wilson Woodlock's party. She was something more. Something astonishing, and he didn't know how to cope with what she had become.

Before he'd met her, when he'd thought of marriage at all, he'd thought of it in terms of his parents. He'd loved his mother, but she had been a woman who deferred in all things to Vic Marshall.

He'd known Olivia would never be like that. Still, he'd hoped his special talents gave him an edge that would make up for the Woodlock position of power.

Now he knew there was no way he could ever be her equal. Not in this lifetime. And he understood on some deep, emotional level that his ego was rebelling against the role reversal. So he was crawling back into his cave and shutting the door behind him.

Some part of himself stood back, telling Sam Morgan he was a fool to let Johnny Marshall rule his life. But he couldn't stop himself from driving away.

He was almost at the turnoff to San Marcos Pass when a jolt of psychic pain and fear hit him like a million megawatt bolt of lightning, sizzling along his nerve endings.

Sam. Oh God, Sam, help me.

The physical and mental anguish were so searing that he almost skidded into the car in the next lane.

CHAPTER
THIRTY-TWO

THE SOUND OF the other driver's horn blared in Sam's ear as he fought to stay on the road.

"Olivia?" he shouted.

But she couldn't hear him because she wasn't there. After that one frightening call for help, he heard only a terrible silence.

All his self-serving thoughts of escape fled his mind. Fear for Olivia clawed at him as he sped to the next exit, took the off-ramp, and turned back in the other direction.

"Olivia. Love, I'm coming. Just hang on," he raged into the empty confines of the car.

He didn't know what had happened. He didn't know if she could hear him. But it helped to keep talking to her.

"Love, I'm so sorry. Forgive me. I never should have left you. Just hang on. Do that for me."

Then another jolt of pain hit him, worse than before. In that moment, the car skidded out of control, onto the shoulder, gravel crunching under the wheels, and he knew that disaster was less than a second away.

OLIVIA lay on the cold ground. In the illumination from the floodlights, she stared up at the man who towered over her.

She blinked, trying to make her mind work, trying to understand what her eyes saw when every cell of her body shrieked in pain.

"Don't . . . please," she managed to get out before he bent down and pressed the weapon against her shoulder, hitting her again with a blast of electricity that vibrated through every cell of her body. She knew what it was. A stun gun. Her father had kept it in a locked cabinet, along with his other weapons. Now he stood over her, holding it.

For days, he had been too sick to get out of bed, and she had been afraid he was going to die.

But the Astravor must have worked, and now he was on his feet again. His body was under his control, but his mind was still . . . sick.

She wanted to ask why he was doing this to her. But she couldn't make her voice work. She couldn't move. And the burst of pure terror she had sent to Sam had drained the last of her psychic abilities. But she could hear her father raging at her.

"I won't let him have you, not that lowlife Sam Morgan. Darwin called him a demon. He was right all along. The demon Morgan came to steal my daughter from me."

If she could have spoken, she would have told him Sam had left. But communication was beyond her.

Her father's voice rose as he stood over her, gun in hand. "You and Colin hired him to do a job. But you ended up in his bed. How could you? After the way you were raised."

Words formed in her mind, but she couldn't move her lips.

"I know he left. I heard the bastard drive away like he was leaving you. I wish to hell it were true. But he's coming back. Or you're going to throw yourself on his mercy. You. A Woodlock, groveling at the feet of a man who isn't fit to shine your shoes. Don't bother to tell me differently. I have my power back. I can see your future. I can see you and him and your brood of little bastard demon thieves. But I won't let it happen. I'll fry your brains with this thing before I let that happen."

No. Oh, God, no. Please.

Her father reached toward her with the weapon again, but the sound of running feet made him stop and whir.

Sam.

"No!"

She heard her brother's voice. "Dad! What are you doing?"

His question rang out into the awful stillness of the night, as still as the eye of a hurricane.

Her father swung away from her. "Stay away from me."

"Dad, put down the gun."

"I'm the head of this family. I make the decisions. You were all working behind my back. Taking over. And you think you can still defy me."

"We weren't working behind your back. We kept you informed. We had to do it, because you were too sick to take charge."

"I was never too sick to make decisions. I did what needed to be done. I let Darwin out of his room, so he could help Irene escape."

"Why?" Colin gasped.

"So she'd go back to Ethridge. I knew he'd kill her. I let

him do the dirty work. But now I'm back in charge. So I'm warning you. Stay away from me."

"Dad . . ."

Colin leaped forward. The gun made a sizzling noise. Her brother screamed and fell to the ground.

Her father bent over him, and the gun hissed again. She knew, in some twisted way, he was doing what he had to. In his mind, he was preserving his family values.

Every scrap of her concentration now was on fighting her father. She had to get away. She had to save herself. And save her brother.

But she couldn't do it. Dad had disabled her body and disabled her psychic ability with the blasts from the stun gun.

As a silent scream welled inside her, a breeze sprang up, ruffling her hair. It picked up force, making the branches of a nearby tree shake with astonishing violence.

"Darwin?" her father called. "Is that you? Are you with me or against me?" The wind answered with a howl.

SAM roared into the driveway, pulled up in front of the house, and slammed on the brake.

He knew where Olivia was. She hadn't told him, but somehow he knew she was still out in back of the house, where he had left her.

He raced around the mansion, stopping in the shadows, because he realized that leaping into danger before he understood what was going on could be fatal, both to himself and Olivia.

The night had been calm. Out here, the wind roared, and lightning crackled in the dark sky.

In the illumination from the floodlights, he saw Olivia lying on the grass. Colin was sprawled nearby. Both of them looked limp and lifeless. And their father crouched over them. Had he hurt them? Or had Darwin knocked them to the ground?

Wilson bent toward his daughter again, his hand extended, and Sam felt his heart leap into his throat as he saw the weapon in his hand. The sick reality of what he was seeing snapped into focus. All along, he had thought Wilson might attack him. Instead, he had gone after Olivia.

"No!" he shouted. "Get the hell away from her."

The older man whirled, the weapon pointed toward the interloper. Sam's considerable training told him what he was seeing. A stun gun.

His mind made a quick assessment. There were several versions of the weapon. One used an air charge to fire two bolts over a fifteen-foot range. But it only had two shots before the whole system had to be reset.

The other kind fired electrical charges directly into a person or animal, but only with direct contact.

Either Wilson had reset the weapon, or he had to be on top of the victim.

A flash of movement made him swing his head to the right. Jefferies stood outside the French doors, holding a pistol, and Sam fought a new spurt of panic.

"Don't shoot," Sam called out, pitching his voice to carry only as far as the doorway. "You could hit Olivia or Colin."

When Jefferies nodded, Sam switched his focus back to Wilson and raised his voice. "Over here. Come and get me, you bastard. Or are you a coward?"

"You! Stay away from my daughter."

"Make me," Sam challenged. He thought about the night he'd started to change in front of Darwin. He thought about the trick he'd pulled on Ethridge. Every fiber of his being urged him to change into a wolf. But if he followed his instincts now, he wouldn't be able to speak to Wilson. And he needed to lure the man away from Olivia.

Heart-stopping moments dragged by before the head of the Woodlock family started moving toward him, looking a lot more fit than the last time Sam had seen him. He was old, Sam told himself. He was no match for a thirty-year-old. Yet Sam felt his muscles clench. He had underestimated Darwin that night in the sunroom. He could be just as wrong now. He plowed ahead.

"Come and get me," he shouted again. "Hurry up."

When Wilson charged toward him, he felt a spurt of triumph. Every step toward Sam Morgan was a step away from Olivia.

But the wind impeded the man's progress, whipping at his shirt and pants.

Wilson stopped, and Sam shouted a curse into the night. "Come on, you bastard."

The head of the Woodlock clan wasn't focused on his daughter's lover now. He was looking quickly around, then up at the sky.

"Darwin?" he shouted as the wind tore at him. "What the hell are you doing, Darwin?"

There was no answer. Not with words. But a shower of hail fell from the sky, not over the whole lawn but just on Wilson Woodlock's head and shoulders.

He screamed, raising the weapon, turning in a circle, looking for an enemy he couldn't see.

"Stay away from me," he cried out. "Stay the fuck away."

Sam watched as a bolt of lightning cut like a jagged knife across the dark sky.

The wind howled with a man's voice. And Sam realized there were words shrieking in the air. "Wilson, put down the gun."

"No! Leave me alone, you old fool. You don't know anything."

In answer, a savage gust of air raked across the lawn, catching Wilson and spinning him around.

Sam saw the stun gun discharge as another lightning bolt formed in the heavens, then speared down like the wrath of Zeus.

It hit Wilson in the chest. His scream rang out, followed by the smell of burning flesh. And then absolute quiet filled the night.

SAM sat rigidly in the chair beside Olivia's bed.

A blast from a stun gun wasn't fatal. He kept telling that to himself. But how many times had her father shot her?

The moment she stirred, every muscle in his body tensed and he leaned over her. "Olivia? Thank God."

"Sam," she breathed.

"How do you feel?"

"A lot . . . better."

A choking sound rose in his throat. "Forgive me."

"For what?"

"Leaving you."

"I called you back. And you came."

He told her what he had ached to say. "Yes. I heard you, love. And I would have walked barefoot across broken glass to get to you when you needed me."

"Oh, Lord, Sam." She tried to push herself up, and he put a gentle palm on her shoulder. When she reached to cover his fingers, he felt himself relax a fraction.

His vision blurring, he turned his hand and clasped hers, and a little sigh breathed out of her.

She tugged at his hand. "Come here."

He came down on the bed, gathering her in his arms, holding tight, and for a long moment cradling her against himself was the only thing that mattered.

Then he felt her swallow. "Is my father . . . dead?"

"Yes." Sam heard his own voice hitch. "Killed by a thunderstorm that looked like it blew up out of nowhere."

"That's what Jefferies thinks?"

"Yes."

"What about my Uncle Darwin?" she whispered.

"He's . . . resting."

"Does he know about my father?"

"I think so. But he's not quite himself."

"What's going to happen to him?"

"That depends on what kind of recovery he makes."

They were talking in a kind of code.

Finally, she spoke directly. "I wish Dad had . . . made it."

Sam couldn't hold back his outrage. "He hurt you! Why would he do that to his daughter?"

She tightened her hold on him. "Have you ever heard the phrase power corrupts? And absolute power corrupts absolutely."

"Yeah."

"Well, that was his big problem. His parents treated him like a king. He thought he was entitled to anything he wanted. And he wanted things the way they were."

"But he . . . attacked his own family."

"I just told you, he was raised to expect the world to turn at his command. And he didn't know how to cope any other way." She sighed. "He knew you and I were going to take his place."

"How could we . . . when I left?"

"You left today. But he could see the future. He told me he saw us together."

"Jesus. He hurt you because of me . . . because of us?"

"It wasn't just seeing the future. He knew you had already rescued me from him."

"I was too late for that," he reminded her, his tone gritty.

"No," she said softly, "you already saved me."

"When?"

"It started the night of the party. I saw you, and I knew my life was never going to be the same."

"Olivia." He gathered her closer, allowing himself a moment to clasp her tightly before easing away so he could look into her eyes. "While we're being brutally honest, you know I would have done *anything* I had to do to stop him from hurting you."

"Yes. I know that," she said, her tone very serious. "But I'm glad you didn't have to be the one." She dragged in a breath and let it out. "How did you handle the cover-up?"

"Jefferies called nine-one-one and reported that lightning had struck your father. Before they arrived, we took you and Colin inside."

Just then, the door opened a crack.

They both looked up and saw Colin's anxious face. "I heard you talking. Are you all right?"

"Yes," Olivia answered. "What about you?"

"Not too bad, considering." He gave them an assessing look. "I just wanted to make sure everything was okay. I'll leave you alone."

"Wait. What about Barbara—and Ross and Thurston?" Olivia asked.

"They came back a while ago. Ross said he'd like some downtime. So he's at the Biltmore."

Sam nodded. "He knows when to stay out of the way." He laughed. "At the best hotel in town."

"Yes," Colin agreed. "And Barbara is going to stay here for a while. She and Brice are out on the sun porch comparing notes on Mozart operas."

"I think you and Brice will be good for her," Olivia murmured.

"Right. We're two non-threatening males. I believe we

can tell people she's our cousin. If anybody asks what she's doing here."

"Yes."

He looked at Sam. "I haven't thanked you . . . for everything. We'd still be sick, if it weren't for you."

"I'm glad it worked out. Very glad," he added.

"I'll go tell Barbara and Thurston you're okay."

"And call Ross," Sam added.

"Yes." Colin stepped back into the hall, leaving them alone again.

They lay on the bed in silence for several moments, Sam cherishing the chance to be close again. Then Olivia cleared her throat, and he tensed.

"What about us?" she asked. "I mean the rest of our lives."

He felt his face contort. "If you mean, am I going to cut and run again, I think I acquired a big dose of maturity in the past few hours. I mean, I would have eventually figured out I was acting like a jerk. But I had some incentive to hurry up the process."

"So you've decided you can live with a woman who . . ."

"A woman who called out to me—and nobody else—when she needed help," he finished, his voice gritty.

"When I was in danger, I reached out to you." Before he could respond, she went on quickly, "But I want to be clear. You know I'm . . . different from the Olivia Woodlock who hired you a couple of months ago."

"I see you don't want any misunderstandings," he answered.

"No. I don't."

"Well, then, let me put it this way. You're the woman I love. My mate. The mother of the children we're going to have together."

"And you can accept my . . . talents?" she murmured.

"I think so. I'm going to work hard at trying not to be a lower-class male chauvinist wolf." He laughed. "You can kick me when I forget that we're partners."

She reached for him again, and he gathered her to him.

"Oh, Sam. I want what we've made together. So much."

"Yes." He swallowed. "While you were sleeping, I was sitting here, daring to think about our future."

"Good."

"I was thinking about where we'd live."

"It doesn't have to be in this house."

"We don't have to decide yet. But we should talk about my profession."

She cocked her head to one side. "What about it?"

"It was suitable for a lone wolf. It's not so great for a family man."

"I wouldn't ask you to give up the job you love."

He laughed, feeling better by the moment. "I did get considerable pleasure from it. But I think I can reduce it to the status of hobby. I can support you very well on my investments. But maybe I can get a job with one of the environmental groups."

"Or maybe you'd like to help bring Woodlock Industries into the twenty-first century. Maybe you'd like to turn a major polluter into a model company."

He knew he must look startled. "You'd trust me with the family business?"

"I trust you with my life."

"Would it be okay with Colin for me to stick my paws in Woodlock Industries?"

"Colin and I already talked about your joining the company. He likes the idea. He didn't approve of what Dad was doing. But he particularly appreciates the notion of letting someone else take the responsibility of fixing it."

Sam laughed. "Convenient for him, to have a tree hugger for a brother-in-law."

"Yes. And a brother-in-law who can give him nieces and nephews to spoil." She cleared her throat. "Which brings up an important point. It would be nice if we got married before I get pregnant."

He felt like his heart would burst, but he managed to say, "Not a bad idea."

"Do you mind a quiet ceremony? I mean . . . because of my father."

"Just so the world knows you're mine."

"Oh, I am. Body and soul. And . . ."

"What?"

"How would you feel if I wanted to try having you use the Astravor?"

He blinked. "How could I? I'm not a member of your family."

"I think I have the power to . . . condition you. A tiny bit at a time. I think we might be able to do it."

"You'd want to share that with me?"

She wrapped her arms around him again. "Yes. I want to share everything with you that I can. Starting with . . . I'd like to find out what making love with you is like, now that I'm well again."

"Oh yeah." He struggled to rein in his enthusiasm. "But you just took a couple of bad jolts from a stun gun. You need to rest."

"I think I know what medicine I need. Let me show you."

Under the covers she slid her hand down his body, making him instantly hard.

"Maybe I'd better lock the door first," he murmured.

He got up and quickly turned the lever, then came back to the bed.

Even as he stretched out beside her, her lips touched down on his, settled, melded into a long, hot kiss—a kiss that told him they could work through their problems because they had a bond too strong for anyone or anything to break.

NAT JENNINGS WAS going to have to stop for gas. The
mustang had been running on fumes for the last twenty miles.
She'd planned on stopping at the Citgo station on the highway
only to find the windows boarded up, the pumps gone, and
knee-high weeds sticking out of the concrete. Now, unless she
wanted to backtrack all the way to the interstate, she was going to have to fill up in Bellerose.

"So much for anonymity," she muttered as she drove
slowly down Main Street, past the courthouse on the square,
Boudreaux's Corner Drug Store, and Jenny Lee's Five and
Dime.

She tried hard not to notice the double takes and shocked
expressions of the people who recognized her. But then
she'd known before ever coming back that the upstanding
citizens of Bellerose had long memories when it came to
murder.

Ray's Sunoco was located on the bayou side of town. The
service station had only one pump and hadn't yet made the
technological quantum leap of accepting credit cards. Nat slid
out of the car, careful to keep her back to the highway, and
pumped the gas in record time.

Once the tank was full, she grabbed her purse and went inside to pay. A teenage boy wearing a dirty work shirt and a sour
expression sat behind the counter, eyeing her with unconcealed

curiosity. A pregnant woman in a bright green maternity top was eyeballing the candy bar display.

Nat smiled at the boy. "Take a check?"

"'Slong as you have a driver's license."

Tugging her checkbook from her bag, she crossed to the counter.

"Sixteen fifty-three," he said.

Nat began making out the check. She could hear the low hum of the RC Cola machine out front. The hiss of the occasional car as it passed on the highway. Behind the counter, wooden shelves with peeling white paint displayed cans of 10 W 40 motor oil and filters and various sizes of engine belts. One of the cans was rattling, blending with the buzz of a fly trapped against the window.

The dizziness struck her like a sledgehammer. Too late she realized the buzzing wasn't from the soda machine or the can of oil or even the fly in the window. The high-frequency hum was inside her head, as powerful as a jet engine, the vibrations jolting her body all the way to her bones. Dread and alarm coiled inside her as the warm shock of energy penetrated her brain. Sensations and thoughts and images flew at her in dark, undulating waves.

Dear God, not now, was all she could think.

She tried to finish writing the check, but her hand fumbled the pen. Her arms drooped as if they were paralyzed. It was a terrifying sensation to be trapped inside her own body and unable to control her limbs. She was aware of her left hand grappling for the pen. Her nails cutting into her palm. Her knuckles going white as her hand swept across the check.

"Lady, are you okay?"

She heard the words as if from a great distance. Vaguely, she was aware of the boy looking at her strangely. She wanted to answer, to reassure him that she was fine. But the breath had been sucked from her lungs. Words and thoughts tumbled disjointedly inside her head. She tried to focus, but his face kept fading in and out of her vision.

An instant later her legs buckled. Her knees hit the floor with a hollow *thump!*

"Oh, good Lord!"

Nat heard alarm in the pregnant woman's voice. She heard the shuffle of shoes against the floor. Felt a gentle hand against her shoulder. "Honey, are you all right?"

Slowly, she became aware of cool wood against her cheek. She was lying on her side, still gripping the pen. She wanted to get up, but she was dizzy and disoriented and an inch away from throwing up all over the woman's Nikes.

"Ma'am, are you sick?" came the boy's voice.

Bracing her hand against the floor, Nat pushed herself to a sitting position and shoved her hair from her face. "I'm okay," she heard herself say.

Her checkbook lay on the floor next to her. She picked it up, saw that her hand was trembling violently.

"You need me to call Doc Ratcliffe for you?" the woman asked.

Nat shook her head. "I'm fine. Really, I just . . . got a little dizzy."

Shaken and embarrassed, she rose unsteadily to her feet and brushed at her jeans. The vibrations had quieted, but her thoughts remained fuzzy and disjointed. She felt as if she'd just stumbled off some wild amusement park ride and had yet to regain her equilibrium. She glanced at the boy behind the counter to see him staring fixedly at the check, his expression perplexed.

"What's that?" he asked.

bad man take ricky. kill again. hurry.

Gasping, Nat snatched the check off the counter. "Nothing," she muttered.

The woman shot her a wary look. "It said something about killing."

Unwilling to explain—not sure she could, even if she knew what to say—Nat shook her head. "I just . . . must have gotten confused for a second, right before I blacked out." She tried to smile, but was too shaken to manage. "I have epilepsy."

"Oh." But the woman didn't look appeased.

Nat knew it the instant the woman recognized her. Her eyes widened, then she took a step back, as if she'd ventured too close to something dangerous. "You're Nat Jennings."

Sliding the ruined check into the pocket of her jeans, Nat began writing a second one. She had wanted anonymity for her return home. She should have known that was the one luxury she would never have in a town the size of Bellerose. "That's right," she said.

The clerk and the pregnant woman exchanged startled looks. Nat did her best to ignore them, but her hand was shaking when she tore off the check and handed it to the clerk. "Thanks for the gas."

"If I'da known who you was, I never would have let you pump here," the clerk muttered.

"Yeah, well, it's too late to do anything about it now." Nat started toward the door.

"Bitch," he said to her back.

Nat felt the word as keenly as if he'd thrown a rock at her. She'd known her return would be met with hostility, but she wasn't going to let that keep her from doing what she'd come here to do. She'd waited three unbearable years for this moment.

Once in her car, she pulled the note from her pocket and read it again.

bad man take ricky. kill again. hurry.

A chill passed through her as she studied the child-like scrawl. Aside from seeing that justice was done, there was nothing she could do for the ones who were already gone. Nat knew all too well that the dead could not be resurrected. But if she could prevent the death of a single child, whatever she faced in the coming days would be worth it.

Staring at the note, she set a trembling finger beneath the words.

kill again.

"Not if I can help it you son of a bitch," she whispered and jammed the car into gear.